TWIN STONES

Book 1 of the World Walkers Chronicles

Ryan Shriver

Copyright © 2025 Ryan Shriver

All rights reserved

No part of this book may be reproduced, stored in a retrieval system, or transmitted in any form or by any means, electronic, mechanical, photocopying, recording, or otherwise, without the express written permission of the publisher.

To my beautiful wife and four beautiful daughters. Thank you for your support and boundless patience with me. I love you dearly.

And to Robyn, thank you for taking the time to proofread this manuscript! I could not have finished this without you.

CONTENTS

Title Page
Copyright
Dedication
The Prophecy
Prologue   1
Chapter 1   5
Chapter 2   25
Chapter 3   41
Chapter 4   58
Chapter 5   72
Chapter 6   97
Chapter 7   106
Chapter 8   117
Chapter 9   131
Chapter 10   143
Chapter 11   159
Chapter 12   176
Chapter 13   201
Chapter 14   214
Chapter 15   228
Chapter 16   238

Chapter 17	248
Chapter 18	257
Chapter 19	268
Chapter 20	280
Chapter 21	285
Chapter 22	294
Chapter 23	309
Chapter 24	321
Chapter 25	332
Chapter 26	342
Chapter 27	356
Chapter 28	366
Chapter 29	374
Chapter 30	383
Chapter 31	393
Epilogue	403
Sneak Peak	405
Know Your Chances	412
Riv'el	415
Summary	425

THE PROPHECY

Twin chosen foraged from fallen stone
Will rise in ash what none have known.
They'll fracture fate where patterns bind,
And craft anew what ruin left behind.
From world to world their steps shall tread,
Through ancient lands and halls of dead.
Until the root of darkness dies,
In their wake, worlds shall rise.

PROLOGUE

The Hollow Realm

The pack of dogs finally arrived at the Wild Awakening Circle, drawn to it by some deep instinct. They slept at the edge of it that day. But when the sun sank, they stirred. Muscles rippled. Heads lifted. Joints cracked as they stretched from sleep. One by one, their shapes seemed to morph. Their fur darkened and began to glow faintly with soft green light, pulsing in patterns across their flanks and shoulders. Their ears pricked higher. Their fangs extended subtly. As the changes took effect, they arched their necks into a howl, long and wild.

They were no longer canines; they were something wilder, and given a purpose as protectors.

By night, they circled the stones. They formed a silent perimeter, walking and prowling slowly spiraling outward, like moons that had lost their orbit. No one was close to the circle. So they wandered further and further out. By the time dawn came, their wandering led them far away from the circle; they lay down, one by one, at the base of the twisted oaks. Curling close to the earth, they waited until sunset to restart their wandering.

Some part of them knew if they stayed close to the circle again, they would change even more. The wild beasts did their jobs well; they kept people away from the circle. The pack twitched in their sleep as the sun rose and heated the ground. Even in their new state, they could feel something was coming. The wild was calling its champions. And they would come to the circle, just like the new wild pack would protect it from people. It was instinct. The Hollow Realm was sick. And the cure-whatever it would be-would begin here.

On the other side of the Painted Peaks in Elarith, the glass vials clinked as 10-year-old Cass tried to steady her hands. Her father, Tavuv, was standing beside her, watching her every move. The thick black oil moved slowly into the mixing bowl. Beside the mixing bowl was some resin and a few other powdered ingredients, each giving off its own smell. Cass wrinkled her nose.

"This stuff stinks," she muttered, turning the metal spigot her mom made a little too far.

The oil splattered out, leaving a thick black trail down her tunic and onto the floor. She looked at her father, who stood not even a head away, perfectly clean, without a dot of oil on him. Not the first time she was jealous of his Earth Mage ability to stay clean while working with earth-related materials. He literally built the home and workshop they were in, but Cass was most jealous of his ability to stay clean while doing it.

Tav laughed. "That's one way to fill it."

Cass glared at him, cheeks red. "It's not funny!" she snapped, stomping off toward her room. "I liked this outfit!"

Still grinning, Tav cleaned the spill and climbed the narrow hallway to the top of the lookout. His wife, Miruv, stood at the edge of the cliff, looking through a brass scope she made, wind pulling at her hair.

He wrapped his arms around her from behind, and she jumped.

"You okay?" he asked.

Her voice was tight. "We may have an issue."

Tav frowned. "Where?"

She handed him the looking glass. "Smoke. A lot of it. It may be from Varnhollow. That raiding group you spotted a few days ago could have been heading in that direction."

He pressed the scope to his eye, jaw tightening. "Yeah, that's a lot of smoke."

"Still no word from the King?" he asked.

"Only a confirmation of receipt," she said bitterly.

"Poor Varnhollow. There's nothing there to steal, and no one there to defend."

For a moment, they stood silent, watching the faint gray haze in the distance. It may have been their imagination, but they swear they could hear screaming on the wind, even though it was too far away for that to be true.

"The closest garrison is Darrowmere," Tav said. "If the king's too busy daydreaming, we'll answer for him."

"What's going on?" Cass asked, padding up behind them, now

in a clean tunic.

Mir exchanged a glance with Tav, then knelt to meet her daughter's eyes. "The King still hasn't answered us, and one of the towns, Varnhollow, looks to be under attack. We're going to Darrowmere to convince the lords there to send their troops."

"I thought you didn't like the Lords of Darrowmere," Cass said.

Mir gave a half-smile. "We don't. But some quarrels can wait when people's lives are at stake."

She turned toward the stairway. "I'll send another message to the capital. Tav, start packing. We will leave as soon as we can."

Cass tugged at her father's sleeve. "How long will you be gone?"

Tav smiled softly, resting a hand on her shoulder as they walked back inside. "A few days, maybe a week. Don't worry, you're safe here. The King sent too much food and supplies for us when he ordered us out here, and you know as well as I do that the traps your mom and I set up around this place will keep you safe."

Less than an hour later, Cass's last memory of her parents was the warmth of their arms around her, and the sight of them vanishing into the woods below the cliff, heading toward the city of Darrowmere.

CHAPTER 1

Five Years Later

Finn-to-ring-your-neck. That's what the fishmonger called him. The Darrowmere City guards had their own names, streetrat, shadowbrat, wastelet. He'd heard worse. Everyone in the market knew who he was, thirteen, quick, too skinny, with hair like hay and gray eyes that never stayed still. Raised by his Aunt and bad luck.

But Finn didn't care. He lived by three rules, don't get greedy, don't get caught, and think faster than the guards.

The bread stand near the north fountain was loud, busy, and perfect. Two guards leaned on their pikes by the jewelry merchant, sweating through their armor, yawning like wolves with nothing to chase. Finn didn't look at them. He watched the baker's son, who was arguing with a woman over whether her coin was real.

He didn't go for the loaf. That would be obvious. He went for the heel, the one that sat alone at the corner of the stall, dry, rough, forgotten. He slipped it under his tunic, but the baker's son wasn't that distracted. His eyes snapped to Finn's hand, and he took a step forward.

Finn had a choice-run from the baker's son, right next to him, or run from the guards farther off.

He dodged the Baker's son and whistled as loudly as he could.

"Oi!" one of the guards barked. "It's him!"

Chaos bloomed like fire. The baker's son hesitated, not wanting to get caught between the guards and their prey.

Finn bolted-not into the alley, but straight through the fountain, kicking water high enough to soak a merchant's silks. The woman screamed. The merchant cursed. A cart full of kindling tipped just enough to block the path behind him.

The guards were big, but they weren't fast. And they were already tired from roasting in the sun all afternoon.

Finn zigzagged in between a horse's legs, slipped through a drainage hole in a wall, and popped out three buildings down, soaked, grinning, and a lot dirtier, but the heel of bread was still warm and dry under his tunic.

Not bad. Not great. But better than the carrots he picked up yesterday.

He eventually made it across town, ducking into a crooked stairwell past the shaking steam pipes and climbing up to the attic above the cooper's shop. The boards creaked, but only a little. The room smelled of oil, dust, and boiled mint.

"Got something," he said, holding up the bread like a trophy.

With some help, his aunt sat up in bed and propped herself against the wall on a stack of folded blankets, a shawl around her shoulders. She was pale, her breath thin, but her eyes crinkled when she smiled. "You always do."

"Not much today," Finn muttered, tearing it in half and offering her the bigger piece.

She took it, tore it again, and returned the larger bit. "I'm not very hungry. You're a growing boy. You need this more than I do."

He didn't argue.

"I don't know how you keep ahead of those guards."

"Because they're dumb," he said with a smirk. "I do what they don't expect me to do."

She laughed, soft and warm. "I wish we weren't in this position." Her voice turned quieter. "You need to be careful with them. People in power don't like being made fools of. One day they'll stop chasing-and they'll really come after you."

"They might get mad," Finn said, shrugging. "But they won't catch me."

They sat in silence, chewing slowly. Finn watched her as she leaned back against the wall, her hands trembling as she reached for the water he'd left earlier. Her lips barely touched the rim.

"I'm not a kid anymore," he muttered, eyes on the floor.

She opened one eye. "No, you're not. But I still get to love you like one."

He groaned, but not too loudly.

That night, the coughing wouldn't stop.

It started like it always did-soft, hollow, like the beginning of a storm. But it didn't pass. It came in waves. Finn sat cross-legged by the wall, blanket around his shoulders, counting the seconds between each breath. Five… four… seven… three… There was no rhythm to it tonight. Just a dry, desperate rattle that scraped the walls and stole the sleep from his eyes.

He hated this part. The waiting.

The not knowing.

She was getting worse. He could feel it in the way her cough shook her frame. In the way her hand trembled when she reached for water and missed the cup. She was still warm, still breathing-but every night, the line blurred a little more.

He pulled the blanket tighter and stared at the floorboards, heart hammering like it used to when he was small.

When he was eight.

When they hadn't come back.

They had left in the spring-his parents. His mother wore a green sash that day, the one she used when she meant business. His father had carried three satchels-one for goods, one for trade, and one for bad weather. They were headed west, past the hills. The name of the town had sounded funny to him back then.

Varnhollow.

They were going to trade dyes. Velvet-blue. A pigment that caught the light like oil on water. His mother had been excited-she said it could fetch silver from the weavers. Maybe gold, if they got lucky.

He'd kissed them goodbye. He remembered that.

They never came back.

A week passed. Then another. And another.

His aunt had told him gently, with a whisper like she was trying not to break something already too fragile

"Varnhollow was attacked by raiders," she said.

Some people said they were still alive. That they'd run off, or lost their way, or started over in some far-flung corner of the world.

But Finn knew better. Even at eight, he'd understood what it meant when no one returned.

The roads were not safe anymore. The roads ended more dreams than they inspired.

The coughing died down. Not stopped-just resting. A silence settled in the attic.

Finn stood slowly and crossed to his aunt's side. She'd fallen into a shallow sleep, jaw slack, breath ragged. Her face looked older in the moonlight, the lines carved deeper, like something was hollowing her out from the inside.

He sat beside her and placed a hand over hers. It felt small. Too small.

"Don't go too," he whispered.

She didn't stir.

After her coughing quieted and her breath fell into its usual, shallow rhythm, Finn slipped out, like he had so many nights before.

Not to drink. Not like the old drunkards who forgot their names between swallows.

He went to listen.

To eavesdrop on the songs, the arguments, the half-truths passed between spilled mugs and flickering lamps. To listen for news from the west. For someone, anyone, who had returned from where his parents never did.

Tonight, he was more desperate than usual. More raw around the edges. He needed something. Hope. Distraction.

Maybe tonight would be one of those nights.

He walked the narrow, winding street known as Lantern Row, a crooked stretch of alley-lit taverns and cracked-stone stoops. The flickering oil lamps above each doorway gave the illusion of welcome.

A meat vendor stood at the corner where the cobbles dipped into a shallow drain, hunched over a sputtering brazier. The smell of smoke and grilled meat wrapped around Finn like a coat, burnt edges, pepper, and smoke. The kind of scent that made his mouth water even when he wasn't hungry. Borek stood at his stand waiting for the drunkards to stumble out so he could relieve them of any coin they may have left.

Borek was a rough man with a gray-streaked beard, arms like boulders, and a permanent furrow in his brow that softened only when he spotted Finn.

"Well now," he said, voice gravelly. "If it isn't Finn-to-pick-your-pockets."

Finn offered a tired grin. 'Didn't steal anything today,' even though technically that wasn't true.

"That so?" Borek snorted. "Must be a holiday."

He flipped a skewer on the grill and leaned closer, peering at Finn's face. "How's your aunt?"

The grin vanished.

Finn looked away. "She's... not great. Worse than this morning. Her hands won't stop shaking. She didn't eat more than a bite. The coughing won't stop."

His voice cracked.

He hadn't meant to say that much. But once it started coming out, he couldn't seem to stop. His throat tightened. His eyes burned.

"She-she looks so tired."

He tried to laugh, but it came out as a shudder instead.

Borek didn't say anything at first. He just stepped around the cart and placed a heavy hand on Finn's shoulder.

The touch was solid. Real.

It snapped something back into place.

Finn wiped at his face, embarrassed. "Don't tell anyone I cried, alright?"

Borek smiled. "Won't if you don't tell anyone I gave you this." He handed over a stick of skewered meat, warm and dry, but it smelled so good.

Finn took it, holding it like it was gold. "Thanks."

"Go on now. I'm running a business, not a soup line. If word gets out, I'll have a dozen gutter kids swarming me by dawn. Tell your aunt that Ann and I said hi."

Finn gave a small, genuine laugh. "Deal."

He took a bite, chewed slowly. It helped. Not enough to make the fear vanish, but enough to dull it around the edges. After a few bites, he slipped the last half of the meat into his pocket, wrapped in the cloth.

For her.

He twirled the stick between his fingers as he walked the row, letting the noise guide him. The bars were louder now, singing, shouting, stories spilling out into the street.

He didn't go inside. He never did.

He'd learned quickly. Shop owners didn't want boys like him unless they came with coin, and drunks didn't care who you were when their fists started flying. Once, a man had stumbled out and spotted Finn sitting near the steps. Got spooked, maybe. Kicked him hard in the ribs like he was a stray dog.

Since then, Finn stayed low. Stayed quiet.

If he wanted to listen, he had to blend into the dark. Had to disappear.

It was a painful lesson. One he hadn't forgotten.

Now he sat against a low wall just outside The Crooked Tankard, knees drawn up, ear tilted toward the doorway, eyes half-lidded. His hand gripped the meat stick like a dagger, just in case a stray dog tried to take a bite of him.

The old men were already rambling about lost deals, about wars from before the Twisted Shadows, about the King's long dead dragon. Most of it was nothing. Just the made-up stories of old men.

But maybe tonight…

Maybe tonight, hope would sound like a slurred sentence.

So he listened.

And waited.

And held onto what little warmth he had, and the meat stick like a dagger.

After a few hours of listening to the usual slurred tales and bar bickering, something changed.

A man seated close to the open window leaned forward, voice thick with ale and gossip. "Did you hear? That lordling Kaelen, the one from House Morrowind, he's going to try to awaken with Malachite, tomorrow."

The men around him erupted with laughter, one nearly falling off his stool.

"Fool's gonna end up in a ditch," someone said.

"Or worse, twisted," another added, voice low. "Guards'll have to put him down before lunch. Now, nearly every awakening ends in death or them becoming a Twisted Shadow. Foolish boy."

They jeered, argued, and called the lordling ten different bad names, some were pretty creative. But Finn's ears were tuned to something else.

Awakening.

Someone was actually going to try it.

It had been months, maybe even a year, since he'd heard of anyone attempting a bonding, especially with malachite. The green stone wasn't rare, but it was risky. He'd heard whispers, stories: those who succeeded gained power over earth itself, stone, dirt, and dust. Not flashy like flame or wind, but solid. Unbreakable. Terrifying.

And beautiful.

A real malachite awakening. Tomorrow. At the awakening circle in the Keep.

Finn's heart thumped against his ribs.

He'd never seen one, only heard scraps of description from old merchants and half-drunk hopefuls. But the circle was supposed to be carved into the center of the main hall, where it was guarded and ancient. A relic from before the dark things crept down from the peaks. A place where magic recognized those who dared to touch it.

He leaned back against the wall, breath shallow.

Could he get close?

Maybe slip past the guards at dawn, hide in the stonework, or find a crack in the outer hall. Just close enough to see. To hear. To know if the lordling Kaelen, really becomes a Mage.

Two hours past sunrise, they said.

That wasn't far off.

He stood slowly, one hand still holding the stick from his meat skewer, twirling it with restless fingers. The streets were quieter now, but the night hadn't ended. The dark could still cover him.

In the morning, if he was clever, he might see something no

one in Lantern Row ever would.

A real awakening.

Wow.

The city was still asleep when Finn started moving.

The sky was shifting from black to bruised purple, and the oil lamps along Lantern Row had burned themselves out. Only the moon and the rising blush of dawn gave him light, and he stayed close to the walls, where the shadows still held.

The keep sat in the center of Darrowmere, a fortress-turned-palace-turned-prison depending on who you asked. It rose above the city like a rotting tooth, wide, heavy, and wrapped in legend. Finn had never been close. Not this close.

It would take nearly an hour on foot, longer with the dodging.

He moved like water through alleys, over fences, under carts, ducking between washing lines and crumbling archways. Twice, he had to flatten himself against stone to avoid a patrol, their armor clinking and boots echoing with lazy authority. Once, he dove behind a stack of crates just as a guard rounded a corner, heart thudding so loud he thought it would give him away.

The closer he got, the cleaner the roads became. The stones were tighter-laid, the trash less frequent. Houses were still falling apart, but not as badly as before. The poor here weren't starving; they were just uncomfortable.

And then, just before the second sunbell, he saw them.

A small party walking up the central road toward the Keep. Two guards at the front, one at the rear. A woman in a long, emerald cloak. A man with gray at his temples, walking with dignity and distance. And at the center, a boy, not much older than Finn, maybe fifteen.

Kaelen of House Morrowind.

Finn ducked behind a wagon and watched, jaw tight.

The boy's clothes were spotless, stitched with silver thread at the seams. His cloak was clasped with a polished stone. His boots were soft-soled leather. And on his left hand, a gold ring caught the morning light, like it was trying to outshine the sun.

His mother adjusted his collar. His father said something, and the boy laughed. He wasn't afraid.

Finn's stomach twisted from jealousy.

That boy had everything Finn had lost. A Family. A future. And now he would walk into the keep, into the awakening circle, and maybe, just maybe, he'd come out a Mage.

Finn pressed his palm to the stone wall beside him to calm his nerves. He didn't have a ring like Kaelen. Or fancy clothes. But he could still find out what was going to happen; he could find a way inside.

It took another ten minutes of climbing the outer walls and creeping through servant paths before he found a half-opened stained glass window on a hinge, wide enough for someone small to squeeze inside. He slipped through it and found himself in a narrow corridor in the keep, where his footsteps echoed like whispers and the air smelled of wet rock and dust.

He followed the sound of voices down a hall, heading towards the interior of the keep, and finally into a long corridor lined with old statues. One of the stone archways opened just enough to give him a view of the main hall.

He froze.

The awakening circle was carved into the floor at the hall's center, humming faintly with energy. Pillars loomed on all sides, and banners bearing house symbols hung heavy with age and pride. Guards stood at the hall's edge, still and silent.

And at the edge of the circle stood a man in ceremonial robes, dark and flowing, edged with copper threads.

He turned toward the lordling and his family as they stepped into the hall.

The family, having just entered the hall, appeared to be struggling with something. His mother held tightly to Kaelen's sleeve as if she were trying to keep him from entering. Tears in her eyes and her lips moving quietly, speaking with her son. Lord Morrowind was stoically walking ahead of his wife and his son, both ignoring his wife's tears, for all appearances, as if he were heading to an unpleasant meeting.

As they approached the circle, the man spoke to Kaelen.

"Kaelen of House Morrowind," the man said, voice loud and calm, echoing off the marble walls. "You hold in your possession a shard of malachite. You stand here of your own will?"

Kaelen nodded once. "I do."

"You understand the risk? That the stone may take you? That it may twist what it cannot bind?"

"I do."

His mother sobbed and covered her mouth, shaking and barely holding herself together.

"You understand also: should you survive the Awakening and forge a true bond, your life no longer belongs to you or to your house. You will be bound in service to King Theron IV and his bloodline until your final breath. Do you accept this burden?"

"I do."

At this, Finn saw the first reaction from Kaelen's father, who rolled his shoulders and then grasped his hands behind his back, as if he were trying to restrain himself.

Finn held his breath. He had always thought Mages were free, not servants. Not sworn tools of the Crown.

"Then step forward. Place the stone against your heart. And let fate judge your worth."

His mother tried one last time to pull her son back, and Kaelen pulled his arm free.

The lordling stepped forward and took one last look back at his parents. He stood alone now, clutching the green stone in both hands against his chest like it was both sword and shield.

He moved slowly. Measured.

And Finn watched, unblinking from the shadow of a statue.

Unbeknownst to Finn, he wasn't as hidden as he thought.

One of the guards stationed along the hall's edge had spotted him five minutes ago-a wiry shadow tucked behind a statue alcove, still as a mouse and twice as quiet. The boy thought he was invisible and, for some reason, was holding a thin stick like a sword.

The guard, Ser Jorran, just smiled to himself and didn't move.

Let the rat watch. He didn't want to disrupt the Morrowind family anyhow.

He remembered being like that once. Thin. Hungry. Eyes too big for a life too small. Always looking for an adventure.

Better the boy was here, watching something important, than picking pockets or starting fights. At one time long ago, half the city would be here witnessing the event. But now, most awakenings end badly.

This one won't, everyone knows it.

The air in the Keep carried the scent of confidence. Guards

leaned back slightly in their stances. Hands rested lightly on hilts. No tension. No readiness. Even the Bondwarden's voice, solemn as it was, lacked true warning.

Awakenings often ended in failure, or worse, but that shouldn't happen with this one. Not with names like Morrowind and stones like malachite. Twisted bonds came from lesser families, from gutter kids who stole stones they couldn't understand and tried to squeeze power from a pebble.

But this?

This was proper. If any awakening would forge a Mage, it would be this one. The Morrowinds were an old family that had historically produced many notable and powerful Mages.

Jorran folded his arms over his chest, shifting slightly to the side. He didn't want the boy to get the wrong idea and try to get closer.

Let him watch. Then scare him off.

He'd give the kid a start after it was done enough to make him bolt and remember that guards were always watching, even when you didn't think they were.

Still… Jorran glanced toward the circle, where Kaelen of House Morrowind stood poised at its edge, the stone in his hands glowing faintly as he drew closer.

Even with all that confidence, he thought, there's always a risk.

Finn reached into his pocket and pinched off a small piece of greasy, cool meat, starting to dry at the edges. He popped it into his mouth, not to eat, not really. Just to suck on. Just to keep his nerves from buzzing out of control.

In the center of the hall, the malachite stone pulsed with green light. From this distance, he couldn't see the patterns decorating the circle, but he imagined them. What did it feel like to hold that power in your palm? Was it heavy? Warm? Or humming?

He imagined himself in Kaelen's place, stepping into the circle with steady feet and proud shoulders, a golden ring on one hand and a future waiting on the other side. He imagined what it would feel like to belong there.

Instead, he was an intruder, not even meant to witness this, crouched behind a pillar with half a scrap of meat in his mouth and a wooden stick clenched tight in his hand.

So close.

And yet the distance between them felt too wide.

Kaelen stepped into the circle.

The air throbbed, a deep pulse that Finn could feel in his chest.

Kaelen cried out in pain.

He arched backward, spine drawn tight, arms trembling. The stone didn't fall; it began to sink into his chest, slow and steady, shrinking as it vanished beneath his skin like it was being sucked in by his body.

The light flared again, and his shirt tore down the back. His skin darkened, but not like bruising, like shadow, like his body was starting to blur, each edge fraying and unraveling into something that wasn't quite flesh anymore.

Someone screamed.

The mother. Then the father.

And then the guards.

A man sprinted past Finn, robes fluttering, fear on his face. He didn't even glance down at him, just barked, "Run! Hide! Twisted bond!"

The words crashed through Finn's skull like cold water.

Twisted bond.

He looked back toward the circle in time to see Kaelen, or what had been Kaelen, rise from the center, a human shape made of shadow and ash, limbs pulsing in and out of focus.

Panic swept the room.

Guards moved. Strings twanged as archers loosed arrows from the balconies. Javelins were hurled through the air. Some struck the creature, but most passed right through, disappearing into the swirling darkness.

The lordling's parents dropped to the floor, his mother sobbing, his father trying to cover her with his body.

Finn's head snapped around, wild, looking for escape. He couldn't run back through the storm grate, the way he came would be swarming with guards by now. The only chance was to vanish again.

There, tucked beneath the base of a massive pillar, under a draped tapestry, was a stone crawlspace. In the space where a few unlit torches lay on the ground, it was a storage space, and Finn could fit. Finn dove in, pressing himself against the back with his legs bent to his chin. His shoulders scraped against rough stone. He barely fit.

His heart hammered. He gripped the meat stick like a dagger, knuckles white, tip pointed outward, ready to stab at whatever found him first, be it guard or monster.

Then the throbbing stopped.

And the screaming began.

Wet noises, rips, splashes, thumps. The kind of sounds you couldn't explain but could never forget because the nightmares wouldn't let you.

Men yelled. Steel rang. Someone cried out prayers.

The lordling's mother wailed, grief-stricken, then cut off suddenly. Finn squeezed his eyes shut.

All around him, people died, and he, just a boy, trembled in the dark, holding a stick.

The thing that had once been Kaelen shrieked, not like a person, but like stone being torn apart by teeth.

The creature grew.

Twisted limbs stretched upward, nearly doubling its height, warping its frame beyond anything human. Its torso fractured outward like tree bark splitting under pressure. Both legs bent backwards, birdlike. Its flesh was shadow and ash, patchy and dense, flickering like smoke that couldn't decide whether to vanish or harden.

Guards moved fast, shouting to one another. They weren't amateurs, not green recruits trembling at the unknown. They formed ranks, attacked in measured waves, flanking from the edges of the chamber. This wasn't the first Twisted Shadow they'd fought. But it had been a while.

Even if the last several awakenings were twisted, they were certain this Lordling would be different.

One guard lunged with a spear, but the creature caught it mid-thrust and hurled him across the chamber, sending the man crashing through a tapestry with a dull, wet thud. Another was snatched off the floor and thrown directly into a marble pillar, the sound of bones shattering echoing through the Keep.

And still, they fought. Archers fired from the balconies, aiming for its legs and head. Two halberds caught its side, slicing deep, letting loose a spray of thick, black blood that hissed as it hit the stone.

Then, finally, a heavy blade connected, chopping through the creature's upper arm at the shoulder.

The arm was kicked across the room by the Twisted with a wet slap, within view of Finn's hiding place.

He recoiled, clutching his stick, frozen in a crouch behind the stone ledge. The limb twitched once, reflexive and horrifying. It was long and gnarled, part muscle, part ash, with clawed fingers twice the length of his own. The flesh shimmered at the edges, like it couldn't fully decide whether it belonged in this world.

And around the ring finger hung a snapped thin gold ring.

It was bent now, twisted by the transformation, but still clinging to the bone like it refused to fall off.

Finn stared in horror. But it didn't move.

Not yet.

The fight dragged on. Screams and howls filled the chamber. Steel rang. Men swore. One guard yelled something about the legs, "Go for the knees!" and five of them converged with long spears, timing their strikes like a hunting pack.

With a final roar, the Twisted lurched backward. It staggered, limbs flailing, body shedding shadow like smoke off burning tar, until it collapsed onto the awakening circle-half-human, half-myth, and finally… dead.

The only sound that remained was the yelling of survivors.

Men barked orders. Some called for medics. Others ran to the fallen. Blood spread in slick pools across the stone. Someone stuck a spear through the head of the Twisted. The air still crackled faintly from whatever magic had once surged in the room.

And Finn, hidden in his narrow crawlspace, held his breath and waited.

Minutes passed. Then the chamber filled with more adults, soldiers, medics, runners, all crashing into the chaos like a second wave. The world above was noise and panic.

Now or never.

Finn shifted, slow and silent, crawling out from under the stone recess toward the nearest pillar, trying not to knock over the few torches in the hole, keeping low. He crouched beside it, heart pounding. The severed arm lay within reach nearby.

The ring gleamed dull gold in the torchlight. Bent. Warped. But gold nonetheless.

He hesitated.

It wasn't his.

But it wasn't the lordling's anymore either.

Finn reached out and pried the ring from the flesh on the hand. His fingers came away slick with black blood, sticky and clinging to his skin. He wiped them against his kilt, staining it dark. An unfamiliar stench clung to him. He pocketed the ring and pressed himself back into the shadows, watching. Waiting.

No one even noticed.

Finn crept along the courtyard's edge, sticking to the shadows, slipping behind a statue. His breath came quick and shallow, but no one called out. No one pointed. No boots thundered after him.

He darted down hallways, out the open window, and over the outer wall, the gold ring still warm in his pocket, blood drying on his fingers, and the meat stick in his hand. His legs ached, but he moved fast, quiet as always. One more bend, one more alley, and he'd be gone.

◆ ◆ ◆

High above, across the courtyard, a medic wrapped a bandage around a soldier's arm. The man sat against a broken column, face smeared with blood and soot, armor scuffed and torn.

Ser Jorran. He didn't speak. He didn't move much, save for turning his head slightly.

And he saw Finn, for just a moment, sneaking away.

There was no shout. No order.

Just a faint breath through bruised lips.

And, maybe, the hint of a tired smile. Every survivor of a Twisted awakening is lucky. Even if it's a street rat. Then the medic said something, and Jorran turned away.

CHAPTER 2

No Options

The attic was still and dim when Finn climbed the stairs, every joint in his body aching.

He didn't even realize how heavy he felt until he collapsed onto his bedroll. The light had changed, slanting through the single window in the attic apartment. The city was wide awake now, voices rising faintly from the alleys, carts rolling past below, but it all felt far away.

His aunt was still in bed.

She hadn't moved.

Still breathing. Barely.

But not waking up either.

"I'm back," he mumbled, unsure if she could hear him. "I got out. It's done."

He rolled onto his side, muscles giving up.

The warmth of the attic made his eyes heavy, and his head fogged with the crash of too many sleepless hours. His fingers were still sticky with dried blood, and his kilt stained from the creature's arm, but none of it felt urgent anymore.

Just for a bit, he told himself. Just a minute to rest.

Then darkness took him.

He woke slowly, like his body had to climb out of something heavy.

No dreams. Just a thick, dark nothing that felt more like drowning than rest.

His skin was damp, and the blanket twisted around his legs. He blinked against the light, squinting at the beams that cut through the attic, too bright and hot.

His head ached.

Everything ached.

His limbs were slow to listen, like he'd been buried and had to dig his way up. He coughed once, dry, and wiped at his face, only to notice the dark smears on his fingers.

Blood.

But not red.

Dark. Oily. Wrong.

He stared at it, the memory slow to return.

The arm. The ring. The scream. The shadow twisting in the circle.

Twisted Shadows can bleed, he thought, dazed.

And if they bleed… they can die.

Everything dies.

The attic was boiling now, thick with stale air and sweat. The heat pressed in from all sides, suffocating and still.

Then it hit him.

His Aunt.

He sat up too fast. The attic tilted. A rush of dizziness swelled behind his eyes, and his knees nearly gave out.

He staggered across the boards to her bedroll.

She was still there. But something felt wrong.

Unmoving.

He dropped to his knees beside her, his fingers reaching for her arm before he even realized what he was doing.

No response. No breath. Her mouth hung open just slightly. She wasn't asleep. She was gone.

Finn sat there, hands in his lap, the warmth of the attic clinging to his skin, the sound of the world outside muffled and far.

He didn't cry.

Not yet.

His chest felt tight and full and empty all at once, like there was something trying to push its way out but finding no space.

He called her name once.

And when she didn't stir, he stood.

Finn stood for a long time in the silence of the attic, staring at her still body.

She'd spoken yesterday.

Her voice, thin but warm, told him to be careful. To stop teasing the guards. To eat more. To sleep. And now she is gone. Just like that.

He sank to the floor beside her, head in his hands.

What had he been thinking?

Running off to watch some lordling become a monster, risking his neck to see something he didn't even understand, when she was here, dying.

Alone.

He could've been there. He could've held her hand. He could've done something.

Panic crept in behind the grief-sharp and cold, wrapping around his chest. His breath came in short, shallow bursts.

He was alone now. No family, few friends, and no one to take care of him any longer

It took everything he had to stand, to pull on his belt, to move like his bones still worked. He stuck the thin skewer through the threads of his kilt on the side of his hip like a makeshift scabbard, so it stayed in one of the folds without poking him. His hands trembled as he wiped the sweat and blood from his face, smearing more shadow-stain across his skin.

There was only one person he knew who dealt with death. A man on the far side of the city, known for his rough attitude.

They called him Murn, the grave digger. Strange. Harsh. Quiet. People said he spoke to the bodies while he buried them. Finn didn't know if that was true. He just knew he had no one else.

So he walked.

Unwanted and silent tears streaked his face as he moved through the sunlit streets, barely registering the shouts of vendors, the clatter of carts. He kept his eyes low, fists clenched, feet dragging.

Two city guards on patrol near the tannery saw him pass-a skinny boy, his kilt stained, hands blackened with what looked like oil… or maybe blood.

They looked at each other and began to follow.

Murn's place was tucked into an alley beside the east wall-a sunken structure of dark wood and stone with a crooked sign above the door.

Finn didn't knock. He just pushed the door open and stepped inside.

The air smelled of dust and rot.

Murn stood at a long slab table, engraving something onto the headstone. He didn't look up.

"What do you want?" the man said, voice like gravel and smoke.

Finn tried to speak, but the words tangled in his throat. Then they rushed out all at once.

"It's my aunt, she's dead, I fell asleep and she, she didn't wake up, and I didn't know what to do, I didn't want to just leave her there, I thought you could, could help, please, I just-"

Murn finally looked at him.

Finn froze under the weight of the man's cold stare. His eyes were sharp, sunken deep into a face like cracked leather.

"You didn't bring her?" Murn said, voice flat.

Finn shook his head. "I-I didn't know if I should. She's upstairs. Still in bed."

Murn frowned. "Where are your parents?"

"Gone," Finn whispered. "They died years ago. She raised me."

"How'd she die?"

"I don't know." Finn's throat was tight again. "She was coughing for weeks, and then she just… stopped."

The silence that followed felt longer than it was.

Murn grunted and tossed the chisel into a bucket. "So who's paying for the hole, then? You got coin rat?"

Finn hesitated.

Then, slowly, he reached into his pocket and pulled out the twisted gold ring.

He unwrapped it from its cloth and held it out.

"This," he said. "It's real. You can sell it."

Murn's expression changed into something hungry. He reached for it, fingers twitching.

Just then, a gloved hand came down on Finn's wrist from behind.

"What's this, then?" a voice said.

Finn gasped, twisting to see the guard who had followed him. The second one stepped around his other side, eyes narrowed.

The first guard plucked the ring from his palm, holding it up to the light.

"House Morrowind," he muttered. "This is their crest."

He looked down at Finn like he'd just stepped in something.

"This rat must've lifted it off one of the family members. That family's been through enough without gutter scum picking them clean."

"No, I didn't steal it!" Finn stammered. "I-I found it, after the circle, he dropped it, I swear-"

"He's lying," the second guard grunted.

Hands reached for him again.

But Finn was already moving.

He ducked under the slab table, burst past a stack of crates, and slammed through the door. The alley exploded around him as he ran, sandals skidding on loose stones, lungs burning.

Behind him, one guard cursed and another shouted for backup.

Finn didn't look back.

He ran until his legs buckled, until the buildings thinned and the alleyways no longer offered cover.

But there was no safety left in Darrowmere.

Within hours, the guards were everywhere, not just the two who'd chased him from Murn's place, but patrols from across the city. Word had spread fast, and twisted faster.

"The boy with the blood on his hands." They said he'd killed her.

He heard it from behind shutters and half-open doors as he darted through back streets. Heard merchants whispering it behind their carts. He was beginning to panic, he knew it, but struggled to control himself. Borek, the meat vendor, his friend, was gone when Finn passed the old stall.

The only place he found to hide was a crumbling root cellar beneath an abandoned house in the coal quarter. The door was broken, and what was left of the building was covered in ash.

However, it opened with a soft groan, and Finn slipped inside.

The space was low and damp, the air stale with mold and rot. Cobwebs brushed his cheeks. Somewhere nearby, water dripped steadily. The floor was nothing but packed dirt and a few broken crates.

He crouched in the shadows and did not move.

Finn bit into the cold meat in his pocket. It had gone soft, with a strange sour edge that curled his stomach. But he ate it anyway. Slowly. Each bite was harder to swallow than the last.

He was starving. But that wasn't the worst of it.

The worst was the feeling in his chest, like something had hollowed him out and left shame in the shape of his heart.

He wanted to bury her.

To wrap her in her blanket.

To carry her to a quiet place.

To tell someone who cared.

But he couldn't. He couldn't even go back.

He chewed the last bit of meat and sucked on the gristle, wiping his mouth with the back of his shaking hand.

At night, when the patrols thinned and the city lights flickered low, he made his decision.

The drainage tunnel behind the tannery was old, built of brick, and had a rusted metal grate at the mouth. The drainage throughout the city gathers here and in a few other locations to funnel the rainwater and mess outside the walls. This caused the land on the other side of the walls to resemble a swamp more than a field. Finn had found it years ago while playing with some younger kids through the alleys. Back then, he hadn't thought much of it. Now, it was his only door out.

He knelt at the entrance of the large and very smelly drain and peered through the iron bars. Too narrow for a grown man. But he wasn't a man yet.

He turned sideways, pressing one arm through the gap first,

then his shoulder, gritting his teeth as rough stone and iron scraped his ribs and hips. With a final shove, he slipped through into the narrow brick tunnel beyond.

The ceiling was low, barely enough for him to crouch, and the air reeked of tanner's runoff, a choking mix of urine, rot, and things better left unnamed. He ran hunched over, feet slapping the damp stone, ignoring the rats and slick, wriggling things that glinted briefly in the pale light streaming through iron grates on either side of the tunnel.

At the far end, another set of bars waited, closer, tighter. He squeezed through with effort, scraping skin and snagging his clothing. Then suddenly, he was free tumbling down a short drop, landing hard in a bed of mud, briars, and cold, sucking earth.

But he was outside for the first time that he could remember.

No one was in front of him either. For the first time in his life, he was truly alone, not even strangers were around him. His whole life, the sound of people had been constant. Now that the noise was distant, coming from the tunnel behind him and in front of him, there was nothing but wild sounds. He didn't stop to savor it.

He stood and ran.

The land around Darrowmere was clear-cut for defense, flat and open for a hundred heights in every direction. He sprinted across it, his sandals slipping in the damp grass, getting stuck in the mud, his breath ragged.

The forest loomed ahead, dark and tangled.

By the time he reached the trees, his legs were burning. His lungs felt scraped raw. He fell once, hard, on a root he didn't see, but caught himself before he could cry out.

He pushed on, just far enough to feel the trees close around him, and he couldn't see the fire lights from the city any longer. Then he collapsed with his back against a broad, rough-barked trunk.

His body shook.

From fear and exhaustion.

He hugged his knees to his chest and let the dark press in around him. The woods whispered with distant leaves and insect calls. The wind moved like a soft voice, and somewhere far away, a bird called out once and fell silent.

He whispered nothing. Not a prayer. Not a name. Not even goodbye.

Just one more breath.

And then another.

Then, he slept.

Finn woke to the sound of leaves crunching.

He blinked, disoriented, the rising sun filtering through the trees in pale shafts of light. For a moment, he wasn't sure if he'd imagined it, just the tail end of a bad dream.

Then he heard it again. Closer.

His eyes snapped open fully, scanning the underbrush.

Not a guard. A dog.

Thin. Mangy. All ribs and teeth. It crouched low, hackles raised, staring right at him, tail still, ready to lunge.

Finn's hands scrabbled blindly through the dirt, searching for anything, stone, stick, anything he could throw. He flung a handful of soil and pebbles at it. The dog flinched, darted back a step, uncertain.

It thinks I'm armed, Finn realized. But not for long.

He reached for his hip and grabbed the broken meat skewer that had cracked when he'd fallen the night before. The shaft was splintered, but it still had a sharp end. Short, crude... but a weapon.

The dog lunged.

Its teeth caught the sleeve of his tunic, yanking him sideways. Finn drove the thin jagged stick forward, jamming it deep into the dog's ear. The animal howled, thrashing wildly, foam at its jaws. He hadn't killed it, but he had caused it significant pain.

It's still alive.

Finn scrambled to his feet, heart hammering, and grabbed a rock as big as he could lift, rough and wet with morning dew.

He lifted it, muscles shaking, and slammed it down.

Once.

Twice.

Three times. And the dog finally stopped moving.

Finn fell to the ground, chest heaving, hands trembling, blood splattered across his forearms and tunic. His ears rang, his breath sharp and uneven.

He stared at the dog's body.

He'd survived.

Barely.

But he had.

Not again, he thought, wiping the sweat from his brow with a bloody sleeve.

Never again. He'd never let himself be caught off guard like that.

Another layer of blood on him now.

Not a Twisted. This time, a dog.

And the sun kept rising.

A pale gold light spilled through the branches, brushing the tops of the trees and warming the forest floor. His back ached from sleeping against the roots and lifting the rock so quickly, and his legs were sore, scraped from the night before.

But he was alive.

Not in a cell.

Not dead.

Still free.

He sat up slowly, brushing away the dirt, leaves, and crushed bugs that clung to his tunic and kilt. A beetle scuttled off his leg. His arms were streaked with mud and dried blood, his hair tangled with grass.

He looked back, over his shoulder, toward where he knew the city sat behind the trees.

Still too close.

He stood.

Now what?

The forest stretched wide and empty before him, damp with dew and humming with the early breath of day. He had no food, no water, no blanket. Nothing but the clothes on his back.

But he had a direction.

West towards the sunset.

Varnhollow.

The name filled his head like a whisper. The place his parents had been traveling to. The place they had vanished.

Maybe he'd find their names etched into a grave site.

Maybe he'd find someone who knew them.

Or maybe... maybe he wouldn't find anything at all.

But it was the only hope he had left.

He avoided the road. Everyone said the same thing-that the roads west of Darrowmere were haunted by twisted things, creatures that moved like men but weren't, that hunted after sunset and walked without sound.

It was why no one argued when people disappeared heading west.

It was why no one came back.

So Finn walked through the woods instead, the tangle of brush and uneven ground slowing him, but giving him cover. It would take longer, three or four days if he were lucky, but it was better than being seen.

Or caught.

Or worse.

He needed a weapon.

He needed food.

And he really, really needed to wash.

The blood on his hands was drying, so he used leaves and dirt to clean himself as well as he could, but it still clung to him. The stink from the drain, sweat, fear, and blood had soaked into his skin and clothes.

He moved carefully through the trees, ears alert, eyes searching. Somewhere out here, there had to be some water to wash with, even a shallow creek would do. He was desperate for clean water to drink, to scrub the gunk from his hands.

He pressed on, the forest growing brighter around him with each step. The trees grew taller and spaced further apart.

Birds chirped above. The wind stirred the leaves.

And in the distance, just faintly, he thought he heard running water.

The sound of running water grew louder, drawing Finn forward through the thick underbrush until he reached the stream, a narrow, clear ribbon cutting through the forest floor. Sunlight dappled its surface, and the water moved fast enough to be clean but slow enough to enter safely.

Without hesitation, he stripped down, wincing as the cool morning air hit his skin. The still breeze made his wet, dirt-caked clothes stink worse than he realized.

He stepped into the stream, gasping as the cold bit into his legs, then pushed himself in deeper until he was waist-high. The water closed around him, and he exhaled slowly, letting it rinse away the sweat and stink from his skin.

Bending low, he scooped handfuls of the gritty sand from the streambed and used it to scrub his arms, chest, and face. The sand scraped away dried blood and dirt, and after several minutes, he finally felt clean. Cleaner than he's felt in a very long time.

Then he turned to his clothes.

Dragging them into the stream, he soaked the fabric, scrubbing hard, focusing on the worst spots first-his kilt, the hem of his tunic, the sleeves. It took longer than he expected, but eventually the black stains thinned into faint brown blotches, no longer recognizable for what they were.

He wrung everything out, piece by piece. Then he spread his clothes across a boulder that was tilted just enough to catch the full sun. As the warmth rose, Finn turned his focus to the next two things he needed: food and a weapon.

The banks of the stream were scattered with smooth stones, some could be made sharp, and the water danced over them in sparkling ribbons. As Finn crouched to search for anything edible, something small scuttled under a rock near his feet.

He froze.

Another movement, then a third.

Crabs. Small ones, half the size of his palm, but something.

He waded in up to his shins and waited. When one darted into a pool between two rocks, he lunged, pinning it with a flat stone. It fought hard, legs kicking against his fingers, but he got it. It snapped at him, but he didn't mind. He had food. Not much, but enough.

He returned to the shore, dripping wet, mostly nude, and breathless. He sat down with the crab in his hands and looked it over, trying to remember what to do next. He had neither a fire or a pot.

People eat fish raw sometimes, he reasoned.

He cracked the shell with a nearby stone and scooped out the flesh, slimy and pale.

One bite.

The texture turned his stomach immediately. It was cold,

sandy, and slimy. Still, he forced himself to swallow-

Then he vomited into the reeds.

His body rejected it outright.

Shaking and shamed, he sat for a long moment, staring at what was left of his crab.

His head still throbbed. His stomach churned.

He needed something else. Anything.

He threw the crab in the stream close to the shore and searched the underbrush nearby, eyes sharp for movement, color, or nests. Eventually, he found a couple of low thorny bushes, their vines twisting like black wire.

He thought they were blackberries.

Most weren't ripe, small, hard, bitter, but he didn't care. He picked the ones that looked even close to ready and shoved them into his mouth, one after another. The sweetness was faint, overpowered by sourness, but it lingered.

He kept picking until his fingers were stained purple and his tongue ached from the tang. The thorns snagged his hands a few times, but he was hungry enough not to care.

Near the thorn bushes, half-sunk in the mud, Finn spotted a curve of rusted metal.

He knelt beside it and dug carefully with his fingers. It was a fragment of an old cooking pot or pan, the edge split and curled where it had broken. One piece still had part of a rounded handle, just enough to tell what it used to be.

Someone must've camped here once. Maybe long ago. He glanced around, suddenly alert and aware that he was still mostly nude, but saw no sign of anyone nearby. No ashes. No shelter. Just the fragment, forgotten and half-swallowed by the forest.

I wonder what broke it, he thought. And where the people went.

The shard had a forked point, with each point bent in separate directions and a slight curve bending to the side. "It must have been a shallow pan, not a pot." The metal was rusted but not pitted through, about half the thickness of his finger, and longer than his hand. Its base had the broken looped handle and a flat, smooth end that was the edge of the pan. It was about three fingers wide and narrowed to a dangerous-looking, curled dual-tip. When he carefully ran his thumb along the edge, it could be made sharp. As it was, it was sharp enough to stab if he needed to.

It wasn't a knife.

But it had the shape of something that could be made into one.

He turned it over in his hands, picturing it lashed to a stick or wrapped in cloth to give it grip. It wouldn't last long, not against anything armored, but for cutting bark, slicing twine, or even against another dog?

It was enough.

Rough. Ugly. Left behind by someone who either didn't need it anymore or hadn't made it out of the woods to take it with them.

Finn didn't care which.

He'd take what he could get.

He turned it over in his hand.

With a good grip and some wrapping, maybe…

Just maybe, it could serve as a blade.

Not much, but better than nothing.

He searched for a hard piece of wood that he could use for a handle. But he couldn't find anything near the stream. Everything was rotting here.

He returned to the boulder with his clothes and noticed that a couple of small fish were in the shallows picking apart what was left of his crab. He tried to creep closer, but they darted off, seeing his shape through the water.

Back at the sun-warmed stone, Finn found his clothes mostly

dry, damp around the seams but wearable. He put them on quickly, the fabric cool against his skin, and turned back to the rusted shard.

He found a fist-sized rock nearby and began tapping the forked ends of the metal against the boulder, trying to flatten the bend. Gentle taps were enough on this soft metal. Once the tips looked straighter, he turned his attention to the edge, tapping and dragging the shard against the stone, trying to narrow it, to pinch the iron into something that might slice instead of scrape.

It was slow work. But when he was done, it felt different in his hand.

He gripped the base, pressing the bit of curved handle flush to his palm. The curved handle was broken and pressed sharply against his hand. The blade jutted out between fingers in his closed fist.

"A punch dagger," he muttered, surprised at himself. He laughed once, short and quiet. "Kinda."

It would probably bend or snap the first time it hit anything solid. And the grip was not good. He would need to find a good handle soon. But as it was, it could still cause some harm. That was enough. It was better than a skewer, and that skewer ended up being very useful.

For now, it was his.

He'd eaten a little bit.

And the forest no longer felt quite as hostile.

He still didn't know what he was doing.

But for the first time since his aunt died, he felt like he could think again. He was not safe, but he was feeling more confident. That was enough for now.

He adjusted his belt, slid his new blade under his belt, looked west, and took what felt like the first step forward of his adventure.

CHAPTER 3

A Girl Named Cass

The sun hung high by the time Finn settled into his rhythm, pushing west through the dense forest. The ground sloped gently in places, and the underbrush thickened with brambles and dry leaves. His legs ached, but he kept moving.

Somewhere along the way, he found a sapling thin enough his make-shift blade could cut, it was long, straight, and smooth enough to hold once the thin branches were removed. It fit well in his hand, and walking with it made the trail feel a little less lonely. A little steadier. His blade eventually did the work, and with his new walking stick, he felt safer.

Birds flitted from branch to branch high overhead. More than once, he heard rustling in the distance, brush-sharp and sudden, just out of sight. His heart would seize, hand tightening on the walking stick... but nothing came of it. Maybe a bird. Maybe not.

And yet, the feeling wouldn't leave.

He felt a crawling weight between his shoulders, like someone- or something-was watching from behind the trees. He spun around more than once, eyes darting between trunks, only to find the forest just as he left it.

Empty.

Still.

Too still. But he was used to the city, where there was always noise and people. Here it was just him.

The sun began to drop, and Finn's throat burned. No streams. No blackberries. He hadn't seen anything edible since morning, and now even the bugs seemed quieter.

His lips were cracked. He kept glancing at tree trunks, hoping to find wet moss or maybe a puddle somewhere. Nothing.

He pressed on.

As the shadows deepened, his nerves climbed. He kept seeing the dog in his mind, those eyes, that sudden lunge, and the idea of sleeping on the ground again sent cold needles down his spine.

He couldn't be that vulnerable. Not again.

When he spotted a tangle of thin vines snaking up a nearby tree, he grabbed hold and yanked, pulling several strands loose and coiling them together. They were fibrous and strong, not rope, but enough to wrap with. Maybe enough to bind his blade to the walking stick.

It wouldn't be perfect, but it might be a spear.

Something longer. Something he could trust more than a jagged piece of rust held in his palm.

He needed a place to rest.

And all around him: trees.

Tall, narrow, clustered close together, until he spotted one that stood out.

A sprawling tree, low to the ground at first, then climbing

upward with a dozen thick branches that curled and twisted like reaching arms. The trunk split in places, forming natural seats and small hollows where he could tuck himself in and stay hidden from below.

He stepped closer and pressed a hand against the bark.

This might work.

A dog couldn't reach him here. Probably nothing short of a bear could. And bears, at least, would probably make a lot of noise.

Finn spotted a low branch and pulled himself up, clambering carefully from limb to limb, each one creaking faintly beneath his weight. After a short climb, maybe five body heights up, he found a nook where two thick trunks split apart, forming a natural seat.

He settled in, his back pressed to one trunk, knees bent. He could let his legs dangle or sit cross-legged if he needed to shift. It wasn't exactly comfortable, but it felt secure.

Looking around, he took his walking stick and wedged it horizontally between a smaller branch and the opposite trunk, forming a sort of makeshift railing. It might not hold much weight, but if he slipped in the night, it could steady him. And if something tried to climb up after him…

He'd have at least a second to fight.

It wasn't comfortable. But it felt safer than the ground.

He unwrapped the blade and the vines, setting them in front of him in the nook between his legs. Tomorrow, he'd try to bind the two together to make a spear.

Tonight, he just needed not to die.

The forest whispered around him, darker now.

He leaned back into the crook of the tree, hand on his walking stick, tried not to fall asleep too quickly, and thought about bread and cakes.

Finn jolted awake, heart pounding, arms flailing slightly as if he'd been falling. His hand scrambled for the walking stick, but nothing was moving.

He froze.

Listened.

The tree was still. No rustling below. Nothing was climbing up to reach him.

Just a dream?

But something was wrong.

Eventually, he realized he could smell something he'd known all his life and only now noticed had been absent all day.

Smoke.

Faint, but unmistakable. Woodsmoke. There was a fire somewhere nearby.

That meant people.

He twisted slowly in his perch, scanning the forest below. And then he saw it, a soft orange glow flickering on the underside of a distant branch. The light was faint, filtered through and bouncing off leaves and branches, but it was undeniably firelight.

He weighed his options. Fire meant warmth, maybe food. But it could just as easily mean danger, or worse, bandits, men who'd kill a boy for sport, or worse, maybe the Twisted like fire also.

Still… the cold was deep in his bones, and his stomach hadn't stopped aching since yesterday. And he doubted the Twisted liked fire.

He had to risk it.

He secured the rusted blade and vine bundle, then carefully braced himself against the trunk. He dropped the walking stick to the forest floor. It thudded softly into the brush below, and he began climbing down branch by branch.

The night was still, unnervingly so. Each step he took felt too loud.

And behind him... something shifted. Leaves moved. Not wind, too steady. Too deliberate.

He glanced back more than once, but the shadows were thick, and the firelight ahead kept drawing his attention forward.

Was something following him?

Or was it just the forest being the forest?

He pushed forward, each footstep faster than the last, until the trees thinned and he broke into a small clearing.

There. The fire.

A crude pit ringed with stones, embers crackling, small flames licking low over blackened logs. There was a rabbit on a spit over the fire. There was a pad and a pack. But... no people. No voices.

Just the fire.

Finn circled the clearing slowly, turning on the balls of his feet, eyes darting into the dark.

No one. "Whatever kind of magic this is, I'm just hungry enough to fall for it," he said.

The warmth and the smell of the roasting meat called to him. He moved closer, hands outstretched, fingers spread toward the food. The pain in his fingertips dulled for the first time all day.

He set the walking stick down beside the fire and leaned in, letting the warmth wash over his face.

Then everything changed.

A cold edge pressed against his neck.

Steel.

And a voice, sharp, female, furious, growled directly behind his ear:

"Move one finger and you die."

Finn froze with his hands still reaching for the meat.

The blade at Finn's neck was sharp enough to raise a bead of blood. He froze, heart thudding in his ears.

"I-I'm not here to steal anything."

"Then why are you stomping around my camp like a bull?" the voice snapped. Female. Older than him. Calm, but coiled tight.

"I saw the fire. I was cold. And alone."

There was a long pause. The blade didn't move.

"I could hear you in the woods for ten minutes, stomping around like a fat merchant lost on his first hike."

Finn swallowed. "I-I'm not fat."

Silence. Then the pressure of the blade lifted. "Turn around," She ordered.

He turned slowly.

A girl, maybe a couple of years older, stood. Her clothes were rough but tightly fitted, layered with stitched hides and dark fabric. Her hair was tied back with something that looked like dried cord. Her eyes didn't blink, just narrowed, scanning him like he was a threat.

"You have nothing," she said flatly. "No pack. No bow."

"No," Finn said.

She raised an eyebrow. "You brought nothing to a forest full of monsters?"

"I'm not a monster," he muttered, a little too quickly.

"No," she said. "You're worse. You're clueless."

He scowled. "I made it this far, didn't I?"

"By the looks of you, barely."

The fire snapped quietly between them. Finn's stomach growled, loud enough that even the girl heard it.

Cass tilted her head. "Sit," she said, already turning to the fire. "If you lunge for me, I'll stick you in the throat. Understand?"

He sat fast.

She pulled the spit from the fire, the scent twisting his gut into knots. She studied it for a moment, then grabbed a knife and cut it in half mid-spine and broke the spit in two, each with half the rabbit on it.

She handed him the back half.

In shock, he quickly said, "Thank you." His hands were already shaking as he tore into it.

The flavor barely registered. It was hot. Greasy. Real.

For a moment, nothing else existed but the act of chewing and swallowing. He tried not to cry while eating, but his eyes stung anyway.

Cass said nothing, just watched him from across the fire. Sharp eyes. Measuring. Judging.

Her gaze dropped briefly to the shard at his belt, then to his feet.

"Why are you wearing sandals in the woods?"

"It's all I had."

"You're from a city," she said.

He didn't answer.

"You're alone."

Still no answer.

"You're running from something," she added softly.

That one hit.

He looked down at the small pile of bones on the ground. Each one licked clean. His stomach no longer hurt, but his throat still burned.

"Where?" she asked. "Where are you from?"

He didn't mean to. He didn't plan to.

But it came out anyway.

Everything.

Darrowmere. The ring. The guards. The twisted boy. His aunt.

Her body. The escape. The pipe. The forest. The dog. The blood. The fear. The walking. The silence.

By the time he finished, he wasn't sitting upright anymore. He was hunched forward, arms wrapped around himself like he could squeeze the ache out of his chest.

Cass didn't speak for a long while.

Then, finally, her voice was quieter now. Less steel. More stone.

"Well," she said, "you're still alive. That counts for something."

"Can I stay here tonight?" Finn asked, voice low.

Cass didn't answer him right away. The fire popped between them, sending sparks into the air like fleeting stars.

"Yes," she said at last. "But if you even think about coming to this side of the fire, you will die."

Finn nodded quickly. "Of course."

He wasn't sure if she was joking. He didn't think she was.

But it didn't matter.

He was warm. He'd eaten. And he'd found someone who, at least for now, probably wouldn't try to kill him.

That was more than he'd expected from the forest.

He lay on his back looking up at the stars and the smoke from the fire.

"Cass is a nice name," he mumbled.

No answer.

His limbs were heavy. His heart still hurts. But he was too tired to stay awake any longer.

He drifted off mid, thought the edge of his tunic dangerously close to the fire's outer ring.

Cass watched him, silent.

She frowned and leaned forward to use his walking stick to nudge the fabric of his tunic away from the flames.

He didn't even stir.

She watched him a moment longer. Then stood, pulled her bedroll loose, and spread it out near the far edge of the fire. She laid it flat, shaping the blanket like a body tucked inside, a decoy, just in case. She didn't know this boy, and she wouldn't trust him so easily.

Then she turned and stepped silently into the woods, vanishing into the underbrush without a sound.

From the shadows, she watched.

Watched the other shadows.

And watched the boy.

To her, both were potential threats.

The shadows could kill her.

The boy… she wasn't sure yet.

But she wasn't about to take her eyes off either one.

Finn woke late, the sun already climbing, gold light filtering through the canopy above. His hay-colored hair stuck out in every direction, except it was flattened on one side. He blinked against the brightness, rubbed the sleep from his eyes, and stretched with a groan.

Cass was already up.

She crouched beside the fire, feeding thin sticks into the coals with practiced care. She glanced at him, just once, then went back to her work.

One eye on the fire. One eye on the woods.

Finn sat up slowly. "Thanks," he muttered. "For letting me stay."

Cass gave a noncommittal grunt. "Hmm."

He hesitated, then cleared his throat. "I, uh… I'm heading to Varnhollow."

That got her attention.

She stiffened slightly, and though she didn't turn to face him, he saw the way her shoulders tensed, fingers tightening around the stick in her hand.

"I mean," he added quickly, "that's where my parents were going. Before they disappeared."

Still, she said nothing.

"I don't know if they made it," Finn continued, voice lower now. "I just… I need to see it. Even if it's just ruins. Even if there's nothing left."

He looked down, picking at the frayed edge of his sleeve. "Darrowmere was full of ghosts. I couldn't stay there."

The silence hung heavy until Cass finally spoke, her voice quiet, but sharp.

"There's almost nothing left of Varnhollow. When did they leave for there?"

He said, "4 years ago, I knew they were probably dead, everyone said they were, I just have to know if it's true."

She tossed another stick into the fire.

"The path to and from that town is plagued by Twisted Shadows. Doesn't matter if it's day or night. Anyone who travels it dies."

Finn swallowed. "I know, that's why I'm walking in the woods.

Cass turned just enough to glance at him.

"Then you're as stupid as you look, Finn."

But her voice had softened. Slightly.

She didn't look angry. If anything, she looked… amused. Maybe even impressed.

"I have to know what happened to them."

Cass sighed, jabbing the stick into the fire until it crackled.

Then she leaned back on her heels.

"The roads aren't the only place with shadows," she said. "They're out here too. And you're lucky, really lucky, you haven't already been killed." Her eyes narrowed. "You have no stealth. No supplies. And barely a plan."

Finn hesitated. Then, carefully said, "Can you help me?"

She studied him for a moment. Long enough that the silence grew awkward. But Finn didn't mind. Thinking, he figured, was good for her.

Finally, she nodded.

"I'll teach you a few things. Enough to not die so easily."

She looked back at the fire.

"That's it. I'm not going to Varnhollow. I'm not going anywhere near a city. But I'll show you how to survive long enough to get there on your own."

Finn's face lit up with a genuine, lopsided smile.

"Deal."

Cass began burying the fire with slow, practiced movements, scooping dirt with her boot and pressing it down until the last ember vanished beneath the ash. Then she stood, adjusted the worn straps of her pack, and threw it over one shoulder.

Finn watched her for a moment, then looked around, confused.

No words. No warning. Just movement.

"We're leaving?" he asked.

She didn't answer. She just started walking.

He scrambled to his feet. Lucky for him, he didn't have much to pack, his makeshift blade tucked into his belt, the coiled vine in his pouch, and his walking stick in hand. He fell in behind her.

They moved northwest, deeper into the forest.

The trees here were denser, their trunks twisting upward like pillars holding up the ceiling of green leaves, bark slick with moss. Ferns brushed against Finn's legs as they passed. The sunlight barely made it through the canopy, fracturing into long, slanting beams that painted everything gold and green.

Finn glanced around as they walked.

The boulders were getting larger now, some taller than a

man, some half-buried like sleeping giants. The ground sloped gradually upward, just enough to feel it in his calves.

Cass walked ahead without a sound, gliding like she belonged to the woods. Her boots didn't snap a single twig. Her shoulders never twitched. She didn't look back. Didn't speak.

Finn, on the other hand, tripped over a root and went down hard. His palms stung from the fall, and his sandals, already worn thin, bent backward as he got up.

He grumbled, dusted himself off, and gripped the walking stick tighter.

After that, he started using it more purposefully, leaning into it with each step, bracing himself when the trail narrowed or when loose stones threatened to roll beneath him.

Still, the silence stretched, and the thirst in his throat turned sharp.

Finally, he spoke up. "Do you… maybe have water?"

Cass glanced back, eyes narrowing. She gave a long, dramatic sigh, rolled her eyes, and then, without a word, tossed him a dented metal canteen. The cap was warm from her hand.

He took a quick drink, cold water sloshing into his mouth, and nearly choked. She didn't wait. Just kept walking.

Finn wiped his mouth and hurried to catch up. "I don't mean to sound whiny, Cass, but… where are we going?"

Still walking, she answered:

"You make too much noise. We are going somewhere safe."

That was all she said.

Hours passed. The sun crawled higher, then began its slow descent. Finn's legs ached from the constant climb, every muscle burning. His breath came in short, huffing bursts. Sweat soaked the collar of his tunic.

And then, at last, they broke through a gap in the trees.

Before them rose a stone cliff face, tall and uneven, with a scattering of shrubs growing from its cracks. Its surface was broken in places where weather or time had peeled layers away, revealing pale streaks of white stone that shimmered faintly in the light.

Finn dropped his hands to his knees, panting.

"Please tell me we're not climbing that."

Cass didn't answer.

She just looked at the cliff, then at a narrow path winding up beside it, barely more than a game trail, half-hidden by brush and boulders.

And she started walking again.

The trail wasn't just worn earth, it had once been carved. Stone steps, uneven and weathered, wound upward in tight switchbacks. From the forest floor, they'd been nearly invisible, swallowed by moss and roots. Now, high above the trees, Finn realized just how far they'd climbed.

They were higher now than any rooftop in Darrowmere.

At the top, the steps ended at a narrow crack in the cliff face. It didn't look like much, just a deep shadow between slabs of rock, but Cass stepped toward it without hesitation.

Finn blinked. Only when she reached into the darkness did he see the outline of a narrow door, cleverly concealed by the natural lines of the stone. A slab of wood reinforced with iron hinges, sunk just deep enough to avoid notice unless you knew exactly where to look.

Cass opened it and slipped inside without a word.

Finn hesitated.

He stood there, one hand still clutching his walking stick, staring at the hidden entrance.

He wasn't sure why, but something about stepping into that shadow made him pause. Maybe it was the silence. Or the strangeness of it all. Or maybe it was the fact that Cass wasn't exactly warm company.

Did he really want to follow her there?

Yes.

Yes, he did.

He stepped through.

Inside, the air was cool and still. The heat of the forest vanished as if swallowed by the stone.

The cave was larger than he expected, and the ceiling arched high overhead. Slender shafts of light poured in from thin slits carved in the cliff face, windows, hidden from outside view. The light turned the dust in the air to soft gold.

There was a table set near the center, with three mismatched chairs around it. A woven rug, faded but clean, rested beneath it, and animal hides were draped along the walls like old tapestries. They muffled the echo of his footsteps.

To one side, a small fireplace had been built into the corner, cleverly funneled so the smoke would vanish up through the rock. A neat stack of dried wood sat beside it. Cass crouched near the hearth, striking flint against the back of a knife until sparks caught on the tinder.

The fire kindled slowly, glowing brighter with each breath of flame.

Beyond the main chamber, Finn saw openings in the stone, doorless thresholds that led deeper into the shelter. Bedrooms, maybe. Storage. He couldn't tell.

Against one wall, counters had been chiseled from the cave itself, smoothed by years of use. Wooden bowls and rough metal cookware were arranged neatly, each in its place.

This wasn't a hiding place.

It was a home.

Finn stood near the entrance for a moment, letting it all settle in.

"You live here," he said, softly.

Cass didn't answer right away. She just added another log to the fire, watching the flames with her back to him.

Then, finally: "For now."

Finn leaned against one of the smoothed stone counters, still watching Cass tend the fire. The cave's flickering light made the space feel cozier than it should have, given that it was carved into the side of a mountain.

"You live here alone?" he asked, cautiously.

Cass nodded once without looking at him.

That was all. No elaboration.

Finn felt the weight of silence settle in. That topic, he could tell, wasn't welcome, not yet. Maybe not ever.

He shifted. "If you live here… why were you in the woods last night?"

This time, she answered more easily. "Scavenging. Hunting."

He blinked. She hadn't carried any meat. No sacks of supplies. No weapons larger than her knife.

What kind of supplies was she scavenging? And where?

Still, he said nothing. If he was going to make this work, if she was going to keep helping him, he'd have to wait. Let her speak when she was ready. Whenever that was.

Instead, he offered, "Do you want me to look for some food? For us?"

That got her attention.

She looked over, one brow raised in surprise. Then, unexpectedly, she smiled.

"You think you'd catch anything worth eating?" she asked, a small glint of amusement in her voice. "You're a little loud for a hunter."

Finn grinned. "I'm willing to try."

She gave a faint snort, then turned and walked into one of the shadowed side chambers. He thought they didn't have doors, but he couldn't see clearly inside. She came back with a wrapped bundle and set it down on the stone counter.

Finn stepped closer, watching her unwrap the bundle to reveal strips of dried meat, dark and peppered, alongside a few small clumps of dried berries.

Without a word, she cut the meat and berries into two piles and put them both on a wooden plate from the counter. Then she crossed to the nearest chair and dropped into it, sitting with her knees pulled up, chewing slowly.

"Thanks," Finn said, genuinely. He took his share and moved toward the thin, natural window slits that overlooked the world below.

The view made him pause.

Far below, the forest stretched like a sea of shadow and green, curling around the base of the cliffs. In the distance, the Twisted Peaks loomed jagged and dark, like ancient teeth waiting to bite the sky.

"Why haven't the Twisted Shadows come here?" he asked, more to the view than to her.

Behind him, Cass spoke around a bite of dried meat. "They don't climb well. And even if they did, I've set traps. They wouldn't make it far."

Finn glanced back at her.

He remembered the chaos at the awakening circle, the shadow thing that tore through armored men like paper, the screaming, the blood.

And here she was, a girl not much older than him, saying she'd kill one if it came close.

He didn't say anything. He didn't question it.

Instead, he sat and ate in silence, letting the food and safety sink in like warmth.

As the sun dipped below the horizon, painting the cliff walls in dusky orange and purple, Cass stood. She pointed to the woven rug.

"Make a pad there. Don't go into the other rooms."

He nodded and gathered a pillow from the corner of the room, placing it in a basket.

Cass crossed to the door and dragged a thick wooden crossbar into place. It settled into its notches with a heavy, final sound. She tested it once, firm.

"Nothing's getting in without a lot of noise," she said without looking at him.

Then she turned and walked to her own chamber. Finn heard the soft creak of wood, and to his surprise, a door slid into place, one he hadn't noticed before. A metal latch clicked shut.

And then he was alone.

Finn spread a blanket on the rug, the stone floor surprisingly smooth beneath it. He lay back on the pillow slowly, still listening to the fire crackle.

Maybe he could sleep tonight. Really sleep. For the first time in what felt like forever, he felt safe.

He closed his eyes and drifted to sleep, thinking about better memories of family and friends, and a girl named Cass.

CHAPTER 4

Home

The next morning, Finn rose slowly, stretching the stiffness from his limbs as sunlight streamed through the narrow windows carved into the cliff face. The fire had burned low overnight, little more than a nest of red coals now. He placed a split log gently on top, hoping it would catch. The cave was quiet, too quiet, and for a moment, he wondered if Cass had left while he slept.

He spent the next hour seated near the window, legs pulled to his chest, staring out across the endless forest. Mist clung to the tree canopy in the distance, curling over the jagged peaks beyond. It was almost peaceful until he remembered why he was out here at all.

Just as he was starting to worry, the door to her room creaked open. Cass stepped out, calm and composed, her hair tied back, eyes scanning the room.

"Morning," she said casually.

"Morning," he echoed.

She gave a short nod. "Today I'm going to show you a few things you need to know out here."

She crossed to the wall and tossed something at him. He caught it awkwardly; a pair of soft, brown leather boots was tied together by the laces. The stitching was clean, and the soles were thick but flexible. The leather was worn enough to be supple but well cared for. They looked like they'd been made for someone just his size.

"These are for you."

Finn blinked at her. It had been so long since someone had given him anything that wasn't food or a hard time.

He untied his fraying sandals and slipped the boots on. They were comfortable, snug, but with room enough to grow into. He grinned up at her.

"Thanks. Really."

She didn't say anything, just held out her hand. "Give me that shard of metal you call a dagger."

Finn hesitated, his fingers brushing the rough, jagged edge of the makeshift weapon he'd shaped days before. Then he handed it over.

Cass inspected it once, then casually tossed it onto the counter.

Without a word, she turned and walked into the storage room. When she returned, she was holding a real dagger, simple in design but solidly built. It had a polished wooden handle, a leather-wrapped pommel, and a clean, double-edged blade. A scabbard hung from it, well-worn but intact.

"I'll trade you," she said. "Your dagger for this one."

Finn's eyes lit up. "Yes! Of course! Thank you!"

She handed it over and watched as he removed the blade to inspect it from the scabbard and strapped the scabbard to his belt. Now dressed and armed, they headed out the front door and began their descent down the cliffside path.

As they moved, Cass stopped at intervals, pausing to tie cords between trees or slip spears and arrows into near-invisible notches along the trail. Finn watched in growing amazement. He hadn't noticed any of this on the way up; he'd been too tired, but now he realized: she had dismantled several traps on their first climb. Traps meant to kill or push someone off the edge of the trail.

They moved north through the woods, weaving around massive boulders and over fallen logs. The forest thinned in places, opened in others, and always the wind whooshed through the leaves above.

Nearly an hour later, they came upon a river, fast and deep, the current carving a silver band through the trees. Cass led him to a shallow pool off the main flow, where the water stilled and shimmered. It barely reached his ankles.

Beneath the surface, several large fish darted between stones, some as long as his forearm.

Cass crouched low beside him. "No talking. The Twisted hear as well as we do. Better, sometimes. Noise draws them."

He nodded, heart thumping.

Cass unstrung her bow and drew an arrow tipped with a four-pronged head, shaped like a narrow trident. She showed him how to notch it, how far to pull back on the bow, and how to steady his aim.

She had him practice first, firing at a stick propped against a log two heights away. He missed. Again. And again.

Fifteen times.

The sixteenth arrow struck the targeted stick.

After that, he started hitting the target every fifth shot. That was enough for her.

She led him to the water's edge.

"Now the fish," she seemed to say, through a simple movement of her chin towards the new targets.

Finn took a breath, aimed, and missed. Again. And again. Seven fish evaded him before one finally didn't.

His arrow struck home, and he yanked the fish from the water, thrashing and heavy.

He nearly shouted in triumph, but her glare stopped him cold. He clenched his jaw, shaking with excitement.

Cass nodded in approval and gave him a quiet applause.

She showed him how to string the fish through the gills and lay it back into the water to keep it fresh. Then she pointed.

"Do it again." She seemed to say.

By day's end, Finn had caught three large fish, and though his arms ached and his shoulders burned, he couldn't stop smiling.

Cass led him back to the edge of the woods and showed him how to gut the fish. He handled the second and third himself with his own knife. It was messy and clumsy work, but he managed.

As he wiped his hands on the grass, a strange thought crept into his head. He remembered the dog. The weight of its body. The fear. The blood.

He shook his head, trying to shake the memory out also. That was then. Today, he hunted fish. Today, he ate.

They made their way back to the shelter, and as they approached the trail up to the narrow entrance, Finn noticed Cass reach behind a fold in the stone and tug a chain he hadn't seen before. It was cleverly hidden, nearly invisible in the shadows. She didn't say anything about it, just gave it a quick pull before heading up the stairs. Even then, she paused now and again to check her traps with a practiced eye.

Inside, the air was cool and a little smoky. She shut the door behind him. He noticed that she went to the right-hand wall and stepped on a metal bar about a head's height off the ground, connected to a pulley system. It slid down and nestled into the floor, still visible but not poking out. He looked at her oddly, she noticed, and told him to lay the fish across the metal grill over the fireplace and to add a log. There's no way she made a security system like this. It's too much for anyone, let alone a teenage girl. His answers could wait.

As the fire caught and the smoke began to rise, the scent of slowly cooking fish filled the room. Without another word, she motioned for him to follow her. They passed through her room, which was neat and spare, and toward a second door he hadn't noticed before. She opened it, revealing a steep, narrow passage slanting upward into darkness. Every 10 steps or so, there was a small hole in the ceiling letting light in. Each window appeared to be covered in glass and was only 4 fingers wide. The hall was maybe 50 steps long.

She led the way, and he followed. The air was close and smelled of earth and old wood. After several minutes, they reached a heavy wooden door, thicker and older than the front one. Covered in iron supports. Together, they pushed it open, and light spilled in. They walked up another 10 steps until they were at ground level again.

They stood on a wide, flat plateau at the top of the cliff. Wind tugged at their clothes, and the view stretched endlessly, across the Land, across the Painted Peaks, where storm clouds brooded like sleeping giants.

She walked to the edge and waited. When he joined her, she said quietly, "My dad built this place with the help of the King."

She didn't look at him when she continued.

"They were sent here as lookouts, to watch the Land and the Painted Peaks. To sound the alarm if the Unbound Kingdom ever stirred again."

"Four years ago," she said, her voice low and steady, "there was an attack."

Finn turned toward her, but she kept her eyes on the horizon.

"My parents sent word to the King. Begged for help. But none came." Her hands tightened into fists at her sides. "They told me to stay here while they went to the city, said they'd try to rally troops to protect the town of Varnhollow."

She paused. The wind tugged at her hair.

"They never came back."

Finn didn't know what to say. His throat tightened.

"I'm guessing your parents died in that same attack," she added softly.

Neither of them spoke for a long time. They stood in silence, the weight of memory pressing down on them like the sky before a storm.

Finally, without a word, she turned and started back toward the hidden door. He followed.

Together, they closed it behind them, dropping the great bar down tight to keep it secure. They set the latch, making sure no one could open it if they could get to the top of the plateau.

Then they descended into the shelter, the scent of smoked fish still hanging in the air, and sat down for dinner, two survivors, brought together by loss, bound by something unspoken.

After they ate, the fire crackling low and steady, Finn glanced over at Cass. The warmth of the food hadn't taken the edge off the questions building inside him.

"Have you been there?" he asked. "To the town... after the attack?"

Cass didn't look up right away. She poked gently at the coals with a stick. "I've seen it. From a distance."

"And?"

"The first time I went, weeks after it happened, there were a few survivors," she said quietly. "But the second time I checked... There was no one."

Finn frowned. "Why didn't the King help?"

She shook her head. "I don't know. My parents sent word. But he never answered. They were... really upset."

Finn genuinely confused, thought it and said, "Maybe he didn't get the message?"

At that, Cass froze. Her hand stopped moving. Her eyes flicked to the fire, then dropped. Finn said nothing, just waited.

He was learning; she sometimes needed these silences. In the city, fast talkers and quick lies had gotten people through doors and around corners. But not here. Here, patience mattered. And Cass... Cass had answers. Real ones. He wasn't about to ruin it by rushing her.

After a long moment, she looked up and met his gaze.

"My parents were Mages," she said, voice low and steady. "My father was an earth Mage. My mother was a copper Mage."

Finn's eyes widened. "A real Mage?" he asked. "I've never met one."

She gave a small nod. "Do you know what a copper Mage does?"

"No," he admitted.

"They connect things," she said. "They build the awakening circles. Link the power in the earth to the focal point in the circle. My mother... She could connect this lookout to the Pale Keep in Crownshade."

He stared at her, barely breathing, and hoping that she would continue.

After a moment Cass said, "My mom told the King instantly when the attack happened. He could have answered. Should have. But he didn't... They told me that he was ignoring them... that he had been different after his dragon died. And that I needed to be very careful around him, to not draw attention to myself. There were very few Mages left in the Kingdom, that's why my parents were surprised when he ordered us here to act as an outpost. They weren't sure if it was a kindness or maybe a punishment. But still it didn't make any sense why he would send us here to act as a scout, and then ignore us when we report on an attack."

Finn wasn't sure what he felt. Betrayal and anger at the King or awe at Cass's personal knowledge of magic. But beneath all of that there was still a burning question that he needed answers to.

He looked at her.

"I need to go to Varnhollow," he said. "To find out if there's any trace of my parents. Any sign that they… that they made it."

Cass didn't answer immediately. Her expression darkened with worry, lips pressed tight. But then, resolve appeared in her eyes. She gave a short nod.

"Okay," she said. "I'll come with you."

The next morning, the sun had just crested the horizon when Cass and Finn shouldered their packs and stepped out into the cool morning air. Each carried a bedroll and pad, dried food tucked away, and a canteen sloshing with water. Cass had slung her bow across her back with a quiver of arrows, while Finn gripped his dagger with more confidence than he'd had just days before.

They moved west, toward the ruins of Varnhollow. Mist clung to the underbrush, curling around tree trunks. Moss blanketed the rocks, and tangled roots sprawled across the trail like veins under the forest's skin. Sunlight filtered down through the tall canopy in soft golden beams, lighting their path in fractured pieces.

The hike was smoother this time. Finn felt it in his body, stronger legs, steadier steps. The boots Cass had given him made a huge difference; he was quieter now, more surefooted, able to follow without tripping every few steps. The forest seemed to accept his presence in a way it hadn't before.

After two hours of steady hiking, Cass suddenly dropped into a crouch, her eyes locked on something up ahead. Finn froze, then quickly mirrored her movement. He followed her gaze to a dense thicket of dark brush, but at first saw nothing, just shadow and bramble.

Then something moved.

It was large, too large. A branch snapped. Whatever it was, it didn't look natural. It was a Twisted Shadow.

Cass reached behind her and pulled an arrow from her quiver. Finn noticed the strange glass bottle strapped to the arrowhead, filled with some kind of mixture. She nocked it quickly and reached for a flint.

Finn gently tapped her arm and shook his head. No way an arrow would take down a Twisted Shadow, not even close, he thought. He'd seen the guards in the city shoot dozens of arrows into one, and it barely staggered.

But Cass just pressed a finger to her lips, motioning for silence.

"Watch," she whispered.

So Finn watched, gripping his dagger just in case.

Cass struck the flint and lit the arrow's tip. Only then did Finn notice the small wick curled at the base of the bottle. The flame caught immediately, dancing along the shaft. Without hesitation, she loosed the arrow into the thicket.

It struck true.

The glass bottle popped, and in an instant, the contents ignited with a violent roar. Flames exploded outward, devouring the bramble in a sudden burst of heat and smoke. The fire crackled furiously but didn't climb high enough to reach the canopy.

Then came the screech from the beast.

High-pitched. Inhuman. Agonizing.

The creature inside, now clearly a Twisted Shadow, thrashed as fire engulfed it. Its massive form became visible through the smoke and licking flames, limbs flailing and mouth open in a howl that turned Finn's blood to ice.

Cass calmly drew a second arrow, this one ordinary with a stone tip, and released. It sang through the air and struck the creature in the throat, piercing straight through to the spine.

The beast collapsed with a sickening thud, like a sack of wet stones.

For several minutes, they waited, frozen in place, listening for any more sounds. The forest was silent again, aside from the fading hiss of dying flames.

Cass stood first and slowly approached the smoldering thicket. Finn followed, quiet and wide-eyed.

"Why did that work?" he asked. "The one I saw in the city... it was so much harder to kill."

She pulled another glass-tipped arrow from her quiver and held it out for him to see. The mixture inside glimmered faintly in the sunlight.

"It's made from Black oil and pine resin," she said. "My dad had a reservoir of the black oil in the shelter, Earth Mage, remember? I just had to collect the resin from the trees. He showed me how to mix these a long time ago. I guess this is common knowledge in the Capitol."

Finn stared at it, awestruck. He handed it back carefully. It was mostly because that was the most he had heard her talk at once.

"Two shots," he whispered. "That's all it took."

He looked at her, oddly.

"I'm really glad I ran into you."

Cass just gave him a small smirk and nudged his shoulder.

"Stick close," she said. "You're just getting started."

The teenagers stayed at a safe distance while the last of the flames burned themselves out. Smoke curled upward through the trees in thick gray plumes, clinging low to the ground before disappearing into the canopy above. The air still shimmered with heat. Neither of them wanted to get closer until they were sure the fire wouldn't spread.

They sat quietly, backs against the base of a thick pine, nibbling at strips of dried meat and bits of hard fruit. Every few minutes, Cass's eyes swept the treeline, bow resting across her knees, while Finn kept his hand near his dagger. The silence wasn't uncomfortable, more like the forest itself was holding its breath.

Finn broke it softly. "Why did the fire work? I mean… why did that work when nothing else does?"

Cass didn't look at him right away. "While they're burning," she said, her voice low, "they can't shift. The flames anchor them to this world. No slipping into shadow."

Finn let that settle in. It made a strange kind of sense.

Another stretch of silence.

Then, quieter still, he asked, "Are you a Mage too?"

Cass let out a breath that was almost a laugh, shaking her head. "No," she whispered. "I was too young to try before my parents disappeared. And now…" Her voice trailed off, then returned with a bitter edge. "Now I'm not sure I want to serve a king who sent us out here and then turned his back when we needed him most."

Finn looked down at his boots, thinking. The leaves rustled faintly above them.

"I'd become a Mage if I could," he said. "Even if I died in the process. I'd rather die trying to become something stronger than live the rest of my life wondering if I could've done more."

Cass looked over at him, her expression unreadable. Something flickered in her eyes, surprise? Concern? Respect? He couldn't tell.

Feeling the weight of the moment, Finn stood abruptly and brushed off his pants. "Well… break's over," he muttered. "Let's go."

Cass shook her head with a faint smile, but didn't argue. She slung her pack over her shoulder, and Finn did the same.

Without another word, they moved deeper into the forest, toward the silent bones of Varnhollow, watching for more shadows, and hoping they wouldn't find any.

Two more times that day, they encountered Twisted Shadows. Both times, the creatures had been lying in wait, hidden in brush or crouched low behind fallen trees, ready to strike at the first careless traveler to pass. Finn hadn't seen either of them until Cass pointed them out, her hand flashing up silently to stop him mid-step, her eyes narrowing toward some shape or movement he would've overlooked completely.

She may not have been a Mage, but she had an uncommon awareness of the world around her. Every breath she took seemed measured, every glance intentional. The longer Finn traveled with her, the more he respected her, her skill, her calm, her confidence. There was no panic in her, even when monsters waited just heights away.

As with the first beast, she used one of the glass-tipped arrows to ignite the creature. The fire stripped them of their shifting power, and once they burned, a well-placed arrow ended them. The second one didn't go down quite as fast. It had been struck in the chest instead of the throat, and though it burned, it thrashed and screamed longer than the others before finally collapsing in a heap of smoldering flesh.

As the forest grew darker, Finn found his thoughts drifting. A few days ago, he was just a city rat, stealing crusts of bread, ducking patrols, trying not to freeze at night. Now he was trekking through wild woods, helping kill monsters, talking about Mages and kings. Everything had changed so fast that it didn't feel real.

They continued hiking all day. The trees thinned slowly as the sun began its descent, casting long shadows over the path. Finally, nearly two hours before sunset, Finn saw it.

Varnhollow.

They climbed the last hill, and as they reached the crest, the ruined town stretched out before them in somber silence. From this distance, there was no smoke, no signs of life. The bones of buildings clustered around what looked like a town square, with crooked roads branching out like veins.

But it wasn't whole. Not even close.

The town had clearly been burned. Most structures bore the blackened scars of fire. Some buildings still stood in part, walls half-collapsed, roofs caved in. Others were nothing but piles of bricks and rotting timber, consumed entirely. It was quiet in a way that made Finn's skin crawl.

He looked over at Cass. "Should we camp down there tonight or outside the town?"

Cass studied the ruins for a moment before answering.

"We'll find a place in town," she said. "The walls may not be strong, but it's better to have something at your back than nothing at all."

Then she added, almost to herself, "Either way... I don't think we're going to be sleeping much tonight."

Finn shook his head in agreement. No way would he be able to sleep tonight, regardless of where they stayed. Certainly not in an empty village.

The way down the hill was simple, steady, and open, with loose gravel crunching beneath their boots. There were no trees around the perimeter of the town, just tall grass swaying in the evening breeze and the broken outlines of stone and charred wood. With no forest cover, the Twisted Shadows had fewer places to hide. If any were here, they'd be inside the wreckage of buildings or buried in the rubble.

That gave them a small window, maybe a couple of hours, to search and find the safest spot to camp for the night.

Finn stayed close to Cass, eyes scanning every shadow, every alley between collapsed walls. The silence of the town felt heavy, thick with memory and untold stories. He kept telling himself that answers might be close, maybe tonight, maybe tomorrow.

But everywhere he looked, there was no sign that his parents were ever there.

It was possible, wasn't it? That someone had survived? That his parents had made it to Varnhollow before it fell? Had Cass's parents passed through or left a sign of where they went?

He wasn't sure what they would find. But the thought that tonight might bring answers kept his legs moving and his grip tight on the dagger at his side.

Tonight. They may finally get answers tonight.

CHAPTER 5

Varnhollow

As they reached the beginning of the path that led into the ruined town, Cass pulled her bow from her back and nocked an arrow without a word. She glanced at Finn and pointed her chin at his dagger. He understood, ready your weapon.

Finn drew his dagger.

He wasn't sure what good it would do if one of the Twisted leapt at him, but Cass was right. It felt better in his hand than at his side. The weight gave him a fragile sense of control, even if it was a thin one.

Their footsteps echoed through the empty streets, bouncing off the broken walls and crumbling storefronts. The wind threaded its way through the wreckage, rustling torn cloth that still clung to beams and shattered windows, curtains, or maybe once someone's clothing left behind in panic.

Each building on the town's edge was half-collapsed, roofs

caved in, and only portions of walls were left standing like a map of bones hinting at where homes or shops had once been. No doors, no signs. Just ruins.

Overhead, crows called out with sharp, echoing caws, flitting from beam to beam, watching. Their cries cut through the silence like warnings to the others in their murder.

It felt like Varnhollow belonged to them now.

Cass moved forward slowly, head on a swivel, scanning every doorway, every pile of stone, every alley choked with debris. Her shoulders were tense, her fingers always just barely away from the string of her bow. Finn followed closely, trying to match her quiet footfalls and breathing.

They were trespassers in a graveyard. And every instinct Finn had screamed that the dead here might not stay buried.

They moved carefully through the ruined town, eyes on every doorway, every shadow, assessing each building they passed for any sign it could offer shelter. Finn kept scanning the ground, hoping, desperately, to spot fresh footprints, some indication that someone else had been here recently. But the only marks he found were from animals.

They made their way toward the town square, but hope dimmed with each step. Nearly every structure around the square had been gutted by fire. Blackened beams jutted out like ribs from the earth, and most places that once offered protection had long since caved in. Almost nothing stood strong enough to shelter them for the night.

As they continued moving, the sun sank lower behind the remains of the town, and long shadows began to stretch across the streets. The wind had cooled, and each gust carried the scent of old ash and rotting wood. Neither of them wanted to be out in the open when darkness fully claimed the town.

Cass caught Finn's eye and gave a quick nod of her chin

toward a building that still had part of its roof intact. They stepped inside, only to find the back wall completely collapsed. Exposed. Vulnerable. Without a word, they turned back into the street, picking up their pace.

Time was slipping away fast.

Finally, they found it.

A squat, leaning structure tucked between two other ruins, its roof still intact, walls mostly intact. It wasn't perfect, but it was better than anything else they'd seen.

They eased through the warped wooden door, which creaked faintly on a rusted hinge. Inside, dust blanketed the floor like snow. Strips of cloth and old bedding lay in scattered piles, and a broken table leaned against the far wall, just in front of what looked like the remains of a loom. Against the back wall, a narrow bed frame sagged beneath moldy fabric, and a door to what had likely been a washroom stood slightly ajar.

Finn looked around and exhaled. "It'll do."

They quickly got to work. Cass checked the walls and corners, while Finn gathered what fabric was still dry enough to burn. The table, battered as it was, could be wedged against the door to block anything from entering quietly.

With purpose, they moved from ruined building to ruined building, gathering bits of broken chairs, dry cloth, anything they could use to build a small fire or reinforce their temporary refuge.

The night was coming fast. But for now, they had four walls, a roof, and a plan.

Cass found a few flat beams nearby, half-buried beneath rubble, and together they dragged them inside. Finn propped them up against the window frame and wedged them in place with stones and broken chair legs. It wasn't perfect, but it would let them know if something tried to get in.

The front door had been useless, swinging outward and refusing to latch. So they tore it off its rusted hinge, brought it inside, and leaned it against the doorway from within. Cass found a solid beam just long enough to wedge between the door's base and the ground, creating a bracing angle that held it steady.

Within thirty minutes, they had scavenged enough dry cloth, splintered wood, and broken furniture to build a small fire in the middle of the building. The ceiling still stood, but several bricks were missing, letting the smoke out. The flames were kept low, just enough to take the edge off the cold and bring a little light into the room. The crackling glow danced over the stone floor and cast flickering shadows across the boarded window and makeshift barricades.

Two doorways blocked. One window sealed. They weren't safe, but they were as locked in as they could be.

And for now, in this haunted town full of ash and silence, that would have to be enough.

They settled across from each other near the low-burning fire, each finding a spot against opposite walls where they could lean back and keep their weapons within reach. The flickering light cast shifting shadows across their faces, and neither of them spoke much, so that they could listen for noises in the street.

Both pulled out dried meat from their packs and chewed at it absentmindedly. The taste barely registered, smoky, salty, tough, but it gave their jaws something to do, a rhythm to distract from the weight of the day.

Today has been both productive and disappointing. Finn had finally reached Varnhollow, something he'd been wanting to do since his parents went missing years ago, but the rushed search had turned up nothing. No signs of survivors. No clues about his parents. Nothing but silence and ruins.

Cass glanced up from her spot and said softly, "You rest. I'll take first watch."

Finn opened his mouth to argue, instinctively not wanting to fall asleep in this place, but the look she gave him was calm and firm. He understood. She wasn't being kind; she was being practical. They both needed to have their heads clear tomorrow.

Don't be stupid, he told himself.

He nodded slowly and pulled out his roll, spreading it on the relatively dry floor near the fire. "Wake me in a few hours," he said. "We'll trade shifts."

She nodded once, already watching the door.

Finn lay down, dagger in hand, keeping it close beside his roll. He doubted he'd sleep, but he had to try. The firelight danced on the walls, and the occasional pop of sap cracked the silence. Whether he actually slept or just drifted in and out of half-consciousness, he wasn't sure. He dreamt about not sleeping, or maybe he didn't sleep at all.

Then he heard her voice.

"It's time."

Finn sat up, heart thudding. The room felt colder now. He took a moment to stretch, then moved to her spot as she rolled her shoulders and settled in where he'd been lying.

Outside, the streets whispered with strange noises, creaks, distant thuds, the occasional shuffle of something too light to be dangerous, but too strange to ignore. Not Twisted Shadows. Just the nighttime sounds of a ruined town.

The fire had burned low, crackling quietly. Smoke drifted up through the ceiling, where it pooled thickly in places like dark storm clouds caught under the roof. Some of it slid out through the gaps in the brickwork, curling like fingers through the holes where the structure had begun to give way.

Finn kept his hand near his dagger and his eyes on the door, listening.

Finn's eyelids grew heavier with each passing minute. His head bobbed once, twice, then jerked upright. His heart thudded as adrenaline spiked through him again. He knew better. Falling asleep on watch in a place like this could mean death for both of them. One mistake, and the nightmare waiting outside might step through the cracks.

He stood up, forcing himself to move, and wandered toward the back of the building. The fire cast long, jumping shadows in front of him, and the warmth faded at his back with each step. He looked around the space, not as someone searching for a secure place to camp, but as an investigator. Someone had once lived here. This had been a home. And everyone died in this town. Maybe he could figure out what happened.

It was a quiet, simple home and a shop.

The loom, the table, the bed, someone had woven life into this place. He imagined an older couple, maybe a small family. Hard-working, the kind of people who took care of what they had. That would explain why this building still stood while so many others had crumbled. The others may have had bigger walls, but this one had been loved.

And now... it was ash and silence.

His eyes caught something, stains on the floor, faded but familiar. They looked too much like the ones that covered his tunic. It was dried and faded blood.

They may have died right here.

He crouched, inspecting the area more closely. In the front of the building, there was little else, just a bird's claw print near the window, etched faintly into the dust. He hadn't seen it earlier. Maybe the crows really had claimed this place.

Finn moved quietly to the back again, scanning for more. Near the place where the bed had once been, before he and Cass had torn it apart to barricade the doors, there was debris. Cloth, stone, scraps of wood. But something caught his eye: a narrow board, maybe two hands long and nearly as wide. It looked thinner than the rest.

He knelt down, brushed the soot and dust away, and examined it. No, not thinner, inset. A hidden panel.

He pulled his dagger free and carefully worked the blade into the edge, scraping, prying, until it caught. After a few tries, the wood creaked loose and lifted, revealing a hollow beneath the floorboards.

A hidden compartment.

He leaned closer, trying to see inside, squinting in the dim orange light of the fire. But before he could make anything out, a new sound sliced through the silence.

Sniffing.

Heavy, wet, guttural. Not quiet. It was loud, too loud. Something was at the front, pressing up against the door. Smelling. Searching.

Finn's heart leapt into his throat. He snapped upright, dagger in hand, and bolted for the fire.

Cass was already on her feet, eyes locked on the door, bow half-drawn.

Finn hesitated for just a second, then acted. He kicked a glowing coal from the edge of the fire towards the door, spraying embers across the room. Running up to it, he tapped the coal closer to the cracks, almost touching the wood that made up the barrier, nudging it toward the sound of sniffing at the corner of the barricade. Close enough that smoke curled into the cracks.

The sniffing stopped.

There was a low huff, then a sneeze, heavier now, retreating. A few sharp hacks echoed from farther down the street, followed by a soft, pitiful whimper.

If it were a dog, it had just gotten a lungful of smoke and heat.

Finn stood still, heart pounding, the sound of blood roaring in his ears. He stepped backward, slow and steady, keeping his eyes on the door until he felt the warmth of the fire against his back. Then he turned and locked eyes with Cass.

She let out a slow breath and relaxed just slightly, realizing it wasn't a Twisted. Just a dog.

Then her eyes narrowed. "Why weren't you watching the door?"

Finn swallowed the guilt rising in his chest. "I was looking around, trying to stay awake," he said, gesturing toward the floor. "There's a bloodstain here, and it got me wondering about the people who lived here. And I found something, Cass."

Cass's serious expression deepened, and she gave a quick nod with her chin. He was beginning to understand Cass's movements better. This one meant, "Show me."

He led her back, crouched down beside the hole, and looked into it. In the dim firelight, Finn bent down and pulled out what he saw, a wooden box the color of pale birch. It was about a hand and a half long, half a hand wide, and roughly the same in height, but heavy for its size. The thought flashed that it might be filled with coins. Twine had been wound tightly around it, and despite the years, it held firm.

As he looked back into the hole, something else caught his eye, a flat leather folio tucked neatly beside where the box had been. He pulled it free and handed it to Cass without hesitation. She took it, already unwrapping the cover, and walking back to the fire.

Finn was quietly relieved. He could read a little, but it had been years since he practiced, and truthfully, he was more curious about what was in the box.

They returned to the fire and added more wood. The flames had already saved them once tonight; they wouldn't let it die now. They wouldn't let the fire die now. Neither of them thought they'd be able to rest tonight.

Cass sat near the fire, fully immersed in the pages from the folio, her brow furrowed in focus or confusion. Finn took a seat beside the box, carefully working the dried twine loose. It cracked and flaked in places, but eventually, it gave.

He lifted the lid.

Inside, the box was lined with soft, thick wool. Nestled inside were two stones, each roughly the size of his palm. One was a red and grey stone, smooth and slightly oblong; he'd seen rocks that had similar colors to it near the Cliffside house. The other was pale green and irregular, almost bark-like in texture, but stone all the same.

Finn stared at them, confused. Were these treasures... or trash?

If someone had gone through the trouble of hiding them in a secret compartment, they must have meant something.

He glanced up. Cass hadn't looked away from the papers once. Finn set the box down and picked up the pale green stone first. It wasn't like the malachite he'd seen the lordling holding before; the color was too light. As he turned it, the firelight passed through it; it was transparent but not as clear as glass. But still it glowed, ever so slightly. Translucent. Weird.

He set it back and lifted the red and grey stone. At first, it felt like an ordinary rock... but then he realized something was off.

It was heavy. It was much heavier than it should have been for its size. It is much heavier than if it were even iron.

Finn had assumed the weight had come from the box. Now he knew it had come from this.

It wasn't a rock.

Finn glanced across the fire. Cass hadn't moved, still absorbed in the paper, eyes scanning back and forth with quiet intensity.

"Cass... you may want to see this," he said.

She tilted her head slightly toward him but kept reading. Whatever she was focused on must've been important.

"They're stones," he added, louder this time, not hiding the curiosity in his voice.

That got her attention. She blinked, pulled herself out of the document, and looked up first at Finn, then at the open box between them.

"Let me see," she said, standing and walking around the fire. She didn't just hover nearby this time; she sat down beside him.

It was the first time she had done that. No fire, no gear, no space between them. Just the two of them, shoulder to shoulder.

Finn slid the box closer to her with the green stone in it while he held the red and gray stone. She leaned forward, setting the paper and folio aside for the moment. With both hands, she lifted it and studied it as if it were some ancient relic.

Her brow furrowed in focus. She ran her fingers along the surface, turning it in the firelight.

She returned it to the box and asked, "Where's the other one?"

Finn passed her the heavy stone. She took it, then nearly dropped it.

She grunted and adjusted her grip.

Finn replied. "Neither of them is normal."

She gently placed the stone back into the box. Finn hesitated, already feeling a strange pull to hold it again. There was something comforting about it… or familiar. He couldn't explain it, only that letting go of it felt like losing something important.

"This place, it wasn't just a shop. It was a trading outpost," she said. "For adventurers heading into the wilds around the Painted Peaks. Kind of like a last supply stop before going deeper into the wilds."

She picked up the loose piece of paper, then tapped a line with her finger.

Says here, "Two stones.

The first one's absurdly heavy. Rust and dull gray, slightly metallic… They are calling it Skysteel.

The second stone is greenish, with a rough surface, but it catches light. With a rough texture. They are calling it Moissanite. What's weird is that there is a note for them to use this paper as a proof of purchase in case they are discovered."

Silence settled between them, heavy, curious, and electric. The fire crackled, its light dancing over the box and the strange treasures it held.

Finn broke the silence. "Okay… let's see what else it says."

Finn pulled a sheet of paper from the leather folio, determined to make sense of it on his own. But after a few lines, the words started to blur. He squinted, trying to make sense of the uneven handwriting and faded ink, but it was like trying to climb a mountain with no legs. Every sentence was a struggle.

Meanwhile, Cass read with ease, line by line, eyes moving across the documents with quiet intensity. Finn gave up with a half-smile and leaned back. Let her have her fun, he thought. She was clearly in her element.

So he waited, watching the fire die down and the light slowly shift from the hearth to the cracks in the walls as the sun began its slow rise. The air grew warmer, and soft gold filtered through the gaps in the wood and stone.

Eventually, she helped him dismantle the barriers they'd built the night before. Bit by bit, they loosened the boards and beams, always checking for movement or sounds before fully exposing the opening. Nothing waited for them this time, just the morning air and the burnt scent of the ruined town.

When Finn asked if she'd found something important, Cass didn't look up.

"There's a lot in here," she said. "I want to keep reading before I say anything. This could be important, or it could be a joke."

Finn nodded, respecting that. He left her to it and stepped out into the morning light, eyes scanning the area around their makeshift shelter. There had to be more, more stories, more remnants, maybe even more hidden treasures.

A short walk down the street and just outside the boundaries of the town, something caught his eye, rows of grave markers, most worn and simple. He walked closer.

The earth was uneven and overgrown. Most of the markers were blank, just stones driven into the ground. Some had names on them. None were his mother's or father's names.

That was it. No sign of his parents. No sign of Cass's either.

He stood there for a while, then turned back and returned to the shelter/shop.

They both sat just outside the shelter, with the Stones and folio, the morning sun warming their faces and the weight of unanswered questions settling around them like fog.

"What do you want to do?" Finn asked.

Cass didn't answer right away. She stared off down the road, thoughtful.

"I want to go home," she said finally. "But… I think we should stay one more night."

Finn raised an eyebrow. "Why?"

"I think I found something interesting in the documents," she said, lifting the folio, voice quiet, steady.

He didn't press. Probably nothing, he thought, but he trusted her instincts. He gave her a small nod.

"I'll start gathering supplies," he said. "Another long night then."

She gave him a small smile, and he stood, stretching. With luck, the dog, or whatever it had been, would leave them alone this time.

Cass was still staring at the documents, eyes locked onto the fading script, her fingers tracing the margins as if the words might vanish if she looked away. Finn left her to it and went back out, wandering the town's ruins with purpose. He scavenged from collapsed homes, picking through splintered beams, shattered chairs, and burned crates, anything dry enough to keep a fire going another night.

An hour passed. When he returned, the fire had faded inside to embers, and Cass had slumped against the wall in front of the shop. Her head was tilted slightly to the side, a lock of hair falling over her eyes, and in her hands was a page she'd clearly been reading when sleep overtook her.

Finn stepped quietly up to her, gently taking the paper and the folio from her grip. She stirred, but didn't wake. Without a word, he helped guide her to the bedroll, laying her down and covering her with her cloak.

Then he sat outside against the wall, the daylight warming the ground around him right next to the folio and the box of stones. He placed the box next to him and opened the folio, flipping carefully through the pages. Most were filled with notes and records of some kind, until one caught his eye.

It was a drawing.

He slid the other pages back into the folio and held up the page with the sketches. In the upper left corner was a map. He recognized the Painted Peaks immediately, jagged lines drawn like teeth across the parchment. Near the Peaks was a dot that must have been Varnhollow, though it wasn't labeled.

But farther north, beyond the Peaks, were more dots, some labeled, some not; lines wormed their way between and touched the dots, indicating that those must be rivers. A small "X" was marked just next to what he assumed were the Painted Peaks. What's that? Finn wondered. Is this a map of Elarith… or of the Unbound Kingdom? Maybe he was confused; this was the first time he had looked at a map like this. But if these were the Peaks, then that should be the Unbound Kingdom.

Below the map, another sketch showed a clearing in a forest. Tall, triangular stones jutted from the ground, arranged in a wide ring around the clearing like blades buried in the earth. Around the ring were tall trees exemplifying the size of the stone. They looked massive, even in a rough drawing; he could feel their weight.

Next to the drawing was a block of dense writing. And under that, in thicker, darker ink, were a few large words. They stood out, clearly meant to be read.

Finn squinted. Reading still didn't come easily. He sounded out each letter, slow and awkward.

"W… a… i… l… d…"

He sighed in frustration, almost ready to give up. He should've kept practicing, he thought bitterly. After his parents disappeared, survival had felt more important than learning letters. But now, here in this ruined town, next to a box of strange stones and a sleeping friend, he wished he'd kept going.

"W... i... l... d... Wild."

He slowly made his way through the sentence. But after he was finally done, he had forgotten what he had read. Frustrated, he read it again, a little faster this time. Then again. Slowly, the full message came together:

"Wild circles can make powerful awakenings and powerful Twisted Bonds. Use at your own risk."

He read it three times before the meaning finally clicked.

Wild circles... like awakening circles?

Could there really be circles outside the King's reach? One's not bound by his laws, or his control?

Finn stared at the street, the weight of the thought settling over him.

Cass had said she didn't want to serve the King. And after everything he'd seen, after his own parents had gone missing and no help had come, Finn didn't want to either. The idea of giving loyalty to a man who may have abandoned them made him feel uneasy.

But this? A wild circle? An awakening that didn't require them to become slaves?

This felt clean, right, good. This could change everything for both of them.

He slid the paper carefully back into the folio, tucked it shut, and placed it beside Cass inside while she slept, next to the box of stones. She didn't stir.

Finn stood and walked toward the edge of the ruined building, watching the shadows of the morning shift into day. There was more scavenging to do, more preparation to make. But he would stay close.

In case she needed him.

And when she woke, they had a decision to make, one that could shape their futures forever.

After a few hours of scavenging, Finn had already checked every building surrounding the old shop. He'd managed to find a few straight boards to reinforce their barricade and a small pile of wood that, with luck, would burn clean. Nothing valuable, but enough to make one more night possible.

Cass stirred and woke, blinking in the dim light filtering through the cracks. She sat up slowly, realizing with some embarrassment that she had somehow ended up in Finn's bedroll. She didn't remember lying down, much less falling asleep, but the warmth and stillness had clearly claimed her.

She stood, brushing off her cloak, and stepped outside.

Finn was there, stacking the scavenged wood and boards near the doorway. He looked up and smiled. "Hey, you're up."

"Sorry," she mumbled, still brushing sleep from her eyes. "I didn't mean to crash like that."

"Don't be silly," Finn said, waving it off. "You didn't sleep at all last night. It's been a rough few days."

She nodded quietly, grateful, and helped carry the materials back inside.

With the sun beginning its slow descent toward the horizon, they had maybe two or three hours of light left. They made the most of it, walking further down the street to explore a few shops they hadn't yet searched. Finn kept his dagger in hand; Cass had her bow at the ready.

Sure enough, they spotted signs of dogs paw prints and nearby droppings confirming that the creature sniffing at their door last night had likely been a canine. Not too dangerous. But nothing worth hunting either.

They returned to the shop and began rebuilding their barricade. This time, they used the heavier beams to wedge firmly between the door and floor, and the straighter boards Finn had found helped transform their haphazard defense from the night before into something that looked and felt solid. They both felt better about it.

The fire was stoked again, flickering strong and steady. They sat near it, each chewing slowly on the remaining dried meat and fruit. Supplies were running low, they hadn't planned on staying a second night, but they had enough to last, and if needed, they could hunt tomorrow.

Finn glanced at Cass.

"I looked through one of the papers in the folio earlier," he said.

Cass's head turned quickly, curiosity flashing in her eyes.

"It looked like a map," he continued, "and a description of something called a Wild Awakening Circle."

Cass's expression changed. Her shoulders stiffened, and her gaze dropped for a moment.

"I saw that too," she admitted. "I hadn't had a chance to really read it yet, but… yeah. Everything in the folio seems to point to those two stones being important to the King and the Unbound Kingdom."

She leaned forward, her voice dropping slightly. "It doesn't explain exactly why. Not in detail. But it suggests they've been looking for the stones. There's wording I couldn't quite understand, but the message is clear: they knew the stones existed."

She paused, then added quietly, "There's a warning on one of the pages. It says the Unbound Kingdom will stop at nothing to get them."

Finn stared at the fire, the weight of that settling in his chest.

"So... the stones might be the reason the Unbound Kingdom attacked the town?" he asked.

Cass nodded. "It makes sense. Varnhollow had nothing strategic, no resources worth fighting for. But if they could have known the stones were here..."

Finn felt a chill crawl down his spine. The attack had always seemed random, brutal without reason. But this, this makes some sense.

And now, they had it.

Finn held the stones in his hands again, turning them over thoughtfully in the firelight. The Skysteel, dense, dark, and rough. The Moissanite had a faint shimmer, but its pale green color wasn't striking. They didn't look magical.

"Sure, they're unusual," Finn said. "But they don't look all that special. The colors aren't bright. The Skysteel's heavy, yeah, but it looks like a lot of rocks near the Cliff House. Would the Unbound Kingdom really risk a war for this?"

Cass sat quietly for a moment, considering. Then she nodded toward the fire. "One of the pages described the stones. It didn't read like a record or inventory, more like... history. Lore."

She reached into the folio, pulled out a folded sheet, and placed it beside them.

"Both Skysteel and Moissanite were found in the same place, according to this," she said. "Skysteel, apparently, can be found here and there, but usually it's small, the size of a finger nail. But this-" she tapped the stone still in Finn's hand, "-this is huge in comparison and the color is off."

Finn lifted it again. It was heavy. Solid. Maybe too solid.

"And the Moissanite?" he asked.

Cass's expression grew more serious. "Very rare also. When it's found, it's always near Skysteel. And this one is… huge."

"So they're like… a matching set?" Finn said.

Cass giggled quietly. "Yeah. That's actually a good way to put it."

Finn smiled slightly. "Have you ever heard of anyone using either of them to awaken? Skysteel? Moissanite?"

Cass shook her head. "I've heard of Skysteel. It's sometimes used in forging weapons, but never as an awakening stone. And Moissanite? I'd never even heard the name before last night."

Finn looked down at the two stones nestled in the wool lining of the box.

"Do you know what kind of magic they could bring out?" he asked. "What kind of powers a Mage might gain from them?"

Cass was quiet for a moment, then shrugged. "No. Not yet.

There might be more in the documents. But the one I read... it made it sound like the Unbound Kingdom believed there was something prophetic about them. Like they weren't just powerful, they were destined for something. Someone."

Finn's stomach turned slightly. Prophecy. Destiny. He wasn't sure he liked the sound of that.

But he couldn't shake the feeling, like the stones had found their way to them on purpose.

Cass was quiet. "It'll be dangerous," she said. "It'll take time to find. And even if we reach it... there's no guarantee. It may not work. Or worse..."

She trailed off.

"We could die," Finn finished.

"We could become Twisted," she said softly.

Silence wrapped around them like a thick blanket. The fire crackled, casting long shadows on the walls.

Minutes passed.

Then Finn spoke, his voice quiet but full of certainty.

"I don't ever want to be weak again. I need to become stronger. I need to awaken."

Cass stared into the fire.

She had only known Finn for a few days, but he was the first person in a long time who made her feel not alone. Before him, she had been drifting, watching, surviving, but uncertain of what came next. And now, here was someone who had lost just as much as she had. Someone who saw the world differently, but who understood.

They were different, yes but their wounds had been carved by the same blade.

And the Moissanite… it felt right to her. The more she read about it, the more she understood. The stone wasn't just rare, it was unique. Resonant. It called to something deep inside her. She would never have this chance again. If the King or the Unbound Kingdom discovered she had it, they'd take it. Or worse.

But once she awakened, once the bond was made, no one could take it from her.

She made her choice.

Cass looked at Finn and nodded. "Let's do it."

The rest of the evening passed in rare peace.

After making their decision, Cass and Finn sat near the fire and began planning. They talked through supplies, mapping out what they had and what they needed, food, water, tools. They discussed potential paths north through the Painted Peaks, where the wild circle might be, and how long the journey could take.

Then came the more awkward conversation.

Cass was going through her mental checklist when she paused, looked at Finn, and said, "We're going up into the mountains, which means… we need to get you some pants."

Finn blinked. "Pants?"

Cass nodded firmly with a knowing smirk on her face.

He glanced down at his kilt. "I've climbed cliffs and rooftops since I could walk. What do I need pants for?"

Cass raised an eyebrow. "Because it's going to be cold. Really cold. And windy. And because you're not impressing anyone freezing to death with bare knees in a snowstorm."

Finn frowned and crossed his arms. "It's not that bad. I've got boots now."

"It's not a want, Finn," she said. "It's a need."

He sighed dramatically, shoulders slumping. "Fine. Pants."

Cass gave a satisfied nod and returned to the list.

There were other essentials, too. She needed to make more oil-filled arrows. Finn needed a bow of his own. Right now, he was relying on Cass's aim and a dagger that, while useful, wasn't much help at a distance.

That meant they'd have to return to the Cliffside shelter first. Stock up, regroup, maybe spend one more night there before beginning the journey north. The wild circle wouldn't go anywhere, but they needed to be prepared before they chased after something that could change their lives, or end them.

As the fire crackled low and the shadows lengthened, Cass pulled the folio back into her lap.

"This time," she said, "I'm going to read aloud. We both need to know what's in these documents."

Finn nodded, grateful. Reading had always felt like a chore, but listening, listening he could do. And now, with everything ahead of them, he wanted to understand. The lore. The risks. The full weight of the choice they had made.

Together, they leaned closer to the firelight, the stones resting between them, and the future quietly unfolding in the margins of old, forgotten pages.

Cass began to read, a letter that was on thicker paper and had large swoopy lettering "To the Council of the Dark Circle, In fulfillment of the binding pact and in payment of the blood debt owed for Caldreth's subjugation and my continued station, I offer the twin stones, retrieved at great cost from a frozen caldera in the far south.

Their discovery came only through great research on my part, finding mentions of pillars of fire that cause earth shaking to the south in old stories. The recovery of the twins required the deaths of many, and the sacrifice of the slaves who first cracked the glacier floor. Let this gift stand as final payment.

Now that the debt is fulfilled, I trust your agents stationed within Crownshade and the Pale Keep may withdraw in discretion; their continued interference in Elarith's awakening circles only fractures our front and risks seeding further corruption, where unity is needed now more than ever.

Elarith, for all appearances, may remain sovereign, but my heart, and my allegiance, will always stand with the Dark Circle and its mission: the subjugation of the Shadow Beasts and the unbound.

Whether these stones are the prophesied pair or merely relics of incalculable worth, I trust their delivery will settle any question about my loyalty. Let no further debt be named between us. - Theron IV"

"That rot-marked coward has no spine at all," Cass said, voice sharp with fury. "These stones were his, his and somehow they ended up here in Varnhollow. They were meant for some group called the Dark Circle." She scanned the letter again, eyes racing. "How did they get here?"

Finn shook his head, jaw tight. "No idea. But I really don't like the sound of what he said. The Dark Circle has agents in Crownshade, inside Pale Keep, and he lets them do whatever they want? He says they've been weakening the kingdom and he still does nothing."

His voice dropped, more disbelief than fear.

"And they subjugated Caldreth... I remember that name."

Cass turned to him, eyes narrowed.

"That was the King's dragon," Finn said quietly. "The old stories always said Caldreth was the one creature that protected the throne when all else failed. The last living known dragon who was bonded to the King."

He stared at the fire, the weight of that realization sinking in. "Who can subjugate a dragon?"

The question hung in the air like smoke, thick and choking. For a few moments, neither of them spoke.

Then Cass jolted, eyes wide. "Did you hear the part about the stones? The twins. He said he found them from stories about a pillar of fire and earth shaking. He thinks, maybe they're the prophesied pair."

Finn's stomach twisted.

Everything felt suddenly... larger. He had thought the stones were just tools, powerful, yes, but not legendary. Not fated. But prophecy? A subdued dragon? A king's betrayal?

He'd spent so long surviving, scrounging, keeping his head down, never imagining that he could be caught up in something like this. And yet... he was. They both were.

He reached out and opened the box again, heart pounding harder now. The soft wool lining cradled the stones like they were sacred.

Finn reached for the heavy red-gray stone, the Skysteel. It pulsed with silent weight in his hand. Cold. Solid. Ancient.

Cass, without hesitation, picked up the pale green Moissanite. It shimmered faintly in the firelight, catching shadows and turning them soft. She held it delicately, reverently, like it might whisper if she listened long enough.

They didn't say anything. They didn't have to.

They had chosen.

Or maybe, Finn thought with a shiver, they had been chosen.

He looked at Cass. She looked back.

In that moment, it didn't matter if the prophecy was real, if the king was corrupt, or if the Dark Circle was watching. What mattered was this:

The stones were no longer lost.

They were theirs.

CHAPTER 6

Near Death

As night settled in again and the fire crackled low in its circle of stones, Cass and Finn agreed to take shifts, just as they had the night before. Finn would sleep first and would take the second watch.

Finn curled up near the fire with the cloak over his shoulders and the weight of the day pressing down hard. Sleep came faster than he expected, but it wasn't peaceful.

His dream was about his aunt and parents. Everywhere he turned, more shapes emerged, Twisted Shadows, armies marching under a hot sun, and voices chanting something.

He woke with a sharp breath, Cass's hand gently shaking his shoulder.

"Your turn," she whispered.

He sat up slowly, shaking off the cold sweat. The fire still burned softly, and the barricades remained quiet. No movement. No sound beyond the gentle whisper of the wind.

"Everything okay?" he asked.

Cass nodded and yawned. She laid down the bedroll, his bedroll, and was asleep almost instantly.

Again.

He gave a small, amused sigh. Somehow, she keeps falling asleep in his bedroll.

Finn settled near the fire, watching the flames flicker. He kept his ears sharp, his eyes drifting across shadows.. But nothing came.

So his thoughts came instead.

He thought about King Theron. How he'd betrayed them all. Finn's parents had trusted the kingdom. Believed in it. And now? Gone. With no answers. Just ashes and secrets.

Then came the anxiety, creeping in like mist.

The Painted Peaks were no joke. People died trying to cross them, even with supplies. He wasn't a soldier. He wasn't trained. He wasn't even sure he knew how to live in the wilderness, much less survive it for days.

What if I can't do it? What if I slow Cass down? What if I fail before we even reach the circle?

Then his mind turned to the stones, and what might be waiting at the end of their journey.

What powers does a wild circle give you?

Would he control the ground like Cass's father had? Become as strong as an army of soldiers? Call down storms?

Or maybe he'd breathe underwater. Maybe speak to animals. Maybe he'd be able to see through lies. Send his voice across the world like Copper Mages could.

Anything sounded better than the feeling he had now, this powerless, uncertain half-life.

But... the Skysteel didn't feel like any stone he'd heard of.

It was heavy. Grounded. And yes, there was a feeling of

ancientness over it.

Finn had the strange, quiet feeling that whatever powers came from it wouldn't be like anything he'd heard of. They'd be different. Maybe even dangerous.

He made a note to ask Cass, really ask her, how Mages learn. Was it instinct? Like waking up and knowing what to do? Or was it like school? Study and discipline? He hoped it wasn't school.

He stared into the fire again, jaw tightening.

Then, without meaning to, his thoughts darkened.

The Dark Circle.

Who were they? Were they in Crownshade right now, smiling behind masks, whispering into the King's ear? Were they the true power behind the Unbound Kingdom? Or something else entirely?

Could it be a coincidence, the attack on Varnhollow, the missing stones, the prophecy?

Or did someone know the stones were here all along?

Finn didn't have the answers.

And they had no idea who, or what, was waiting on the other side. Right now, they have a glimpse of the truth surrounding the powers in the world. But what he feared was the powers in the world getting a glimpse of them.

Eventually, Finn reined in his thoughts.

He'd learned how to do that back in the city, on those long, hungry nights when his stomach was empty and his fear ran wild, spiraling like drain water through a gutter. He used to let his mind drag him down into what-ifs and hopelessness. But one day, he learned a truth no one taught him:

You can't control the world. But you can control yourself.

And now, as he stared into the fire while Cass slept behind him, he called on that same discipline. He closed his eyes, took a deep breath, and pulled his mind back from the edge. He realized that he did not have food for tomorrow; they had only planned to be traveling for two days, maybe this anxiety that he is feeling is because he knew at some level that there was no more food.

No more thoughts of kings or betrayals. No more circles or shadowy prophecies. No more imagining the Dark Circle waiting in the mountains or whispering inside the Pale Keep.

Focus on today. It was a trick his Aunt taught him when she was getting sick and he was just learning to "borrow" from food vendors.

Today, they were going back to the Cliffside shelter. They might face more Twisted Shadows along the way, probably would. They would hike hard, work harder. But they could do it. He knew that now.

They had faced Shadows before. And lived.

He might not be a Mage yet. He might not know what power waited inside the Skysteel. But he could fight. He could protect. And he would not break.

Another breath.

Finn rolled his shoulders, adjusted his posture, and let his thoughts narrow into focus. Just today. The next step. The next hour.

Today was enough.

The rest of the night passed with only a single disturbance. Hours after Cass had fallen asleep, Finn heard what sounded like a dog fight far off in the distance. He tensed, hand on his dagger, but nothing came closer. Eventually, the noise faded, and morning arrived in a quiet, misty gray. Cass did not wake.

In the morning, Cass stirred and opened her eyes.

"Good morning," Finn said.

"Good morning," she echoed, sitting up slowly.

They packed quickly, lifting the beams and planks that had sealed the shop for the night. Cass took the folio, Finn put the box and the stones in his pack, and together they stepped out into the cool morning air. The town was still quiet, ruined, but peaceful in its silence.

Instead of walking back the way they came, they took another, more direct way to leave the broken town. As they walked, they continued to peek into the buildings on either side of the street, searching out anything useful. They passed the square and moved further down a side road, nearing the edge of town.

Then Finn saw it.

A flicker of movement, a shadow that darted between the collapsed remains of a house. At first, he thought it might've been his imagination, but then it moved again, faster this time.

Before he could call out, it lunged.

A blur of claws and teeth. Finn staggered back, instinct and reflex barely saving him from a full-on mauling. The swipe shredded his shirt and snapped the strap of his pack, but only grazed beneath his ribs—a touch so faint it was hardly more than a brush.

"Stupid, stupid," he hissed to himself. "Just because we've been staying here doesn't mean it's safe."

He drew his dagger and braced as the beast lunged again. Finn slashed forward, the blade bit into the creature's arm, partially. He knew that the beast's arm went to partial shadows, but it felt like the dagger struck something beneath the surface, something too solid, but with a little bit of give. The beast pulled back, taking the dagger with it. It snarled, but was still unfazed.

Another strike. Finn dodged, barely, stumbling over a loose brick. He hit the ground hard, his breath knocked out of him, arms flailing for balance. His right hand landed on a pile of loose stones. Without thinking, he grabbed one and hurled it.

It wasn't much of a throw, but the weight surprised the beast and made it flinch back a step.

He grabbed another.

The creature lunged again.

Cass's voice rang out. "Get away from it, I can't shoot it with the oil if you are this close!"

Easier said than done. Finn scrambled, trying to find his footing, but the creature was on him in an instant, claws lashing. He managed to throw the second stone, but it barely mattered. The beast's full weight crashed into him.

He slammed on his back between two broken sections of wall. Finn threw his legs up, keeping its snapping jaws from his face. Its claws tried to rake him, trying to reach him past his legs, the wall sections, and his arms.

An arrow hissed through the beast and nearly struck the side of Finn's head. Cass is trying to shoot the beast, but it's going to pass through it and hit him if he's not careful.

It didn't stop.

Cass screamed a curse. Then, before Finn could react, she leapt onto the creature, one arrow in each hand. She plunged them down, stabbing wildly. The beast shrieked, spinning and clawing to reach her.

Finn saw his chance.

His dagger was still embedded in the creature's arm. With all his strength, he reached up, yanked it free, and began to stab upward, at the throat, the chest, the face. Some strikes hit the shadow and passed through like smoke. Others bit into something solid, tough, resistant.

The beast snarled, eyes wide and angry, teeth snapping inches from his face.

Cass drove one of her arrows down with a sickening crunch, and a spray of dark, oily blood hit Finn's chest. At the same time, his blade drove deep into the creature's throat. This time, it didn't pass through; it sank in.

The beast screeched.

Then it collapsed, its weight slumping entirely onto Finn. Its jaw was still open and shutting as if it were still trying to bite him.

Black blood smeared across his cheek, on his chest, arms, everything.

Cass rolled the beast off of him with a grunt, helping him to the side.

Finn lay there, gasping for air, his legs trembling. His entire body shook.

Cass was breathing hard, blood on her hands and pants. She checked him quickly, no wounds but a faint scratch on his stomach, no more serious than a cat scratch.

Scraping and flicking the blood off himself, Finn said. "This is disgusting."

Cass nodded, still panting. "We need to be more careful. That... we could both have died there."

Finn nodded wordlessly.

After a few minutes, he stood and tried to clean himself the best he could, wiping at his face, arms, and neck with grass, dirt, whatever he could find. The black blood was thick, sticky, and reeked of death.

They gathered their things. Checked the dagger, the folio, the box, and the stones.

Everything was still there.

Without another word, they turned and left the ruins of Varnhollow behind, heading toward the cliffside shelter, stronger, bloodied, and still alive.

Finn was irritable. Frustrated. Sore.

Every step after the attack seemed harder than the last. His pack, now missing one of its straps, sat crooked across his back, pulling painfully against his torso. The scratch was barely visible, but it stung with every movement. The blood didn't seem to dry; it just stuck to his skin, sticky and uncomfortable. His shirt clung to him.

Cass, meanwhile, was focused, silent, arrow nocked, eyes constantly scanning the trees, rocks, shadows. She didn't speak unless she had to, and Finn understood. They couldn't afford to be careless again.

Two hours after they'd left the ruined town behind, they reached a small stream. The moment Finn heard it, he nearly broke into a sprint.

"I have to clean up," he said. "Please, just a few minutes. I'll scrub all this off me, wash my clothes, and I'll be able to actually focus again."

Cass hesitated, clearly still on edge, but finally nodded. She found a rock and sat with her back toward the water, giving him a little bit of privacy without lowering her guard.

Finn dropped the pack, the box with the stones thumping softly inside, peeled off his bloody, sticky clothes, and stepped into the ankle-deep stream.

The cold shocked his system at first, but within seconds, relief flooded him. He knelt, scooped up sand from the bottom, and started scrubbing. The black, oily blood didn't come off easily. Just like last time, it clung with an unnatural stubbornness, but eventually it started to give way.

After several minutes of hard scrubbing, rinsing, and wringing out fabric, he finally felt like himself again.

He looked down at the scratch on his torso. It was red and puffy, swollen slightly around the edges. Not life-threatening, but painful. And no doubt vulnerable. He didn't have anything to treat it with, no bandage, no ointment. Just water and grit. So he splashed it, cleaned it as best he could, and hoped.

He pulled on his wet clothes, better cold than bloodstained, and stepped back up the bank.

"I'm ready," he told Cass.

She stood, gave him a quick once-over, and nodded. They set off again.

The rest of the journey was quieter but not without tension. As they retraced their steps, they passed the places where the bodies of the Twisted Shadows had been that they had killed on the way to Varnhollow. Nothing stirred now.

No movement. No sound but the wind.

They saw carcasses that they hadn't noticed before, bones half-buried in dirt, fur still clinging to sinew, skulls in patches of black earth. Too many. And too varied. Pig, squirrel, rabbit... dog.

Maybe even human.

Maybe the Shadows were territorial.

Maybe the last ones they'd fought had cleared the area.

They stopped twice more, just long enough to rest, drink from the stream water they'd carried with them, and push back the gnawing hunger in their stomachs. The food was long gone. The water only dulled the pain.

Still, they pressed on.

And finally, about three hours before sunset, the cliffs came into view and with them, the shelter.

Almost Home.

Finn stopped walking for a moment when he saw it. Cass slowed too. The weight of the trip, the attacks, the fear, the cold, the hunger, it all came crashing down at once.

They didn't cry. But they could have.

One hour later, they were climbing the last stretch of the trail. The air smelled familiar again. Wild. Cold. Clean. The kind of place where something could begin.

And for the first time in days, they didn't feel like they were running from something.

They proved that, yet again, they could survive in the wild. It was hard, and they needed to build new skills, but even without the burning oil arrows, they could defeat them.

CHAPTER 7

Fever

Finn and Cass finally stumbled into the shelter, dragging their battered packs behind them. They dropped everything just inside the door and immediately moved to secure the space. They bolted the door, pushed the metal bar into the floor that set the traps on the stairs, and listened carefully for any sign that something had followed them.

Once they were sure they were safe, exhaustion caught up with them like a crashing wave. But hunger was stronger.

Cass led the way down a set of narrow stairs carved into the stone, a lantern flickering faintly in her hand. Finn hadn't seen this part of the shelter before, and when he followed her into the dark room, he blinked in surprise.

It was much bigger than the shelter above, and the air was cool, almost like a cave.

"How is it so much colder down here?" Finn asked, his voice echoing softly.

Cass smiled faintly. "My father dug it deeper into the rock. Then he lined the walls, floors, and ceiling with stone, marble, I think. It traps the cold and keeps the food from spoiling."

Finn ran his fingers along the smooth wall, marveling at it.

They made their way toward the shelves lined with dried meat, preserved fruits, and sacks of grain. Finn's stomach rumbled at the sight. But something else caught his eye first: large, sealed stone vats arranged neatly against one wall.

"What are those?" he asked.

Cass glanced over. "My dad's old project. He collected liquids there for making arrows, treating tools, and... other things. He didn't get to teach me everything before he..." she trailed off, then shook herself. "But he showed me how to make the exploding arrows. That much I know."

They gathered food, dried strips of venison, some dense travel bread, a few dried apples, and hauled it back upstairs to the main room. They ate in silence, the kind of eating that was purely for survival, shoving food down until the hunger pangs dulled and they could finally think straight again.

It was only then that Finn really noticed the throbbing pain at his side.

The scratch from the Twisted Shadow was worse than before. Angry red, swollen, burning.

He told Cass he was ready for bed. She didn't argue. She disappeared into her own small room, shutting the door behind her. Finn rolled out his bedroll in the main room near the firepit, too tired to do much else.

For the first time in what felt like days, he was safe.

He thought he would sleep soundly.

But that night was anything but restful.

Finn tossed and turned, kicking off his blankets, mumbling in his sleep. He dreamt he was falling, tumbling endlessly off the cliffs near the Painted Peaks, the wind tearing at him, shadows laughing in his ears. He dreamt of dark corridors, of teeth and claws, of something tearing at his heart. He dreamt of his aunt's body, still lying in her bed.

He woke up gasping, heart hammering, freezing cold despite the fire still burning low.

Something was wrong.

Deep down, he knew it.

Cass woke to the sound of his restless movements and low, broken words. She crept out of her room, instantly alert.

What she saw made her heart sink.

Finn was drenched in sweat, his face flushed an alarming shade of red. His body trembled, and his eyes fluttered beneath closed lids. He was burning with fever.

Cass hurried to the pantry, grabbing the jug of filtered water that had passed through limestone and sand filters her parents had carefully built. She pressed a cup of it to Finn's lips. He drank greedily but remained feverish and incoherent.

Worried, she knelt beside him, pressing her hand to his forehead, then lower across his stomach.

He flinched violently when she touched the side of his torso.

Carefully, Cass lifted the blanket and saw the wound.

Her stomach clenched.

The scratch was worse than she feared, red, angry, leaking pus. The infection had spread rapidly.

She cursed under her breath.

She sprinted back to the storage room, grabbing a bottle of strong grain alcohol her parents had left behind for emergencies. She cleaned the wound as gently as she could, but when she poured the alcohol over the swollen flesh, Finn cried out in agony, half-awake, half-dreaming.

That night, Cass didn't sleep.

She stayed with him in the main room, checking his fever,

cleaning the wound over and over, forcing him to drink water when he was coherent enough. Once, he woke screaming, thrashing against invisible enemies. His eyes were wide but unfocused, seeing things Cass couldn't.

She gripped his hand, steady and firm, whispering soothing words until he drifted back into uneasy sleep.

By morning, the fever had broken.

Finn slept deeply now, his face no longer twisted with pain. His breathing was slow, steady. Peaceful.

Cass, on the other hand, was bone tired. She sat slumped near the fire, staring into the embers, fighting to stay awake in case he needed her again.

She looked at him, at this boy who was younger, stubborn, reckless, and felt fear gnaw at her heart.

How had he gotten under her skin so fast?

A few days ago, he was a stranger. Now, the thought of losing him shook her more than anything the Painted Peaks or the Twisted Shadows ever could.

He wasn't just a traveling companion anymore.

He was the brother she never had.

And she would fight to keep him alive. No matter what it took.

That day passed in a haze of slow, careful movement.

It wasn't the day of hard traveling and supply gathering they had planned for, but it was what they needed. Rest. Recovery. A chance to breathe.

They spent most of the day inside the shelter, eating small portions of dried meat and apples, drinking cool water filtered through stone, and repacking their supplies. Every movement was deliberate, every decision quiet. No rushing. No pushing. Just preparing.

A few hours after midday, they finally stepped outside, blinking against the bright sun. They walked to the edge of the cliff and sat side by side, legs dangling over the empty expanse.

The wind was gentle, carrying the scents of pine, rock, and distant earth.

Finn leaned back on his palms, the warmth of the sun soaking into his skin. He still felt weak, his muscles hollow and his limbs sluggish, but he was stronger than he had been that morning. The fever had broken. He was healing.

Cass looked just as worn. She hadn't slept properly since the day before yesterday, and the exhaustion clung to her movements like an invisible weight. But there was peace in her posture now, and a small, tired smile on her face.

They sat in silence for a long time, taking in the view, the sweeping Painted Peaks rising in the distance, the endless blue sky overhead, the world wide and wild before them.

Finally, Finn broke the quiet.

"We need to bring some of that alcohol," he said, his voice rough but steady. "In case one of us gets scratched again."

Cass nodded without hesitation. "Agreed. That was a nasty fever."

Finn picked at a loose thread on his new pants that were originally Cass's mother's. Cass's father was a large man, and nothing of his would fit Finn for several more years yet. Even her mother's pants were slightly baggy around his waist, and tighter than he would prefer in other places. They would take some getting used to, but they fit.

"I kept seeing things that weren't really there," he admitted after a moment, his voice softer. "I don't remember much, but... it was like everything I was afraid of was crawling into my head. Like I couldn't tell what was real anymore."

Cass turned her head slightly to look at him, her expression serious but kind.

He met her eyes.

"Thank you for helping me," he said. "I'm not sure I would've made it without you."

Cass shrugged lightly, but there was something tight in her throat that kept her from speaking right away. She nudged his shoulder with hers, small but firm.

"We take care of each other," she said simply.

And for a few minutes longer, they just sat there in the sun, letting the world be big and beautiful and still, before they would have to rise again and face it.

That night, after the sun slipped behind the Painted Peaks and the cliffs grew cold, Finn and Cass finished packing their gear for the journey ahead. Finn got a new pack and they each packed carefully, stuffing canteens filled with fresh water, blankets, and tightly rolled bedrolls into their packs. They rationed out enough dried meat and fruit to last them about a week, more if they stretched it. A small bottle of grain alcohol and a few clean bandages were tucked away carefully, just in case either of them was wounded again. Each carried a metal fire starter and a little coil of twine, already shaped into simple snares, ready to be set when they needed food.

Cass still carried the folio, keeping the precious old documents protected in the back of her pack. As for the stones, they both agreed that the wooden box was too large and would draw too much attention if anyone ever caught sight of it. Instead, they each slipped their stone into a small leather pouch, tucked deep within their supplies, out of sight, but always close.

Both of them would carry a dagger, and both would wear bows across their backs with quivers full of arrows-fifteen firestarter arrows treated with oil, and twenty standard arrows for hunting or fighting. They even packed a few extra bowstrings, just in case one snapped. Cass reminded Finn that they would need to recover any arrows that weren't broken after a fight, no matter how tired or rushed they were. Every piece of gear mattered now.

Finn spent several minutes admiring his new bow, running his hand along its polished curve, adjusting the grip, testing the weight. At one point, he laughed and said, only half-joking, that he might just sleep with it like a kid clutching a favorite toy. Cass smiled at that, a real, genuine smile. She was glad to see him excited about something after everything they had endured.

The pants, though, were another matter. Finn still walked stiffly, awkwardly tugging at the rough material as if it were trying to strangle him. He muttered complaints under his breath every so often, but Cass said nothing. She knew he would be grateful for them once they started climbing into the Painted Peaks, where cold winds would whip through the rocks and every bit of protection would count.

They fell asleep that night, Finn in the main room by the fire, Cass in her small bedroom, for the last time in what would surely be a long while. Finn felt much stronger now; he had cleaned the wound on his torso twice more with the grain alcohol, just to be safe. The scratch had scabbed over, swollen and ugly, but it no longer burned the way it had before.

They were as ready as they were ever going to be.

Tomorrow, they would begin their trek into the unknown to find the Wild Awakening Circle, and whatever destiny waited for them beyond the Painted Peaks.

The next day, just before dawn, they both rose and began preparing for the journey. Daggers hung at their hips, bows slung across their backs, packs loaded with everything they could carry. They set out just as the first sliver of sunlight broke over the horizon.

This was a trail neither of them knew. A path neither of them was fully prepared for. The best they could hope for was that the rough sketch of a map they found was accurate. The worst was that it was a hoax, and they were chasing a ghost.

Cass led the way, and they moved in silence, heads on a swivel, every sense alert. If the trip to Varnhollow had taught them anything, it was that the Twisted Shadows would not make their journey easy. Every day, they would likely face more of them.

Spotting the Shadows from a distance was always the safest way to fight. Unfortunately, these creatures were masters of hiding and ambush.

By midday, they spotted the first threat of the trip.

A massive, rotting tree stump stood by the trail, its sides spiking upward like broken spears. The hollow of the stump, easily three times the height of a man, had a deep, rotted U-shaped section, and crouched inside, half-blended into the dark wood, was a Twisted Shadow. Watching. Waiting.

Cass didn't hesitate. She drew an arrow from her quiver, and Finn lit the tip with the metal lighter. Within seconds, the arrow was flying through the air.

It struck the stump, splashing flames across the inside of the rotted wood. The fire roared to life, and the beast, caught in the center, shrieked as it burned, though the flames didn't fully engulf it.

Cass pulled a second arrow and fired quickly. It struck the creature in the chest, but passed through partially, as if meeting something not fully solid.

The Shadow screeched and turned its furious gaze straight at them, but the fire hemmed it in. Cass loosed a third shot, this time aiming for the heart. It struck true.

The beast collapsed in the middle of the flames.

Finn felt a rush of relief. He'd helped, at least a little, but it also sharpened the growing realization inside him: he needed to learn to shoot better. If he was going to be anything more than a glorified pack mule, he had to be able to fight.

Cass, however, looked frustrated.

"We lost three arrows on that kill," she said grimly, already checking her quiver. "We need to do better."

Finn understood. She was right. Arrows were precious; they

couldn't afford to waste them. But part of him wanted to remind her: they had just killed a Twisted Shadow with three arrows. It had taken trained soldiers in the city, dozens of arrows, and attacks without fire. They weren't perfect, but they were doing well, far better than most would have.

The fire, fueled by the oil, burned quickly. Trying to avoid the smoke, they built a small barrier of loose dirt and stones around the stump to prevent the fire from spreading.

When the flames died down and there was nothing left but charred remains, Cass and Finn adjusted their packs and continued walking, the long road ahead still waiting.

The day wore them down like a grinding wheel against stone.

By the time the sun hung low over the hills, Finn's entire body ached. His legs were rubbed raw from the unfamiliar roughness of the pants Cass insisted he wear, and sweat stuck the cloth to his skin in miserable patches. Every step made him itch and sting at once, the chafing along his thighs a constant, slow-burning misery.

Cass moved ahead steadily, but even she wasn't immune to the day's toll. Her shoulders sagged under the weight of her pack, and her movements, normally quick and alert, had become sluggish, mechanical.

The path cut through a sparse stand of trees, the last stretch before the land dropped into a shallow ravine. Near the bottom, sheltered by jagged stones and dense brush, they found it: a shallow cave, little more than a hollow gouged into a small cliff. It wasn't much, but it would give them cover, and tonight, they'd take anything they could get.

Finn dropped his pack with a grunt and immediately set about clearing the space. As he kicked aside dried leaves and broken branches, he uncovered several bloated, sickly-looking insects, each the size of his thumb. He shuddered, smashing them with a rock and scraping the remains outside the cave mouth. Better now than in the middle of the night.

Cass returned from a short scout of the area carrying an armful of dry sticks and branches for the fire. Finn, trying to distract himself from the burning irritation of his legs, wandered and found a little stream.

On the shore, he found a cluster of dewberries, their dark purple fruit plump and ripe where they curled along the ground. Grinning, he called Cass over, and together they filled a spare cloth with the fresh berries. It wasn't a feast, but it was something sweet and alive, and it meant they could stretch their dried food a little longer.

Back at the cave, they ate by the fire, chewing strips of dried meat and popping the tart berries between their teeth. It was the best meal they'd had in days.

Finn, still feeling the sting of travel, begrudgingly admitted to himself that the pants were maybe worth it. As miserable as they were, they'd at least make it harder for bugs, or worse, to bite him in the night.

After they finished eating, Cass pulled out the folio, carefully unrolling the old sheet with the rough map drawn on it. She set it across her knees and read aloud to Finn, the firelight making her voice seem heavier, more ancient somehow:

"Begin from the town of Greyfen, in the borderlands of the Unbound Kingdom.

Follow the river Kestril, whose waters are said to hide the silverback eels of old, creatures that pull men under and are rarely seen again.

Travel upriver for three days until the Kestril bends sharply south at the foot of the Painted Peaks.

Head south toward mountain called King's Fang for three days until you reach the waters of Gravenmere Lagoon. Do not bathe in the lagoon. The dark things beneath the surface wait for victims.

From the Gravenmere lagoon, travel southwest for two days to the Red Mound, a great rise of earth and stone. They say it was piled high with the dead from an ancient battle whose name has been forgotten.

Beyond the Red Mound, between it and the cliffs of the Painted Peaks, the Wild Awakening Circle lies hidden. Only the brave may find it."

Cass finished reading and stared at the fire for a long moment.

"Well," Finn said after a beat. "Sounds cheerful."

Cass gave a faint, dry chuckle.

They set up camp carefully. Finn volunteered to sleep first, and Cass agreed. He drifted off to the steady crackle of the fire, exhaustion dragging him down like a heavy tide.

Cass kept watch for the first few hours, silent and watchful at the cave mouth. When her turn ended, she woke Finn with a gentle nudge.

He rubbed sleep from his eyes, pulled on his damp boots, and sat near the fire, bow across his lap and dagger tucked into his belt.

The night stretched out, long and restless. The forest beyond their little cave whispered and rustled, unseen things shifting just beyond the firelight.

At one point, Finn heard something, a low crack, the crunch of a heavy step. His body stiffened. He reached for the bowstring with one hand, his dagger with the other, heart hammering.

For a long minute, he listened, tense and ready.

But whatever it was, beast, shadow, or simple wind, it didn't come closer.

Eventually, the sound faded into the restless breath of the forest, and Finn remained at his post, staring into the darkness.

Waiting.

CHAPTER 8

Strangeness

The next morning, Finn insisted they take some time to practice.

The scare from the night before had hammered the truth into him: he wasn't ready. Not really. He could fight with a dagger if he had to, but with the bow? In a real attack, he doubted he could hit anything except maybe a tree.

He needed to be better. He had to be better.

It took some convincing, but Cass wasn't thrilled about delaying their march, but she finally agreed. They chose a small clearing a few minutes off the trail, just hidden enough that they could practice without advertising their presence.

Finn picked three arrows, only three, carefully inspecting the shafts and heads before setting them aside for practice. He didn't want to waste any more than he had to.

He found an old, half-rotted stump that gave a little when he pressed against it. Perfect.

Arrow after arrow, he shot, retrieved, shot again. The rhythm was calming. Draw, breathe, release. Draw, breathe, release. He focused on steady hands, smoother releases, and aiming small. Cass watched from the shade, occasionally offering a sharp correction about his footing or draw.

For nearly an hour, he practiced until sweat dripped into his eyes and his shoulders burned. Eventually, Cass called an end to it.

"That's enough for today," she said.

When he inspected the arrows, he found one shaft had cracked near the fletching. Not surprising. He'd have to replace it, which was good practice and a useful reminder that every piece of equipment could fail if pushed too hard.

Despite his fatigue, Finn felt a little closer to being useful. He made a quiet promise to himself: by the time they reached the awakening circle, he would shoot as well as Cass. Maybe even better.

They packed up and moved on.

The trail grew steeper as the day wore on. The trees still hid the view of the peaks, but the breeze grew cooler. Their legs ached from the constant incline, but both Finn and Cass could feel it: they were getting closer.

After midday, they heard a strange noise ahead.

A series of shrill, warbling cries, Reeek! Reeek! echoing from the trees up the trail. Both of them froze, exchanging a wary glance.

The cries didn't sound like anything Finn had heard before.

Moving even more carefully, they crept forward, feet silent against the earth. The sounds grew louder, more frantic.

Then Finn saw movement, a flash of green and blue among the branches.

They edged closer, and what they found stole the breath from Finn's lungs.

High in the trees, flitting from branch to branch, were a group of creatures unlike anything he'd ever seen. Their feathers shimmered in vivid emeralds and deep blues, iridescent in the light. They were not birds; they didn't have beaks or wings. They had arms, legs, and a tail. Some jumped branch to branch; others seemed to glide more than fly, their long, feathered limbs catching the air in slow, graceful arcs.

Cass's mouth parted slightly in surprise, her bow lowered.

The creatures were clustered above something on the ground, staring down, calling out again and again with those sharp, metallic cries.

Finn and Cass crouched low, hidden among the brush, watching.

Something below them had caught their attention, and it clearly wasn't good.

Cass and Finn crouched low in the underbrush, peering up at the flashes of green and blue weaving through the trees. The strange creatures flitted from branch to branch, their brilliant feathers gleaming like scattered jewels in the light. Their sharp cries, Reeek! Reeek! echoed through the forest.

It wasn't playfulness, Finn realized. They were watching something.

They crept closer, careful to keep to the thicker shadows.

Then Finn spotted it.

In the brush under the creatures, crouched low was a Twisted Shadow.

Its limbs twitched as it shifted its weight, head jerking toward every movement above it. Its cracked, blackened skin blended with the rot of the forest floor. It looked feral, twitchy, waiting.

Finn's stomach turned. Another one. Another fight.

He glanced at Cass, expecting her to already be reaching for her bow.

But instead, she was shaking her head.

She motioned sharply with two fingers. Go around.

Finn hesitated for half a second, then nodded.

Neither of them wanted to waste more arrows if they didn't have to. The day was still young, the journey still long, and their supplies were not endless.

Moving slowly, they circled the clearing, keeping low, stepping only where the ground was clear of twigs and dry leaves. Every breath sounded loud in Finn's ears, every heartbeat like a drum. His new pants, annoying all day with their chafing, at least kept the rough branches from cutting his legs as they slipped through the undergrowth.

The strange green and blue creatures, whatever they were, kept the Twisted Shadow's attention locked upward, giving Finn and Cass a precious, narrow window to move.

At one point, Finn's foot caught on a half-buried root, and he stumbled, catching himself with a hand pressed into the dirt. His breath froze in his throat.

The Shadow's head snapped toward the sound, its body tensing.

Neither of them dared to breathe.

Finally, after what felt like hours but was only a few seconds, the beast's attention shifted back to the flashes of green and blue above, distracted once more.

Finn and Cass didn't wait. They moved.

Ten minutes later, they were deeper into the woods, the cries of the strange creatures fading behind them. Only then did they finally straighten and let out long, quiet breaths.

"That was close," Finn muttered.

Cass didn't answer, but she gave him an approving nod.

They hiked through the rest of the day, their boots grinding against the rocky trail, the weight of their packs a constant pull against their backs. The land grew rougher, the trees thinner, and by the time the sun began to sink behind the hills, they hadn't found any obvious shelter.

Cass said, "Prioritize firewood. A big fire and plenty of smoke might keep the worst things away." And Finn nodded.

They gathered what they could, armful after armful, building a towering pile of branches and sticks near a shallow hollow in the earth. It wasn't a cave. It wasn't even a real barrier. But it would have to do.

They ate quickly, chewing dried meat and fruit from their supplies without talking much. Neither of them felt safe enough to go scavenging. Out here, with no walls and nothing but the fire between them and the wild, every sound felt sharper, every breath tighter.

They rolled out their bedrolls facing the fire, backs to the open woods, weapons close at hand.

Cass mumbled something under her breath as she lay down. Finn caught the words: "Fire blind."

He understood. The fire gave light, but beyond its reach, they were nearly blind. Anything could be out there, and they wouldn't see it coming.

For a long time, they listened to the crackle of burning wood and the occasional shifting of wind through the brush.

Finally, Finn broke the silence.

"Why do you think," he said quietly, "that when we first went to Varnhollow, we saw three Shadows… but now we only see one a day?"

Cass didn't answer right away. She turned onto her side, facing him across the fire.

"They must be more common near the cities," she said slowly, thinking it through. "Closer to where… people are."

Finn frowned. "Do you think it's because of food? That they're drawn to cities because that's where people are?"

Cass shook her head. "We don't know if they eat anything. We only know they kill. We don't know what happens after."

She sat up a little, leaning toward the fire, her voice serious.

"Remember all the bones we saw near the Shadows we killed at Varnhollow?" she said. Finn nodded. "They weren't scattered. They weren't chewed on. If wolves or bears kill something, the bones get crushed and dragged off. But those bones were just... left where they fell."

Finn shivered slightly, despite the heat of the fire.

"If Shadows are failed awakenings," he said, "then maybe they are coming from the cities. From people. They used to be human."

He thought about it, confused.

"But back in Darrowmere... they hadn't had anyone try to awaken for a long time before the one I saw fail. There shouldn't have been new Shadows... right?"

Cass stared into the fire, her brow furrowed.

Pieces of the puzzle shifted in her mind, but none of them fit cleanly yet.

"Maybe one day we'll understand," she said softly. "But not tonight. We need to sleep."

Finn nodded, though unease sat heavy in his chest.

As always, Finn slept first, with Cass keeping watch.

When Finn woke hours later, the fire had burned lower-but not out.

He sat up, blinking blearily, expecting to see Cass's silhouette by the fire.

But she wasn't there.

Panic gripped him.

He scrambled to his feet, snatching up his bow, peering into the darkness. His heart hammered against his ribs.

He opened his mouth to call out, but then a shadow moved, and Cass stepped back into the firelight.

"I'm here," she said, her voice calm.

Finn exhaled sharply, lowering his bow.

"Why weren't you by the fire?" he asked, voice still tight with leftover fear.

Cass shrugged, setting her bow down beside her bedroll.

"I kept hearing things. Small noises. The fire made it hard to see beyond the light, so I moved over by that tree." She pointed to a thicker, dark shape a few yards away. "Let my eyes adjust to the dark. I could still see you, and anything that might have come near."

Finn nodded, respect creeping into his expression.

It was a good idea. Smart.

"What was making the noise?" he asked.

Cass shook her head. "I couldn't ever see anything."

Finn wasn't sure if that made him feel better or worse.

Without another word, Cass lay down and tugged her blanket around her shoulders. Within minutes, she was asleep.

Finn sat by the fire, bow laid across his lap, staring into the dark woods, listening.

By the end of the first hour of his shift, Finn was absolutely certain he had heard voices in the woods.

At first, he thought it was just the wind, but no, the longer he listened, the more sure he became. There were two, maybe three voices, low and whispering, carrying strangely through the cold night air.

He crept over to the tree where Cass had kept watch earlier, hoping that if he let his eyes adjust to the dark, he might catch the faint flicker of a distant fire.

But there was nothing.

He could see further now; the trees were spaced wider apart than they had been yesterday, but no lights, no glow, nothing but shadows shifting gently under the stars.

Whoever was out there, if they were real, either they were far away... or they were moving through the dark without fire.

Finn strained to listen, his heart pounding.

He couldn't make out what was being said; the words blurred together, but sometimes he thought he caught snatches of crying. A soft, broken sob, cut short.

Even creepier, the voices didn't seem to stay in one place.

One moment, they drifted from the south, then from the north, then from the east, and the west.

It was like the sound was bouncing off the trees and rocks, or twisting through the night itself.

The longer it went on, the more his skin crawled.

And then, suddenly, the voices stopped.

A heavy, oppressive silence filled the woods.

Finn stayed crouched by the tree, his bow ready, nerves stretched thin.

He didn't move. He barely breathed.

That's when something flew out of the dark, straight toward the fire, toward Cass.

Finn reacted without thinking.

He already had an arrow notched. He drew and fired in one smooth motion.

The arrow struck the thing mid-chest with a sickening thud.

The impact sent it sprawling to the ground, writhing, wailing, a sound that made Finn's blood run cold. It sounded human... but it wasn't.

Cass was on her feet in an instant, bow drawn, eyes wide.

They moved toward it together, weapons ready.

In the firelight, Finn got his first good look.

The thing on the ground wasn't a Twisted Shadow. But it also wasn't human. Its body was human-like, but its limbs were too long, its eyes clouded and wrong, and its teeth were sharp like fish bones.

It let out another shrill cry and lunged at Finn from the ground.

Without hesitation, Finn loosed another arrow, the shaft striking it directly in the face.

The creature spasmed once, then went still.

Dead.

The woods went silent again.

Finn stood there, panting, heart hammering in his chest, the firelight flickering off the ruined body at his feet.

Cass slowly lowered her bow, still staring at the thing. "Why do these things always happen on your shift?" she said half jokingly.

Finn was proud that he had taken whatever this thing was by himself this time. The practice had done him well. "I think it was making sounds in the woods like people having conversations. I kept hearing people talk." He said.

Cass stood over the body for a long moment, her face unreadable in the flickering firelight.

"Maybe a mimic," she said finally. Her voice was flat, tired. "I heard that word somewhere. Things that sound human, but aren't. They call out. Cry. Try to lure people to them."

Finn shivered slightly. He tightened the grip on his bow without even meaning to.

"Do you want to go back to sleep?" he asked.

Cass turned and gave him a look, a tired, sharp look that made Finn immediately regret asking.

Right.

Who could sleep a few heights away from a dead creature that had once sounded like a sobbing human?

They shaped Finn's bedroll into the rough form of a sleeping body, placing it close to the fire, just enough to fool anything watching from the dark. Then they both retreated to the tree line, hidden in the deeper shadows where Cass had kept watch earlier.

They sat side by side against the broad trunk, bows in their laps, arrows ready.

No more voices came.

No more shadows moved.

But neither of them truly relaxed.

Cass managed to sleep a little, leaning her weight against the tree, drifting in and out of shallow, dreamless naps. Finn stayed awake, watching, ears straining for every rustle, every crack of a twig.

The night dragged on slowly.

Finally, the first thin light of dawn appeared in the sky.

The fire had burned down to little more than embers, and the body of the mimic still lay sprawled near the ashes, twisted and unnatural.

After a brief inspection, poking it with a stick, recovering and cleaning his arrows, checking its strange limbs and glassy eyes, they decided not to waste any more time. There was no telling what else might be out here, drawn to the smell of blood and burning.

Silently, they packed up their things, double checked the leather pouches carrying the stones, and tightened their boots.

Without another word, they set off, continuing their trek northward toward the Painted Peaks, and whatever waited for them beyond.

The road was still long.

And the wild was only growing stranger. Before, Finn thought their only threats would come from men and shadows, but now there is a "mimic", and who knows what else, trying to kill them. They will need to find a safe place to sleep tonight. They did not want a repeat of last night.

The land changed as they moved northward.

The thick forest began to thin, the dense green giving way to patches of open, craggy ground where the roots of the world showed through. The trees, once towering and close together, grew smaller and more twisted, their bark darkened by the harsher winds that rolled down from the peaks ahead.

It was colder here.

Finn tightened the straps on his pack, feeling the sting of the chill against his still, healing wound. Every breath came sharper now, edged with the clean, biting scent of stone and old earth.

Mid-morning, they spotted something that made them both freeze in their tracks.

Across a shallow ravine, standing against the backdrop of rising hills, was a herd of deer. But not ordinary deer.

The stag that led them towered above the others, his antlers branching wide and burning faintly with a pale golden flame. It wasn't fire as Finn knew it. The flames didn't consume the wood or grass nearby. They clung to the antlers like wisps of living light, almost too delicate to believe.

The does gathered around him, their coats shimmering faintly as if brushed with silver.

Finn and Cass crouched low behind a fallen log, watching in silence.

Neither spoke.

Some part of them both understood instinctively that this was not something to interfere with. This was the kind of thing you witnessed and remembered for a lifetime.

After a long minute, the herd drifted away into the trees, and the moment was gone.

They pressed on.

By midday, hunger gnawed at them again, but fortune favored them. Cass found a patch of wild purple tubers, and they packed them carefully. It wasn't a feast, but it would stretch their supplies a little longer.

The ground grew rockier as the afternoon wore on, and every step became a test of balance and endurance. Loose stones shifted underfoot. Jagged ridges rose to either side, forming narrow passes where visibility was limited.

Finn and Cass moved carefully, heads on constant swivel, scanning not just the ground ahead, but the cliffs and ledges above them.

Any attacker could easily gain the high ground here.

Late in the afternoon, as the light began to slant golden through the peaks, they found it.

A narrow gash in the side of a hill, barely large enough for a man to stand upright inside, a cave, hidden between two sharp crags.

Cass spotted it first, raising her hand to signal Finn to stop.

Something inside moved.

Shadows twisted just inside the darkness, and a low, throaty growl echoed out.

A Twisted Shadow, lying in wait. Poised to ambush anything that dared to pass.

No hesitation now.

Cass lit an oil arrow from her firestarter, and Finn nocked a normal arrow.

Cass loosed the shot first. The flaming arrow hissed through the air and struck just inside the mouth of the cave. Flames spilled outward, igniting the low brush at the entrance.

The Shadow shrieked and lunged forward, straight into Finn's waiting arrow, which buried itself deep in its chest.

The creature staggered, burning, howling in a high, broken voice. It collapsed just outside the cave, its body writhing in the flames until it went still.

They waited a long moment, bows ready, scanning the cliffs and rocks for any others.

But nothing came.

The wind howled through the pass, carrying the scent of smoke and ash away with it.

Cass and Finn moved on, stepping around the bodies of the beast's previous victims, their steps steady but cautious. They were deep into wild country now, with no one around to help.

A few hours before sunset, they found a cavern tucked into the side of a ridge.

It wasn't much, just a shallow hollow with a firm back wall and a narrow entrance barely wide enough for them to slip through. But it was enough. It would allow them to build a small fire and have a defendable position for the night. Exactly what Cass had been hoping for.

They set to work immediately, gathering firewood from the sparse brush nearby, mostly sun-bleached branches, twisted and dry, perfect for burning. Neither spoke much. Their movements had become automatic by now: one scanning the area while the other gathered supplies, switching without needing to ask.

As the sun dipped lower, casting long shadows across the broken ground, they built a low fire in the center of the cavern, carefully shielding it from view with stacked stones around the entrance.

For dinner, they grilled some of the arrowroot they had dug up earlier. It blackened and cracked over the flames, giving off a faint, nutty scent. The root was hard and chewy, but the warmth of it filled their bellies, and it tasted sweet compared to the dried meat they supplemented it with.

Finn volunteered to take the first watch. Cass didn't argue. She rolled out her bedroll against the back wall and was asleep within minutes, her bow resting within arm's reach.

Finn sat near the entrance, back against the stone, bow across his knees.

He listened to the crackling fire, the occasional whisper of wind curling through the rocks. The world out here felt sharper at night, every sound a possible threat, every shadow something that might move.

But the hours passed quietly.

When it was time, Finn gently woke Cass for the second shift. She rubbed the sleep from her eyes, nodded, and took his place without complaint.

Finn barely managed to pull his cloak tighter around himself before sleep swallowed him whole.

For once, he slept deeply, without dreams, without waking, the exhaustion of the journey finally winning out.

Outside the shallow cave, the stars turned slowly overhead, cold and bright above the Painted Peaks.

CHAPTER 9

Quiet Moments

The next few days blurred into a steady rhythm of survival.

They would wake with the cold dawn, pack their things in silence, and move northward. Each day was the same: travel, scan, watch. Occasionally, they spotted a Twisted Shadow lurking near the trail, but it wasn't like it had been before.

Slowly, Finn realized something important: he wasn't as afraid of them anymore.

The Shadows were still deadly, there was no question about that, but they were also predictable. Each one they found was hidden in a shaded hollow or crouched inside a den, waiting. There were always signs if you knew how to look, animal carcasses nearby, the faint sour smell of death thickening the air.

Twice, Finn and Cass found dead animals and braced for an attack, only to discover no den nearby. It was frustrating, but it was also proof: they were getting better. Their instincts were sharpening.

Three days after the night they killed the mimic, they found something that made them both stop short.

Half-buried in a scree of loose rocks was a skull, huge, bigger than both of them put together. It had broad, flat molars like a mirrgoat, but from its forehead jutted two thick, spiraled spikes like twisted horns.

There was no sign of the body. No bones. No remains.

Just the skull.

They couldn't even guess what the creature might have looked like alive. But one thing was certain: it would have been larger than a house if the rest of it matched the size of its head.

They moved on in silence after that, a little smaller under the vast, empty sky.

Two days later, they made camp for the night and realized, only as they settled near the fire, that they hadn't seen a single Twisted Shadow all day.

The next day, they killed one, lurking in a cleft of stone.

But after that, nothing.

Two more days of clean travel. No Shadows. No sounds but the wind and the grit beneath their boots.

The air grew colder. Drier. Their water supplies ran low, dangerously low. They had no reliable source, no streams, no pools.

They learned to squeeze moss against flat rocks to catch the few drops it would give. They explored caves for hidden puddles, licking moisture from the cracks of stones like desperate animals.

They found patches of shaded snow once, packed into a crease between two boulders. They filled their canteens with handfuls of it, melting it carefully over fires or warming it with their own body heat against their skin.

Nights were brutal, cold enough that even huddled together

near their small fires, the chill still seeped into their bones.

The shelters they found, small caves, wind-carved hollows, helped to trap some of the heat. But twice, they had only enough firewood to cook what they scavenged before the flames died down to embers, leaving them to shiver through the long dark hours.

By the ninth day, Finn and Cass decided it was time to rest.

They had been pushing hard for days without real shelter, real food, or real rest, and it was starting to show in every heavy step and aching muscle.

Their campsite this time was better than most: a deep cave carved into the side of a rocky slope, half-hidden behind a thicket of low, twisted bushes. The cave extended back farther than either of them could see at first, its walls cold and slick with moisture, the stone veined with dark streaks of mineral deposits. Near the back, the air grew colder, and the sound of dripping water echoed faintly in the dark.

It was defensible, mostly dry, and large enough to build a fire without fear of smoke trapping them inside. Exactly what they needed.

Before settling in, Cass spotted some fresh animal scat near a patch of grass, likely hares or some other small creatures surviving the cold terrain. She showed Finn how to set simple snares, twisting the twine they'd packed into loops hidden among the tufts of grass and near rocky paths where tracks showed.

Then Cass grabbed her bow and disappeared around the boulders to hunt. Finn, left behind, busied himself with another task.

Near the cave entrance, they had found a shallow pool of water collected between the rocks, clear enough to see the muddy bottom and the tiny creatures scuttling just beneath the surface. Finn knelt at the edge, letting the cold water numb his scratched hands, and filled their canteens.

He took the time to wash, removing his clothes and scrubbing the worst of the grime from his face, arms, pits, and legs. Cleaner now, he inspected his body and the reflection in the still water. His chest and stomach were gaining muscle, his arms were lean but were also thicker, his face was also changing, but he couldn't quite put words to why. Things were changing, and he didn't know how he felt about it.

His pants, still new to him, held up well through all the travel and hardship. The rough cloth that once felt like a prison was beginning to feel like armor, stiff but reliable, protecting him from thorns, rocks, and biting insects.

While stirring the mud at the pool's bottom, he noticed sudden bursts of movement. Tiny shrimp, no longer than a finger, burrowed into the silt. With a little patience and a lot of splashing, Finn managed to catch five of them, trapping them in his full canteen before transferring them carefully to a pot for later.

By late afternoon, Cass returned carrying a fat quail slung over her shoulder.

A rare prize.

Together, they checked the snares and found one had caught something: a wiry, struggling rabbit. Cass showed Finn how to quickly dispatch it with a swift, practiced hand.

As the sun began to slip toward the horizon, they set about preparing their feast.

Finn built up the fire with brush and dried wood, feeding it carefully while Cass cleaned the rabbit and quail. Finn gutted and rinsed the shrimp, threading them onto a green stick to roast over the fire.

That night, they cooked the shrimp and quail together, the smells of roasting meat and woodsmoke filling the cave.

The taste was better than anything they had eaten in days, sweet, smoky, rich.

The rabbit they treated differently. They set the skinned meat closer to the fire but not directly over the flames, letting the smoke dry it out through the night. It would be their food for tomorrow, or maybe longer if they rationed it carefully.

As they sat by the fire, Finn and Cass allowed themselves to relax a little. Their stomachs were full, and their bodies warm for the first time in days.

Finn looked across the fire at Cass.

In the flickering light, he realized something he hadn't noticed before, or maybe hadn't let himself see.

She was changing, too.

This journey, this endless climb through wild lands and cold nights, was a proving ground, and she was meeting the challenge without flinching.

She was dirty, tired, and bruised from the trail, her hair tangled from days without washing. She could use a bath, sure. They both could.

But none of that mattered.

Cass wasn't just the wary, guarded teenager he had first followed into the cliffs above Varnhollow. She was becoming something more. Something stronger.

A young woman who carried herself with a quiet strength.

Someone who could face monsters in the dark and still stand at sunrise without breaking.

And for the first time, Finn saw her not just as his friend or his teacher, but simply as Cass.

Beautiful, in a way he didn't have the words for yet.

After a while, when the fire had settled into a steady crackling, Cass pulled out the worn leather folio she carried so carefully. Without a word, she pulled out one of the old sheets and began to read aloud, her voice soft but steady against the hush of the cave.

Finn leaned back against the cool stone wall, the warm weight of food in his belly, listening carefully.

Cass read,

"Right now, if you're reading this, I am already gone from town. I handed you this folio and, more importantly, the stones, and then hopefully vanished. I will do everything I can to draw attention away from you and Maedra. I wish I could have explained everything face to face, but I'm being tracked, and I couldn't risk them finding you.

I need you to understand the seriousness of the burden I just handed you. You must never tell a soul what I just gave you. Not Maedra. Not your friends. Not anyone. If someone comes asking, you know nothing. You have nothing. Deny it until your dying breath.

People whispered about legends, about relics hidden in the frozen south, but this isn't just a story. Months ago, I heard whispers stirring in the ports, rumors of something real discovered deep in a caldera. Stones found under glaciers, bought with blood and lives. Stones the King himself took an interest in, and so did others.

Once the King had them, he didn't keep them. He sent them north toward Unbound Kingdom lands. They called it diplomacy, but it wasn't peace they were sending; it was a gift to the Dark Circle in Velmirath.

Powerful forces have always pulled the strings behind nations. You know this. The Dark Circle was already waiting for these to appear. The King was delivering the stones directly into their hands. They have long sought them. Read the notes inside the folio to understand why.

Everything changed when I realized what the stones truly were. These are not ordinary Awakening stones. They don't just choose a wielder like the ancient stone in stories. They have the potential to reshape worlds. The powers they grant are not meant for any kingdom or the Dark Circle to control.

Night after night, crossing the Peaks, I planned. When the

Ambassador's company grew complacent, I struck. During a storm, when their fires were low and their Mages heavy with sleep, I stole the stones.

From the moment I held them, I knew I couldn't keep them with me long. Their weight was more than physical. They would draw attention, Dark Circle, King, worse. That's why I trusted you. Distant enough. Honorable enough. Smart enough.

Only you could hide them the way they need to be hidden. Only you would understand what's really at stake.

Life as we know it, free and unbound, will vanish if the stones fall into their hands. You have to protect them at any cost.

If anyone comes looking, wearing smiles or threats, you must refuse them. The Dark Circle's agents are not who they seem. Neither are the King's men.

Open no doors to strangers. Speak no truths to liars. For the sake of all the Unbound. I hope you can see the importance of this letter.

-Kellan Torren"

A moment of silence fell between them as they stared into the fire, the weight of what they had just read settling heavily on their shoulders.

"Every time we learn more about the history of these stones," Finn said quietly, "the greater the mystery gets."

"You're not wrong," Cass replied, her voice thoughtful.

She turned the letter over in her hands, as if hoping some extra secret might fall out.

"But this at least confirms how the stones got to Varnhollow," she added. "Eddin must have been the shop owner."

Finn leaned back, resting his arms across his knees.

"He traveled across the Peaks, too," he said. "What if... what if he walked the same trails we're on now?"

The thought sat between them for a moment, comforting and

unnerving all at once.

It would be good, Finn thought, so good, to find someone who knew something, someone they could ask real questions without worrying about a dagger in the back.

Cass nodded in agreement, her expression guarded but hopeful.

Without saying anything more, she reached back into the leather folio, replaced the letter, and pulled out another sheet, carefully unfolding the brittle paper.

The firelight flickered across the worn words as she began to read.

"Heard rumors from traders in Elarith's lower ports:

The King is quietly paying large coin for any scrap of information about a strange event over a decade ago in the Frozen South, something about fire in the sky.

Not a common bounty. Sparks my interest.

Began asking around. Found:

First account (spice runner out of Coldharbor):

"Saw a pillar of fire tear across the sky. Looked like a burning lance falling into the glaciers east of the Riftline. The whole ground shook like an earthquake several hours later."

Second account (a fur trapper in Ice Hollow):

"Something bright struck the ice fields near the Singing Cliffs. A blast of wind and light knocked us flat even from miles off."

Both accounts point to the same region. I have direction.

An informant under the King's pay passed me a message:

The King's priests unearthed scraps of an old prophecy in the Deep Vaults of Pale Keep.

First fragment:

"Twin hearts of fallen sky, fire streaking and earth shaking, wild awoken, will rule all."

Second fragment (from second informant):

"The stones that rule not by choice, but by power. When found, they will rule worlds."

Third fragment:

"Were the Twin Stones destined for the Red Mound, or the Red Mound for the Twin Stones? The Wild Awakening Circle was forged for both."

Month of Deep Frost

Offered money for information about what a wild awoken is. I've never heard of this. I've gotten some pretty crazy responses to this request, but the most plausible one I will look into is that awakening circles can occur naturally around dragon burial sites or other natural wonders. I don't know why it would be better or worse than the circles in the cities.

I also wrote to Torn asking for information about any "twin stones".

Torn's reply (delivered by trusted hand):

"The Dark Circle has sought two stones fitting that description for generations. If they exist, they are truly dangerous. The Circle believes whoever wields them will break the kingdoms and shackle the Unbound.

You must not allow them to find the stones.

If they do, it will be the end of everything."

Month of Deep Frost, 2nd Week

Found the King's recovery team encamped on the edge of the Frozen Caldera.

Slipped into camp during blizzard cover.

Saw it myself, hundreds dead: soldiers, slaves, Mages. Bodies frozen where they fell. Stones torn from a crater in the glacier's heart. No regard for life.

Day After Stones Freed

The King's men massacred Braventhorn, a small village west of the Caldera.

Burned every house.

Slaughtered every man, woman, and child.

No witnesses left alive.

3rd Week of Deep Frost

Tracked the stones to Crownshade.

Informants reported:

The King is overjoyed. Boasts of his fortune. Assembles a trusted company to move the stones north to the Unbound Kingdom. Makes no sense. They are not going to Stonehollow the capital. I'm still trying to find out where they are sending the stones to.

I got a description of the stones that one of the slaves saw: Skysteel and Moissanite. I've never heard of either, but they must be valuable.

Final Days Before Departure

Double checked through contacts in Crownshade.

Confirmed the town: Velmirath - a known Dark Circle stronghold.

He's serving the Dark Circle.

My informant inside the palace confirmed:

The Ambassador's company leaves at first light tomorrow. Planning an ambush."

"We've had that the whole time?" Finn exclaimed, staring at the rough map and crinkled papers in disbelief.

"Yes," Cass said calmly, though she sounded just as shaken. She brushed her hand over the folio, frowning. "There are still a couple more sheets I haven't looked through yet. This one was folded tight... I must have overlooked it."

Finn leaned forward, the firelight flickering across his face. "What did those prophecies say again?"

Cass nodded, almost absently, as if repeating the words helped her believe them.

"Twin hearts of fallen sky, fire streaking and earth shaking, wild awoken, will rule all," she said slowly.

"And... 'The stones that rule not by choice, but by power. When found, they will rule worlds.'"

Silence dropped over them like a weight, heavy and absolute.

It pressed down like the pressure under a waterfall, stealing the words from their mouths and forcing them to sit there, thinking, feeling the enormity of what they had just uncovered.

For several minutes, neither of them spoke.

The fire popped and crackled. The cold wind whispered outside the cave mouth.

"I'm not going to rule the world," he said flatly.

Cass looked up at him across the flames, a rare smirk tugging at her exhausted face.

"Well, I'm not either," she said. "I can barely keep up with the chores around the cliff house."

Finn snorted, the first real laugh he'd had in days.

Cass leaned back, exhaling slowly. "Still," she added, her tone darkening again, "it did say 'wild awoken.'"

She glanced toward the hidden map, the battered folio, and the stones packed deep in their gear.

"Maybe that means," she said softly, "that this choice... this path... is the right one."

Outside, the cold crept closer.

Inside, by the fire, two young souls sat between what they were and what they were about to become.

They both reached into their packs, feeling through layers of worn supplies until their hands closed around the leather pouches tucked deep inside.

Finn pulled out his stone first, the palm-sized chunk of

Skysteel. It was heavy for its size, dense and cold against his skin, as if it held a weight beyond just the physical.

Cass followed, lifting her own stone into the firelight.

The Moissanite shimmered like a shard of pale green glass, rough and bark-like, catching the glow of the fire in ways that seemed almost alive.

Finn turned his stone slowly in his hand, studying it.

"This just... feels right," he said quietly, more to himself than to her.

Cass was silent for a long moment, her eyes locked on her own stone.

Then she nodded once, firm and sure. "It does. To me too."

She tucked the stone back into its pouch carefully, as if it were something fragile despite its strength.

"Hopefully we'll be there soon," Cass said, glancing out at the darkness beyond the cave. "This trip has already taken longer than we prepared for."

Finn nodded, gripping his stone one last time before stowing it away.

"We need to read the rest of the documents in the folio," he said.

Cass gave a small, tired smile. "Tomorrow," she agreed.

For tonight, it was enough to sit by the fire, the stones safe in their keeping, and let the quiet night settle around them.

CHAPTER 10

Small Victories

The next morning, they started hiking at daybreak.

The trail grew steeper, but they managed it well enough until the rain began.

Cold, stinging rain, more like knives than water.

They pressed forward without shelter, hunched against the wet and wind. Eventually, the trail wound them into a narrow area with jagged overhangs, small ledges, and stone alcoves barely big enough to stand under. They crowded together under one rocky lip, shoulder to shoulder, trying to stay dry.

It wasn't working.

Cass was shivering hard, her teeth chattering uncontrollably.

Finn hesitated, then reached out and wrapped his arms around her, pulling her into a hug.

Cass didn't fight it. She just leaned into him, still trembling.

That was how Finn knew she was truly, dangerously cold.

She would never have allowed it otherwise.

The rain lasted nearly an hour before finally easing into a mist.

Once it stopped, they both peeled themselves away from the rock, clothes soaked and heavy.

Cass cursed under her breath, frustrated.

"I need to get these off if I'm going to wring anything out," she muttered.

"Turn around," she ordered Finn.

Blushing furiously, Finn turned away without argument and found a nearby stone to sit on. He focused on wringing out his shirt and pants while still wearing them, twisting the fabric hard to squeeze out the cold water.

Ten minutes passed before Cass finally called out, her voice steadier, "Okay. You can turn back now."

They resumed their hike, but the wet clothes clung miserably to their skin. Every step was a battle against the cold wind biting through the soaked fabric.

Another hour of hiking passed before their clothes dried enough to take the worst of the chill away. It was miserable, slow going, and they both silently promised themselves: next time, they would find shelter before the rain.

By midday, the trail plateaued, and for the first time in days, they could see.

They stood together at the edge of a wide overlook.

To the left, monumental peaks towered into the sky, jagged and wrapped in mist.

Straight ahead, forests spread out like a sea of green and silver, with the glint of distant bodies of water tucked between the hills.

To the right, more peaks and more endless mountains.

They weren't through the Painted Peaks yet, but they were getting close.

The trail would lead downward now, but while they had the

height, they took the opportunity to scout the land below, squinting into the distance for any landmarks.

Far to their left, just barely visible through the thinning mist, they spotted it—a massive, rounded rise that almost looked like another mountain.

But it wasn't peaked. It was round.

The Red Mound.

Cass stared at it for a long moment before speaking.

"That's another four or five days away," she said, her voice steady but heavy.

Finn sighed deeply. His legs already ached just looking at the distance between them and their goal.

"At least we know where we're going," he said.

They stood there for a few more minutes, catching their breath, feeling the cold wind against their faces, and then, wordlessly, they adjusted their packs and started down the trail again.

Toward the Mound. Toward the Circle. Toward whatever came next.

As they started down the winding trail, Finn shifted his pack higher on his shoulders, feeling the familiar, uncomfortable weight against his back.

"We still have the rabbit from yesterday," he said, half to himself, half to Cass.

"It'll last us today. Maybe tomorrow if we stretch it."

Cass nodded but didn't slow her pace.

She was already scanning the trail ahead for anything: a trickle of water, a small game trail, a stand of bushes with berries. Anything.

"But not four or five days," she said bluntly.

"Not enough."

Finn already knew it, but hearing her say it out loud made it heavier somehow.

They would need more food.

A lot more.

"We'll have to hunt again tonight," Cass added, glancing up at the lowering clouds.

"Set snares if we can. I'll try for birds."

Finn glanced sideways at her, then out at the endless forest and stone before them.

"We're not starving yet," he said, forcing a little bit of stubborn hope into his voice. "We've been through worse."

Cass gave him a thin smile, one that didn't quite reach her eyes.

The wind picked up as they moved downhill, carrying the smell of rain still clinging to the rocks, the distant, cold scent of pine, and somewhere, faintly, the iron-tinged smell of wet earth.

Every step toward the Red Mound would cost them.

They knew it now.

As the day wound down, Finn and Cass began scouting for shelter.

There were no caves nearby, not like the last few nights, but they found a long stone wall pressed against a cliffside. It wasn't perfect, but at least it would protect one side from an ambush.

They set to work immediately. Finn gathered what dry brush and sticks he could find, while Cass went out to set their snares and try her luck hunting something bigger than another rabbit.

There wasn't much wood at this site.

The wind had scoured the rocks clean, and while they could see woods far below them, dense and dark, they were too far away to reach tonight. Worse, the trail they were following was leading them away from the Red Mound, not closer.

They would have to talk about that later, once the fire was lit and their bellies were full.

Before sunset, Cass returned, her arms laden with a small handful of dewberries and a turtle.

Finn had never eaten turtle before.

But tonight, he would have eaten just about anything. The rain seemed to make him hungrier than normal.

They built a small fire, barely more than a flickering glow, just large enough to cook by and keep the worst of the cold away. They didn't have enough wood to build a real blaze. Every stick counted.

Cass carefully placed the turtle on the hot stones near the fire, letting the shell blacken and crack.

The smell of roasting meat filled the small camp, a mix of sweet and earthy, different from the rabbit or quail they were used to.

When it was ready, Cass cracked open the charred shell with her dagger, and the two of them picked out the meat with fingers and a thin stick.

The flavor was rich and oily, almost like fatty chicken crossed with river fish. Tough, but filling.

It wasn't much, but it was food. And it warmed them from the inside out.

After they ate, Cass insisted on taking the first watch.

Finn didn't argue. His eyes were already heavy with exhaustion as he pulled his blanket tighter around himself and drifted off against the cold stone wall.

He didn't know how long he'd been asleep when Cass woke him.

A hand on his shoulder, sharp, urgent.

Finn jolted awake, his hand already scrambling for his dagger as he stumbled to his feet, heart hammering.

But there were no Twisted Shadows.

No Mimics.

No monsters hiding in the dark.

Instead, he saw something far stranger.

Two glowing orbs floated in the cold night air, spinning lazily around each other. Each was about the size of his head, pulsing with a soft white light.

They hummed, not loudly, but deep enough to feel in his chest. A low, vibrating thrum.

Finn couldn't tell if they were being carried by the wind or if they moved by some will of their own.

He watched, wide-eyed, as small bugs drifted up from the ground toward the orbs, only to burn away instantly when they touched the light, vanishing like ash in a flame.

The orbs spun tighter, pulsing brighter, before finally drifting away over the rocks, swallowed by the night.

Finn let out a breath he hadn't realized he was holding.

"What were those?" he whispered.

Cass shook her head, her voice low and serious. "I have no idea."

Finn stared out into the dark after the orbs.

"I have a feeling we're going to see a lot of things we don't know about... now that we're on this side of the Peaks."

Cass nodded.

"Sleep if you can," she said. "Your shift's not for a little while yet."

Finn nodded back, though sleep felt a lot farther away now.

Still, he lay down again, closing his eyes against the strange new world waiting just beyond the firelight.

Finn woke and took his shift through the rest of the night, but unlike Cass's watch, nothing strange appeared.

No creatures, no orbs, no trouble.

When the first light of dawn crept over the jagged rocks, Cass stirred from sleep.

"Good morning," Finn said, handing her a strip of dried rabbit from his pack.

"Morning," Cass answered groggily. She accepted the meat gratefully and began picking at it while Finn sat down beside her, chewing his own piece.

"I think the trail's taking us the wrong way," Finn said after a while. "It's pulling us further from the Red Mound."

Cass nodded. "I noticed that too. I don't think we should climb down just yet, but if there are shortcuts we can take, we should consider them. Otherwise, we'll end up somewhere we don't want to be."

The trail felt like it was man-made, where the trail on the Elarith side felt like it was an animal trail.

Finn frowned, realizing something he hadn't thought about.

"This trail may lead to a town."

Cass gave a grim nod. "Maybe. And we don't want towns. Not here. We're not in Elarith anymore. We're outsiders. If anyone sees us, we are going to get questioned."

Finn tightened the straps on his pack. She was right.

Better to avoid people altogether.

They double-checked their supplies and began their hike. They still have a bit of rabbit; hopefully, they will find some food here soon.

Two hours later, they came across a shallow stream, water glinting silver as it snaked between boulders. They refilled their canteens gratefully.

Cass scanned the water and spotted something moving, sleek shapes flashing under the surface.

Long and thin, about the length of her arm and no thicker than two fingers, silver eels.

She crouched, wondering if they could catch one. They looked fast, but food was food.

For half an hour, Cass tried to line up a shot with her bow, but the eels blurred through the water too quickly. Every time she thought she had a chance, the eel darted away. Shooting one with an arrow would just result in her losing an arrow. Maybe with a net, but they didn't have one.

Frustrated, she stood up and they began to cross the stream, and that's when Finn yelped.

He stumbled out of the stream, clutching his calf.

Cass barely had time to react before she too felt a sharp, brutal pain in her ankle.

They scrambled onto the rocks, both of them shouting, each with a thrashing eel clamped onto their legs.

Finn yanked out his dagger and stabbed his attacker through the head. The eel writhed once, then went still.

Cass struggled, trying to kick hers off, but it was latched tight.

Finn rushed over, still dripping wet, and stabbed hers through the skull as well. It finally released her.

There was blood on both of them, but Cass's wound was worse.

Blood ran fast from her ankle, soaking into her boot and dripping onto the rocks.

Finn cursed and dropped to his knees, pulling out the bandages and grain alcohol they packed.

He worked quickly, wrapping Cass's ankle tightly to slow the bleeding, then splashed the alcohol over the wound.

Cass winced but said nothing.

Finn tended his own wound too, but it was in the meat of his leg; he wasn't worried about the damage. Cass lay back against a rock, foot elevated, her face pale and tight with pain.

And then, without warning, Cass started to cry.

Not loudly.

But real tears slipped down her face, and she made no effort to stop them.

It was the first time Finn had seen her break.

She had always been the strong one, the steady hand, the sharp eyes, the voice of reason when things went wrong.

Finn didn't touch her. He didn't say anything.

He just sat down next to her in silence, guarding her the only way he could.

When Cass's tears finally slowed, Finn stood and went to the dead eels.

With a grim sort of determination, he gutted them both like fish. Their bodies were slimy and metallic, almost shining in the dim light.

Once the eels were cleaned, he scrounged for dry brush and driftwood and managed to light a small fire.

He wasn't about to push her to hike again, not yet.

Cass eventually sat up, drank from her canteen, and wiped her face.

"I'm sorry," she said quietly, voice thick. "I don't know what got into me. I just... they scared me. I wasn't ready."

Finn shook his head. "Neither was I. Don't worry about it."

He poked at the fire with a stick, adjusting the stones so they could roast the meat.

"We're in an impossible place," he said. "Everything out here either wants to kill us or eat us. We just have to be smarter."

He looked at her seriously.

"You bled a lot. How do you feel?"

Cass flexed her foot slightly, grimacing. "A little sore. But if I can eat, I'll feel better."

Finn gave a crooked grin and nodded at the sizzling eels.

"Good. Because I've got just the thing. Two ankle biters, grilled and ready."

Cass let out a short, half-hearted laugh. But even that was better than nothing.

When the meat was ready, they tore into it.

And despite everything, the blood, the cold, the fear, the eel was amazing.

Tender, a little oily, but rich and filling. Far better than the turtle from the previous night.

They sat a little straighter after eating, feeling warmth and energy returning.

"If we see more of those things," Cass said, "we hunt them properly next time. Spears. Bait. Not our legs."

Finn grinned. "Deal."

They packed up slowly, Cass leaning on him for support until she could walk mostly on her own again.

This time, they didn't follow the old trail.

They forged their own path off-road, cutting across the broken land, straight toward the distant curve of the Red Mound.

Straight toward whatever fate waited for them at the Wild Awakening Circle.

Cass walked with a stagger for a while, leaning heavily on Finn's arm until he spotted a thin sapling just off the trail.

Without a word, he used his dagger to clean it, stripping away the rough bark and trimming it down to a usable size, and handed it to her.

Cass wasn't thrilled about needing a walking stick, but she accepted it anyway, offering a quiet, "Thank you," before using it to steady herself.

The staff helped.

Her steps became a little more sure, a little less painful.

Finn's injury wasn't as bad, just a flesh wound where the eel's teeth had missed anything important. Still, he insisted that both of them clean their wounds again with the grain alcohol.

He remembered all too clearly what had happened after the Shadow Beast scratched him back in Varnhollow. They wouldn't survive another infection out here.

A few hours later, the trail brought them to a small clearing.

A massive fallen tree lay cracked and rotting across the center, surrounded by several towering oaks.

Above the clearing buzzed a strange, living cloud-at first, they thought it was just gnats or mosquitoes, but as they moved closer, they realized it was something else entirely.

The air was filled with insects unlike anything either of them had ever seen.

Tiny creatures, their wings and bodies glinting in the light like shards of glass.

Not dull or soft, but sharp, brilliant, colorful, moving so fast they blurred into glittering trails between the trees.

Finn caught a better glimpse as one darted close. The wings looked like razor-thin slivers of crystal, spinning so fast they could easily slice flesh.

He didn't need to get closer to know: they didn't want to find out what kind of damage those things could do.

Cass raised her hand, signaling: Go around. Quietly.

Finn nodded immediately. They didn't need this fight.

The insects were beautiful, hypnotic, almost human in their intricate movements-but here, beauty and death seemed far too closely related.

Carefully, they backed away from the clearing, moving slowly through the brush.

Twice, a few of the glittering insects zipped dangerously close to them, their wings humming sharply in the air, but neither Cass nor Finn made any sudden moves.

They simply kept moving, slow and steady, giving the swarm a wide berth.

The insects didn't seem to care, so long as they weren't disturbed.

It was nerve-wracking, inching around the clearing with both of them still limping from their injuries, but eventually the glittering cloud was behind them.

The humming faded into the misty woods, and they continued their long, slow trek toward the distant curve of the Red Mound.

They moved quietly for a while after the clearing, their boots crunching softly against loose stones and dry leaves.

The woods seemed to hold its breath.

No more glass-winged insects.

No more buzzing or shimmer in the air.

Just the low, steady beat of the wind pushing through the narrow gaps in the rocks.

Finn adjusted the weight of his pack and glanced sideways at Cass. She was leaning heavily on her walking stick, but she hadn't slowed. Not yet.

They were both tired, hurt, cold, pushed to the edge, but they kept going.

Finn turned his gaze back to the trail ahead.

Everything feels different now. Not just harder. Wilder.

It was as if the land itself had changed once they crossed into the far side of the Painted Peaks.

The air was sharper. The sky felt closer.

The animals, the plants, even the stones, were not like anything he had grown up with. They didn't belong to the quiet towns or familiar woods of Elarith.

Finn tightened his grip on the strap of his pack.

This is what it means to be Wild Awoken, he thought.

Not just to survive the wild, but to walk straight into it, and still come out stronger.

He didn't say it aloud.

But he thought maybe Cass was feeling it, too.

The Red Mound loomed in the distance, and with every step, the land itself seemed to hold more secrets, waiting for them to find, or to be swallowed whole.

Either way, they kept walking.

That night, they could finally say it; they were back in the woods.

They had broken from anything resembling a trail hours ago, choosing to leave the safer descent that led in the wrong direction and blaze their own way toward the Red Mound. The slope was still downward, but now they were surrounded by thick trees and brush.

It wasn't the bare, rocky faces of the Peaks anymore, and that brought a small measure of comfort to both of them.

They knew how to survive in the woods.

The stone and thin air of the Painted Peaks had nearly broken them.

But even here, things felt different.

The trees were twisted and unfamiliar.

The grass grew in strange colors.

The herbs, the vines, even the scent of the forest floor, it was all different, wild in ways they didn't recognize.

It was like stepping into a new world.

They had to be careful.

Finn and Cass set up their snares around the clearing, uncertain whether the tricks they knew from home would even work here.

Maybe the animals were different, too.

Finn hoped for a quiet night's sleep, but part of him stayed tense, remembering the mimic, the glowing orbs, the glass, winged insects.

He rested one hand on the hilt of his dagger, Cass doing the same across the fire.

Cass found a sprawling oak tree nearby, its low, wide branches perfect for climbing. She decided to try her luck; maybe some birds had nested up there.

While Finn prepared the fire, she climbed up into the branches and searched.

A while later, she returned with a small bundle, a handful of tiny eggs, and a few foraged nuts.

It wasn't much.

They would eat the last of the rabbit tonight, stretching their supplies one more day.

Cass set the eggs near the edge of the fire, hoping they would cook gently in their shells. They toasted the nuts, cracking them open to get at the meat inside.

The meal was simple but good enough.

Finn was exhausted, but so was Cass.

He told her to sleep first, and she didn't argue. She only nodded in thanks, wrapped herself in her blanket, and lay down by the fire.

Finn took the first watch.

But the fire was too bright.

He couldn't see much beyond its circle of light, and the woods around them seemed darker than they should have been.

Worried about another mimic, or something worse, he left the fire behind, moving about five body lengths away to lean against a tree.

There, his eyes adjusted, and he could see the shifting shapes in the darkness better.

Several times during his watch, small creatures came close to their camp, shadows slipping through the brush, curious about the fire.

But whatever they were, they stayed distant.

Finn never got a clear look, and eventually, they wandered off.

When it was Cass's turn, she woke on her own, moving quietly in the firelight.

Finn met her halfway, giving her a quick nod.

"I'm here," he said softly.

Cass nodded back, and they switched places without speaking. She walked out toward the same tree Finn had used, while he returned to the fire, pulling his blanket around him.

As he lay down, Finn exhaled slowly, staring up at the thick weave of branches overhead.

He'd lost track of how many days they had been out here now.

The mountains, the woods, the endless dangers, they all blurred together.

But he knew they were getting closer.

Closer to whatever future was waiting for them.

Finn didn't know exactly what that future would look like.

But somehow, despite everything, the cold, the blood, the terror, it still felt right.

And for now, that was enough.

When Finn woke the next morning, the fire had burned down to little more than ash and a few faintly glowing embers.

The forest was quiet. Still. The kind of stillness that made him uneasy.

Cass was already up, stretching her injured leg carefully, testing the strength in it. She nodded to him in greeting but said nothing.

Finn sat up slowly, pulling his boots on with stiff fingers, and that's when he noticed it.

Tracks.

Dozens of them.

All around the fire, pressed lightly into the dirt and fallen leaves, half-moons and sharp toe-marks, like a strange blend between a claw and a hoof. Some of them were no larger than his hand, others nearly as wide as his chest.

He stood slowly, scanning the ground.

The tracks hadn't been there last night.

They were fresh.

Whatever had made them had circled the camp during the dark hours, close enough to see them, close enough to smell them, but had never crossed into the ring of firelight.

Finn knelt down to get a closer look.

The footprints were scattered and disorganized, almost as if whatever had made them wasn't sure whether to approach or flee.

Cass limped over, following his gaze.

"What are those?" she asked.

Finn shook his head.

"I don't know."

He poked at one of the deeper prints with a stick.

"But there were a lot of them."

Cass's mouth tightened into a hard line. She looked out into the woods, at the trees shifting in the early morning breeze, the mist curling low over the ground.

"We need to move," she said.

Finn agreed.

Whatever had been out there last night, it had been watching them.

And next time, it might not hesitate.

They packed quickly, gathered their empty snares, every sense on edge, and struck out again toward the Red Mound.

Every step forward now felt like stepping deeper into a place where the world's old rules no longer applied.

CHAPTER 11

Red Mound

They kept moving, hiking carefully through the woods, both painfully aware of how little they had left.

No food.

Almost no water.

The priority was survival now.

Their heads stayed on a constant swivel, watching the trees, the sky, the ground. Any hint of food or danger.

They spotted a few small blackberry bushes growing between the rocks.

Finn and Cass quickly gathered handfuls, splitting them between themselves, snacking as they walked.

The berries helped. A little.

The ground was rocky and uneven here, and Cass was still limping, though she had abandoned her walking stick. She moved slowly but steadily, refusing to lean on Finn. His own leg, bitten days ago by the eel, showed no sign of swelling or lingering damage. They were both battered, but they were still moving.

Up ahead, the forest grew thinner.

More light filtered through the trees.

They walked faster toward it, hoping maybe for another stream, a break in the trees, something good.

Instead, they found the edge of the world.

They reached the treeline and stopped dead.

Ahead of them, the ground simply ended.

A cliff, sheer and jagged, plunged fifty body lengths straight down.

Far below, the forest resumed like a rolling sea of green.

From this height, they had a wide view of the surrounding land.

To the left, the Red Mound loomed larger than ever before.

Massive. Monolithic.

They were getting closer.

But to the right, something they hadn't expected.

An encampment, about half a day's walk away if the terrain were flat.

The encampment was huge.

They hadn't seen it from the Painted Peaks, hidden by distance and terrain. But now, sprawled out across the valley floor, was a living sore against the earth, thousands of people, tents, fires, wagons, and smoke twisting into the sky.

Cass and Finn both dropped low to the ground, crawling to the edge on their bellies, trying not to draw any attention.

They stared in silence.

Finn turned to Cass, whispering, "What are they doing out here?"

Cass shrugged tightly, her eyes locked on the camp.

"I don't know," she said. "Maybe... maybe they're the same ones who attacked Varnhollow years ago."

Finn shook his head.

"But why stay out here for years? That doesn't make any sense."

They crouched there, watching.

Could an army be preparing to attack?

"Last we heard," Finn said, "Elarith and the Unbound Kingdom were basically allies. At least... because of the Dark Circle."

Cass nodded grimly.

"It didn't make sense for them to attack us the first time either."

They didn't have enough information.

That was the truth.

Everything out here was built on guesswork and fear.

A heavy silence passed between them.

Finally, Cass spoke, her voice low.

"We have something else we need to worry about first."

She pointed downward.

"Do you see a way off this cliff?"

Finn scanned the rock face carefully, but there were no paths, no easy slopes. Just jagged drops and broken ledges.

He shook his head.

Cass frowned. "I don't see one either."

"Are we going to have to climb down?" Finn asked.

Cass thought for a moment, measuring the cliff and their supplies.

"I don't know. Maybe. We can walk the ridge for a while and see if there's a better spot to descend. But right now..."

She glanced at their small bundles of gear.

"We don't have enough rope. Not even close."

They sat there a few moments longer, gathering their breath, staring at the camp and the endless cliff below.

One way or another, they'd have to find a path down.

Because the Red Mound and the Wild Awakening Circle waited somewhere beyond.

Finn and Cass stayed low as they crept along the edge of the cliff, following the ridge westward.

The ground was uneven, crumbling in places where the stone gave way to loose dirt. Several times, they had to step carefully around cracks that looked ready to split wider with a single misstep.

The cliff beside them fell away in sheer drops, jagged and merciless.

There was no easy climb down.

Not yet.

They pushed forward, cautious and deliberate.

After half an hour, Finn spotted something different.

A break in the cliff wall, not a true trail, but a long, narrow slope of broken stone and gravel, almost like an old landslide. It wasn't smooth. It was steep and treacherous, with plenty of chances to slip and fall, but it wasn't a sheer drop.

And near the edge of the slope, Finn knelt down and pointed.

Tracks.

Small ones at first, animal prints. Maybe mountain goats or deer.

But it meant a path existed, at least for the daring or the desperate.

Cass crouched beside him, studying the slope.

"It's not a real trail," she said grimly. "But it's better than climbing straight down a cliff."

Finn nodded, though his stomach twisted just looking at it.

"If we're careful," he said, "we can make it."

They sat back for a moment, breathing hard, listening to the wind tear across the open ridge.

Below them, the distant fires of the encampment glowed against the gathering twilight, a reminder that time was running short.

"We'll wait until full dark," Cass said.

"Then we move. We don't want anyone down there seeing us on the way down."

Finn agreed.

For now, they sat in the shadow of the rocks, gathering their strength.

Soon, they would risk everything, scrambling down a crumbling mountainside toward a forest, a mystery, and whatever destiny waited at the Red Mound.

While they waited for the sun to sink fully behind the mountains, Finn and Cass stayed busy.

They combed the woods near the ridge, eyes sharp for anything they could gather or hunt. They knew this was going to be a long night, and they needed whatever strength they could scrape together. The climb would be hard enough; doing it on an empty stomach would make it even worse.

They moved carefully, speaking little.

Most of the bushes were barren this high up, and small prey must have fled deeper into the woods long ago.

Cass eventually found a scattering of nuts beneath a gnarled tree.

Its trunk twisted sharply against the wind, with thick, tough leaves like spears and deep, armored bark scarred by weather and time.

It wasn't a familiar oak or maple; it was harder, rougher, like everything else that survived out here.

Finn thought it might be a kind of ironbark tree, the kind that only grew in wild places too rough for ordinary forests.

Cass gathered a handful of the nuts, pocketing them carefully.

It wasn't much.

But it would have to be enough for tonight.

As the light faded, Finn and Cass returned to the cliff's edge and crouched low, watching.

The encampment sprawled below and to the east of them like a living beast, massive and busy.

Now, in the lower light, they could see more details.

Thick earthworks had been built around its outer edges, high, sloped walls of packed dirt and stone, separating the fires and tents from the forest beyond.

Along the walls, crude watchtowers rose at regular intervals, manned by sentries.

It wasn't just a camp.

It was nearly a city.

Finn and Cass traded a worried glance.

The earth walls meant Mages, powerful ones. Shaping stone and ground into defenses wasn't something ordinary men could do.

The towers meant trained soldiers, too. Scouts. Lookouts.

They were being cautious because they weren't from the Unbound Kingdom. But even so, it was unlikely anyone would see them this far out, especially once darkness fully covered the ridge.

Still, neither of them wanted to risk it.

Too much movement, even a single figure scrambling down the cliff, could catch a watchful eye in the daylight.

That meant no fire tonight.

No warmth.

No light.

No safety net.

They needed to climb down by moonlight, eat whatever they could without a fire, and sleep in the dark.

It was not an exciting thought.

But it was necessary.

Cass crouched near the cliff's edge, tightening the straps on her pack until it hugged her back snugly.

Finn did the same, making sure nothing loose would swing or catch while they climbed.

Every piece of gear needed to be tied down or stowed securely. One mistake, a strap snagging, a buckle catching, and the whole climb could end with a fall they wouldn't survive.

Finn stripped off his outer cloak, rolling it tight and lashing it across his pack. It would only weigh him down and get caught on the rocks. Cass adjusted the grip on her walking staff, then thought better of it and tossed it aside. It would be useless on the cliff face.

They checked their boots.

Checked their belts.

Checked their weapons.

Ready.

Finn glanced up at the darkening sky. Only the faintest glimmer of twilight remained, and the first few stars had started to appear. The world was shifting into true night.

He tightened the straps on his shoulders one last time and met Cass's eyes.

No words were needed.

They both knew: get down quietly, get away unseen, survive the night.

One last breath, and they began moving toward the broken slope that would be their path into the unknown.

They moved in near silence, feet crunching lightly over loose stone as they approached the slope they had found earlier.

The ground fell away before them, a long, broken spill of rock and gravel leading down into the darkness below. It wasn't a path. It was a wound in the earth.

Cass went first, testing each step carefully.

Finn followed a few paces behind, crouched low to keep his center of gravity steady.

The gravel shifted underfoot almost immediately.

Each step was a battle to keep balance, boots sliding on loose rock. Their fingers scrabbled against the cliff face, finding shallow holds, cracks, rough stone edges, anything they could clutch to steady themselves.

The only light came from the stars overhead and the faint, shifting glow of the fires far below from the enemy camp.

It wasn't much.

Just enough to see the worst drops, but not enough to see how far they might fall.

About twenty body lengths down, Cass slipped.

Finn's heart leapt into his throat as she lost her footing, but she managed to catch herself against a jagged boulder jutting from the slope.

She froze for a second, breathing hard, then nodded once and pushed onward.

Finn didn't call out.

No shouting.

No noise.

They were aware of how the noise could echo off the rock around them.

He moved after her, boots slipping, sliding a little with each step.

More than once, he felt the gravel give way under him, sending small stones bouncing and skittering into the void below.

It took everything, balance, instinct, and stubbornness, to keep from falling.

The air was cold here.

The cliff radiated chill through the rock, through their clothes, through their bones.

Down.

Step by step.

Breath by careful breath.

The forest at the base of the cliff still seemed impossibly far away.

But they had already passed the point of no return.

They had to keep going.

It took the better part of an hour, but finally, finally, they reached the base of the cliff.

The last stretch was brutal: sliding down loose stone, crawling over sharp ledges, dropping the last few body lengths to the forest floor with jarring thuds.

When they stood again, bruised and shaking, the forest seemed to swallow them whole.

The trees here were thicker and darker, and the air colder and heavier.

Nothing moved.

No birdsong.

No wind.

Just a heavy, suffocating silence.

Cass and Finn didn't speak.

They just tightened their packs, pulled their weapons, and pushed forward, needing to put distance between themselves and the cliff face in case anything, or anyone, had seen their descent.

They moved carefully through the undergrowth. The ground was soft with layers of fallen pine needles and black soil.

It smelled wrong here, like rot and iron.

After about ten minutes of cautious walking, Finn stopped short.

He heard it first, a rapid, rhythmic thudding through the brush.

Low to the ground. Fast.

Cass heard it too.

She pulled her bow from her shoulder and notched an arrow silently.

Then they saw them.

A pack.

At first, Finn thought they were massive frogs, bodies broad and low to the ground.

But no frog ran like that.

These creatures sprinted on four elongated, clawed legs, moving with terrifying speed.

Their mouths were massive, stretching nearly as wide as their heads, full of short, brutal teeth built for tearing.

Their skin was a slick, dark green, shining faintly in the low light.

There were six of them, weaving between the trees, tongues flicking, mouths snapping open and shut.

They didn't hop or jump.

They ran.

Fast and silent except for the pounding of their clawed feet against the earth.

The pack began to circle, spreading out through the trees, eyes glinting in the dim light, calculating.

Finn tightened his grip on his dagger.

Cass pulled her bowstring back to her cheek, breath steady despite her limp.

They couldn't outrun these things.

They couldn't climb back up the cliff.

They would have to fight.

The creatures kept circling, faster now, closing the gap with every heartbeat.

Cass whispered, "We hold here. Hit them before they rush."

Finn nodded, already pulling an arrow from his quiver.

His hands were steady. No panic.

He knew how to do this now.

The first frog-creature lunged from the underbrush, sprinting low, claws tearing into the earth.

Cass loosed an arrow, clean and sharp.

It struck the beast square between its wide-set eyes.

It tumbled forward, dead before it hit the ground.

Finn didn't hesitate.

He drew back and fired at another sprinting shape.

The arrow caught it in the throat, an ugly, wet sound, and the creature crumpled, legs twitching.

Another two charged from the side.

Cass spun and released, her arrow driving deep into one's gaping mouth as it snapped at the air.

It dropped mid-leap, skidding across the dirt.

Finn took aim at the second, closer now, and shot it through the shoulder. It staggered but kept coming, so he calmly nocked another arrow and fired again, this time sinking it into the soft underside of its jaw.

Four down in the span of seconds.

The remaining two skidded to a halt just beyond Cass and Finn's reach.

They hesitated.

Whined, an eerie, croaking sound, and then turned, bolting into the darkness between the trees, their clawed feet kicking up sprays of soil.

Finn kept his bow raised for another few seconds, scanning the woods, heart pounding.

Nothing else moved.

Cass lowered her weapon slowly, exhaling hard.

"Good shooting," she said, voice tight but proud.

Finn allowed himself a small grin.

"Not bad for almost dying six times in the last two days."

They stood there for a moment longer, listening.

But the forest had swallowed the runners completely.

The dead creatures lay sprawled around them, their slick skins already starting to dull in the cool air.

Finn walked forward and nudged one with the tip of his boot.

"They're not natural," he said.

Cass simply nodded.

They had won, but it was a small victory.

They didn't waste time.

Cass and Finn quickly pulled their arrows from the fallen creatures, cleaning the shafts as best they could on the grass, wiping off the dark, oily blood.

They couldn't afford to lose good arrows now.

Without speaking, they turned toward what they hoped was the direction of the Red Mound.

Neither of them wanted to stay in this place.

The dead creatures might draw worse things, and the air here already felt wrong, heavy, sour.

They moved quickly and quietly, slipping through the woods, trusting their instincts to keep them pointed in the right direction.

They couldn't see the Mound from here.

Not yet.

But they remembered its position from the cliff.

And for now, they had to believe they were heading the right way.

They traveled for hours through the dark.

Every so often, they heard noises around them, rustlings in the trees, the distant snapping of twigs, but they saw nothing.

Nothing came close.

It was as if their earlier fight had left a scent in the air, a warning.

Danger here.

Finally, after a long stretch of cautious, exhausting travel, they found a spot to rest.

Not a camp.

Just a dip between two large stones, sheltered enough to hide in for a few hours.

They agreed that Finn would take the first watch.

Cass lay down, pulling her cloak around her and closing her eyes almost immediately.

Finn settled against the stones, dagger laid across his knees, bow within arm's reach.

He stared into the darkness.

This was the first time they had intentionally made camp without a fire.

No crackling flames.

No circle of safety.

Just the cold, the dark, and the endless woods.

It was terrifying at first.

But strangely, it also helped.

Without the fire, his eyes adjusted fully.

He could see farther into the night, shapes and shadows among the trees.

Every sound, every small scratch of movement, seemed sharper, louder.

Somewhere above them, he heard small animals skittering through the branches, light, harmless things.

Farther out, something heavier slithered through the brush, moving steadily past.

But nothing came close.

Nothing challenged them here.

Maybe the creatures of this forest were smart enough to avoid them.

Maybe, for once, they were the bigger threat.

A few hours passed in tense silence.

Eventually, Cass stirred.

Without a word, she rose, took up her bow, and nodded to him.

Finn gave her a tired smile, placed his dagger back in its sheath, and lay down.

He closed his eyes, trusting Cass to keep watch.

And for the first time in days, he let himself fall into sleep without fear.

Finn woke to Cass, shaking him urgently. It was maybe half an hour after sunrise, so he had slept in. But Cass's shaking made him feel like there was a threat nearby. He woke with a jolt, her fingers on his lips. She quickly bent down to whisper in his ear, "There are voices nearby."

For a moment, Finn's mind spun out of control. All he could think of was how close she was and the feeling of her breath whispering in his ear. Slowly her words registered. Cass signaled sharply, Finn grabbed his pack and bow, and they both ran into the thick underbrush, dropping low. With the threat, Finn hoped Cass hadn't noticed how hot his cheeks were growing.

Cass and Finn heard something, metal clinking, boots on dirt, which to Finn was a welcome distraction.

Minutes later, a small scout troop passed through the trees below their hiding spot, half a dozen men in rough armor and travel-worn cloaks, talking low but serious.

Finn and Cass could just barely make out their words.

"Keep your eyes open," one of the scouts muttered. "There are a lot more beasts than normal right now."

They passed without ever looking at the brush where the teenagers were hiding.

Finn and Cass waited in silence long after the scouts had gone, hearts pounding in their throats.

When it was finally safe, they emerged and pressed on, more cautious now, but also a little faster, eager to put distance between themselves and the army.

The next two days passed like walking through a dream.

The woods twisted more with every hour. Trees grew taller but stranger, their trunks gnarled and split in unnatural patterns like complex runes. Vines hung like webs. The ground grew soft and warm underfoot, almost vibrating faintly, like a distant drumbeat underground.

Both Cass and Finn felt it: a pulling.

At first, it was just a vague awareness; their packs felt heavier somehow, more important.

By midday of the second day, it became harder to ignore.

Their stones.

Without speaking about it at first, they both began reaching into their packs throughout the day, brushing their fingers against the stones wrapped inside.

They were more certain than usual; the stones wanted to awaken.

The stones themselves felt alive.

By nightfall, both Cass and Finn carried their stones in hand more often than not, hidden inside their cloaks, pressed against their palms as they walked.

That evening, after skirting another rocky slope, they stumbled across a clearing and a prize they hadn't dared hope for.

A huge bird grazed in the low grass.

At first, Finn thought it was a turkey, but it wasn't like any turkey he had ever seen.

It stood nearly as tall as Finn's chest, covered in thick, wool-like fur, as white as a Mirrgoat.

Its claws were long, longer than Finn's hands, and curved wickedly.

It moved with an odd, heavy grace, ripping up grass and small roots.

Cass whispered, "If we're lucky, that'll feed us for days."

They didn't waste time.

Staying low, Cass notched an arrow and aimed carefully. Finn readied a second, just in case.

Cass's shot struck true, piercing deep into the creature's side. It let out a strange gurgling honk, flapped its powerful wings once, and crashed heavily to the ground.

They approached slowly, weapons drawn, but it was already dead.

Food.

Real food.

They hauled the creature back into the woods, far from open ground, and found a hollow sheltered by thick roots.

Here, far from the army and the main trails, they risked it; they built a fire.

For the first time in days, they felt safe enough to cook properly.

They skinned and cleaned the woolly bird carefully, roasting thick slabs of meat over the flames.

The scent of roasting meat filled the hollow, making their mouths water.

They ate until they could barely sit upright.

The rest of the meat they smoked over the low fire through the night, turning it into dried strips they could carry with them.

Enough food for several more days.

It was the best night they'd had in what felt like forever.

By the next morning, they were moving again, packs heavier now with precious food, spirits lifted slightly.

They aimed for the south side of the Red Mound, following the slope of the land, using the last rocky ridges to shield themselves from view. Hundreds of stone spikes poked out of the earth, looking as if they were bowing to the mound itself, each easily 10-12 height tall.

The Red Mound grew larger with every step, vast and round, an unnatural swelling in the earth. It was unnaturally shaped and unnaturally large. Almost like it was a giant soap bubble made of rock and earth waiting to explode.

Once they saw a giant green and brown bear lumbering to the north, so large they could see it from a day's walk away, they were amazed.

And somewhere ahead, hidden between this ancient hill and the mountains they had crossed, waited the Wild Awakening Circle. The wind was at their back, almost like the whole world was taking a deep inhale, waiting for them to step into the circle. They slept that night between the two megaliths. They thought that tomorrow they would awaken, finally.

CHAPTER 12

Awakening

They had hardly slept, but when the sun rose, they were ready.

There was no hesitation anymore.

Some unseen force pulled them forward, drawing them toward the Awakening Circle like a current pulling them downriver.

It was not fear.

It was inevitable.

The trees around them leaned subtly to the southwest, as if bowing toward whatever power waited ahead.

The ground sloped in the same direction.

Even the air seemed to hum with silent anticipation.

They held their stones tightly now.

It felt wrong not to.

Even though it meant they couldn't draw a weapon, couldn't

defend themselves, somehow, they both knew they wouldn't need to.

Not here.

Not now.

They moved through the woods in silence, each step pulling them closer.

And then, through the thinning trees, they saw it.

A clearing that was wide and wild.

Ancient oaks circled the space like watchful guardians.

And at the center, a ring of massive stones, diamond-shaped and tilted like broken blades, forming a jagged, perfect circle.

Cass gasped, her hand tightening around her stone.

Finn dropped his pack without thinking, eyes wide.

They had made it.

Finally, after everything, they were here.

They turned to each other, faces split with exhausted, stunned smiles.

Both still clutched their stones, feeling them thrum warmly in their palms.

Cass's voice broke the silence first.

"Are you ready? Or... do you want to take a moment?"

Finn shook his head. His heart was hammering, but he didn't feel fear. Only certainty.

"I'm ready."

"Me too," Cass said softly.

She hesitated, then held out her free hand.

"Can we... hold hands?"

Finn nodded without thinking, too happy, too relieved to care about anything but the moment.

He grasped her hand firmly.

Together, hand in hand, stones clenched tightly in their other fists, they stepped to the very edge of the stone circle.

Cass squeezed Finn's hand.

"One... two... three," she said.

They stepped forward.

The moment they crossed the boundary, everything changed.

The sound of the world around them went distant.

Just the crunch of their boots on the brittle grass.

But as they walked deeper, approaching the heart of the circle, the world around them began to unravel.

Step. The birds froze mid-flight, wings locked in the air.

Step. The trees stilled, not even a whisper of wind through their branches.

Step. The clouds in the sky froze.

Step. The very air around them shifted color, turning deep and shimmering, like they were standing inside a vast glass sphere, the shade of pale blue ice.

Step. Time itself had stopped.

For ten long seconds, neither Cass nor Finn could move.

Couldn't even blink.

Trapped between heartbeats, held in a moment of perfect stillness.

Then, all at once, everything changed.

Thump...

A wave of violent energy erupted from the Circle, blasting skyward without resistance, tearing through the clouds and vanishing into the heavens.

It was not light.

It was force, raw, living, ancient.

Cass and Finn cried out as their bodies arched backward. They were lifted off the ground and then moved by something unseen, spun to face each other, five heights apart.

Their stones tore themselves free from their hands.

They hovered, glowing, humming, over each of their hearts.

Thump…

The earth shook with a single, massive heartbeat.

The stones above them pulsed in time, growing brighter, hotter, wilder.

Around Finn, the world shifted.

Dust, leaves, even the faint breeze itself bent inward toward him, as if gravity had shifted, as if he were the center of all things.

Nothing heavy moved, but the world noticed him now. He had claimed its authority.

And it obeyed him.

Around Cass, shimmering shards of crystalline light flickered into existence, sharp, beautiful, deadly.

They spun around her like she stood inside a living prism, fractured reflections flashing in every direction at once.

She floated at the center of the impossible.

Thump…

Another great heartbeat.

Another shockwave of power tore through the air above the Circle, felt even in distant lands.

The stones hovering at their chests began to sink, slowly into their bodies.

Finn gasped as he felt the Skysteel sinking through his skin, into his ribs, into the very marrow of his bones.

At first, it crushed him, pressing harder, harder, but then he found strength.

His muscles firmed.

His bones and skin became unbreakable.

He was not being crushed.

He was becoming the center of everything.

He inhaled, and the pull became a bond.

At the same moment, the shards of light around Cass spun tighter, faster, sharper.

They, too, began to sink into her.

She shimmered with needle, thin blades of energy, feeling the very threads of time, distance, and location fold into her mind with stunning clarity.

She knew exactly where she was, not just in this circle, this kingdom, and even on this world, but she knew where she was in all of existence, down to the width of a hair.

The world no longer hid its secrets from her.

Thump…

The Red Mound itself crumbled and cracked, sinking into itself, into the earth.

Another pulse shot into the sky, stronger than all before.

Images flashed before Finn's eyes while he screamed from seeing and knowing so much.

Visions of fire and ash, of mountains crumbling, of new kingdoms rising from the ruins.

Pain lanced through his chest, his arms, his skull, through every bone in his body.

Cass screamed silently, trying to close her eyes, but still she saw the same visions: cities falling, towers shattering, oceans swallowing land, then green sprouting from wastelands, new life building in the ashes.

The burning in their bodies was total, cleansing them, reshaping them.

Thump.

The Painted Peaks shook in fear.

And within the Circle, a thousand voices, ancient, powerful, beautiful, spoke in unison, filling the world:

"Tuar ven'ul jastel mor'sten falen,
Echo: Twin chosen foraged from fallen stone
Vi'ashar ven'ral nosen ken.
Echo: Will rise in ash what none have known.
Tharnel fate vi'bindral torn,
Echo: They'll fracture fate where patterns bind,
Krafen anew vi'ruen lef'norn.
Echo: And craft anew what ruin left behind.
Mor'wel to mor'wel vi'stepen tred,
Echo: From world to world their steps shall tread,
Thru'nal lands en hallen dred.
Echo: Through ancient lands and halls of dead.
Til'rut darnok dies'nar,
Echo: Until the root of darkness dies,
En'vur nura, mor'wel risar.
Echo: In their wake, worlds shall rise."

The humming grew deafening.

The light built to a terrible climax, and then-

Silence...

The power collapsed in a flash, leaving only a faint, eerie glow behind.

The world returned to motion.

Birds dropped from the sky.

The trees swayed.

The clouds reformed.

But the Red Mound and the closest ridges of the Painted Peaks were gone.

Erased from the land forever.

And in the center of the Circle, two teenagers fell to the earth. Around them, the stone spikes that formed the circle crumbled into ash. There was no more Wild Awakening Circle here. Its singular purpose was to awaken these two stones. A purpose it had fulfilled to its fullest.

Cass and Finn had not just survived the Wild Awakening.

They had become something so much more than they could have imagined was even possible.

Far away from the Red Mound, beyond the wild lands of the Unbound Kingdom, there stood a solitary tower of white stone, rising high above the sprawling city of Auremere in a kingdom called the Ardent Crown.

The structure resembled a lighthouse: tall, slender, crowned with a broad, circular room made entirely of shimmering crystal.

But it was no lighthouse for ships.

It was called the Aurium Spire, built and maintained by the Order of the Shining Veil, a loose brotherhood of Mages and scholars dedicated to preserving balance, understanding magic, and, in secret, gathering intelligence on the use of Awakening Circles.

The room at the top was a marvel.

The room was round, the circular wall was made of smooth crystal, one and a half heights tall, and the dome on its top was made of stone. The crystal was enchanted by dozens of Light Mages over generations to be extremely sensitive.

To the untrained eye, it looked like a massive observatory.

But to those who knew its purpose, it was a listening post, an eye to the world's hidden powers.

From this height, the young Mage Kellen Vey could see everything.

The city below looked like a toy village.

The distant forests were patches of green velvet.

And beyond that, if the day was clear enough, he could almost imagine seeing to the edges of the kingdom itself.

Kellen sat at his assigned position near the crystal pane, elbows resting on a smooth stone rail, chin in his hand, half-daydreaming.

It was mind-numbing work.

Every day, for hours at a time, he was expected to sit here and stare, watching the crystal's inner reflections for any sign of activity.

If there was an awakening, the enchanted crystal would flash a sharp red line, like a spear of light slicing vertically through the crystal, pointing in the direction where the surge originated.

The signal was instantaneous and just as quickly gone, only lasting a few seconds.

Kellen was required to memorize the angle and bearing of the flash the moment it appeared, knowing precisely which Awakening Circle the light corresponded to.

Degrees and azimuths were drilled into him like a soldier memorizing battle maps.

He was also told to never trust only the automated bell that chimed faintly when a red flash occurred.

"If you're caught reading when the crystal flashes," his supervisor had said, "you'll be scrubbing corridors for a year."

So he didn't read anymore.

Not openly, at least.

Sometimes he tucked a book just out of reach behind the stone ledge, but most of the time he sat in silence.

Thinking.

Staring.

Bored beyond belief.

The last real event had been several weeks ago: a weak,

trembling flash from Elarith, so faint and corrupted that it almost certainly signaled another twisted awakening.

Kellen remembered shaking his head at the time.

Poor Elarith.

Once a proud kingdom, now little more than a graveyard of failed Mages and broken Circles.

The Dark Circle's poison had rotted it from the inside, until every Awakening was a gamble between death, madness, or worse.

In the early years, before the kingdoms built domes of copper and stone over their Circles, flashes had been frequent, vivid, and clear.

Back then, the Spire could detect dozens of true awakenings a week.

Now... days passed with no sign at all.

Every kingdom had learned the value of secrecy.

No one wanted their enemies to know when a new Mage had been born.

No one wanted their failures broadcast to the world.

The crystal listening post's glory was fading with the age of hidden awakenings.

Kellen sighed and shifted in his seat, careful to keep his eyes scanning the shifting reflections of the enchanted glass.

He would be here another three hours before his replacement arrived.

Three more hours of waiting.

Three more hours of hoping for something to happen.

Even a whisper of light across the crystal would be better than this dead silence.

Kellen Vey was staring blankly across the endless reflections of the crystal dome, his mind drifting, when the first shift happened.

Without warning, the entire dome dimmed.

The world beyond the crystal turned muted and gray, as if a horribly dark storm cloud settled over the city.

Kellen sat up straighter, all the sleepiness draining from his body in an instant.

He could tell it was the crystal itself darkening as if to protect him. This wasn't normal.

Normally, when an Awakening registered, the crystal would flash a quick red beam, a sharp blink across the glass, and then fade after a few seconds.

But this...

This was something else entirely.

A single white line, bright as burning magnesium, sliced across the crystal.

It was not a flash.

It was a beam, persistent and searing, burning from the bottom to the top of the crystal wall like a lance of pure magic.

Kellen shielded his eyes against the glare.

And then it got worse.

Five times, five enormous blue pulses rose from the farthest visible horizon. Rolling across the land like ocean waves, washing over mountains, forests, cities, and even the ocean itself towards the beam of light. Each pulse struck the world like a drumbeat, a thundering heartbeat across the sky.

Kellen barely had time to process what he was seeing before it happened:

Over the course of a few seconds, twelve high-ranking Mages ran up the stairs in the tower.

They didn't speak, breathing heavily, staring wide-eyed at the crystal.

None of them could move.

None of them could look away.

The beam lingered long enough that it burned itself into the very structure of the ancient crystal.

When, finally, the muted world resumed its color and life, and the dome's magic reset... the white beam was gone.

But it had left behind a black scar, a burnt mark across the treated crystal, as if it had carved itself into the structure of the tower itself.

The room was deathly silent.

One of the high Mages walked up to the scar and touched it.

"...Which circle was that?" he demanded.

Kellen, throat dry, managed to stammer, "Master Torn, I-I don't know, sir. It doesn't align with any known coordinates. It's not on the registry."

Another Mage spoke sharply.

"Impossible. Every Circle has been charted for centuries."

"It wasn't from a city," a third Mage said grimly. "That power signature was completely unique."

Master Torn, robed in pale silver, leaned closer to the black scar burned into the crystal. His voice was almost reverent.

"...Could it be?" he whispered.

"Could it really have been... a wild circle?"

The room fell silent again.

All eyes turned to Kellen, still standing rigid by his post.

The eldest among them fixed him with a cold stare.

"You will say nothing of this," he said.

"No one outside this room is to know."

Kellen swallowed hard.

"Y-yes, sir."

The senior Mages turned back to the burnt mark, already speculating.

What had happened?

Was it an ancient site reawakened?

Could they send scouts before anyone else found it?

One thing was clear to all of them:

This was no ordinary Awakening.

This was power unseen in their lifetimes, something older, rawer, and vastly more dangerous than anything the city, states, or kingdoms had ever known.

Far across the seas, beyond the reach of the Unbound Kingdom and the smoke of the mainland wars, lay the island nation of Saphrelle.

Saphrelle was small compared to the great kingdoms, but what it lacked in land, it made up for in heart.

Here, the people valued peace above conquest, healing above warfare.

And of all the magics honored across the world, it was Mind Magic that ruled Saphrelle's heart, magic that could untangle memories, mend broken minds, soothe griefs and nightmares alike.

The island itself was beautiful: lush green hills rolling down into sandy shores, ringed by craggy white cliffs.

The people of Saphrelle were sun-browned, their clothing loose and flowing to catch the ocean breeze, bright colors stitched with delicate patterns of vines, waves, and stars.

And at the center of Saphrelle's capital, the white city of Veylen, stood the Sanctum of Minds-a place that was both school and hospital.

Students there studied the art of Mind Magic, and citizens came freely, seeking help for every kind of wound unseen by the eye.

Inside the Sanctum's polished halls, Mind Mages drifted like gentle tides from room to room.

There were no loud voices here, no shouts, no clang of weapons, only quiet murmurs, soft weeping, and the peaceful hum of healing magic.

One of the healers working today was Serin Valen, a young Mind Mage dressed in loose ocean blue robes, a silver circlet holding back her dark hair.

Her face was open, kind, but her gray eyes were sharp, trained to notice every small flinch, every tremble of voice.

Right now, she sat in a sunlit room with a refugee named Pen.

Pen had come from the distant mainland, fleeing some battle that had burned half his village to ash.

He bore no visible scars, but his dreams...

His mind was a battlefield even now.

Serin sat with him, palms hovering just over his temples, whispering soft words of calming thought, magic.

She helped him reshape the memory: not to forget, but to survive it.

She peeled away the sharpest edges of the terror, soothed the bleeding places in his mind where nightmares nested.

Her magic wrapped around him like cool, clear water, cleansing, healing.

When the session ended, Pen sat back, breathing easier than he had in months.

Tears stood in his eyes. "Thank you," he whispered, standing to go.

Serin only smiled and bowed her head gently.

He left, and Serin sat there for a moment longer, feeling the peace settle around her.

And then it happened.

The world convulsed.

Without warning, a pulse of pure, raw energy slammed into

the island.

Serin gasped, doubling over, clutching her head as if something had struck her physically.

Around her, in every hallway, every healing chamber, the other Mind Mages fell to their knees, hands to their temples, grimacing in silent agony.

The ordinary citizens, those without magic, noticed nothing.

But the Mind Mages, they felt everything.

It was as if the sky itself screamed.

Another pulse struck. And another. Five times the waves rolled over Saphrelle, from one end of the island to the other, like invisible tsunamis crashing through their minds.

Serin tried to focus, tried to erect a mental shield, but it was like trying to hold back a hurricane with bare hands. The power was too vast, too alien. It bent the very nature of thought.

Those Mind Mages who hadn't passed out from the pressure heard a thousand distant voices say;

"Tuar ven'ul jastel mor'sten falen,

Echo: Twin chosen foraged from fallen stone

Vi'ashar ven'ral nosen ken.

Echo: Will rise in ash what none have known.

Tharnel fate vi'bindral torn,

Echo: They'll fracture fate where patterns bind,

Krafen anew vi'ruen lef'norn.

Echo: And craft anew what ruin left behind.

Mor'wel to mor'wel vi'stepen tred,

Echo: From world to world their steps shall tread,

Thru'nal lands en hallen dred.

Echo: Through ancient lands and halls of dead,

Til'rut darnok dies'nar,

Echo: Until the root of darkness dies,

En'vur nura, mor'wel risar.

Echo: In their wake, worlds shall rise."

When it ended, the Mages were left gasping on the floor, shaking and terrified.

Some wept openly. Some stared blankly at the ceiling, too stunned to move. But several Mind Mages, not just in Saphrelle but all around the world, managed to write down what they heard.

Serin struggled to her feet, pressing a hand against the cool stone wall for balance.

Within the hour, a small group of senior Mind Mages gathered in the inner courtyard of the Sanctum, still pale, still trembling.

Serin stood among them, clutching her robes tight around her.

No one spoke at first.

Finally, one of the elders, an ancient man with dark skin and a shock of white hair, broke the silence.

"What was that?" he whispered.

Another Mage shook her head, wide-eyed. "An attack?"

"But from who?" someone else asked. "There are no enemies left who could command such a strong mental attack."

Serin raised her head.

"I don't think it was aimed at us. I think... we heard something that was not meant for us."

The group murmured anxiously.

The pulses hadn't just hit the island randomly. There had been a direction—a vague but undeniable pull towards the mainland.

One of the scholars drew a rough map in the sand at their feet, using the courtyard's soft dust.

"If we could sail that way," he said, "perhaps we could find the source."

Serin closed her eyes, remembering the power of the pulses burning across her mind.

"Whatever it is," she said softly, "it's powerful beyond anything we have ever known. And if we don't understand it. If we don't learn what caused it, someone else will."

The group fell into uneasy silence.

Deep beneath the city of Velmirath, behind walls blackened with soot and shadow, the heart of the Dark Circle's laboratories pulsed with quiet, terrible life.

Here, in windowless halls carved into volcanic stone, Mages in robes of dark gray and crimson worked tirelessly on projects the world must never find out about.

At the center of it all stood the Obsidian Crucible, a great basin of ancient black stone, shot through with crimson veins of corrupted magic.

Obsidian, yes, but not common.

This was Blood Obsidian: a stone formed from the death of a bound creature in ancient times, infused forever with power over darkness and decay.

It was from this Crucible that the Dark Circle had discovered its greatest secret:

They could influence the Twisted.

Not control them, not fully, but they could push, guide, even unleash the instincts of those failed awakenings, those cursed creatures, those engines of hunger and rage.

Archon Mairev, one of the Circle's leading scientists and rising stars, was jubilant today.

He had been able to push two of their Twisted Shadows to dig deeply into the core of an Awakening Circle in the Ardent Crown and infect it. He just got word that 5 of the last 8 awakenings from that circle resulted in the creation of another

Twisted. As time passes, that margin will shrink to zero, and every awakening will result in death or more soldiers for their mindless army.

Twisted Shadows were amazing tools. Once they drank from the Blood Crucible or got infected by another of their own kind, they became malleable to the Crucible's influence and much more dangerous. In their natural state, the beasts are barely stronger than a man and unable to control their shadow abilities. But with the control that the Blood Crucible gives them, they can move in and out of shadow states as needed.

On a battered map nailed to the stone wall, he marked a half-dozen towns where neighboring nations had quietly suffered outbreaks of Twisted in recent months.

Entire villages abandoned.

Border skirmishes blamed on "natural" dangers or one of the other Kingdoms.

Small wars begin with fear and rumors.

It was beautiful.

They knew that when every awakening resulted in a Twisted Shadow, it would reduce the number of willing candidates.

But that didn't matter.

Fear would fill the ranks.

Promises to save loved ones.

Deals made under threat of death.

There were always ways to persuade the desperate to feed the Crucible.

And every new Twisted soldier made the Dark Circle stronger.

The unbound had always been easy to manipulate.

A little fear.

A little greed.

The Twisted were harder to control in many ways.

But the Circle was mastering even them.

Soon, they would not just command the broken kingdoms; they would expand across oceans, across continents.

Mairev had already been sketching models for introducing their "Gifts" into other lands, smuggled in like seeds into enemy soil.

The Blood Crucible could, of course, control men also. But they needed to drink from it themselves; no scratch would transfer the influence to a human. Many men died from infections, from their attempting to transfer the corruption in this manner. Slave Crucibles were better at controlling men. They were smaller and more mobile. Plus, there was only one Blood Crucible, so they couldn't risk moving it.

He was midway through a report on Twisted acceleration trials when it happened.

At first, it was a small thing, a tremor across the surface of the Crucible, then a crack split it down the side.

He frowned, setting down his pen.

Then came the rumbling in the walls.

The torches flickered, casting wild, leaping shadows.

And then, chaos.

The doors slammed open, and a flood of high-ranking Mages poured into the laboratory.

Their faces were pale with rage and fear.

"What happened?" one demanded.

"Why are the Twisted out of control?" shouted another.

Mairev stood, confused.

"I-I don't know," he stammered. "What are you talking about?"

"You haven't felt it?" a senior Mage hissed.

Outside, through the corridors and past the city walls, Mairev could now feel it:

Something was wrong.

Horribly wrong.

The Twisted, those the Circle had seeded and nurtured across the land, had gone mad.

Their faint bonds of influence had snapped or warped beyond recognition.

Reports poured in:

Twisted left their posts, rampaging out of control.

Entire nests collapsed, devouring themselves.

Some creatures lost their substance, reverting to pure shadow and barely holding form.

It wasn't just in one kingdom.

It was everywhere.

Something had struck them all at once, like a hammer falling across the world.

And they had no idea why.

The high Mages argued furiously, throwing theories like knives.

Had another power found a way to break their bonds?

Was this the result of sabotage? In panic, he thought, "Would the infected Awakening Circles stay infected if the Twisted at their cores rotted away?"

Mairev staggered back to his desk, grabbing at ledgers, notes, anything to explain it.

There was nothing.

Nothing but the sudden collapse of a secret army they had spent generations building.

The leaders of the Dark Circle left the laboratory within the hour, silent, grim, already planning their next moves.

But in the depths of the Crucible chamber, Mairev sat alone, staring at the trembling, cracked surface of the Blood Obsidian basin.

Whatever had happened had not just disrupted their plans.

It had wounded the very source of their power.

And somewhere, he knew, with the sick certainty of a man seeing a storm approach, someone had awakened something far, far older and stronger than the Circle had ever imagined.

And it was only the beginning.

Along the wild spine of the Painted Peaks, the army of the Unbound Kingdom moved like a living scar.

Every day, without fail, the soldiers rose before dawn, marching along rough, broken trails that clung to the ridgelines.

And every afternoon, the Mages began their work.

The army was mobile, but it was not vulnerable.

Earth Mages stomped to the front, their palms pressed flat to the broken ground.

With deep chants and twisting hands, they coaxed walls of stone from the earth itself, raw, angular barricades tall enough to shield against any sudden assault.

Behind them came the Fire Mages, tracing blazing sigils through the air.

Their fires hardened the fresh stone walls, baking them into strength, searing weakness away.

Wind Mages soared into the air, lifting themselves with gusts and weaving long banners of breathable air into the camp, clearing out the dust, cooling the tents.

Mind Mages walked among the ranks, keeping spirits high, whispering calming magic into the minds of soldiers exhausted by grief and rage.

Together, they built a mobile city every day, one that could rise from nothing in an hour and vanish again at first light.

The soldiers knew exactly how blessed they were.

Without the Mages, they would be nothing but meat for the

wolves, or worse, for the twisted beasts that prowled these cursed woods.

They hated the woods.

Everyone did.

Out beyond the firelight, the trees seemed to lean inward, whispering threats too quiet to hear.

The beasts that lived here were not natural.

Each one was different.

Each one more monstrous than the last.

Scout duty was a punishment.

Only the disobedient, the unruly, or the untrustworthy were sent beyond the safety of the walls at night.

Few returned without new scars, if they returned at all.

This wasn't just another border patrol.

This was war without end and without an enemy.

They were stationed here, year after year, because the soldiers of the Unbound Kingdom knew what Elarith had become under its mad king.

Raids were common, brutal attacks where Elarith's twisted forces and armies swept down on border villages, burning homes, slaughtering women and children, abducting the strong for who knew what purposes.

Everyone here had lost someone.

Parents.

Siblings.

Spouses.

Children.

The government of the Unbound Kingdom understood this.

It was why they funded the army so well.

It was why so many Mages were assigned to this endless, grinding duty.

It was not because they believed victory would come easily.

But because they could not afford to lose.

The camp always left scars on the land, a trail of burned earth and half-torn stone walls, marking where it had stood for a night before the march continued.

Today was no different.

By midday, the walls were up.

The tents were pitched.

Fires crackled inside the barricades, and soldiers rested for the evening.

And then, without warning, the earth screamed.

An earthquake struck with the force of a hammer blow.

The walls, freshly shaped by the Earth Mages, buckled and cracked.

Tents collapsed.

Fires overturned, sending smoke and sparks whirling into the air.

The ground heaved underfoot like a ship caught in a storm.

Men and women shouted, grabbing for weapons, for comrades, for anything solid to cling to.

No one knew what was happening.

No one understood.

Even the Mages, usually so calm, looked shaken and afraid.

And then, in the distance-

The Red Mound.

The great looming mystery on the edge of the Painted Peaks-

The Mound that had stood for longer than memory-

collapsed.

With a grinding, deafening roar, the entire mass buckled inward, sending a tower of dust and broken stone skyward.

The soldiers of the Unbound Kingdom watched in horror

as the earth swallowed the Mound whole, leaving only a shattered wound in the landscape.

Men fell to their knees.

Others simply turned away, unable to watch.

They hated this place.

They hated its unnatural beasts, its cursed mountains, and the enemy beyond it.

And now, after this, they knew they would hate it forever.

Most of the Army moved on, but little did they know that their "Red Mound" would become the site of a major power struggle. And despite their strong desire not to return, they would do just that.

Far to the north, nestled along the mirrored edge of Lake Iridan, stood the radiant city of Virelios, capital of the Copper Network.

It was a city built not on conquest or superstition, but on knowledge.

Towers of glass, veined steel rose into the air, connected by sweeping metallic rails that moved silently across the skyline, shuttling citizens from one district to another.

Copper inlays ran like bloodlines through every surface, walls, walkways, and even windows, conducting not only heat and energy, but information.

Here, Copper Mages were the lifeblood of society.

Masters of conductivity and connection, they had turned Virelios into the most informed and interconnected city in the world.

Messages could be sent from the mountaintop to the harbor in seconds.

Awakened students received updates from across the

continent mid-lecture.

Awakened minds collaborated on living archives, etched into metal sheets woven with a code long developed by the Copper Networks to save information.

In Virelios, everyone learned.

Everyone taught.

Even a teenager could quote old philosophers or recite market data from half a world away.

This was a city where magic wasn't wild or dangerous; it was precise, tamed, and structured.

Early that morning, the copper lines buzzed with routine.

In the High Halls of Transfer, where young Mages trained to interface with the world's flow of knowledge, dozens of teenage students were mid-synchronization, hands pressed to their copperwork desks, their minds threading with signals from the network.

And then-

It hit.

Without warning, every Copper Mage in the room screamed and collapsed.

Arcs of blue light snapped from desks. Walls flickered.

Whole channels of thought and communication shorted out, cascading through the city's delicate magical infrastructure like a lightning strike through a spider's web.

In the core district, dozens of Mages staggered in the streets, clutching their heads.

Some convulsed.

Some simply crumpled, eyes rolled back, completely unconscious for minutes.

Across Virelios, every awakened Copper soul felt it, like being burned and frozen at once, thoughts torn loose from their anchors, information itself corrupted by a pulse that didn't speak their language.

When the worst of it passed, the city's information grid exploded into chaos.

The Great Archive was overwhelmed. Thousands of messages surged into the system at once.

"Did anyone else feel that?"

"Are we being attacked?!"

"Where did it come from?"

"We've got outages all over the map!"

Across continents, Copper channels from allied city-states began asking the same thing:

What just happened?

But for the first time in decades, not only were they taken by surprise, but they had no answers for what could have happened.

Nothing had been detected.

No alarms.

No storm activity.

Only the shared convulsion of their entire magical class, like a system-wide seizure that had left no mark.

In the Tower of Echoes, where the city's oldest Mages monitored magical frequencies across the known world, copper-clad elders gathered, still pale and shaken.

"We lost connection with five cities," one muttered.

"The surge wasn't internal," another said. "It came from outside."

"Southwest," someone whispered. "Maybe beyond the Unbound Kingdom…"

They all stared at the map. The threads. The ruptures.

Someone finally spoke what none of them wanted to say:

"Something big just happened."

CHAPTER 13

Ash

Finn slowly opened his eyes. At first, he couldn't see anything. Something soft and warm covered his face, blurring everything into a grayish haze. He shook his head and coughed.

Some light filtered through whatever was smothering him, ash he realized, and his temples throbbed with a brutal headache.

"What happened...?" he muttered.

Slowly, Finn pushed himself to his knees.

He was standing in a field covered entirely in ash, mid-calf deep, endless and gray as far as he could see.

Where am I?

The question rattled in his aching head.

"Ohhh, my head..." he groaned.

And then he remembered.

Cass.

He spun around, heart hammering.

"Cass!" he shouted. "Cass, can you hear me?"

Stumbling through the thick ash, he moved in the direction he last remembered seeing her, until he tripped hard over something solid and fell face-first into the ash.

A muffled groan came from under him.

"Why'd you kick me?" a familiar voice complained.

Finn laughed in relief.

"Cass! Are you okay?"

"I don't know," she grumbled, pushing herself up and shaking her head, sending a cloud of ash flying in all directions.

"Where are we?"

"I have no idea," Finn said, grinning despite the pounding in his skull.

"I'm just glad you're alive."

"Not sure I am," Cass muttered, brushing ash off her arms and legs.

They sat there for a moment, dazed, the world around them muffled and gray.

Everything was wrong.

There was no Red Mound.

No stone circle.

Even the Painted Peaks looked broken and twisted, scarred beyond recognition.

Had they been moved to some different location while they lay unconscious?

Ash blanketed everything.

Finn coughed, gagging on the thick, bitter taste in the air. They both pulled their tunics up over their mouths to help filter their breathing. "This stuff tastes awful," he said, spitting.

"Well, don't eat it, dummy," Cass shot back, managing a weak smile.

Finn laughed again, a short, cracked sound, but it felt good.

Eventually, they staggered to their feet and trudged back to where they thought their packs had been, wading through the ash like trudging through snow.

Eventually, they found their packs, half-buried but intact.

Finn yanked free his canteen and drank deeply. Cass did the same, wiping her mouth with her sleeve. More than the supplies, knowing that they were still in the same location gave them some relief.

"Well," Cass said, staring out across the ruined landscape, "I guess we survived."

"Yeah," Finn agreed softly. "That's good."

They stood quietly for a while, both feeling the weight of it.

"So... now what?" Finn asked.

Cass ran a hand through her ash-covered hair, grimacing as it clumped together.

"We talked about this before, but getting to the circle was always the most urgent thought at the time. I guess we head back to the Cliff House," she said. "Find a place to rest. Regroup. Figure out what just happened to us."

Finn nodded slowly. "Yeah... that's a good idea."

They looked around again, but nothing felt familiar.

It was hard to believe this was the same place they'd entered just a short time ago.

Together, they decided to backtrack toward the campsite they'd left before the Awakening.

Cass led the way, moving carefully.

As they walked, the ash slowly thinned.

After a while, they stepped back onto normal ground, though even here, the landscape looked changed, bent and broken by whatever force had been unleashed.

Where the Red Mound had once loomed unnaturally large, now they could see nothing.

A few hours later, just as the light began to shift to midday, they reached their old campsite.

They dropped their packs and collapsed to the ground, exhausted.

No words passed between them for a while.

Then Cass turned to Finn. Finn turned to Cass.

And without needing to say a word, they both knew:

Everything had changed.

And somehow, their journey was only just beginning.

Cass eventually stirred and turned to Finn. "We should talk about where we will go next."

He looked up. "You mean… Cliff House?"

"Maybe," she said. "But I've been thinking."

"About what?"

"There's an Unbound city not far from here," she said. "I remember it from the folio-five days, maybe six."

Finn frowned. "You're sure?"

"I think, I'm sure."

He hesitated. "I don't know. After everything that happened…"

"I'm not saying we go now," Cass said. "But we should think about it. If we go back to the cliff, we'll be alone again. Out here… there might be answers."

Finn nodded, still unsure.

Then he glanced up at the sky, still pale blue and quiet, and muttered, "Plenty of daylight left."

Cass smiled faintly. "Let's eat," she said. "Then we'll see what else the world has waiting for us."

As they ate, both of them were thinking the same thing-

What had just happened wasn't simple.

It wasn't normal.

It was something rare, something enormous.

Something that had changed them.

Cass looked up at Finn, her expression uncertain.

"Did you… see anything when the awakening was happening?"

Finn flinched slightly, like she'd poked a bruise he hadn't realized was still sore.

"Yeah," he said quietly. "A lot of things.

Some looked good. Some… not so much.

I'm not sure how I feel about it yet."

Cass nodded, arms wrapped loosely around her knees.

"Same. I saw cities burning. People dying. Battles.

But I also saw-" she hesitated, "-beautiful things.

Cities where Mages and regular people lived together in peace.

Kids playing in the streets.

Trade routes open and safe.

Whole communities that felt… good."

Finn's eyes met hers. He nodded slowly.

"I saw that too. All of it."

They sat in silence for a while, the fire crackling softly beside them.

"I just hope," Finn said, "that if those things really do happen, if we're part of them, we'll be strong enough to do what we're supposed to do."

Cass didn't answer right away.

But after a long pause, she whispered,

"We have to be."

A while later, Finn glanced at her. "So… do we have magic now?" he asked.

Cass laughed softly. "I don't know. Maybe?"

Finn looked around, then pointed at a small, dry limb lying nearby.

It was lightweight, half-buried, probably flammable.

"Let me try something," he said.

He stared at the stick. Concentrated.

Nothing.

He pointed at it.

Still nothing.

Cass smirked. "Was that it? The whole spell?"

Finn sighed, still squinting at the stick like it might give in under pressure.

"Well, how are we supposed to make this work?"

Cass shrugged. "I don't think it's about pointing."

"Maybe I'm just out of power," Finn muttered.

"Or maybe," she said, "we have no idea what we are doing."

"Well, that's disappointing," he muttered.

They sat in the dirt near their old campsite, the jagged edge of what was left of the Red Mound visible through the thinning trees. The sun still hung above the horizon, casting long golden bands across the ground and stretching its shadows like soft reminders of the day's weight. They hadn't bothered with a fire; there was still light, and the warmth hadn't faded yet. The silence around them no longer felt heavy. Just quiet.

Cass's gaze drifted to where the red mound was in the distance. She stared for a long time, unmoving.

"I want to go look," she said.

Finn glanced up from where he was digging through his pack. "At the Red Mound?"

She nodded. "It's strange. That whole thing… just collapsed. Doesn't that bother you?"

He raised an eyebrow. "I mean, the whole mountain collapsed. I guess that's… strange."

She stood, brushing off her pants. "We're not in a rush, are we? Let's go see it. Just for a minute."

Finn looked towards where the Red Mound was, then back at her. He shrugged. "Yeah, alright. Lead the way."

They shouldered their packs, and Cass set off first, walking straight toward the place where everything had changed.

They didn't talk much as they walked. The trail was quiet, dappled in shade and light, with the low sound of wind threading through the branches. Cass led them northwest, cutting gently down the slope toward the remains of the Red Mound. Her pace was steady, focused.

Finn followed, glancing around more often than he had that morning.

It was too quiet.

Even the bugs were quiet.

After a while, Finn noticed that Cass was walking really quickly, so Finn had to rush to catch up. About an hour after leaving their previous campsite, Finn's neck hair stood on end.

He stopped and turned around, scanning the area.

Two orange eyes glowed from the trees just off the trail, fixed on him.

It stepped forward into the light and jumped onto the ground.

A creature shaped like a large cat, but wrong in every way.

It was larger, about twice the size of Finn, built with coiled muscle and covered in slick black scales that shimmered faintly in the sunlight. Its tail was too long. Its shoulders too wide. It moved with silent precision, claws glinting like obsidian.

"Cass," Finn said tightly.

She stopped, now several heights away from him, turned, and froze.

She saw it instantly and cursed herself for not watching their surroundings better.

The creature crouched low, eyes on Finn. Its muscles rippled.

"Back up, slowly," Cass whispered.

Finn took a step back, and instantly the cat lunged.

It slammed into him like a falling tree, knocking him flat. His breath left him in a single sharp gasp.

Claws tore through his shirt as it pinned him down. Its mouth opened, teeth bared, aimed for his throat.

Finn twisted, barely getting his dagger free.

An arrow thudded into the cat's back. It roared, spinning toward Cass. And it leaped at her.

She didn't move, and a small crystal barrier the size of a dinner plate shimmered into existence just in front of her, floating like a spinning shield of refracted light.

The cat hit it mid-leap, the barrier popped, and the cat dropped to the ground, stunned for just a second. That's all Finn needed.

He jumped on the cat's back from behind and drove the dagger straight into its neck,

With everything he had, he pulled the dagger up through the neck, trying to cause as much damage as possible.

The beast let out a guttural sound, half-roar, half-choke, then crumpled.

Dead.

For a moment, neither of them moved.

Cass ran to him, eyes scanning his body.

"Are you okay? Finn, let me see."

He was breathing hard, but confused. "I... I think I'm fine."

Cass knelt and yanked at the shredded remains of his shirt.

Underneath, his skin was dirty, sweaty, and completely unmarked.

"No blood," she whispered.

He looked down, just as stunned. "It clawed me, I felt it."

"You are fine, no marks," she said, confused. She saw the cat put all its weight on him and tear his shirt. She was certain he was dead, that she had lost her only friend in the world, just like she had lost her parents. She started shaking, from the adrenaline wearing off.

They looked down at the scale-cat. The sunlight hit its body just right, highlighting the black gloss of its armor-like hide. That was a very strong beast. She grabbed her dagger, threw herself at it, and, yelling, she stabbed it two more times as hard as she could. She knew it was dead, but she didn't care. She hated this thing for nearly taking Finn away from her. She stood up and kicked it over and over again until she finally fell on her bottom, panting.

Finn slowly got up, walked to her, and sat down. He didn't know why, since he was the one who almost died, but he put his arms around her shoulders and hugged her. She was still shaking but slowly starting to catch her breath.

"Are you okay?" He said after a moment.

She nodded and said, "For a moment, I thought I lost you, all because I wasn't paying attention."

"Ah, it could have happened with you paying attention too," he said. "You are not responsible for me; we are a team. This whole trip, I've been learning, and I'm capable of spotting things like this Scale Cat just like you. Both of us need to be more careful." After a few more moments, he asked, "Why were you distracted?"

She thought for a moment.

"I don't know," Then she hesitated for a long moment. She looked at Finn and said. "I think I have a map sense now."

Finn frowned, "What do you mean?"

She laughed. "It's like... I know where I am. Exactly. Not just in the world, but in relation to everything else. I don't have to guess. I could walk blindfolded for days and still know where I'm going."

Finn raised an eyebrow.

Cass continued, her voice more distant, "It's weird, I can't see everything, but I know where I am compared to things. If there is something I want to see, I may be able to get a sense of where it is. I also know where the circle is, or was, and I know where the campsite is." She looked at Finn, and he stayed quiet.

"It's more than that. When I think about it, really think, I get this sense that I'm looking down at myself, like I'm not just here, but also above myself. Like I'm both here and way up in the sky looking down."

Finn smiled, "Ah, like a map sense, why didn't you just say so?"

Cass opened her eyes wide, smiled back, and then shoved him over. "Shut up," she said, laughing.

"So that's it?" He said. "Your power is that you have a map sense that will get us eaten by a beast eventually?"

She pushed him over again. "Yes, but also I think… Did you see that cat stop in mid-air?"

He shook his head, "I was still on my back when I got up it was already on the ground, looking around. I thought you hit it with your bow."

She nodded, "It jumped at me, and a very thin shield popped directly its way. It hit it, and it disappeared, but it was strong enough to stop its jump in mid-air."

"That is helpful," he said. "Can you show me?"

Cass tried to focus, but nothing happened. "Maybe it only happens when I need it."

"Well, it's a lot better than my power, which is nothing as far as I can tell," Finn said sarcastically.

She wasn't sure about that still. He was doing a great job of distracting her and pulling her out of the shock she was feeling, but before she was certain he was going to die. She saw its sharp, razor-like claws mauling him from his collar to his hip. And there wasn't a scratch on him. She would keep this to herself for now. But she didn't think she was the only one who was developing powers. "Let's go," she said.

They stood up and resumed their hike, this time moving more slowly and watching for movement around them. Neither of them even thought about using the Scale Cat for meat. As far as either of them was concerned, it was as evil as the Twisted Shadows.

They crested the final ridge just as the sun began to dip low, the light shifting from gold to the first notes of dusk. The world beyond the trees dropped away suddenly, and both Cass and Finn paused at the edge, staring in quiet awe.

The Red Mound was gone.

In its place yawned a vast, irregular, roundish canyon of red stone and jagged ledges. The walls were steep and uneven, as though the earth was a bubble that had popped. The rock faces were striped with dark clay and rust, and thin trails of loose gravel spilled down the sides like old scars.

At the canyon's base, the floor was covered in a sea of smooth red pebbles, worn and scattered, as though they'd been tumbled by water long ago.

And at the very center of the canyon sat a building.

A squat white stone structure, stark and geometric, like it had been dropped into the world from some other place entirely.

Two heights tall. Ten heights wide. Maybe twenty long.

No windows. No seams. Just a single door.

Finn squinted down at it, then glanced at Cass.

"What do you think that is?"

Cass shook her head slowly. "I don't know," she murmured. "I just… felt like something was here. I didn't know what."

Finn grunted. "Map sense, my butt."

Cass smirked and pointed to the right. "There. That slope looks like we can get down from there."

The path wasn't really a path. More of a jagged line where the earth had slid into the canyon. They moved slowly, boots crunching on loose stone. Every few steps, a pebble would skitter away beneath their feet and rattle down the slope into the basin.

The drop wasn't sheer, but it was steep. The walls were crumbling, brittle. Red dust coated their boots, filled the air, and clung to their hands when they reached out for balance.

They didn't speak much as they descended.

The sun sank lower behind them, and half the canyon fell into shadow. The light painted the other half in deep orange, setting the white building at the center aglow against the darker stone around it.

By the time they reached the floor, the shadows had grown long and cool.

The structure loomed before them, silent and still. It had no visible seams. No carvings. No decoration. Just pure, pale stone. It was solid in a way that felt deliberate. Timeless.

Like it had been waiting.

The only thing they could discern from the uniformity of the building was a door in the center of the near wall, perfectly flush with the surface. There was no handle, only two hand-shaped depressions carved into the stone.

Cass stepped closer and frowned. "That's... weird."

Finn tilted his head. The handprint on the left was shaped for a right hand. The one on the right was clearly for the left.

"They're meant for two people," Cass said quietly. "Standing shoulder to shoulder."

They exchanged a glance.

Finn shrugged. "We've already come this far."

They stepped forward and placed their hands on the stone.

For a heartbeat, nothing.

Then, suddenly, their hands stuck.

Not painfully, but completely. The air around them felt thick, charged. A faint hum vibrated through their fingertips.

They both looked at each other, uncertain.

Then-

Click.

A soft whoosh of air escaped from the sealed edge, and the stone door shifted with a low, grinding sound.

Their hands came free as the door slid inward, revealing only darkness within.

Finn exhaled.

Cass took a step forward.

"This is either a great idea or the worst we have ever made," Cass stated.

"Well, let's see."

CHAPTER 14

The Mausoleum

Inside the building, the air was cool and fresh. A soft strip of light ran along the top edge of the ceiling, casting a faint glow that stretched the length of the chamber. It wasn't bright, just enough to reveal the space as pale and seamless as the outside.

The walls, floor, and ceiling were made of the same smooth, white stone, unblemished, polished, uncracked, and eerily clean. There was no dust, no spiderwebs, nothing natural. Just silence and stone.

At the far end of the room stood a rectangular box, one height long and half as wide and tall, perfectly centered against the back wall.

Cass and Finn stepped inside, cautious but curious.

As soon as they crossed the threshold, the door closed behind them with a heavy click.

They froze as the pressure inside the room pressed on their

eardrums.

Cass spun around and rushed back to the door. "Did it just-?"

Finn stared at it, jaw tight. "It closed."

Cass pressed her hands against the door, searching for a seam, a catch, anything. "It's sealed. There's nothing here. No handle, no switch."

Finn stepped toward the box at the end of the room.

"Finn?" Cass called. "I think we're locked in here."

"I think..." he said slowly, "this is a mausoleum."

Cass flinched and turned to look at the box more carefully. Her shoulders slumped. "Yep. That's coffin-sized, alright."

"Fantastic," Finn muttered. "Trapped in a tomb."

They exchanged a look, half nerves, half disbelief.

Whatever this place was, it hadn't brought them here by accident.

They both started scanning the walls, pressing, tapping, even knocking, trying to find anything that resembled a button, a lever, a seam. For a few minutes, the only sound was their feet scuffing against stone and the soft thuds of hands on walls.

Then a shimmer caught Finn's eye.

"Uh... Cass?"

Above the stone box, a thread of light twisted into the air. It flickered, wavered, then slowly began to condense into shape, a man, no more than a few heads high, standing on the lid of the coffin.

An old man.

His back was hunched, his frame wrapped in layers of robes. He leaned on a crooked staff. The image was faint, translucent like smoke, and barely held its shape. But it was there. And it was looking, not at them, but at the sealed door.

"Well," Finn muttered, "this isn't freaky at all."

Cass said nothing, too busy staring at the image, circling

slowly to see if it was flat or fully formed. It looked real. Real enough.

After a few moments, the figure lifted its head and began to speak.

The voice was distant, muffled like sound through a wall. But it was loud enough to hear and understand it.

"I am Edrin, last Seer of the Fourth Meridian," the figure said. "When I was young, during my own Awakening, I was shown a vision of the twin stones, and the two who would carry them."

He paused, head slightly bowed.

"I saw your arrival, not as names or faces, but as forces, opposing and entwined. Heroes born from wild power. My life, my death, my legacy... all shaped by preparing for this moment."

The image flickered, then resumed.

"The circle where you awakened is not ordinary. It was not built for the masses or the average person. It is wild magic, untamed and dangerous. Unlike the circles guarded in cities, this one was never meant to be controlled. The wild magic the circle leaks is enough to change living things around it. Because of this, it repels civilization. That was always its nature. The Dragon that died and created it was a matron of great power, wild and unbound. She died 1000s of years old and died here in order to fulfill the prophecy."

Cass and Finn looked at each other. Finally, they were getting information that they desperately needed.

"But in my vision, I saw this: the twin stones would brave the wild. You would find the circle. And when you did, everything would change."

He leaned forward slightly, his voice low and deliberate.

When I was young, I was too liberal with my tongue, and I shared parts of my visions with others.

"I spent much of my life hiding the rest of the truth. That this circle was the one. I did the unforgivable. I altered records. I misled scholars. With time, even the most curious forgot its importance. But the wild cannot be erased, and neither can prophecy."

The Mage straightened again.

"You must understand: the energy this circle pulls, especially during your awakening, is immense. Too immense to ignore. The world will notice. They may not know why, not yet, but they will come. They will scour the land. They will search for you."

Finn and Cass exchanged a glance.

"I have two gifts for you, one you will get today in your need. The final gift you will get in one year from this day, when you are strong enough to have them, but you both must return to this place to get it. The mausoleum will not open again until then, and only for the twin stones."

"For now… you have time. Time to grow, to learn, to train. You must use it well. Because in one year's time, when you return to this place… you will not be alone. My vision was clear that the second gift would be visible in front of Kingdoms. The powers of this world will be watching."

The old prophet's voice softened.

"I wish I could have met you. I feel like I already know you. I've seen fragments of your future, it will be glorious, terrible, and unfortunately necessary. The world will change, and you will shape that change. But the cost will be great. Be careful who you trust. There are evil forces in this world that would destroy the potential you hold in your grasp right now."

The image dimmed, dissolved, and disappeared into the air above the stone.

Then, with a low click, several drawers slid open from the wall.

Inside: new clothes, several swords, several bows, several strings for the bows, and a small leather pouch filled with gold coins.

Cass exhaled slowly.

"He really meant it."

Finn nodded, staring at the drawer. "Why would he do all this just for us? It seems like this Mausoleum took a lot of resources to create and sustain. Just to give us these supplies?"

Cass said, "I don't know about you, but these new clothes are worth more to me than the gold is right now." She laughed.

Both chose a set of clothing that was close to their size.

Finn agreed. "One year," he said quietly. "Between now and then, we need to get a lot stronger."

As they turned their backs to each other and changed their clothes, the air between them felt charged. They'd changed near each other before, out of necessity, behind trees or near campfires. But this felt different, for some reason.

Finn tugged off his ash-stained, shredded tunic and Cass's mom's pants that he'd been wearing for weeks now. He could swear he felt her body warmth through the still air. It was probably his imagination, but still, his ears burned.

The new shirt was a little stiff, but clean and well-made. The pants were loose at the waist, a bit long at the legs, but he folded them at the cuff so they wouldn't trip him. They'd clearly been sewn without the person knowing his size, or for someone still growing, like him. The fabric was light and breathable, a dull charcoal color that wouldn't draw attention. Practical.

Next, they looked over the weapons. Finn chose a sword, and Cass a new bow and string.

Finn adjusted the belt and slid the scabbard and his new sword into place at his hip. The sword nestled inside was simple, nothing ornate. The hilt was wrapped in rough leather, enough to feel comfortable in the hand. The blade itself was short, no longer than his forearm, made of unpolished steel with a dull gray sheen. Just enough to defend, not to dazzle. It felt heavy, but not unmanageable. Solid. Honest.

He glanced down at himself and let out a breath. For the first time in a long time, he felt...prepared.

And yet, the moment of quiet stirred something else.

His thoughts wandered, to his parents, to his aunt, to the life that had vanished like smoke. What would they say if they saw him now? Dressed like a fighter, with a sword.

A flicker of sadness tightened his chest.

He shook it off before it could drag him down.

No time for that. Not now.

He cinched the belt tighter and gave the scabbard a tug, testing its hold.

Then he turned to Cass, now dressed, and said, "How does it look?"

She said, "You still need a bath, but the clothes are nice."

He smiled at the jab and took the belt off; they were going to sleep after all. They laid out their bedrolls and sat eating a bit of the woolly turkey that hadn't turned yet. This would be the last day they could eat from it, and they would have to find something else tomorrow. The lighting inside stayed constant, but it was still soft. They eventually drifted off, both sleeping at the same time for the first time in a while.

They both woke up at the same time. Even though they couldn't see the sun, they knew it was before sunrise. They quietly organized their new and old supplies into their packs. Finn put on his new sword, and Cass her new bow. Her old bow she decided to leave here in a drawer. She strung her new bow with the bow string in the drawer. It was tight and required more strength to draw, but she said that she was eager to try it out.

Finn's new weapon caused a discussion between the teenagers. If he was going to use a sword now, the bow would just get in his way. He decided to keep them all for now. His bow saved them a few times, and it was a hard decision to give it up. He packed his dagger, chose to only keep a few normal arrows (and one oil-filled arrow) to lighten his load. Cass took the rest in her quiver.

Cass looked up and offered a faint smile. "We should go."

Finn nodded, rubbing his arms to shake off the cold. "Right."

As they gathered their things, Finn handed the coin pouch to Cass.

"You hold it," he said.

"If I hold it, I'll drop it, or lose it."

Cass laughed and tucked the pouch into her pack. "Fair."

With one last look around the silent tomb, they stood at the door, and Cass tried to open it without success. She stood back, and Finn tried without success. *Maybe we need to both touch it like we did to enter, shoulder to shoulder.* When they did, their hands stuck and the door clicked open, swinging outward this time, letting the fresh morning air inside.

They stepped outside into the chill of dawn, the great door closed behind them, and clicked shut. "See you in a year," Finn said. The canyon that once held the Red Mound was quiet now, and the path back up the rim, though steep, was manageable with careful steps.

Their destination was a town named Greyfen, mentioned in the folio. Cass believed it was real and felt certain she could lead them there, straight and true, without having to take the roundabout way of travel described using landmarks. She didn't know what lay between them and the town, only that based on the directions in the folio, the direction felt... right.

Their pace was steady through the morning. The trees thickened around them as they descended the far side of the old mound. The land was no longer as ominous as before; it was even vibrant with odd plant life and winding animal tracks. Birds called to each other with sounds the two teens hadn't heard before, and strange insects shimmered on leaves with bright colors.

By midday, they paused near a wide stream to refill their flasks. The water was icy and clean, and they sat for a moment in the shade of a low, branching oak.

"Feels weird," Finn said.

Cass looked over. "What does?"

"Just... being out here. After everything."

Cass nodded. "We are still hiding, the ghost-guy said some groups would soon be looking for us. But for now, we have somewhere to go."

They walked until the sun began to dip, eventually finding a small rocky alcove nestled in a hillside to make their first camp. Cass gathered sticks while Finn cleared space for a fire.

After, Cass then went to hunt, Finn set two snares, collected firewood, and foraged for whatever he could find before the sun set. Finn found some nuts with hard shells. Each was egg-shaped and about half his finger length; the animals and birds seemed to love them based on all the different kinds of scat around the tree. He gathered so many nuts that he had to use his shirttail to hold them all. Cass returned with a hare that had a clean arrow hole through its back. "First kill with your new bow." Said Finn. Cass said, "Truth is, I missed the first time, we're just lucky that when we heard the shot, it froze rather than ran. I was able to take the second hit." They both were starving and ready to get some food in their stomachs.

The nuts were good and could be eaten raw. They ate half of them with the rabbit and kept the other half of the nuts for the trail.

The first night was uneventful, save for the occasional snapping of twigs in the dark. Finn took the first watch, bow in hand, while Cass slept. The moonlight made everything look silvered and distant. At one point, Finn thought he saw a flicker of movement in the trees, but nothing came close. When his turn ended, he gently nudged Cass awake, who rose wordlessly and took his place, sharp-eyed and still.

They woke to pale light and the crackle of cooling embers. After packing their few things, Finn slipped off to check the snares. One had done its job–a squirrel, small but enough. By the time he returned, Cass had rekindled the fire. They skinned and cooked the animal carefully, eating what they needed and wrapping the rest in cloth for later.

Finn also pulled out a handful of the nuts he'd foraged the night before. They ate slowly, savoring the light meal. Food wouldn't last long, but for now, it was needed.

By mid-morning, they were on the move. The woods thinned as they went, and the soft forest floor gave way to scattered rock and sloping terrain. Climbing grew more frequent. Heat rose off the stones, and their packs felt heavier with each step.

Around midday, they stopped under the twisted shade of a leaning pine. Cass dropped her pack with a groan and stretched.

Finn sat nearby, chewing the last of the squirrel. "You notice something weird?"

She raised an eyebrow. "Just one thing?"

He smirked. "No more wild, crazy monsters?"

Cass tilted her head, thinking. "Yeah. The animals feel... normal. Birds. Squirrels. A few old deer tracks."

"Back near Darrowmere, it was one thing after another," Finn said.

Cass frowned, looking off into the hills, "It does feel different here."

They didn't speak much after that.

Unfortunately, they spoke too soon.

The sun had dipped low when it happened. The slope ahead narrowed between two broken spines of rock. It was the perfect place for an ambush, which is why Finn and Cass were on guard. Cass moved first, bow in hand. Finn followed, fingers resting on the hilt of his sword, though he still hadn't drawn it. Then, without sound or warning, the thing was upon them.

It erupted from the rocks, black and glistening like wet stone, with too many limbs and a mouth that split sideways. It was a Twisted Shadow but different from any other they had seen. Its presence felt wrong in the gut, like it didn't belong in the world but had clawed its way in anyway. And it looked out of control compared to the others they've seen. Rabid.

Finn stumbled back as Cass loosed an arrow. It missed, shattering against stone. The creature lunged, jaws wide, and Finn raised his sword in a shaky grip. He swung wide and missed. The thing slammed into him, jaws aimed for his neck.

But the bite never landed.

Its fangs struck his left forearm, and it stopped cold. Finn gasped, watching in disbelief as his skin was hard and unbroken. The beast bit his arm over and over, like a reflex in a series of rapid bites, then it reeled, confused.

Cass nocked again and fired. This time, the arrow sank deep into its ribcage. It didn't turn to shadow, like those near Darrowmere would have. It shrieked, twisting toward her, but Finn surged forward and drove his blade into its side. The sword caught, slid between ribs, and Finn pushed to angle it up through its chest.

The creature staggered. It shivered violently, then collapsed with a heavy thud, its jaw still working as if it were chewing on something as it died.

Silence followed.

Both of them stood there, panting, wide-eyed.

Cass lowered her bow slowly. "Well," she muttered. "Maybe I should have practiced with this thing."

Finn looked at his arm, flexing it. "Did you see that?" he said, grinning now. "It didn't even scratch me."

She looked at him. "You were nearly killed."

"But I wasn't."

She rolled her eyes, but she smiled.

"This Shadow is different from the ones by Darrowmere. Why was it so easy to kill?" Finn asked.

"I don't know. It's like it forgot or couldn't turn into shadow." Cass said, "Maybe they are just different here."

Finn nodded, and they gathered their things with renewed urgency, nerves still humming from the encounter. The rest of the evening passed in wary silence, and when they made camp that night, neither of them slept deeply. That night, Finn and Cass noticed several shooting stars; one was so bright it looked like a beam of light pointing in the direction they had just come from. Finn thought they were something wonderful to see.

The road ahead, they knew now, was not as quiet as it seemed.

The third day was warmer. The trees returned, but they looked different now, taller, older. The ground sloped gently downward as if guiding them. Cass said they were making good time, that they'd likely reach Greyfen sometime the next evening.

But the day wasn't without issues.

Midmorning, they encountered signs of an old battle, broken spears, rusted metal, and bones long picked clean. The forest had nearly swallowed it up, but the feeling of violence still clung to the place. Neither of them spoke as they passed through.

By midday, the woods gave way to a grassy plain. Wind tugged at their clothes, and the sun beat down from a cloudless sky. Cass shaded her eyes, pointing. "There. Those hills. We should camp there tonight."

They reached the hills by early evening and found a shallow cave. It wasn't deep, but it was dry and gave them some cover from the open plain. They went hunting, set snares, and foraged for wood and food. They ended up with a young boar, and they feasted on it.

"Think we should use fake names in the city?" Finn asked, nudging a coal with a stick.

Cass shook her head. "No one's looking for us. Better to keep it simple."

He nodded. "Alright. Less to remember."

Cass leaned back, watching the fire. "We need to be careful. We don't know anything about these people. The first thing we do is find a vendor. Buy something, ask questions. Let them talk."

"Figure out what kind of place Greyfen really is," Finn added.

"Exactly. What's safe. What's not. Where people like us go."

They were quiet for a moment.

"Do you think we'll find anything useful there?" Finn asked.

Cass shrugged. "Food. Rest. Maybe some answers. If we listen close enough."

Finn nodded again, more slowly this time. "I'd settle for being able to rest for a little while."

Cass gave a small smile. "Let's try not to stand out, and maybe we will."

A moment passed in silence. He hesitated, then added quietly, "I've been thinking about my parents. And my aunt a lot."

Cass looked over. "Yeah. Me too. I miss mine all the time."

The fire crackled between them, soft and steady. They sat in silence, the weight of the world briefly lifted.

Later, they took turns keeping watch, but sleep came more easily than it had in days.

Tomorrow, they'd reach Greyfen. And they both had a feeling that nothing would be the same.

The next morning, they woke early, eating the last of the smoked boar before breaking camp. The sky was overcast but dry, and the breeze carried the scent of grass and far-off water.

By midday, they saw it.

Greyfen.

It was larger than either of them expected, sprawling out over low hills beyond a wide, winding river. Stone walls surrounded the city, but they could see rooftops and smoke stacks rising high beyond the battlements. The gate was busy with traffic: wagons, merchants, travelers on horseback, and foot. People flowed in and out like currents in a stream.

Finn stared, wide-eyed. "It's bigger than Darrowmere."

Cass nodded. "Looks like it."

The whole time they watched it, people and carriages were entering and leaving the city. They even saw little kids running in and out of the gate. So they decided to take the chance and try to enter it. They crossed a long stone bridge over the river. The water below was fast-moving, clear, and cold. Two guards stood by the entrance, tall and armed, their expressions sour. The teens kept their heads down, walked side by side, and said nothing.

But no one said anything to them. It took several minutes for Cass and Finn to stop themselves from bracing for an attack. There were no beasts here except humans. The guards saw them, looked them up and down, and let them pass without challenge. They were speechless and surprised that they may now be safe. It took them several minutes to notice what was around them.

Once inside, the city exploded into motion and sound. Vendors shouted over one another from colorful stalls, selling everything from fruit to fabric to clockwork trinkets. Children laughed and darted through the crowds. Music played somewhere nearby, and the air smelled like baked bread, roasted meat, and not-so-pleasant smells of a city.

It was the happiest and busiest place either of them had ever seen.

Cass looked around with wide eyes. "Alright," she said,

glancing at Finn. "Let's see if we can find a place to rest tonight."

"And some food." Said Finn

Nodding, Cass said, "And some food too."

CHAPTER 15

A Day After

It was early morning in a fortified military encampment positioned along the edge of the Painted Peaks. The sun had only just begun to rise, casting a copper glow over tents and worn banners that snapped lightly in the wind. Soldiers moved quietly, some sharpening weapons, others tending to mounts, but there was an unspoken tension hanging in the air.

A day earlier, they had all seen the unnatural collapse of the Red Mound from several days' walk away. A mountain of earth folding in on itself without sound, without warning. It had shaken even the veterans. Now, everyone waited for orders.

Inside the largest tent near the center of camp, the grizzled Unbound General Fash leaned over a table crowded with maps and text. He was in his 50s, with deep scars running down his neck and across his left cheek, but his eyes were sharp.

A Scout Commander Saren entered, tall and lean, his travel cloak still dusty from his last patrol.

"You summoned me, sir?"

The general looked up, nodded once. "You're going to the Red Mound."

The commander stiffened. "You think it's an attack?"

"I think it's something. And I don't like not knowing what. Take a small team. Stay a few days there. Send a report after you scout the area well. I want to know what you find, and I want your eyes on that place until you hear back from me. You will leave tomorrow."

"Any engagement rules?"

"Just observation. But if you see anything magical at the sight, anything at all, you don't touch it. I'm not sending any Mages with you."

The scout commander gave a sharp nod. "Understood."

General Fash looked him over once more before returning to his map. "Go."

That day, a small party of 20 was mobilized and sent out. And as the sun climbed higher over the peaks, the team rode out toward the ruins of the Red Mound, and whatever mystery waited inside the canyon.

The scout team reached the site on the fourth morning.

Their journey through the Painted Peaks had been grueling, three and a half days of rough terrain, thick woods, and treacherous ridgelines. They crossed broken stone paths that hadn't been used in decades, forded two rivers swollen from spring runoff, and maneuvered around sinkholes hidden beneath carpets of moss. One scout twisted his ankle on the second day and had to be supported by another for most of the journey. At night, the howls of unseen creatures haunted their campfires, and strange clawed prints greeted them come morning.

But the men of the Unbound army were seasoned. Tired, bruised, but unbroken, they pressed forward, driven by the urgency of their orders and the haunting sight of the Red Mound's collapse from afar.

What they found when they arrived brought even the most battle-hardened among them to silence.

The mound was gone. In its place yawned a massive canyon of jagged red stone, as if the mountain had been punched inward by some unseen fist. Sheer walls, formed of broken but naturally fused rock, ringed the hollow in a rough oval, nearly circular. Down in the center of that bowl sat something impossible.

A perfect rectangular block of white stone. Squat. Seamless.

It looked completely untouched by the collapse. No dust clung to its smooth surface, no debris piled against its walls. The structure was two heights tall, ten wide, and twenty long, perfectly rectangular, with no visible seams, no windows, and only a single door facing the slope.

The team remained at the canyon's edge for several long minutes, just staring.

One of the younger scouts asked. "Was it under the mound this whole time?"

"Can't say."

The leader crouched, brushing his fingers across the cracked earth. "Look here," he said. Faint impressions marred the dust; there were light bootprints nearly erased by the wind, leading up to the edge and then away again. "Someone beat us here."

He motioned for a sweep of the area.

The scouts spread out in silence, combing the canyon rim and checking the surrounding tree line. They found no signs of a camp close by, no fire pits or discarded gear, but further to the southeast, hidden behind a rise, they came across the remnants of a campsite: a burned circle of blackened stones, disturbed ashes, the faint scent of old smoke. Small footprints circled the clearing, and a few snapped branches showed where someone had passed through in a hurry.

They followed the trail until it vanished into a field of ash.

The ash was strange. Deep, silky, and unnaturally still. It clung to their boots like flour and muffled every step.

"Not from a fire," one of the men said, kneeling to sift the powder through his fingers. "This... this is from something else."

"Must be magic," another muttered. "Or something worse."

As dusk fell, they returned to the canyon and made camp near the rim. A fire was lit, watch rotations were set, and all eyes kept glancing at the white structure down below. Even in darkness, it seemed to glow faintly in the moonlight, cold and indifferent, like a bone waiting to be unearthed.

That night, they debated in low voices over steaming mugs of bitterleaf tea.

"Could be Elarith scouts. Maybe they got here first."

"Why would Elarith send kids?"

"Kids?"

"The footprints were small."

"Locals, maybe women. Deserters. Runners. Or worse, Unbound gone rogue."

"Or bait," someone else said. "To lure us in."

The scout leader said nothing, staring at the structure from his seat on a nearby rock. The wind tugged at his cloak, and the firelight danced across his scarred face.

"We don't touch it," he said at last. "We wait."

The next day, the scout team expanded its search radius. They moved methodically, in pairs and small groups, spiraling out from the canyon like spokes on a wheel, careful to mark every turn and trail. The land around them was quiet, unnaturally so. The usual chirping of birds and rustling of small creatures in the underbrush had dulled to silence, as though the earth itself was holding its breath.

Each clue deepened the mystery. The team logged everything in field journals, taking measurements, sketches, and observations. One scout made note of a strange sensation-a pressure in his chest whenever he neared the white building. Another reported seeing distant glimmers in the sky, like falling stars that vanished before touching the horizon.

Their appearance and direction were added as a side note. Orders were clear. They were only to observe and report.

On the second night, the scout leader penned a short dispatch in scout-speak. He described the canyon and the precision of the stone building in the center of it. He included descriptions of the area, distances covered, and, perhaps most importantly, the signs of recent passage.

He emphasized the field of ash, the light bootprints, and the building's lack of any door seam or mechanism. He mentioned the way the canyon seemed to repel animals, and how even the wind carried an uneasy stillness. Finally, he included a short note:

"The structure is unlike anything in the Kingdom. It appears to be new, not as if it were buried under the Red Mound. Its very presence seems to alter the behavior of the wilds. Recommend Mage inspection immediately. We are maintaining distance as ordered."

He sealed the report in a light oilskin, tied it to the leg of a messenger hawk, and released it into the cold morning sky.

Then they waited.

The evening on the next day a response arrived, and it was not what they expected.

The men's cloaks were stiff with dust, their bellies hungry for more than rations, and tempers were beginning to fray. Every crack of a twig in the woods turned heads. Every shift in the wind stirred hands to weapons. They were seasoned scouts, trained to endure far worse, but this waiting, in a place so strange, so quiet, was beginning to wear on them.

Then, a sharp cry pierced the stillness.

A hawk spiraled down from the northern sky, its powerful wings slicing the air. It landed on the outstretched gauntlet of the lookout stationed on the northern ridge, a heavy parchment tube no bigger than his finger, strapped to its leg, sealed in wax emblazoned with the crest of the Unbound Kingdom.

The scout leader broke the seal with steady hands, even as his heart thudded in anticipation.

He unrolled the scroll and read it twice.

The message was brief, but its implications were enormous:

"Scout Commander Saren,

By order of General Fash:

Secure the site immediately. Reinforcements en route. Mage support authorized. No tampering with the structure. Do not attempt entry.

You are to maintain a twenty-height perimeter. The white stone structure is now classified as a priority.

Good Job."

-Command

Commander Saren lowered the scroll, expression unreadable.

Around him, his lieutenants waited.

"Well?" one asked.

Saren exhaled through his nose, handed the scroll to his second-in-command, and said flatly, "We're not going anywhere."

"What do they want us to do?"

"Guard and do not touch it. Reinforcements are coming. And Mages."

That last word hung in the air like smoke.

Mages meant attention. Serious attention. That building, the one squatting like a forgotten god in the middle of the red canyon, was no longer a curiosity. It was a symbol. A threat. Maybe even a weapon.

The scouts exchanged glances. Some looked worried. Others intrigued.

One muttered, "So we're babysitting a rock."

"No," Saren said. "We're babysitting whatever secrets the rock is holding."

He ordered double watches set on all sides. The camp perimeter was redrawn, wider and sharper. Lite fortifications were built with whatever the land could offer, fallen trees, carved stakes, trenches lined with fire-hardened poles. Signal fires were prepped at three lookout points.

Then came the hardest part.

Waiting again, but this time, under new orders, with the weight of the Kingdom bearing down on their shoulders.

Three days later, as dusk fell, Saren stood alone on the canyon's edge, gazing down at the seamless white stone building, its surface still untouched, unmoved, and maddeningly silent.

For the first time in days, the wind stirred around them again and carried with it something new. The first sign of Mage support came in the form of dust on the horizon.

They arrived at dusk, two dozen soldiers clad in polished armor escorting a covered wagon flanked by six mounted Mages. The caravan moved with purpose, banners of the Unbound Kingdom fluttering high above the lead rider's lance. As they entered the scout encampment, all conversation quieted. The mere presence of the Mages turned the air stiff.

Commander Saren stood at attention as a stern-faced officer dismounted and approached him. He was an older man with a weatherworn coat and a sharp bronze insignia clipped at the collar. Without ceremony, the man produced a scroll, cracked the wax seal, and read aloud:

"By order of General Fash, the location heretofore known as

the Red Canyon Outpost is now designated a forward post under military jurisdiction. Commander Saren, you are hereby promoted to Field Captain. You will secure this site until relieved."

Field Captain Saren said nothing. He only nodded and saluted. The camp around them sprang into motion.

The stone Mages got to work immediately, their hands glowing with muted light as they began pulling walls from the earth itself. Stones cracked and rose, forming a perimeter around the rim of the canyon. Shale formed into guard posts. Dirt became packed walkways. In a matter of hours, the crude trenches had evolved into the beginnings of a proper outpost.

Meanwhile, a copper Mage, young, sharp-eyed, and already bristling with copper coil jewelry and charms, bent down and touched the ground. Her eye rolled back in her head the way that Copper Mages do when they are reaching for metal in the earth to form a connection. After an hour, she pulled her hand upward, and with it came a metal rod until it stopped around hip high.

"We can send messages to Command now, Sir," she told Saren without looking up.

But it was the light Mage who drew the most attention.

He was tall, draped in white and gray robes that shimmered subtly in the growing starlight. He approached the white stone building alone, arms crossed behind his back, and simply stood before it for a long time. Then, slowly, he began to circle it, fingers twitching, eyes distant.

Hours passed.

Eventually, he returned to the fire where the officers were gathered.

He said. "I can't sense any traps, in, on, or around the building, and the canyon itself appears to just be a normal canyon."

A silence settled over them.

Someone muttered, "Good."

But curiosity has a sharp edge.

The next morning, after creating a dome of stone over the suspected campsite and the field of ash to protect them, one of the earth Mages, a burly veteran with slate-colored tattoos carved across his arms, stepped forward.

"I want to test the wall of the building," he said, staring at the building.

Saren frowned.

"Not to enter," the Mage corrected. "A surface test. Something small."

Reluctantly, Saren allowed it.

The earth Mage approached the side of the structure, knelt, and summoned a narrow drill of stone, about the width of his fist. It hovered in the air, rotating slowly, and then thrust forward to scrape the wall.

The moment it touched the surface, the Mage screamed.

The drill shattered.

Blood sprayed from his side as if something had carved a wound clear through the side of his chest, the diameter of a fist. He staggered back, hands pressed to his side, eyes wide in disbelief.

Several men ran towards him to help. Whatever force connected the building to the Mage had acted too swiftly, too violently.

He died within moments, bleeding out beside the very structure he tried to scratch.

The camp fell still.

No one moved. No one spoke.

From that moment on, any testing on the building would be approached with extreme caution.

The first message the Copper Mage transmitted back to central command was a grim one: One Mage was dead, and the cause was the building itself. Her report included every detail she could gather, the mirrored injury, the lack of visible magic.

As she encoded the message, her hands trembled slightly. At first, she'd assumed this post was a quiet punishment, a reassignment for her gossiping about an officer's love life. But now?

Now she wasn't so sure.

Whatever this structure was… it might be tied to the magical surge the world had just felt. The events happened at the same time after all.

And if that were true, then this was no backwater posting.

After transmitting her formal report to central command, the copper Mage lingered at her relay node, fingers hovering over the copper rod. She pretended to adjust the connection, casually, deliberately, shifting frequencies. The secondary message she prepared was brief, vague, and encoded in a common inter-Mage cipher. It wasn't treason. Not really.

But every copper Mage on the planet had felt that surge. Whatever had caused it wasn't normal.

She sent the message to a relay far beyond the Unbound Kingdom, directing it toward Virelios, the City of Signals, the shining capital of the Copper Mage academies. Virelios had the infrastructure, the reach, and most importantly, the hunger for information. If anyone could make sense of what had happened, it was the Mages there.

She kept it simple:

"Unusual structure found under the Red Mound in Painted Peaks. Possible connection to the Surge."

No names or personal information were included. Just enough to flag curiosity. And if Copper Mages were anything, they were curious. This was just enough to plant a seed.

CHAPTER 16

City Life

Finn and Cass walked slowly through the crowded market of Greyfen, eyes wide, trying to take everything in. It was louder than anything they were used to: people haggling, bells ringing, carts clattering over cobblestones. The scent of roasted meat mixed with sweet pastries and the tang of tannery smoke. Color was everywhere: bright fabric banners, polished copper kettles, and rows of fruit, some of which they had never seen before.

They stopped at a modest stall run by a middle-aged woman with braided hair and sun-worn skin. Her table was loaded with baked goods, sugar-dusted rolls, meat-stuffed hand pies, and thick loaves of still-warm bread. Finn's stomach growled.

He glanced at Cass, who gave a nod.

Finn stepped forward and picked two meat pies. The vendor smiled and named her price, "One copper for both."

He reached into the pouch and pulled out one of the silver coins from bag of coins given to them at the mausoleum. It caught the sunlight, heavier, cleaner, older than anything else on the table, and set it gently down.

The vendor's smile faded. She didn't reach for it.

"That's... not from here," she said, lowering her voice.

Cass's hand drifted toward her pack.

"It's silver," Finn said quickly. "We just... found it."

The woman didn't answer. She glanced up and down the street. A vendor two stalls away paused mid-sale, frowning at the coin. Someone nearby leaned closer to whisper.

The woman cleared her throat and slid the coin back toward them.

"Don't use that here," she said quietly. "You'll draw too much attention. There are pickpockets, and worse, who notice things like that."

Finn's mouth went dry. "Oh. Thanks for the-"

"You're not in trouble," she cut in. "But if you're smart, you'll find someone who knows what they're looking at."

Cass leaned in. "Do you know someone?"

The woman hesitated, then gave a small nod. "Four blocks that way," she said, pointing down the street. "Then turn right. Another four blocks. You'll see a house with white walls and wood beams over the gate. The man's name is Lord Tovin Brenrick. He deals in collectibles. Keeps to himself."

Cass nodded. "Thank you."

"Don't thank me. Just be careful." She hesitated, then added more cheerfully, "Now, got anything smaller?"

Cass passed her the same coin. "If you'll take it for the pies, you can keep the change."

The vendor accepted it quickly, this time without hesitation. "Done."

They walked away quietly, pies in hand, back into the crowd.

"Too much attention," Finn muttered.

Cass nodded.

They ate as they walked, hot, flaky crust wrapped around slow-cooked meat and thick, peppery gravy. Finn let out a low hum of satisfaction. Cass smiled through her first bite. It was the best thing they'd eaten in weeks.

The winding road led uphill to a tall white wall and a gate framed by wooden beams. Cass tugged a rope bell, and a distant chime echoed inside. Moments later, a tall man in a layered coat, clearly a butler, appeared.

"We were told Lord Brenrick might be interested in this," Finn said, holding up the coin.

The man stepped forward, inspected the flash of gold, then said, "Oh my, I see he might just at that." Then turned silently to open the gate.

Inside was quiet and cold. Stone floors, heavy rugs, and glass cabinets filled with oddities: pressed flowers, bone tools, a fist-sized fossilized snail. They waited in a sitting room that smelled faintly of parchment and lemon polish.

Eventually, a side door opened, and in walked Lord Tovin Brenrick.

Middle-aged, tidy, with ink-stained fingers and a bookish air, he moved with the confidence of someone who studied more than he spoke. Cass and Finn instantly liked the man. He gave off a feeling as someone who was only interested in learning and not in politics or fighting. He gave them a polite smile and introduced himself before asking to see the coin. After glancing at it, he placed it beneath a lens.

"Remarkable," he murmured. "This might predate the Split."

He flipped it once, then looked up. "Where did you find this?"

"We're travelers," Finn said carefully. "Found a few near an old watchpost."

"I feel like I owe you an apology. When I first saw you and heard what you were bringing me, well, I didn't believe it. But now I see that I was a fool."

Tovin studied their faces for a beat too long, then nodded. "How many do you have?"

"How much are they worth?" Cass countered.

"I'll give you fifty silver for each."

Cass said, "Then we have five."

Tovin didn't blink. "Deal." He gestured to his butler, who left and soon returned with a leather pouch and placed it on the desk.

"That's 250 silver," Tovin said. " For five coins. Fair?"

Cass hesitated. "What's the exchange here?"

"In Greyfen? Ten silver to one gold. Twelve copper to a silver. But your coins, these are rare. Worth more to a collector."

Cass nodded. "It's fair." And handed him another four gold coins, and took the pouch that held the solver in exchange.

Before they turned to leave, Tovin asked, "Where are you staying?"

"We haven't found a place yet," Cass said.

"I own a rental house, two blocks east. Quiet. Two silver a week, if you're interested."

The two exchanged a glance, then nodded. "We're interested."

They handed him two silver coins from their new pouch, and he shook their hands.

"My man will take you there. If you find more coins, bring them to me. I'll pay more than anyone else in the city."

Cass tucked the pouch away, and with a final nod, they followed the butler out.

Behind them, Lord Tovin Brenrick was already placing the coins in a velvet-lined drawer.

The guest house sat on a few quiet streets beyond the bustle of Greyfen's markets, tucked behind a wrought iron gate and high stone walls wrapped in ivy. As Finn and Cass stepped through the gate, the sounds of the city dulled to a distant murmur, replaced by the gentle trickle of a fountain at the center of a small inner courtyard. The two-story house was built from pale stone, with thick wooden beams and arched doors worn smooth by time. Sunlight filtered through the leaves overhead, painting shifting shadows across the cobbled ground.

Inside, the house was cool and quiet. A wide sitting room greeted them with deep rugs, a hearth, and a low table set with a clay pitcher and two cups. A wooden staircase curved upward to the second floor, where two bedrooms sat across from one another. Each room had its own shuttered window overlooking the courtyard, and, to both teens' surprise, a private washroom tucked behind a heavy door in the corner.

Cass stepped into the room on the right, dropped her pack, and pushed open the washroom door.

Then she froze.

A deep metal bathtub sat inside, built directly into a stone platform. Above it, a copper pipe curled down from the ceiling and fed into a brass faucet.

She reached out, turned the handle, and a moment later, warm water began to flow. Her mouth fell open in disbelief.

"There's... hot water," she whispered.

Cass erupted into the room. "It has a tub! With hot water!"

Finn blinked. "I think mine-"

Before he could finish, Cass marched over, grabbed his shoulders, spun him around, and shoved him gently but firmly away from her door.

"Don't bother me for the next few hours." She said.

Then she slammed the door, and Finn heard the unmistakable sound of her squealing in excitement.

He laughed to himself and stepped back into his room. Sure enough, his own washroom held a similar setup. A black tank on the roof, the butler had told them, absorbed sunlight during the day, warming the water for evening baths.

Finn turned the faucet and leaned on the doorframe, gazing at the hot water now filling his tub.

It had been days since he'd felt safe. Weeks since he'd felt clean.

And now, for a little while at least, they had both.

Finn leaned back in the tub with a long exhale, letting the hot water seep into his aching shoulders. It stung at first; his skin wasn't used to heat like this, but once the shock wore off, it felt like his entire body started to uncoil. The water quickly became dirty, swirling with ash and grime.

He watched the water darken, turning a murky gray. With a grimace, he pulled the stopper and drained it, watching days of dirt spiral down. Then he filled it again, scrubbing his arms, his neck, his feet, his face and hair, letting the warmth melt away layers of exhaustion he hadn't even known he was carrying.

And still, the water turned cloudy.

So, he drained it a second time.

By the time he filled the tub for the third round, the water stayed clear. So he filled it just enough to lie in for a few minutes longer, then he turned the running water off.

The bathroom was softly lit by two oil lamps mounted on either side of a small mirror above a ceramic basin. The flickering light made the whole space glow amber, shadows dancing along the white walls. It smelled faintly of the herb-scented soap left out on a wooden tray. He didn't know which herb; the only one he was familiar with was mint, because his aunt used to boil it to help her breathe, but this didn't smell like that. Finn reached for the soap again and lathered his hands, watching suds slip between his fingers and trail down his arms.

When he finally stood, drying himself with a rough towel, he caught sight of his reflection in the mirror, slightly warped, its tin backing old and imperfect, but still enough to study himself.

He leaned in.

His face looked thinner. Sharper. Not sickly anymore... older somehow. His cheeks had hollowed a little, and his jaw had definition now. The soft, boyish roundness he remembered from Darrowmere was gone.

He tilted his head, studying the rest.

His ribs no longer stuck out. His arms, while still lean, had shape to them now, cords of muscle just beneath the skin, maybe even a thin layer of fat, earned through long hikes, cold nights, and tight fights. Even his legs, once spindly and clumsy, looked solid now. He ran a hand across his chest and stomach, surprised at how strong he had become.

He thought of the last time he'd seen himself clearly, reflected in that pool in the Painted Peaks. Back then, he still looked like the kid who had stumbled out of Darrowmere, hungry and unsure.

Not anymore.

He'd walked through a storm of ash, fought a scale-cat twice his size, and held his own against a Twisted Shadow. He'd awakened something ancient. Whatever else happened... he wasn't weak.

He turned sideways, flexing just a little, half smiling to himself.

"I'd like to see that drunk try and kick me now," he muttered.

Back in Darrowmere, he'd been the kind of boy people ignored, or worse. The kind of kid someone might shove into a gutter just to feel big. But not anymore. Even without his unbreakable skin, he was someone who could fight back.

He pulled on his shirt from the new set of clothes they'd received at the mausoleum. The fabric was still a little stiff with newness, but it fit well enough. He cinched the belt around his waist and clipped his scabbard into place, letting his hand rest on the hilt of the short sword.

Small or not, he was starting to feel capable and maybe even a little dangerous.

And as he stepped out of the washroom into the quiet of his room, he smiled to himself.

Finn sat in the front room of the guest house, perched on the edge of a cushioned bench beneath a tall, arched window. The fading light of day spilled in through the ivy-covered lattice, casting soft golden stripes across the tiled floor. A gentle breeze drifted through the open courtyard, rustling the leaves, and the trickling sound of the fountain echoed softly through the quiet.

He sat still, clean for the first time in what felt like weeks, his skin still warm from the bath. The new clothes fit better now that he'd moved around in them. The sword at his hip felt heavier than it had back in the mausoleum, but also more real. It wasn't for show. It was his.

He leaned back and let his head rest against the wall, just breathing.

For once, he didn't smell like smoke or sweat or damp forest. And his muscles, usually tight and sore, had relaxed into a kind of quiet readiness. His mind, though, drifted half thinking of what might come next, half watching the shifting light as the sun lowered.

He didn't hear her footsteps until she was already in the doorway.

When he looked up, he froze.

Cass stood there, still towel drying her long hair, which was brushed and neatly braided over one shoulder. Her skin was fresh and flushed from the bath, and for the first time since he'd met her, she wasn't hidden behind layers of travel dirt or tension. She looked... beautiful.

It wasn't just that she was clean; it was the way she moved. The way her shoulders weren't hunched, how her face wasn't braced for the next fight. Her eyes were brighter, her mouth not guarded or tight but curved with the beginnings of a real smile.

"Ready?" she asked, casually adjusting the dagger at her belt.

Finn blinked, stood a little too quickly, and tried to play it off by brushing imaginary dust from his sleeve. "Yeah. Let's go."

She gave him a look, like she'd caught the awkwardness but didn't call it out.

They stepped out into the evening together.

The air was cooler now, touched with woodsmoke and the scent of fresh bread. Greyfen had changed with the light, less crowded than it had been earlier, but still alive. Lanterns flickered to life along the walkways, casting long pools of warm orange light over the cobbled streets. The laughter of children echoed from an alleyway, and the low murmur of late-day merchants packing up their goods drifted between the rows of stalls.

Finn kept a hand resting lightly near his sword hilt, not because he expected trouble, but because it felt right. Cass walked just ahead, her braid swinging slightly with each step, the silver hilt of her dagger catching the lanternlight now and again.

They didn't speak much at first. Just walked.

He wasn't sure how to describe the feeling exactly. It wasn't new, not entirely. But something had shifted.

They'd been through a lot together already. Faced things people twice their age hadn't. But here and now, walking through a city with full bellies and clean clothes and no one chasing them, he realized he was seeing her in a different way.

And he didn't hate it.

"Let's find something easy," she said, finally breaking the quiet.

"Bread. Dried fruit. Maybe a few travel meals."

Finn nodded. "And something sweet if they have it."

Cass glanced back at him, grinning. "After those meat pies earlier? You're getting spoiled."

He shrugged. "I regret nothing."

And with that, they disappeared into the streets of Greyfen again, two quiet figures, half lost in the lanternlight, walking side by side.

CHAPTER 17

Harlen

It had been a week since the awakening. Nearly that long since the ash, the canyon, and the old man's voice in the mausoleum. And though the world hadn't slowed, something inside Finn had. In that time, Finn and Cass hadn't had one issue. But the weight of it all was still there, still Greyfen, with its noise and color and food and music, dulled the edge.

They'd been in the city for a few days now, long enough to know their way around the central market and to understand that wandering without blending in was a good way to get noticed. That morning, they'd gone shopping for a second set of clothes, nothing expensive, just what a local teen might wear. Finn had purchased a dark cotton shirt and a short hemmed jacket. Cass had chosen a forest green wrap and light trousers stitched with reinforced knees.

"Better?" Finn asked as they left the shop.

"Less 'wandering and starving child,' more 'regular teenager,'"

Cass said with a smirk. "Yeah."

The streets were alive, as always, smells of roasting meat, spiced teas, and damp stone mingled in the air. They were headed toward a baker's stall when the shouting started.

A cluster of voices rose near the east quarter, sharp and panicked. People ran, others pointed, and smoke began to rise, curling black over the rooftops.

They followed the sound.

A house had caught fire, one of the narrow homes with timber siding and a cloth canopy, half melted now by flame. The upper window belched smoke. A few neighbors were frantically tossing water from buckets, others pulling children back.

Then he appeared.

A man, maybe in his sixties, strode through the crowd not in uniform, not wearing Mage robes or sigils. He wore workman's clothes and a satchel slung across his chest. But everyone parted for him. They knew him.

He raised both hands as he approached the fire, and the water from a nearby barrel jerked upward, caught in an invisible grip. It swirled in the air, no chanting, no massive arm movements, just raw precision. Finn and Cass froze.

The water slammed into the window, and the fire hissed in protest. Another surge followed, then another, until smoke replaced flame. The crowd clapped and sighed with relief.

The man lowered his arms, said a few kind words to the frightened homeowner, tousled the hair of a young boy nearby, and then turned and walked off, calm as you like, toward a corner tavern.

Cass watched, jaw tight.

Finn could hardly speak. "That was-"

"I've seen magic before," Cass said quietly. "But only from my parents in private. I've never seen someone use magic so openly before."

He looked toward the tavern door where the man had disappeared.

"Think we can talk to him?" Finn asked.

Cass glanced at him. "We can try."

When they entered, the tavern had the smell of stewed onions, damp wood, and the faintest trace of smoke from the fireplace. He and Cass stepped inside, keeping close together as they scanned the crowd.

There, toward the back, seated at a small table with a half-eaten plate and a cup of something steaming, sat the man who had doused the flames with a sweep of his arm and a rush of water that seemed to rise from nowhere.

"That's him," Finn murmured.

Cass nodded.

They approached slowly. Cass cleared her throat as they reached his table. "Excuse me," she said, careful to keep her voice friendly but neutral.

The man looked up, blinking once before his eyes sharpened on them. He had a weathered face that came from too much time outdoors and too many years solving problems with more grit than rest.

"You need something?" he asked.

"We saw what you did," Finn said. "With the fire."

The man didn't smile, but his face softened. "Ah. That. Nobody hurt, thankfully."

Cass tilted her head. "You... used water magic?"

He studied them for a beat, then nodded. "Yeah. Been practicing long enough."

Finn shifted slightly. "So it's true then? That magic is just... used? Out in the open?"

The man raised a brow. "Depends on the city. But here? Greyfen's got room for magic. Most folks don't mind as long as you're not lighting things on fire or price gouging them for service."

Cass gave a small laugh. "And you're not in the army or anything?"

"I'm not," the man said, sipping from his mug. "Worked on fishing boats most of my life. Learned magic to keep the boats balanced and the nets untangled. Just happened to get good at controlling water along the way."

They both fell quiet, absorbing that.

He set his mug down and gave them a more thoughtful look. "You two from around here?"

"No," Cass said carefully. "Just passing through."

"First time seeing magic up close?"

Finn nodded. "Yeah."

The man nodded like he understood. "Greyfen's different. You'll see."

There was a beat of silence as they stood there, and then he said, "Why are you really asking questions about magic?"

Cass smiled faintly. "We're curious."

He let out a soft chuckle. "That's not a bad thing."

Then he reached into a small leather satchel beside him and pulled out a small slip of parchment, setting it gently on the table. "If you're curious," he said, his voice low but kind, "there's a meeting. Happens right here, same place, once a week."

Cass leaned in slightly. "What kind of meeting?"

He replied. "A couple of Mages show up, sometimes more. Folks who've awakened, folks who haven't but are thinking about it. No pressure. Just questions, stories, real answers."

Finn glanced at Cass, then back at the parchment. "Can anyone come?"

"Anyone," Harlen said with a shrug. "It's not official, not run by the Kingdom or anything like that. Just people trying to make sense of what magic really is before they jump into it." He stood, finishing the last of his drink. "You two strike me as the thoughtful type. That's rare. The next one is tomorrow night. The two of you should come."

Cass tilted her head. "What should we call you?"

"Harlen," he said, standing to leave. "And don't worry, I don't ask too many questions back, awakening is too difficult a decision to make to worry about what questions are safe or not."

Then he nodded once and stepped away, leaving them with the invitation.

The next night, just as dusk began to settle over Greyfen, Finn and Cass returned to the tavern.

The warm hum of voices and clinking mugs filled the space again, but the tone was different, quieter, more focused. A back room had been opened, and a sign written in tidy ink hung beside the archway: "Awakening – All Questions Welcome."

Cass led the way inside. A dozen people were already there, some seated on benches, others leaning against the walls. Most looked ordinary. A pair of older men whispered in the corner. A younger woman sat near the front, clutching a satchel as if it held her whole future. Finn noticed the Water Mage, Harlen, sitting casually near the center, a mug in hand and no sign of arrogance on his face.

Cass and Finn found seats near the back.

Harlen stood and greeted everyone with a wave. "Alright. Some of you've been here before. Some of you haven't. Doesn't matter."

He introduced a few of the others, two more Mages, one who was an Earth Mage and the other was a Fire Mage. There was also a man who hadn't awakened but had been studying the theory for years, and was introduced as a pseudo-expert on local awakenings.

Then came questions.

"Does it hurt?"

"Can anyone do it?"

"Do you have to serve the Kingdom?"

"No," Harlen said plainly. "The Unbound Kingdom doesn't force anyone. If you awaken, your power is your own. There are rules, sure, don't destroy anything you can't fix, don't harm people without cause, but no one will draft you."

The stoneworker nodded. "I used to be a mason. Now I use my gifts to build homes by myself. Pay's better, too."

"And I teach glass making," the Fire Mage added. "Kids mostly. Some older folk. You'd be surprised how many people wait until they're nearly forty to try."

A woman raised her hand from the side. "But how do you know if you're ready?"

Harlen smiled. "You don't. Not really. That's why groups like this help. You ask, you learn, you watch. And then, maybe, one day, you just know."

Cass leaned toward Finn and whispered, "This is nothing like Darrowmere."

Finn nodded. "Not even close."

They didn't speak up much that night, just listened, taking in every word, every warning, every laugh that echoed around the small room.

When the meeting ended, Harlen passed out a few more slips of parchment, reading suggestions, contacts, directions to libraries, and Mages who offered guidance. He didn't sell anything. Didn't even ask names.

Cass and Finn slipped out quietly, thoughts buzzing.

For the first time since their awakening, it felt like the world might actually have a place for people like them.

The streets of Greyfen were quieter now, lit by the steady glow of lanterns that lined the plaza. Cass and Finn walked side by side, the meeting still fresh in their minds. Behind them, the tavern buzzed with muffled conversation and laughter, but out here, the city breathed slower, softer.

Cass stopped at the edge of a narrow bridge that crossed one of the city's smaller canals. She looked down into the black water, brow furrowed.

"We can't wait much longer," she said. "We have to start training."

Finn leaned against the railing, arms crossed. "I know."

"It's been a week since the Awakening," she went on, her voice low. "We still don't know how to use what we've been given. That can't go on."

They stood in silence for a beat, the wind tugging at their sleeves.

"I don't want to wait until something forces us to learn," Cass said finally. "We need to choose it. Control it. Before someone else tries to do it for us."

Finn didn't answer right away. His mind kept going back to Harlen, they'd seen putting out the fire. The way he'd been calm, practiced. The way everyone had trusted him, not because he was powerful, but because he'd mastered it.

And now, after what they'd learned at the meeting, everything felt different.

"They train here," Finn said, half to himself. "In the open. They study together. They're not afraid of being found out or locked up."

Cass nodded. "But are we safe here?"

Finn met her eyes. "We've been here several days now. No one's followed us. No one's asked questions that we know about."

"No one's looking yet," she replied. "But they will."

"We still have time," Finn said. "But we can't waste it."

Cass turned to face him fully. "So do we stay? Train here? Find a teacher, maybe a group?"

He hesitated, then said, "If we leave, we're back in the wild. Alone. Chased. Trying to survive instead of learning."

She didn't like it, but she didn't argue.

"I think we stay," he said. "At least for now. If it turns bad, we move."

Cass nodded once, then looked back toward the lamplit streets. "Think we can ask Harlen's help to train us?"

Finn nodded, "I think I trust him enough. Let's go back and ask him."

Together they walked back to the tavern and waited across the narrow street, leaning against a low wall. The night was quiet but not silent; muffled laughter spilled from the bar, boots scuffed on stone, and the occasional cart creaked by in the distance.

Finn shifted his weight, anxious. "You think he'll come out alone?"

Cass nodded. "I don't think he came with anyone. Just wait."

A few minutes later, the door creaked open and Harlen stepped out, adjusting the collar of his coat. He walked a few steps before spotting them. A broad smile spread across his face.

"Well now," he said, hands on his hips. "Didn't expect to see you two again tonight. What'd you think of the meeting?"

Cass and Finn exchanged a glance, then stepped forward.

"We're not from around here," Cass began carefully. "And we weren't sure how things work with Mages in the Unbound Kingdom. We've been… cautious."

Harlen tilted his head, his smile softening.

Finn lowered his voice. "We're both awakened."

Harlen blinked, then let out a short laugh. "Well, why didn't you just say so?"

Cass gave him a wary look. "It's not something we've said out loud before."

"Fair enough," Harlen said. "So what is it you're hoping for from me, then?"

"We need to learn how to use our powers," Finn said plainly. "We don't really feel safe until we can."

Harlen nodded thoughtfully, rubbing his jaw. "I know a body Mage who trains the newly awakened. Works with folks who are still finding their feet. He's steady. Good at what he does."

Finn furrowed his brow slightly. "A... body Mage?"

Harlen caught the look, but didn't comment. "Name's Thomas. I'll tell him to meet you here, midday tomorrow. There is no guarantee that he'll show. He is his own man. But I'll give him your descriptions. If he is available and if you like him, you can talk more then."

"Thank you," Cass said, genuine relief in her voice.

Harlen smiled again. "Don't mention it. Everyone's got a first step. You've taken yours. Now take the next."

He gave them a friendly wave and strolled off into the dark.

Cass and Finn stood still for a moment after he'd gone. The street was quiet again.

Finn let out a breath. "That... went better than I expected."

Cass nodded. "We actually told someone."

"He didn't ask about the stones. Or what we can do. He just wanted to help."

Cass looked down the empty street. "He seems like a good guy."

They turned and started the walk home, the quiet stillness of the town wrapping around them like a blanket. After weeks of secrets and second-guessing, it felt strange, and good, to let a little truth into the open.

For the first time in days, they let themselves feel something like hope.

CHAPTER 18

Expedition

In the northeast, the Copper Kingdom was still reeling from the magical surge, now simply referred to as the Surge, even a full week after it shook the world. Though no physical damage had struck their cities, the event had brought their network to its knees. Entire communication webs collapsed. Long-range links sparked erratically. It had taken hours to restore basic lines, and days before the data streams stabilized again.

It was more than a disruption. It was a mystery.

Using triangulation from relay towers and energy monitors across their territories, the Copper Mages had narrowed down the origin point of the Surge. Somewhere near the Painted Peaks, in the Unbound Kingdom, or, in the worst-case scenario, within the wild and fractured borders of Elarith. The implications of either possibility were... concerning.

Officially, their leadership claimed the investigation was about national safety. About making sure such a phenomenon couldn't threaten their systems again. It was true that they feared what might happen if the Surge's source fell into the wrong hands.

But the real reason?

They didn't know what it was, and that fact alone drove them mad.

The Copper Kingdom was a nation built on knowledge and communication. Secrets were unnatural things in their culture. For something this powerful to remain unknown was unacceptable.

On the seventh day after the Surge, they launched their response: a full research expedition of over three hundred individuals, including elite Copper Mages, specialized researchers, military scouts, and support personnel. They began marching southwest, toward the suspected epicenter.

Simultaneously, their communications guild sent out a flurry of diplomatic messages to every friendly or neutral nation with which they had ties. The wording was precise and polished:

"We are initiating a peaceful exploration mission to investigate the source of the recent global magical anomaly. We invite collaboration from any nation willing to aid in identifying the cause and effects of the Surge. Infrastructure rewards and information sharing agreements will be available to meaningful contributors."

As expected, most responses were cautious. But two nations stood out.

The Ardent Crown replied swiftly, asking for updates in exchange for intelligence they had gathered, an offer that implied they knew more than they were saying.

Saphrelle, however, responded with urgency. Not only were they eager to contribute, but they revealed something no one else had admitted: during the Surge, every Mind Mage in their borders had heard the same thing, a deep, reverberating call, spoken in no known language, yet understood instinctively.

This corroborated what some Mind Mages within their own number had reported, although the Saphrellelian report was much more concise, as if their entire nation had come together to agree on what had happened.

This revelation sent shockwaves through Copper intelligence.

They'd assumed it was a magical overload. An energy discharge of some kind like an explosion. But a message? That changed everything.

The Unbound Kingdom, predictably, remained silent.

Or at least, they offered no formal response. One encoded message had made its way back through the northern relay: a simple confirmation of receipt. What that meant-whether they would help, hinder, or simply monitor, remained to be seen.

Elarith, as always, said nothing at all.

The Copper delegation pressed forward, minds buzzing with theories. Was this a natural event? A weapon?

They didn't know.

And that not knowing was intolerable.

Whatever had happened near the Painted Peaks, it had changed something. Something big. And the Copper Kingdom would spare no expense until they uncovered the truth.

With the new information from Saphrelle, the claim that their Mind Mages had heard something during the Surge, the Copper Network's Communication Division launched into a frenzy of analysis.

They ran every inscription method available. They compared the energy signatures of the Surge against decades of known magical events: elemental quakes, leyline fractures, even controlled detonations. They filtered the waveform data through frequency analyzers and copper-threaded drums.

But no voice. No message.

Whatever the Saphrellian Mind Mages had heard, the Copper Mages could not replicate. And that only deepened the mystery.

If the Surge was a message, why had it spoken to some but not others?

Who could hear it?

Or was the Copper Network simply deaf to that kind of magic?

They needed answers.

Negotiations with the Ardent Crown, already simmering, intensified. The Ardent Crown had not only confirmed they had been affected by the Surge but implied, carefully, that they held intelligence they were willing to trade. The Copper Kingdom, driven by urgency and curiosity, agreed to negotiations and recommended that they send a diplomatic delegation toward the Painted Peaks. Once their research team identifies a location, they would send it to them. The first item they used to negotiate with was the prophecy Saphrelle sent to them.

"Twin chosen foraged from fallen stone,

Will rise in ash what none have known.

They'll fracture fate where patterns bind,

And craft anew what ruin left behind.

From world to world their steps shall tread,

Through ancient lands and halls of dead.

Until the root of darkness dies,

In their wake, worlds shall rise."

Little did they know the war this message would ignite in the Ardent Crown.

Meanwhile, behind closed doors and sealed copper lines, the Copper Network initiated quiet negotiations with the Unbound Kingdom.

Relations between the two nations were... complicated.

The Unbound Kingdom, led by a decentralized council of representatives, was notoriously unpredictable, sometimes cooperative, sometimes isolationist, and often secretive. Sometimes, the Copper Network couldn't understand the Unbound Kingdom's choices and politics. The Copper Kingdom, by contrast, prized clarity and open knowledge. But they needed each other now.

Neither forgot the bloody fractures of history.

Long ago, their lands had all been one, ruled by the iron hand of the King of Elarith's great-great-grandfather, may his soul rot in whatever forgotten pit still bore his name. His cruelty had broken the land. The five great nations that now stood were born from his collapse. But many, many still refused to recognize any government at all.

Whole peoples still wandered the borderlands, loyal only to clan or creed. Dozens of fragmented cultures, speaking in old tongues, still claimed independence.

A few days after the Copper research delegation departed for the Painted Peaks, a private message arrived, encoded, unsigned, and routed through a dozen relays.

"Unusual structure found under the Red Mound in Painted Peaks. Possible connection to the Surge."

The message was brief but precise. The phrasing wasn't military, but it was careful, like someone trained in sensitive information handling. The implication was clear: someone had found something.

And they wanted the Copper Kingdom to know.

The analysts scrambled to verify the sender. No luck. But the energy signature of the encoded spell was Unbound in origin, layered with their standard magical weave, likely sent by someone embedded in their infrastructure.

It was the first real lead since the surge.

And somewhere in the heart of the Copper Kingdom, in

the dim control room beneath the northern relay tower, a young Mage sent two words to the Communications Network's ArchMage.

Site Confirmed.

The negotiations with the Unbound Kingdom had already been delicate, handled through formal channels by the Copper Network's Communication Guild with the utmost care. But after the anonymous lead identified the location of the unusual structure near the Painted Peaks, things started to get… strange.

The Guild sent an official message to the Unbound Kingdom's council. Polite. Direct.

"To the esteemed representatives of the Unbound Kingdom,

The Copper Network wishes to inform you that our research delegation will be traveling through your lands, en route to a region bordering the Painted Peaks. The area is known to be part of Wild Territory, unclaimed, unsettled. We respectfully request passage and guarantee non-aggression. Our purpose is solely research and investigation."

It was, by all accounts, a simple request.

The reply was not.

"The aforementioned territory," the response began, "has recently been brought under formal claim by the Unbound Kingdom. A forward installation is currently under construction to protect the region from wild beasts and possible aggression from neighboring territories."

It was worded with precision. Too much precision. The kind of language politicians used when they didn't want to say something out loud.

The Communication Guild's council gathered in their chamber and read the message multiple times. Finally, one brave soul sent a follow-up.

"Might we inquire as to the location of this newly claimed

forward installation?"

Silence.

For two days, not a single pulse of magic came back through the lines.

Then, finally, a terse message arrived.

"The fortification is located in the southwest region of our domain, at the site formerly known as the Red Mound."

For several seconds, no one spoke.

Then, in the Copper Network's central tower, someone exhaled sharply and muttered, "It's confirmed. We found it."

And then chaos.

Mages and couriers ran through the halls, copies of the message pulsing and fading just as quickly. The entire guild building erupted in celebration.

They had confirmation.

The Unbound Kingdom knew and had control of the site. At least it wasn't in the hands of Elarith. This minor relief changed everything, because, however difficult the Unbound Kingdom was for the Copper Network to understand, the Elarith King would have been even worse.

They were already there, on top of the most important magical mystery in a century. But now, at least, it was no longer just a mystery. It was a location.

The site of the Surge. The epicenter.

And it wasn't hearsay or rumor anymore. It was official.

By evening, a party had broken out in the Communications Guild headquarters. Wine and firefruit liquor flowed freely. Music echoed in the atriums. Someone summoned an illusionist to project miniature dancing lights across the walls of the archive dome. The party had no formal name, but everyone knew what they were celebrating.

The Unbound Kingdom had admitted, perhaps without meaning to, that something real had happened.

They even hinted that something happened to the Mound itself. "Formally named" means that something, presumably the surge, caused there to be a need to change the name.

And the Unbound Kingdom had built at least a fort to defend it, so that meant that it couldn't easily be moved.

Inside the Guild, among half-finished reports and toasts raised with stained-glass goblets, the conclusion was unanimous: They're hiding something. And we're going to find out what it is.

One Guild leader staggered up onto a table and declared loudly:

"Tomorrow, we negotiate our way in. Today, we drink to the biggest mystery since the Split!"

Laughter, cheers, more drinks.

Outside, across the sea of politics and borders, the Unbound Kingdom likely knew exactly what was happening inside the Copper Guild's towers.

Maybe they even smiled.

Let them have their celebration.

Tomorrow will come soon enough.

Unfortunately, the messages with the Ardent Crown took an unexpected and unwelcome turn.

At first, things progressed smoothly. The Crown confirmed that a diplomatic delegation would be dispatched toward the Painted Peaks. But the moment the prophecy was mentioned, the Crown's tone shifted. Their questions became sharper. Their phrasing was more pointed.

What had started as a collaboration quickly began to feel like an interrogation.

They demanded access to the origin of the prophecy.

They requested copies, no originals, of any ancient texts that validated the prophecy's existence.

They pushed for the precise location of the event.

And then came a question that caught everyone off guard:

"Are there any known persons of interest in relation to the surge event?"

It was not a question the Copper Network or even the Saphrelliens had considered seriously. Until now, the surge had been treated as a phenomenon, magical, environmental, perhaps ancient in nature. But the Ardent Crown's question implied something more.

Had this been caused? Were there individuals responsible? Or could it be possible that the Ardent Crown believes in this Prophecy?

Was the Unbound Kingdom harboring them?

The implications were impossible to ignore.

Within hours of the Ardent Crowns' message, the upper leadership of the Communication Guild, who were not drunk, and the Network's historical division called an emergency session. Messengers were dispatched. One of the senior scribes was overheard muttering, "If there's even a chance this prophecy is real, we need to know how far back it goes."

The next morning, just one day after the revelry of their hard-won breakthrough, the party lights had burned out, and the Copper Network turned sober.

A new team was formed.

Their task: scour the deep archives for anything-anything that might resemble a reference to a "twin awakening," of the Red Mound, or a surge of magical resonance. Half a dozen researchers were sent into sealed vaults under the central tower, digging through brittle scrolls, cracked stone tablets, and Mage logs from before the Split.

Meanwhile, the Communications Guild resumed their messaging with the Unbound Kingdom, but now with a strategic cadence.

Step one: Secure official permission for their delegation to enter Unbound territory and reach the Red Mound site.

Step two: Determine the status of the site. What was the site currently called if not the Red Mound?

Step three, and this one was sent carefully: "Are there any individuals presently under observation or in protective custody related to the event?"

They knew it was a long shot. But if the Ardent Crown was asking, it could be a possibility at least.

The response from the Unbound Kingdom came swiftly, and it was blunt enough to leave the Communications Guild in stunned silence.

Permission granted, on the condition that your delegation funds and constructs a transportation rail from Stonehollow to the site.

The location is now designated as the Red Canyon Outpost.

No persons of interest are currently tied to the event.

That was it.

To the trained diplomats and analysts of the Communications Guild, the implications were explosive.

The Unbound Kingdom, known for its secrecy and territorial control, had just rolled over for a rail. No extended negotiations. No security assurances. No territorial disclaimers. Just... permission.

It didn't add up, unless they were desperate.

Desperate for help. Desperate for answers. Desperate to turn this anomaly into something they could control.

The demand for a rail made that desperation even more obvious. A permanent line meant regular movement, supplies, personnel, and equipment. Not a survey site. A permanent outpost.

Something was happening at the Red Mound.

Or rather, what used to be the Red Mound. Now it is being referred to as a canyon. A structure-shattering, landscape-altering event had occurred, and they were fortifying around it. What could possibly remain in that canyon that required an outpost, a rail line, and so much secrecy?

The mystery deepened.

The Copper Network didn't hesitate. They agreed to the terms and relayed updated orders to the research delegation: continue toward the site immediately. Upon reaching Stonehollow, a team would split off to begin rail construction, with Mages, engineers, and enough coin to keep workers moving day and night.

As for the third line of the Unbound message, "No persons of interest are currently tied to the event," no one took it at face value. The word currently hangs in the air like a storm waiting to break.

They would be watching. They would be searching.

And so would the Copper Network.

In two to three weeks, the research delegation would reach the edge of the Painted Peaks. But those weeks would be anything but quiet. The world was shifting beneath their feet, and when they finally arrived at the Red Canyon Outpost… everything would be different.

CHAPTER 19

Thomas

The tavern was quieter at midday, sunlight slanting through the high windows and painting long streaks across the scuffed wooden floors. Finn and Cass sat in the corner near the hearth, their packs tucked close, untouched mugs of water in front of them. The scent of baked grain and spiced meat drifted from the kitchens, but neither had an appetite.

"He's not coming," Finn muttered, eyes scanning the door for the hundredth time.

Cass didn't answer right away. She was watching the street through the window, lips pressed tight. Then she sighed. "Give it a little longer."

An hour passed. Then another. The tavern grew busier, with merchants, apprentices, and two guards off duty, but no one approached them. Finn drummed his fingers on the table. He was just about to suggest they leave when the door creaked open again.

The man who entered didn't seem to belong. He was lean, but not weak; his posture was perfect, shoulders relaxed but alert, the kind of calm that came from years of knowing exactly what you were capable of. His coat was simple but well-made, fastened tight at the waist, but he held no weapons Finn could see. His eyes, though sharp and unreadable, moved across the room once, then locked on them.

He approached with smooth, confident strides and stopped at their table.

"Cass and Finn?" he asked. His voice was low, clear, and dry as sun-baked stone.

Cass stood and nodded. Finn followed suit.

The man extended a hand. "I'm Thomas."

Finn reached for it and felt the strength in the grip, firm but not crushing. It wasn't the handshake of a merchant or a guard. It was the handshake of someone who had trained his whole life. Still, something about the moment made Finn feel like he wasn't a kid anymore. He met the man's gaze and didn't look away.

Cass offered her hand, too. "Thank you for meeting us."

Thomas nodded. "Harlen said you're looking for a trainer."

"We are," Cass said.

Thomas raised an eyebrow. "What stones did you bond with?"

The question hung in the air longer than it should have.

Finn opened his mouth, then closed it. Cass glanced at him, then answered with a shrug. "We're not exactly sure. We… found them. Used them."

Thomas studied them for a moment. "Found them, huh?" His tone was neutral, but something flickered in his eyes, understanding, maybe. "So you survived an uncontrolled Awakening. That's rare. Impressive, even."

"We were lucky," Finn said quickly.

Thomas didn't argue. He leaned a little closer, lowering his voice. "What have you figured out so far? Any powers showing up?"

Cass shook her head. "We'd rather not say. Not yet."

A small smile tugged at the corner of Thomas's mouth. "Careful. That's smart. Alright then, how about you show me instead?"

He stepped back, hands sliding behind his back. "I have a training ground not far from here. Quiet. Private. You want lessons, it's two silver coins a week. I'll train you. But I expect effort, and I don't do this for free."

Both hesitated, but eventually they agreed. They knew they needed to grow stronger and that they needed help to do so.

Cass nodded. "Deal."

Finn echoed, "Deal."

Thomas gave a short nod. "Then follow me."

He turned and walked toward the door without another word. Cass and Finn grabbed their things and followed, the din of the tavern fading behind them as they stepped back into the light.

This was it. No more wondering, no more guessing. They were about to show someone what they could do, and more importantly, learn how to do it better.

The walk from the tavern to the gym was short but winding, threading through narrow alleys and past quiet courtyards draped in ivy. Cass and Finn followed Thomas in silence, the sounds of the city slowly giving way to stillness. After several turns, he stopped before an unmarked wooden gate set into a tall stone wall.

He pushed it open without a word.

Inside was something neither teen expected.

A wide, open-air courtyard stretched before them, surrounded on all four sides by pillars, some cracked, others leaning slightly. Moss clung to the stone bases, and pale sunlight filtered through narrow gaps in the high walls. The ground was smooth, packed dirt, firm beneath their boots, with a faint grid pattern worn into it from years of footwork and repetition.

Weapons lined the interior walls: wooden swords of varying lengths, padded staffs, shields with cracked leather faces. Scuffed training dummies stood like patient sentinels along the edges. Nearby, racks of gear stood organized with quiet precision, coiled ropes, sandbags, lengths of cloth, and armor padding, all kept in perfect order.

It felt… surreal to the teenagers.

Not in a holy way, but in the way of places where things matter, where people come to struggle and to sweat.

Finn stepped forward slowly, his boot crunching softly on the grit. The air smelled of dust, sweat, and oiled leather. He glanced at Cass, who was scanning everything with quiet interest. This wasn't just a gym; it was a place where people came to become something more.

Thomas crossed the space ahead of them, his movements fluid and precise. He didn't strut, didn't perform, but every step, every turn of his heel, spoke of control. He bent slightly and retrieved a padded staff from one of the racks, spinning it lazily once in his hand.

"You two," he said, voice calm, "take something light."

Finn found a wooden short sword, smooth and solid, worn down at the hilt from years of use. It felt a little too real in his hand. Cass picked out a bow and a quiver of blunted arrows, testing the draw with a thoughtful frown.

Thomas pointed to the center of the ring. "Out here."

They moved into position, heartbeats ticking faster. The sunlight was soft and gold now, slanting low into the ring, making the dust sparkle.

Finn swallowed hard.

Cass flexed her fingers.

The courtyard was quiet, the kind of quiet that came right before everything changed.

Thomas walked to the far end and stopped, spinning the staff once, then planting it lightly in the dirt.

"Alright," he said. "Let's see what you've got."

The courtyard felt larger once they were in motion.

Finn and Cass circled Thomas warily, exchanging quick glances, unsure how seriously to take the fight. Thomas didn't posture. He didn't even raise his staff. He just waited, relaxed, like a man watching two puppies figuring out how to walk.

Finn lunged first, an awkward swing aimed wide to test distance. Thomas sidestepped without effort. Cass loosed an arrow a heartbeat later; Thomas turned and let it pass by his shoulder like he had planned it.

"Again," he said simply.

They pressed in, faster this time. Finn ducked low, swinging upward with the wooden sword while Cass moved along the edge, keeping her shots spaced and sharp. Thomas weaved between the two of them, fluid, almost lazy in his precision.

As the pace quickened, Finn started to sweat, not from exertion, but from the strange thrill of trying to hit someone who made it look so easy. Cass loosed another shot, and Thomas ducked it while blocking Finn's strike with the staff, effortlessly.

Then Thomas began closing in on Cass.

He didn't ignore Finn, just managed him, slipping past his attacks like water. His attention shifted more and more to Cass, drawing her fire, stepping in closer and closer. Finn tried to flank, but Thomas never let himself be fully exposed. Every move flowed into the next, evasive, calculating, almost playful.

And then, without warning, Thomas flipped backward off one foot. His body turned in midair, staff spinning behind him, and his free hand snapped forward in a sudden strike, his fist racing straight for Cass's face.

A shimmer of light flared to life.

A crystal clear barrier burst into existence between them, humming softly.

Thomas's fist stopped just short of impact, so close a breeze stirred Cass's hair.

He froze.

His eyes widened, not in fear, but in surprise. His own reflection lightly flickered in the shield, fragile, shining, but gone an instant later.

Cass blinked, but Finn moved.

Finn took the hesitation as an opening and charged. His sword came down in a solid arc, but Thomas turned with it, sweeping his staff in a tight spin. The wooden blade was knocked clean from Finn's hand, clattering to the floor. In the same motion, Thomas stepped forward, and the staff aimed for Finn's temple.

As the staff came down, Finn's skin instinctively hardened, and Thomas's staff cracked in two.

Thoma's mouth twitched with something like amusement.

He stepped back slowly, lowering his half of the staff.

"You're both a little strange," he said, voice calm but tinged with genuine curiosity. "Let me guess, Light and Iron?"

Cass and Finn exchanged a look. Neither spoke.

Thomas studied them both, then shrugged. "Alright. No need to say more."

He smiled and picked out another staff.

And then, without warning, moved.

He twisted on one heel, launching into a spinning kick, both legs flying out, one aimed at each of their heads. Finn ducked with a startled curse, and Cass rolled sideways, hair whipping behind her.

Thomas landed in a low stance, staff out, eyes gleaming.

"Now," he said, grin widening, "let's see what you're really made of."

The tempo of the fight had shifted. Fast.

Finn's wooden sword moved in broad arcs, deflected again and again by Thomas's spinning staff. Cass's blunted arrows flew in tight rhythm, forcing Thomas to shift his footing constantly, but not one of them hit. He weaved between their attacks like fog through the woods.

They pushed harder, finding rhythm in their clumsy coordination. Cass moved wide while Finn closed in. Still, every blow missed. Every arrow sliced the air. Every strike slipped past the mark.

And yet, every now and then, Thomas hesitated.

Just for a fraction of a second. A blink. A breath. His eyes would widen ever so slightly, like something had just surprised him… and then the next attack would come, and he'd snap back into motion.

Cass huffed in frustration, tossing aside her last arrow. She darted to the wall and yanked a wooden dagger from the weapons rack. "I'm done missing."

She leapt into the fray, slashing low and fast, joining Finn in close combat.

But Thomas moved like a ghost, impossibly fast, impossibly smooth. His body twisted in ways Finn couldn't understand, dodging sword, dagger, and fists with almost lazy grace. At times, he seemed to vanish entirely from the space he had just occupied.

Still, no hits landed. Not one.

Then, without warning, Thomas stepped back and raised his hand, signaling a pause.

Finn and Cass froze, panting hard, weapons lowered but still ready.

Thomas didn't look tired. Not even winded.

He stared at them with a strange intensity, brows furrowed.

"Which one of you is the Mind Mage?" he asked.

Finn blinked, still catching his breath. "What?"

"I slipped," Thomas said flatly, pointing at the ground with the end of his staff. "Right there. I never slip. Not since I awakened. My balance is perfect. And if I think I slipped, but I didn't… that means someone is making me believe I slipped."

Cass straightened, hands on her knees, sweat dripping from her jaw. "We haven't noticed any powers like that."

Thomas tilted his head slightly. He studied them both for a moment longer, expression unreadable. Then he gave a one-shouldered shrug and twirled the staff once before stepping back into position.

"Huh," he thought. "Maybe this will be more fun than I thought."

He grinned.

And the fight resumed.

For two weeks straight, Finn and Cass met Thomas in the stone courtyard, sparring under the open sky for three hours each day. What had begun as awkward and uneven clashes had transformed into fast-paced, focused drills, each session more intense than the last.

Thomas hadn't expected much from them at first. Strange kids with half-hinted powers and no real training. But now… he wasn't so sure.

They were getting better. Fast.

And not just stronger or quicker. Smarter. More aware. More dangerous.

Thomas found himself working harder than he had in years,

dodging with sharper precision, countering with cleaner forms. He was still the better fighter, no doubt, but the margin was shrinking. And that wasn't the weird part.

The weird part was the other stuff.

More than once a day, in the middle of a spar, Thomas caught sight of something moving where it shouldn't. A stone sliding across the edge of the courtyard floor, quiet, deliberate, as if nudged by an invisible hand. At first, he thought it was fatigue playing tricks on him.

Then it happened again.

And again.

He even stopped a match once, strode over to one of the displaced stones, and crouched beside it, tracing the fresh gouge it had carved in the packed dirt, a handspan and a half long. He didn't say anything to the teens, but the way Finn avoided his eyes confirmed it.

That's him, Thomas thought. Every time I push him hard, something moves.

Then there was his iron skin.

It remained reflexive and did not shimmer silver when hit, Finn didn't summon it consciously, but it was coming quicker, sharper. Twice now, Thomas had cracked a training staff against him, and both times the wood had splintered. But what really puzzled him was that it didn't slow Finn down. Most Iron Mages moved like statues when armored compared to him. Finn retained his agility.

As for Cass... well, she wasn't a Light Mage. Not even close.

He'd learned that the hard way.

He'd gone in for a high strike during a drill, hoping to break through her rhythm, and slammed his fist into a crystalline barrier that hadn't existed a heartbeat earlier. It stopped him cold. Had he not been awakened, he would have dislocated his wrist.

But that wasn't all. Now, she could summon two shields at once, one to each side, without knowing the attack was coming. Pure instinct. Pure control. That level of precision usually took years of training for Light Mages. And it wasn't just her magic.

She fought with a kind of awareness Thomas usually only saw in fellow Body Mages, always in control of her space, always tracking her opponent even when surrounded. He'd tried to surprise her more than once, but she never seemed truly caught off guard.

They didn't talk much during those sessions. Just sweat, move, and learn.

And Thomas found himself... enjoying it.

He started thinking about bringing in others, specialists who could push the teens in ways he couldn't. Fire Mages. Mind Mages. Someone to test their limits.

Because if things kept up like this, these kids weren't just going to be good.

They were going to be something else entirely.

Not every day in Greyfen was spent sparring.

Though their mornings were still dedicated to training, blunt weapons clashing in the sunlit gym, Thomas shouting corrections, sweat dripping into the dust, afternoons and evenings belonged to something else. Something easier. Something normal.

They explored the city.

Taverns became familiar haunts. They tried every dish they could afford, roasted game soaked in buttered sage, crisped potato stacks with cheese and red salt, creamy fish stews that left them licking the bowls. They ordered seconds. Sometimes thirds. Cass once joked they were trying to eat their weight in gravy.

And the schedule suited them.

Train in the mornings, eat and rest in the afternoons, then walk the streets after sunset when the lanterns flickered to life. They began to recognize faces. Not just vendors and barkeeps, but people in the crowd, blacksmiths and bakers, mothers with loud children, old men with dice cups and strong opinions. A few even started greeting them by name.

Finn was startled the first time a stranger said, "Evenin', lad," and nodded at him like they were old neighbors. Cass just smiled and nodded back, like she'd been waiting for something like this her whole life.

They heard local gossip too, shouted across the square or whispered over a mug of cider.

"Did you hear Jarnie had her third? Another boy."

"Tomas caught his wife with that potter from the west quarter. Threw him in a trough."

It was strange and a little sweet. The kind of community neither of them had ever really belonged to. Especially not Cass.

Greyfen was becoming a kind of home.

Around their second week in town, word started spreading about something new, a rail.

According to a gossipy merchant near the grain stalls, a Copper Kingdom delegation had reached some sort of deal with the Unbound Kingdom, and in a few weeks, a transport rail would be built from Stonehollow, the capital, directly to Greyfen.

Cass's eyes widened when she heard it. "Stonehollow... we could visit the capital without hiking across half the kingdom."

They'd never seen a transport rail up close before. But Cass has heard about how they worked.

Copper Mages were the backbone, crafting the rails out

of metal, mostly copper, and green joints. Massive rails, suspended above the ground by sculpted copper spires, rose like spider legs out of the earth, latticed and arched, winding between mountains and valleys with impossible grace. They were said to shimmer in the sun like a net of frozen lightning.

But the real magic was in the movement.

At the front of the train, Water Mages stood on reinforced platforms, cooling the copper ahead to reduce friction. At the rear, fire Mages superheated the copper, generating the thermal push that propelled the train forward. It was a delicate dance of opposing forces, cold guiding, heat driving.

And it worked.

Sleek railcars glided a few heights above earth, faster than any horse could run, glowing red from the heat of the rail. They said you could cross half the kingdom in a day if the magic held steady.

Now Greyfen would be one of those stops.

A quiet little town with pies, gossip, and a hot bath for bruised travelers would soon become a gateway to something bigger. That was exciting. And also a little terrifying.

CHAPTER 20

Dark Orders

Deep beneath the city of Velmirath, the leaders of the Dark Circle gathered in their chamber of shadow. The circular room pulsed with an unnatural hum of Blood Magic.

Twelve cloaked figures stood around a hip-high blackened pillar, their faces masked and obscured by hoods of different hues: red for war, gray for death, white for manipulation, and black for leadership. Above the pillar, a candle chandelier cast flickering flames upward, shadows lurching across the cold walls like dancing spirits.

The council exuded confidence, the kind born of centuries of manipulation, assassination, and hidden warfare. But beneath the stillness, beneath the cool words and sharp eyes, something stirred.

Fear… hidden underneath bravado.

A cloaked woman in a white mask, her voice crisp, addressed the chamber. "Report."

A man stepped forward from the outer circle, dropping to one knee. He had no mask, but his voice carried weight. He was a High Collector, a spy whose webs stretched across continents.

"My lords and ladies, the world moves."

He unrolled a thin scroll and began to read, his voice flat but urgent.

"The Copper Kingdom has deployed what they call a research delegation, over three hundred strong. They march south under banners of peace. Whispers say they are heading to the Painted Peaks."

Murmurs circled the chamber.

"They've struck a deal with the Unbound Kingdom," the spy continued. "They're building a transport rail. Here. A copper spine running straight from Stonehollow to Greyfen. Which makes no sense unless Greyfen is just a stop on their way to the Painted Peaks."

"More than that," the spy said. "The Unbound Army has ceased its endless patrols against the Painted Peaks. The entire army has stopped their patrol as if they are waiting for something."

The room was silent.

"The Saphrellelians are deploying a diplomatic envoy to the Unbound Kingdom. Ostensibly to 'assist' in understanding the surge, but they've also sent over 100 Mind Mages."

He took another breath.

"The Ardent Crown has closed court. The monarch refuses audiences. He is in session daily with generals. With researchers. And with priests."

The council began to shift in place now, no longer statues.

"And perhaps most bizarre of all… the King of Elarith has requested that we tell him what to do."

That drew laughter, thin and bitter.

The spy nodded. "Yes. Even the puppet has stirred. He asked what course to take, what stance to hold. He wants advice on how to deal with the inquiries he has been getting."

"That means he's scared," someone muttered.

"That means," added the woman in gray, "that even he, in his fever dreams, sees the importance of what is happening."

Silence returned.

The silver masked figure at the head of the council leaned forward, voice a velvet whisper. "What of our agents near the Red Mound?"

They are still trying to get in.

"Send our best team," the silver mask said. "Just get us answers."

The woman in white asked softly, "Do we know what caused this surge the Copper Network and the Saphrellelians felt?"

The spy hesitated. Then said, "No. But we fear…"

His voice dropped.

"…we fear the Twin Stones have awakened."

A chill swept through the chamber.

One of the elders hissed. "That fool of a King let them be stolen over a decade ago and failed in finding them. Worthless is everything he does."

"And now," the spy continued, "there's proof of a powerful event tied to prophecy. A surge strong enough to reach every kingdom."

"Then we must forge a new Crucible soon," said the woman in the black mask, her voice low and sharp as a knife edge. "Or this world will shift out of our control."

She stood from her seat, the folds of her cloak dragging across the floor as she paced slowly around the circle. "Begin the foraging trips. Quietly. Secure six hundred newborns or pregnant women, four months pregnant or longer."

Several figures around the circle stirred in anticipation, already calculating routes, safehouses, and which agents were suited to the work.

She stopped pacing and looked at the man in gray. "We'll move on Caldreth's Grave in two months. That worm is still good for something, at least."

That brought a soft ripple of chuckles through the room, dry and joyless.

The woman in white leaned forward slightly, her voice cold with reverence. "It will be a great ceremony. One to be remembered for centuries."

All twelve cloaked leaders nodded, slow and solemn.

Their masks were expressionless, but the room brimmed with anticipation.

In the weeks that followed, shadows spread across the land like spilled ink.

Cities and towns dotting the hills around Velmirath, quiet, prosperous places that had lived untouched for generations, were struck in the dead of night.

No banners. No warnings.

The attackers moved with ruthless precision. Entire villages were wiped from the map in hours. Soldiers stationed nearby arrived too late to stop it. Too late to understand it.

In each case, the stories were the same: almost no survivors. Houses burned. Even animals are slaughtered. The dead were left where they fell.

Some villages vanished without a sound, only discovered when traders found the roads eerily quiet and smoke still curling from the ruins.

In towns where pregnant women lived or newborn cries were heard, they were taken while everyone else died.

Those who escaped, the old, the wounded, the lucky few, fled toward Velmirath, seeking shelter in the fortified city said to be the safest in the region. The city welcomed them. Its gates opened wide, guards ushering the broken refugees inside with practiced sympathy.

What the survivors didn't know, of course, was that Velmirath was the predator they were running from.

CHAPTER 21

Back at the Fort

The wind carried the dry scent of mortar and sunbaked stone as Captain Saren strode along the high wall walk, boots thudding on the newly laid planks. Below him, the Red Canyon yawned like an open wound in the earth, its sheer red walls as striking as ever, but now framed by towers, watch posts, and lines of Unbound banners flapping crisply in the wind. The wildness was still there, lingering in the air like an old scar, but it no longer held dominion over this place.

Not anymore.

What had once been an exposed ridge of ash and death was now a fortress.

Stone walls, twice the height of a man, ringed the canyon's rim, replacing the makeshift palisades and scattered tents from the early days. At each corner stood a newly built tower, fitted with copper-tipped lightning rods and shaded sight windows, both practical and ceremonial, broadcasting Unbound strength to anyone who might approach.

Barracks had doubled in size. Mess halls bustled at every hour. Even the pathways were laid with cobblestones to keep boots dry.

And at the heart of it all, like the center of a wheel, was the canyon itself. The white stone structure remained sealed as tightly as the day they'd found it. Despite the dozens of tests and attempts to pry its secrets loose, it remained stubbornly silent. But now, it was ringed with a full defensive garrison, three stone towers, and a copper-enforced network tuned to receive long-range messages hourly. If anything changed, they would know.

Saren paused near the north tower and looked out over the rim.

The land had quieted. Where once normal animals refused to linger, small herds had begun returning, careful, hesitant, but present. Birds nested in the crags again. Even the air felt lighter, less charged. Whatever magic had once roiled beneath the surface was still there, he knew, but buried, maybe sleeping.

A junior officer approached, saluting crisply. "Sir, the eastern wall reinforcement is complete. We've begun trenching for the new supply tunnel."

Saren nodded. "Good. No delays. The dignitaries will arrive soon, and I want this place looking like a jewel set in the hills. No excuses."

The officer hesitated, then added, "The men are calling it Redwatch now. They say it's got a better ring to it."

Saren let out a low breath, almost a laugh. "Redwatch, huh?" He glanced back toward the structure in the canyon. "Well… I like it."

He continued down the wall walk, passing laborers and Mages alike, each caught in the rhythm of something bigger than themselves. It wasn't just a mystery anymore. It was a stronghold. A statement.

The whole world was on its way to see it, and he was going to make his little fort into a show of power.

The scent of parchment and candle wax lingered heavily in the war room, a low stone chamber beneath the east tower where maps cluttered tables and sketches lined the walls. A brazier burned steadily in the center, its heat doing little to cut the chill that had settled over the Mages assembled there.

Copper Mage Rennik stood before the council table, his long coat smudged with ash and his eyes shadowed from sleepless nights. Behind him, a table full of diagrams and notes. Around the room, military commanders and Mages leaned in, their expressions a mixture of skepticism and unease.

He took a breath, then tapped the slate.

"Trial One. Light Mage Ethan attempted an illumination spell on the door's surface, no contact, just visual resonance." He paused. "He lost vision in both eyes for three hours. No lasting damage, but he said it was like staring into the sun through ice."

Someone at the table muttered a curse.

"Trial Two. Earth Mage Brella attempted a seismic echo read from a safe distance. No direct tampering. The ground beneath her feet opened in a perfect square and swallowed her to the chest. If she'd been any slower, she would've been crushed. The stone tried to reform around her."

General Tharn growled. "That's a kill trap. Old world magic."

Rennik nodded grimly and advanced the slate again.

"Trial Three…" He hesitated. "Carlie the Copper Mage, he tried a passive probe, just a filament of copper, thin as a hair, to test magical conductivity. He approached the threshold carefully, gently threading the wire through the narrowest crack in the frame."

Carlie is still recovering but should heal with only a ragged scar from his ankle to just below his hip.

The ground itself retaliated. A mirror of the wire, made of copper, shot up from beneath him and drove through his leg. It was like the building anticipated his intent.

Murmurs spread around the room. The flame in the brazier popped sharply.

"The structure seems to overreact. Any invasive effort is countered, not blocked, reflected. And it doesn't matter how subtle the spell is."

Light Mage Arlith leaned forward. "It's almost like it's a beast protecting a nest."

"No," Rennik said. "It has very complex responses. But there is no sign that it's alive."

There was silence for a long moment.

Then General Tharn exhaled, low and slow. "That thing is a fortress. And we don't even know what it's guarding."

Rennik set down the slate with a heavy hand.

"If you want my recommendation, stop testing it. Watch it. Guard it. But for all our sake, stop touching it."

Around the table, heads nodded slowly, some reluctant, others clearly relieved.

The midday sun hung low behind a curtain of cloud, casting the canyon floor in a pale, muffled light. A routine patrol wound along the eastern slope above the white-stone building, keeping their usual distance from the structure's silent, deadly defenses.

It was Private Kest who spotted the body.

"Sir," she called, halting her squad with a raised fist. "There is something poking out of the ground."

They moved in slowly, spears angled low, boots crunching softly over the ever-shifting layer of gravel. The figure lay twisted half into the slope, legs jutting out, the rest buried as if he'd fallen from the rim and been forgotten.

They uncovered the body in silence.

He wore an Unbound uniform, with the correct cut, boots, and even the field sash assigned to this unit. But his face was mangled beyond recognition. The lower jaw was gone entirely, and the skin above his right eye was split open down to the bone. Dried blood clung like rust to the edges of his collar.

Worse, his identity tags were missing. Torn from his neck.

Kest looked to her squad leader. "You recognize him?"

"No," the sergeant said grimly. "Not from my unit."

Back at the command room, the body was laid out on a canvas mat. Commander Arlen stood over it, grim-faced, as report after report from the quartermaster and record keepers came back with the same answer: No one was missing. All soldiers accounted for. No one is on leave. No extra assignments. No new transfers.

Arlen's hand clenched the edge of the field table.

"Damn it," he muttered. "You're telling me a dead man in our uniform shows up inside our perimeter, and we don't even know who he is?"

The quartermaster flinched. "Sir, we've double-checked rosters. If he was part of the garrison, he's not in the books."

Arlen stared down at the corpse, cold fury in his voice. "Then find out where the uniform came from. I want every armory inventory pulled. Every requisition form. If someone's forging Unbound insignias, I want to know how they got close enough to die on my doorstep."

Beneath a false floor in one of the supply sheds, a narrow tunnel lay dark and empty. At its end, a cramped room contained a bedroll, rations, and a tiny hand-sized crucible filled with blood, shattered beyond repair.

The hidden listening hole above it, once angled toward the command tower, had gone unused for days.

The Dark Circle had sent one of their own to infiltrate the outpost. He had orders to observe, report, and only if necessary, interfere.

But the infiltrator never sent his last message. The Dark Circle was waiting. And wondering what had become of their spy.

The wind howled low across the Red Canyon, whipping dust up in thin spirals along the rim of the fort. Commander Arlen stood atop the eastern tower, his arms folded, cloak flaring behind him as the Copper Mage delivered the morning's report.

"Three delegations confirmed," she said. Her voice was calm, but her eyes gleamed with tension. "The Copper Kingdom, Saphrelle, and the Ardent Crown. The first one will arrive within the week. The others soon after."

Harlen didn't respond at first. He simply stared down at the white building nestled in the canyon, its smooth, inscrutable walls unmarked by time or tool.

"That thing draws more power than a crown," he muttered. "And now the world wants a look."

He turned sharply and snapped orders before his boots hit the stairs.

"Double the expansion effort. I want new barracks along the northern wall. A stone receiving hall, polished floors, and banners raised. Have the Earth Mages reinforce the towers and carve formal symbols into the outer walls, Unbound crest, clean and unmistakable. This is our land. Let them see it in the stone."

His aides scattered.

Within hours, the ground thundered with activity. Earth Mages raised larger walls with graceful, sweeping gestures, coaxing stone and soil into precision-cut blocks. Laborers followed behind, setting beams, hanging canvas, and laying down patterned stone in the courtyards. What had once been a scrappy wild outpost was becoming something else entirely, fortress and embassy in one.

The noise of hammers echoed through the canyon. Even the sky seemed to hang lower under the weight of it all.

"This isn't about comfort," Harlen said to his second-in-command as they surveyed the work from a new balcony. "This is posture. They think they're coming to see a mystery."

He smirked.

"They're coming to see our mystery."

The Red Canyon Outpost no longer resembled the raw encampment it had once been. What began as tents and temporary walls had taken root, becoming something solid, deliberate, permanent.

Stone rose from soil in rhythmic pulses, whummm, crack, settle, as Earth Mages shaped the landscape like sculptors with calloused hands. Towers swelled upward from nothing, carved with crisp angles and window slits. Timber creaked under the weight of construction, hauled into place by soldiers and hired builders alike. The scent of fresh turned soil mixed with ash, iron, and sweat, hanging in the air like a promise.

The outpost expanded outward and down, a living structure growing with urgency. In the west quadrant, a new hexagonal war room was formed, featuring stone benches and a polished table carved with the map of the region. In the south wing, reinforced kitchens bustled with activity. Smoke chimneys vented upward into the sky, their curls visible even from the canyon floor.

Staging areas were added beyond the main walls, prepared for arriving delegations. Rows of cots lined narrow barracks beside clean latrines and armories. Even the courtyards were swept daily now, stone brushed free of dust, banners hung high, the Unbound crest etched deep above the gates.

Despite the site's dangers and the constant, silent pressure of the sealed white structure in the canyon, morale had changed.

At first, it was fear. Superstition.

Now it was pride.

"They say no one can even touch it," one guard remarked to another while sanding down the edge of a new stairway. "That no other nation has anything like it."

"I's ours," the other replied. "Let them come and look."

And come they would.

From atop the north wall, Captain Saren watched as Mages and masons worked side-by-side, transforming the wild edge of the Painted Peaks into a bastion of the Unbound Kingdom. Beneath his boots, the outpost thrummed, not just with power, but with purpose.

The air shimmered with heat as the Copper Mage approached the command tower, his robes stiff with road dust and sun, creased at the shoulders. Captain Saren met him at the outer balcony, where the wind carried the scent of dry stone and ash.

"The update?" Saren asked.

The Copper Mage nodded, unrolling a thin sheet of parchment. "The rail line from Stonehollow is progressing faster than projected. The first spires have reached as far as the Forest Cliffs."

He turned the sheet, revealing an etched diagram of the route.

"The Main Copper research delegation will be here soon, but 50 of their Mages split off in Stonehollow to build the rail. The support lattices are holding well," the Mage continued. "Each spire rises a few heights over the forest ground, anchored by stone and reinforced by copper veins woven through the bedrock. They say that from a distance, it's quite beautiful to look at."

"The Fire and Water Mage teams are training and should be ready," the Mage added. "Fire Mages heat the rear coils to create lift, while Water Mages cool the front to pull the vessel forward. It's a delicate balance, but the engineering team in Stonehollow says the ride will be smoother than horseback travel and far faster."

"Timeline?" Saren asked.

"Two more months," the Mage said. "Maybe less, if we avoid more flare-ups or Mage rotation delays. But it will reach us. And when it does, Red Canyon Outpost will be connected directly to the capital."

The commander crossed his arms, considering the implications. What began as a temporary military outpost was quickly becoming something more, something permanent.

"When the rail arrives," Saren said slowly, "we won't just be holding this site. We'll be the gatekeepers. In fact, I wouldn't be surprised if General Fash himself took this place over as his base of operations."

The Copper Mage nodded, already turning to send the next pulse message to Stonehollow. Soon, Mages, merchants, politicians, and spies alike would flood the canyon.

And they would all have to come through him.

CHAPTER 22

Training

The mornings had become a ritual.

No more sleepy, sluggish arrivals or hesitant greetings. Finn and Cass were always early now, and warmed up by the time Thomas stepped through the heavy iron gate of the courtyard gym. The once quiet training space was now a buzz with shields and movement, stone tiles bore new cracks, and the weapons rack had been rearranged half a dozen times to keep up with demand.

Thomas stood near one of the pillars, arms crossed, watching the two teens run through a short series of warmup drills. Cass launched her crystal shields in a slow orbit while Finn rotated through a series of short sword strikes that would've made any soldier proud.

They weren't acting like kids anymore. Not in the way they moved. Not in the way they looked at him.

What started as a favor had grown teeth. He wasn't just teaching them to spar-he was shaping something dangerous.

Something needed.

It was the end of their first month when he approached them, towel slung over his shoulder, sweat still clinging to his jawline.

"You two," he said, not unkindly, "are officially outpacing me."

Finn grinned, rubbing his arm. "That sounds like a compliment."

"It's not," Thomas said. "It's a warning. I can't train you alone anymore. You need more voices. More challenges. I know two Mages who might help, if you're willing."

Cass tilted her head. "Who?"

"Harlen."

Cass smiled before Thomas could even finish.

"And Sparky."

Finn blinked. "Sparky? That's a name?"

Thomas chuckled. "It's what everyone calls him. You'll understand when you meet him."

The next morning, both new Mages arrived at the gym with the same wary look Thomas had worn a month earlier, like they'd just signed up to babysit a pair of cubs.

Harlen, ever composed, brought a cloth-covered tray of warm cheese bread and fruit. Cass immediately claimed half of it, thanking him with an awkward grin that made her look younger than usual.

Sparky laughed when Finn asked him about his name.

"The dome I awakened in was struck by lightning during my awakening," he explained. "Name stuck. I liked it better than Darven."

Cass and Finn decided that if they were going to get new teachers, they wanted to make sure they didn't tell anyone about their abilities.

Cass took Harlen to the far side of the courtyard. "If you're going to teach us," she told them, "you can't talk about this to anyone."

Harlen raised an eyebrow.

"Not your friends. Not the government. No one."

He looked at her for a long moment, then nodded. "Understood. You have my word."

Finn's conversation with Sparky was a little different.

"I'm not good at lying," Finn said. "But we have secrets. Big ones. If you can't be trusted to keep them, then we'll find someone else."

Sparky gave a lopsided grin. "No worries, kid, trust me, you aren't that special."

"You're not saying anything reassuring," Finn muttered.

"I'm saying I'll keep your secrets," Sparky said. "Because I'm too curious not to see where this goes."

By the following week, the gym had become a true training ground! Cass began to control her shields while Finn began to manipulate everything around him. Cass was developing her aim while Finn worked on manipulating weight and direction with greater finesse.

Each Mage took turns pushing the teens, and more often than not, they left sore and satisfied. Sometimes Cass collapsed on the stone bench, crystal fragments clinking into the dirt and then disappearing. Sometimes Finn accidentally launched a loose staff onto a nearby building and had to sheepishly walk across rooftops to retrieve it.

But they laughed more. Ate more. And trusted more slowly.

Thomas watched them one evening, as the sun bled gold across the courtyard. Harlen passed Finn another slice of the sweetbread he always brought. Cass leaned back, breathing hard and hair a mess.

These kids are powerful, Thomas thought.

He hoped they would continue to grow at this rate. Because

they would truly be beasts if they did.

Sparky's boots slid across the worn tiles of the courtyard, kicking up dust. He grinned as Finn lunged again, no hesitation in the teen's movement, no fear of reprisal. Just clean, fast aggression.

Sparky spun his staff low, trying to sweep Finn's legs. The blow landed square against Finn's shin with a sharp crack, but the boy didn't even flinch. The sound echoed like steel on stone. Sparky stepped back, twirling the staff in his hands.

"You sure you're just thirteen?" he muttered.

Finn didn't answer. He was already charging again.

His skin looked normal, bare, even a bit sun-bronzed from the walks to market and the long sparring hours. But beneath the surface, Sparky knew, was something far tougher than any other Iron Mage he had ever met. He'd seen Finn take a strike from Thomas that should've shattered bone. And it didn't even leave a bruise.

More than that, he wasn't just defensive anymore. He was fast. Strong. Dangerous.

Sparky ducked under a punch and jabbed with the butt of his staff toward Finn's ribs. It bounced off with a thunk.

Finn's hand shot out, and Sparky's staff twitched. Not just from the grip. The air pulled at it.

"Focus!" Sparky shouted, stepping back again.

Finn gritted his teeth. Tiles around his feet were beginning to rise, slowly at first, like breath caught mid-inhale. Three of them hovered off the ground, trembling in the air. Sparky glanced at them warily.

"Easy, Finn!"

"I am trying!" Finn snapped.

One of the floating tiles jolted sideways and slammed into a training dummy, knocking it clean off its stand. The crash was loud, echoing through the courtyard.

Cass and Thomas, watching from the side, flinched but unsurprised.

Finn stood in the middle of the chaos, fists clenched, chest heaving. The tiles dropped around him, clattering like spilled dishes.

Sparky exhaled. "You can control that."

"Sometimes," Finn muttered, not meeting his eye.

Sparky walked over, grabbing a towel to wipe the sweat from his neck. He gave Finn a long look, not angry, not amused. Just… serious.

"You're stronger than any Iron Mage I've trained," he said. "And that includes the ones twice your age. I don't know what kind of bond you've got, but it's powerful."

Finn looked up, wary.

"But strength without control?" Sparky's voice lowered. "That's the beginning of a very sad story."

Finn opened his mouth to reply, but Sparky raised a hand.

"I'm not telling you to hold back. I'm telling you to hone. Every hit, every pull, every breath, you have to master it. There may be a time when you will need to let go and let your abilities guide you, but while you are learning the basics of how your abilities work, you need to control it."

Finn nodded slowly, still catching his breath.

From the sidelines, Cass gave him a thumbs-up. "You only launched one dummy today," she said. "That's progress."

He smiled, faintly.

Sparky clapped a hand on his shoulder, hard. "We'll get you there, kid. But don't think you're done learning just because I can't crack your skin."

Finn nodded again.

Inside, he still felt the humming pressure of a thousand tiny weights drifting through the air, like invisible pebbles waiting for his command. His own power was like a coiled spring. But now, for the first time, he felt the itch to master it.

Because just fighting ability wasn't enough anymore.

And he was done feeling afraid of whatever power he had.

The courtyard echoed with the sharp crack of training staves, boots on stone, and the low hum of Cass's power stirring in the air.

Six crystal shields shimmered and spun around her like fragments of a broken star, diamond-shaped, thin as glass, yet harder than any blade. The shields caught sunlight and scattered it in brilliant arcs. They hovered in a perfect circle, adjusting position each time Thomas moved, predicting his angles before he even struck.

Finn dashed in from the left, sword raised. Cass, standing behind him, flicked her fingers and two of the shields pivoted, sliding into position to block incoming blows. One absorbed a snap kick from Thomas, and another deflected a thrown training knife.

Finn grinned. "I like this formation."

"Don't get used to it," Cass called back, sweat beading on her brow. "These take focus."

Thomas blurred forward, his Body Mage reflexes turning him into a streak of movement. Cass tracked him, not his speed, but his path. She sent two more shields hurtling forward to intercept. One clipped his hip, making him stumble. The other just missed his shoulder as he flipped backward.

The shields returned to her orbit, reforming their ring.

"She's definitely not a Light Mage," Sparky muttered from the sidelines. At this point, even the idea of Finn being an Iron Mage and Cass being a Light Mage is a joke."

Thomas paused just outside Cass's range, panting, grinning.

"You're learning fast," he said. "Let's see how far you'll go."

He charged again, and this time, Harlen joined in.

He lifted a hand, and a shimmer of water gathered into blades of ice that shot across the courtyard.

Cass reacted on instinct.

Three shields shot outward to intercept the ice daggers, two more swung toward Thomas to block his advance, and the sixth... shifted into a long, tapering spear.

It launched.

Straight toward Harlen.

The old Water Mage's eyes widened, and he brought up an ice shield just in time. The crystal spear screamed as it struck, embedding itself with a sound like stone breaking glass.

The entire courtyard went still.

Cass stood frozen, her mouth open in horror, arms trembling.

Harlen stared at the glittering shard now lodged in the wall, half a head from his own head. Then he turned, calm as ever, and said, "Well. That one was close."

"I-I didn't mean-" Cass stammered, stepping back. "I'm so sorry, I didn't think-"

Harlen raised a hand gently. "Cass. Breathe."

She did, barely.

He crossed the space between them and rested a steady hand on her shoulder.

"You're strong," he said, "and getting stronger. That's a good thing. But fear will make your magic clumsy. Control it. You're not dangerous because of what you can do. You're only dangerous when you don't trust yourself to handle it."

Cass looked at him, eyes wide, then down at her hands.

Later that evening, the training ground was quiet. Cass stood alone in the fading light, kneeling beside a patch of worn stone.

Around her, six shields floated, smaller now, thinner. She shifted them with slow, careful movements, like a conductor guiding a silent orchestra. They formed shapes: a wall, a spiral, a flower. Then she reshaped them into blades, narrower and sleeker than before. Each moved with a grace that made them seem alive.

She didn't need power. She needed precision

After training, the sky had begun to turn golden from the sunset. Muscles sore and sweaty from sparring, Finn and Cass said their goodbyes and wandered out into the city as they had so many nights before. But this evening, the streets buzzed with a different energy, an anticipation that hummed beneath every step.

They took the stone stairwell behind the baker's shop, climbed up past rows of hanging laundry and wind chimes, until they reached the rooftop that overlooked Greyfen's eastern edge. From there, the horizon glimmered with something new.

The Copper Rail Station, unfinished just a week ago, now stood like a spiderweb of polished spires and metal lattice, rising from the earth with symmetrical elegance. Fire Mages worked the engine at the rear of the rail bed, releasing columns of heat while Water Mages walked the copper rails ahead, cooling the metals and locking them in place. The magic shimmered, cold blue in front, searing orange behind. The track bent across the hills in a long, lifted path, suspended on supports.

Cass sat on the rooftop's ledge, eyes narrowed as she watched the spires thrum with heat and magic. "They're nearly done."

"Another few days, maybe," Finn guessed, folding his arms. "Faster than I thought."

Below them, they saw others watching the oddity crawling towards the city. Here and there, they saw townspeople standing near corners or leaning out windows, even some children pointed, cheering as they saw the engineers work. But there was also tension, subtle, but thick as smoke.

"I heard the rail is coming because of the refugees," one woman whispered to another nearby.

"No," said the man beside her, "it's for the armies. There's going to be a war. Elarith's hitting eastern towns again."

"Greyfen could be next," a vendor muttered.

Cass stiffened, and her hand dropped to her side and rested on her dagger.

"I don't like this," Cass murmured.

"It's just talk," Finn said, but the quiet way he said it meant he didn't believe that either.

Down below, a family rushed through the square, mother, father, and three children. All their belongings were bundled in cloth, and their faces were pale and drawn. Refugees. More of them, each day.

The Copper Network engineers and the city's politicians might smile and wave, but the guards at the gates were doubling shifts. Every time Finn and Cass passed through the markets now, there were new faces, new eyes watching.

"Let's head back," Finn said, finally.

Cass nodded. But she didn't move. Not yet.

She just stared at the copper spires glowing in the night.

Back at the open-air gym, the training courtyard, which normally echoed with the sound of weapons clashing and shouted commands, had fallen into a rare hush.

Thomas sat against one of the central pillars with sweat-soaked clothes. Sparky lay flat on his back nearby, one leg draped over the edge of a weapons rack, still holding a shattered staff in one hand like he couldn't bring himself to drop it. Harlen leaned against the cool outer wall, ice magic coiling in slow spirals around his fingers as he conjured and reabsorbed tiny flickers of water, just enough to stay cool.

The silence lingered.

Then Sparky groaned. "I swear that girl cracked my rib with a broken staff today."

Thomas didn't reply.

"She wasn't even trying to hit me," Sparky muttered. "I swung the staff, and it ricocheted off a shield and hit me."

Harlen chuckled faintly, but it didn't last long.

Thomas tilted his head back against the pillar and stared up at the open sky. "They're not normal."

"No," Harlen agreed, folding his arms. "But they're not dangerous either. Not yet."

Thomas ran a hand over his face. "We're already at the edge of what we can teach them. Both of them have to hold back to spar with us now. Cass's shields are so sharp they can cut through metal swords, and Finn…"

"Felt like an earthquake," Sparky grumbled. "If he ever really tries to throw something… Who knows the damage it would do when it hits."

Thomas looked at both of them. "We need more help."

Harlen frowned. "We bring in more Mages, we bring in more eyes. Word gets out, and it won't just be curious students showing up. It'll be recruiters. Spies. Politicians."

Thomas shook his head. "Then we find the right people. Ones we can trust. We can't train them alone."

Sparky finally sat up, wincing as he rubbed his ribs. "We should be charging them ten silver a week. We're gonna need doctors next."

Harlen looked up at the stars beginning to prick through the darkening sky. "We joke now," he said quietly, "but if we're not careful, we're going to end up training weapons. Not people."

That silenced them again.

The three men sat in the fading light, each holding a different kind of exhaustion, one physical, one mental, and one worn deep in the soul.

Tomorrow, they will train again.

But tonight, they will rest.

◆ ◆ ◆

It was late, the air cool and still, the cobbled streets of Greyfen emptying as the last tavern goers trickled home. Finn and Cass walked in silence beneath the flickering glow of oil lamps, their boots scuffing the uneven stone.

They passed under an archway and entered a narrow garden between rows of quiet homes. Ivy curled over stone walls, and a single bench sat beneath a tree heavy with night blooms. Cass sank onto it without a word, and Finn joined her.

He broke the silence first.

"When the rail is finished, more people will visit here," he said, his voice low. "More people are coming in. More Mages. More eyes."

Cass didn't look at him. "Yeah."

"We've been here almost two months," he added. "And already… people recognize us. Some even know our names."

Cass's jaw tightened. "I don't like that."

"I do," Finn admitted. "Sometimes. It feels… normal."

She turned her head slowly. "But we're not in a normal situation, Finn."

"I know," he said. He picked at a crack in the bench's surface, watching his thumb trace the line. "I like it here. The food. The people. The teachers. But it's not going to stay quiet. Not with that rail."

Cass leaned back, exhaling through her nose. "You think we should leave."

"I don't know what I think," Finn said. "Part of me wants to go somewhere hidden again. Another part wonders if we're stronger because of this place."

Cass hesitated, then said, "If we left… Do you think Thomas, Harlen, and Sparky would come with us?"

Finn shook his head. "I think Harlen would. Maybe. But Thomas and Sparky…" He trailed off.

Finn looked up at the stars. "Do you think they'd betray us? If someone asked?"

Cass was quiet for a long time. "I think… they'd want to protect us. But that doesn't mean they'd succeed."

They sat in silence for a while, watching the wind ripple through the ivy. Somewhere in the distance, a dog barked. A gate creaked shut.

"We've got ten months," Finn said quietly. "Ten months until we go back to the Mausoleum."

"Let's not go too far," Cass murmured. "But maybe… far enough to think clearly."

Finn nodded.

"Tomorrow," she said, "we'll ask the teachers about the other towns near the Painted Peaks. Somewhere smaller. Somewhere we can disappear again… if we have to."

Finn looked over, and for the first time in days, Cass looked tired. Not just from training. From wondering when the world would find them.

"I'll follow your lead," he said.

She smirked faintly. "For once."

They stood and walked back toward the rental house, quiet and watchful.

The city around them was beginning to shift.

And the clock had already started ticking.

The next morning, after a light breakfast and a long silence over lukewarm tea, Cass and Finn made their way through the market district to the courtyard gym where their training always began. Thomas, Harlen, and Sparky were already there, talking quietly. All three men looked up when the teens approached, and Finn didn't miss the flicker of tension that passed between them.

Cass got straight to it. "We've been thinking," she said, her voice calm but firm. "About training somewhere else."

Harlen raised his eyebrows. "Somewhere else?"

Thomas crossed his arms. "You mean leaving Greyfen?"

"We're not sure yet," Finn said, glancing at Cass. "But the city's changing. The rail's almost done. More people are showing up, and not just refugees. Soldiers. Mages. People who may ask questions."

"We were already going to talk to you about something similar," Thomas said. "We think it's time to bring on more instructors. A Fire Mage. An Earth Mage. Your growth is beyond what the three of us can manage on our own."

Sparky nodded. "If we're being honest, it's been hard keeping up. You two push us harder than any other students."

Harlen stepped forward, rubbing the back of his neck. "But going out into the wilds? That's not the solution. It solves nothing. You still need guidance, and more of it, not less."

Cass shifted, uncomfortable. "We're not saying we're running off into the woods. We just... don't feel challenged here anymore, and yes, maybe we don't feel safe also."

"What about going to the Capital?" Harlen asked.

"Stonehollow," Finn said. "It sounds like a fortress. The kind of place where a kid like me wouldn't get a chance to leave if someone decided I was dangerous."

"You think the capital would try to keep you?" Thomas asked, not unkindly.

"I don't know what it would do," Finn answered. "And that's the problem."

The teachers exchanged glances. It was clear they disagreed. But they also understood.

Harlen sighed. "Alright. You want to stay in Greyfen, but away from people. Fine. We'll move the training."

Thomas added, "We'll rent one of the old stone warehouses across the river. It's private, soundproofed by the quarry stone, and no one will bother us there."

"And we'll bring in the two new Mages," Sparky said. "Bruce is our fire guy. Intense, but reliable. Cam's an Earth Mage, strong, quiet, knows her stuff."

Cass and Finn nodded in agreement.

"Just don't shut us out," Harlen said, looking at both of them.

"We're not shutting you out," Cass said quietly. "We're just trying to stay ahead of whatever may come."

And so, the next day, they began training in the warehouse. It was large and cool inside, with high ceilings and dust still clinging to the beams. It's a little dark inside, with the only light coming from the skylights. Cam arrived first, tall, thin, with a silent gaze that seemed to weigh everything. Bruce followed a day later, his hair singed at the tips, his grin full of excitement like he couldn't wait to fight.

The training ramped up immediately. Now it wasn't just sparring, it was small battle formations, blending in some of their elemental abilities, and reflex drills that pushed them beyond exhaustion. Finn practiced controlling his strength without destroying the building. Cass focused on shaping her crystal shields with sharper precision.

But no matter how fast they moved or how powerful they became, the weight never left them.

The fear that they were going to be discounted was always there.

The worry that someone would come asking questions.

They were hidden, but hidden in plain sight, and they didn't

know if that was enough.
But for now, they trained.
They laughed.
They lived.
And they prepared.

CHAPTER 23

Heroes

The two weeks that followed were grueling.

Every afternoon, Finn and Cass faced off against five fully grown Mages in a sprawling stone warehouse at the edge of Greyfen. Fire, Water, Earth, Iron, and Body, their instructors took turns sparring with the two teens, sometimes all at once. What had started as lessons now felt like a battlefield.

Finn held back. Even in the larger space, he could feel how fragile the room really was, how a single lapse could bring the ceiling down or twist the stone floor into something dangerous. Cam, the Earth Mage, was the easiest for him to counter. When she summoned walls of stone, he crumbled them with a glance. When she hurled rocks, they sank into the ground a few heads from her hand, pulled down as if the air itself had rejected them. She took it in stride, grinning through defeat, clearly seeing it as a puzzle she hadn't solved yet.

Bruce, on the other hand, the Fire Mage, was another story.

Finn couldn't stand him.

It wasn't his attitude; Bruce was friendly enough. It was the constant burning. His shirts, pants, and even a new pair of boots, scorched within minutes of the match beginning. Finn had taken to bringing a spare set of clothes every day. And yet, oddly, the flames never touched his skin. Not even his hair would catch. Bruce, half-joking, half-bitter, once muttered, "Must be nice," as he flicked a small flame out on his own sleeve.

The sparring forced Finn to focus. He couldn't make them submit by instinct alone. Their coordination, their constant movement, their combined elements, it was like trying to swat flies while balancing on a rope. And when he did let go just a little, when he thought he had everything under control, it happened.

Every time.

He'd look up to see the other Mages frozen, staring past him with wide eyes. He'd turn, slowly, and find the floor behind him lifted like a wave, a massive arc of dirt and stone hanging in the air, suspended by forces even he didn't fully understand. It looked ready to collapse and bury them all. In those moments, he'd feel the blood drain from his face. He'd take a breath. Slow down. The wave would settle, slowly, the stones returning to the ground in quiet, trembling clatters.

More than once, Cam coughed up dust and muttered, "Let's not drown in dirt today, yeah?"

And Finn would nod, trying not to let them see how hard his hands were shaking.

Cass had grown sharper, literally and figuratively.

Her shields, once flickering and unstable, had evolved into something far more tangible. She could now form multiple weapons at once, sleek spears, curved swords, and even intricate, plate-sized sawblades that shimmered like snowflakes suspended in the air. They spun with eerie grace and cut with terrifying precision.

Walls thrown up by Cam were sliced down effortlessly. Finn once watched one of Cass's crystalline saws carve through a four-head-thick slab of stone like it was paper. Her blades, once fragile and glass-like, now shimmered with a dense, refracted light. They didn't just cut, they cleaved, needing little more than a flick of her wrist to split shields, walls, even the reinforced training posts the teachers kept replacing.

But it was her shields that drew the most awe.

No matter what the instructors threw, flames from Bruce, ice spikes from Harlen, or earth walls from Cam, none of it pierced her defense. Her barriers, forged from interlocking panes of light and crystal, rang out like bells when struck, holding fast every time.

"Unfair," Bruce muttered one afternoon, wiping ash from his brow after a bolt of fire bounced cleanly off one of her shields. "I can't even scare her anymore."

Cass only grinned.

There was strength in her now, not just in power but in confidence. Where she had once hesitated, she now stood unshaken, her glowing arsenal orbiting her like a snowstorm of blades waiting to be unleashed.

During a break between rounds, Finn and Cass slipped outside for some air. Inside the warehouse, their five instructors lay sprawled on the stone floor, groaning in defeat.

"Five minutes," Bruce had wheezed. "Just five... please."

The afternoon sun cast long shadows across the back alley of the training grounds. As they rounded the side of the building, Cass froze mid-step. Her eyes locked on a small group across the narrow lane, near a warehouse they'd been told was empty.

Several men were forcing a woman toward the entrance. She was clearly pregnant and clearly resisting. One man had a firm hand clamped over her mouth, stifling her screams as she struggled. The others pushed her forward, laughing quietly.

Cass caught Finn's eye. With a sharp jerk of her chin, she motioned toward the building, the same silent signal she'd used on their hunts through the Painted Peaks. Finn nodded.

They crept forward, fast and quiet. The warehouse door stood half open. From inside came muffled cries, a woman's screams, and the unmistakable sound of babies wailing.

Finn didn't wait.

He stepped through the doorway, his voice cutting through the noise like a blade. "Hey! What are you doing with her?"

The nearest man turned. His face twisted into a sneer. "Kid, you chose the wrong day to play the hero."

He snapped his fingers.

The shadows around Finn twitched, then lunged. Needle sharp strands of darkness slashed at him, slicing through his shirt, raking into his arms and chest. He staggered but didn't fall.

"Not another outfit," he muttered through clenched teeth.

Then he saw the rest of the room.

Fifteen women, all gagged and bound, sat huddled against the far wall, every one of them pregnant. Scattered nearby, laid out on thin blankets across the filthy floor, were at least thirty newborns, crying, naked, and dirty.

In the corner, a pile of pale, still bodies.

Women. Lifeless. Stacked like discarded cloth.

Finn's breath caught. His fists clenched. Something hot stirred in his gut, deep rage. The air around him grew heavy. Stones on the floor trembled.

For the first time, Finn was able to let a little bit of his control go.

Before him stood enemies, not sparring partners, not instructors, not curious onlookers, but people who had chosen cruelty. People who had bound and gagged pregnant women. People who left newborns crying on a cold, filthy floor. People who smiled through blood and silence.

They looked normal at a glance: clean, strong, confident. But their smirks, their casual posture, the glint of violence in their eyes gave them away. And the shadows that coiled and snapped through the room, living things made of nightmare, made their intent unmistakable.

Something inside Finn broke.

A soundless crack echoed through his core. In an instant, every enemy within his sight was flung backward and slammed into the far wall with bone-shaking force. Some struck low, others high, crumpling like thrown dolls. One flew into a stack of crates, and another crashed through a metal rack that bent under the weight.

Yet the room itself, every floorboard, every suspended lamp, even the blanket beneath the infants, remained untouched. Only the guilty moved.

They couldn't lift their heads.

Each one was pinned flat, arms trembling under invisible weight, spines twisted awkwardly. Their mouths opened in gasps, but most couldn't speak. Several coughed blood onto their own faces.

The air hummed, the walls thrummed like distant thunder. Dust shivered in place.

Finn stood in the center of it all, his breath shallow, chest rising and falling in hard, steady rhythm. The fury in him was hot. Like the walls of flame in his training. All he could see was red.

Cass didn't move. She stood just behind him, hands open at her sides, her blades ready, but not needed.

Cass hadn't hung back.

She had walked in just behind Finn, her expression hard as she saw the horror around them. Finn didn't notice, couldn't. All he saw were enemies. But she saw everyone.

The structure groaned from the weight of Finn's power. Dust

began to tremble loose from the ceiling, with cracks forming along it. Cass extended four shimmering shields, stretching them wide like protective wings to cover the women and crying infants. Falling stone shattered harmlessly against her barriers, bouncing off with a hiss of light.

At the same time, two of her remaining shields reshaped, slimmed into long, glasslike knives with glowing edges. They darted forward, cutting through ropes and gags with surgical precision. The women flinched at first, but once freed, many began crawling to their feet, dazed and sobbing.

Then came the thunder of boots.

Harlen burst through the door first, his massive frame barely slowing as he took in the scene. The other instructors followed close behind, Bruce, Cam, and the others, all wide-eyed but quick to act. No questions, no hesitation. They moved to the women, lifting them gently, ushering them toward the exit. Some carried two infants each, others helped the limping or wounded.

In minutes, the captives were safe. Every one of them.

Only then did Thomas step forward to Finn's side.

He approached Finn cautiously, navigating the space where the air still rippled with invisible weight. He didn't speak until he was beside him, one hand reaching up to Finn's rigid shoulder.

"They're out," Thomas said quietly. "You did it. But we need to talk to these people, if they're still alive. The city will want answers."

Finn didn't reply.

His jaw was locked, breath ragged, arms shaking. The room still pulsed with tension, like the heartbeat of something far too big for his body. The enemies remained pinned, moaning, twitching, some unconscious, some very much afraid.

Letting go wasn't easy. The fury didn't want to leave.

But slowly, Finn forced himself to breathe. Inhale. Exhale. He pictured weight lifting. One heartbeat at a time.

Then, thud. The first body hit the ground. Then another. Then all of them dropped like marionettes with cut strings.

The silence that followed was heavy. But it was over.

Most of the abductors were unconscious, many with shattered limbs or fractured ribs. They lay groaning on the warehouse floor. One of them, in a moment of delirious spite, snarled through broken teeth, "You don't know what you've done. We are the Dark Circle."

As if naming their allegiance were a threat, not a confession.

Thomas, seeing that the others had everything in hand, didn't wait.

He left the warehouse and ran full speed toward the city's main guard watchtower. Bruce stepped outside and launched a series of bright red flares into the air, one after the other, the bursts of light splitting the afternoon sky. A signal no one in Greyfen could ignore.

The rest of the instructors remained behind, weapons ready, standing guard over the surviving Dark Circle members. Even bound and broken, none of them were trusted.

Inside, the women, freed but still trembling, told their story.

Some had been taken from Greyfen itself. Others had been lured or dragged from nearby villages. Some of the babies came in without a mother and had already been a few days old. The women were forced to nurse the babies.

Their voices wavered as they explained what came next. What had been happening in that warehouse. When the pregnancies reached a certain point, the captors would take the babies, cutting them out whether the mother was ready or not. The women who survived the procedure were killed soon after. Others didn't survive at all.

Cass knelt beside one of the women, offering her a blanket and a waterskin. The woman's hands shook as she clutched them, her face pale and hollow. "We asked them why," she whispered. "Why were they doing this. Why wouldn't they just let us go."

She swallowed hard. "They only laughed. Laughed and said we were just wombs. Said we weren't even human."

Finn stood nearby, fists clenched at his sides, staring down at the warehouse floor. The shadows had retreated. The storm had passed.

But the fury remained, quiet and cold, settling in his bones like winter.

Later, Harlen found them sitting a little ways off, near a cracked stretch of stone where grass had forced its way through. Cass leaned against the wall, arms around her knees. Finn sat beside her, elbows on thighs, staring at nothing.

The guards hadn't arrived yet. The teachers were still inside, keeping watch. But Harlen didn't look like a teacher now, more like a man carrying the weight of something too big for his shoulders.

He stopped in front of them and crossed his arms.

"You're a lot stronger than you pretend when we're sparring, Finn."

Finn blinked, slow to register the words. Harlen sat down across from them with a groan and added, "You're holding back. Always have been."

Finn gave a tired, almost dazed laugh. "I was holding back in there, too."

Harlen's brows lifted. "You have more power than that?"

Finn didn't answer right away. He just shook his head, not in denial, but in frustration. They didn't understand. No one really understood.

Cass put her hand on his shoulder.

"Tell him," she said softly.

Finn breathed in deep and let it out slowly. Then, without looking up, he said, "It was all I could do... not to throw the warehouse, with all of them in it, so high they'd never come back down."

Harlen stared at him, stunned.

"So you lost a little control, huh?" the old man said, trying to keep it light. A weak smile tugged at the corner of his mouth.

Finn gave a short laugh. "Maybe a little."

Then his voice lowered. "How are we supposed to hide this now? After what happened there... how do we pretend we're still just normal Mages?"

Cass looked over, her jaw tight. She didn't have an answer.

But Harlen did.

"We don't," he said. "I think it's time we come clean."

Finn turned to him, startled. His heart skipped. This-this was what they feared more than anything. Exposure. Becoming symbols. Or weapons. Or worse.

"No," he said quickly, shaking his head. "We can't."

Around them, the pebbles on the ground began to lift. Blades of grass drifted upward, swaying as if caught in rising water.

Harlen leaned forward and placed a heavy hand on Finn's shoulder.

"I know it feels that way," he said, voice low and steady. "But based on what I've seen today... I don't think there's a soul in this nation, or beyond it, who could hurt either of you. Even if they tried."

The guards began arriving from all directions, drawn by Bruce's flares and, likely, Thomas's sprint through the city. Within moments, the quiet alley outside the warehouse buzzed with armored boots, sharp commands, and the sound of reinforcements spreading out to secure the perimeter.

Luckily, the presence of the teachers smoothed everything over quickly. Harlen, Bruce, Cam, and the others were well known in Greyfen, respected even. Their reputation alone gave Finn and Cass a measure of unspoken credit, at least for the moment.

Harlen stepped aside to speak quietly with the other instructors. "We only tell them what they need to know," he said. "If we can keep Finn's name out of it, we do. But if it comes up... we don't lie."

Inside, the guards swept through the building, and some came out with disgusted looks on their faces. Some checked the bindings on the injured captors; others comforted the women and gathered the crying infants. One of the guards, young, still wide-eyed despite the uniform, froze when she spotted one of the freed women. "Elsa?" she whispered. The woman turned, and in an instant, they were hugging, both shaking but alive.

When the captain finally arrived, Sparky, the Body Mage whose real name no one used anymore, met him near the center of the scene.

"We were training students in the next warehouse over," Sparky explained. "The teens saw something. A group of men forcing a woman inside this building. It looked wrong. So we followed."

The captain's eyes narrowed. "What happened next?"

"They acted fast. The boy confronted them. It escalated... fast. And when one of the men used shadow magic, he told us exactly who they were."

Sparky's expression hardened. "He said it himself. Dark Circle."

The captain flinched at the name. "You're sure?"

Sparky nodded once. "As sure as I am breathing."

That changed everything.

The captain barked orders to his lieutenants. More guards were summoned, this time with explicit instructions, double restraints, constant watch, and secure transport. "They're hard to hold," he muttered. "The Circle always tries to get them out... or silence them before they can talk."

Within minutes, carriages arrived. Five were assigned for

the women and children, and several guards went with them, bound for city healers and safety. The others, heavily reinforced, were for the captives. Shackles, chains, steel-barred doors. It still didn't feel like enough.

As the last of the wounded were loaded, the captain turned back to the instructors.

"Thank you," he said. "If you hadn't intervened, those women, those babies, might've been lost."

The teachers glanced at one another. No one spoke.

Then Cam, brushing dust off her sleeves, let out a short laugh.

"We didn't do it," she said, pointing across the courtyard. "He did."

The captain followed her finger to Finn, who stood beside Cass, arms folded, dirt on his face, and burns on his sleeves. The boy looked exhausted.

The captain raised an eyebrow. "Surely all of you had a part in it."

Cam grinned. "Nope. That was him. Finn."

"And her," added Sparky, jerking a thumb toward Cass. "The only reason those women aren't buried under rubble is her shields."

The captain looked back at the teens, his expression unreadable.

"They're why it takes five of us to train two students," Cam added with a smirk. "They're... weird. But good."

The captain didn't ask many questions about the teens.

He shook hands with the teachers, gave curt nods of respect, and quickly turned his attention to the prisoners and the processing of evidence. With a crime scene this grotesque and Dark Circle agents in custody, it was all hands on deck.

In his mind, it didn't matter who landed the blows or shattered the floor. The only thing that mattered was justice, that the men who had done these terrible things would face trial, and that the women and children were safe.

If the adult Mages claimed credit, he let them. There was no time to ask questions about the details. Not yet.

So the teachers walked the teens home.

The walk was hollow and quiet as the sun dipped low behind the walls of Greyfen, casting the rooftops in blood-orange shadow. The walk was long, and no one spoke until they reached the doorstep.

Inside the small house, Finn sat on the edge of the table, Cass by the window.

"I don't get it," Finn said finally, voice low. "They didn't even ask. Not once."

Cass didn't look away from the street outside. "Maybe he didn't want to know."

"They saw it. The warehouse. The bodies. And all of the guilty are still alive."

"Maybe." She turned to him now. "But it's easier for everyone if they pretend we're just kids who are nearby."

He let the words hang in the air.

It should've been a relief. No crowds. No questions. No rumors. Just… normalcy.

But it didn't feel right.

Cass leaned back against the wall. "Should we run?"

Finn didn't answer right away.

He looked at his hands and thought about how it had felt, not holding back as much. How easy it had been to lose control. And how many people had watched it happen.

Then he looked up.

"Or should we stay?"

The house was quiet. Outside, life in Greyfen returned to normal. But both of them knew it wouldn't stay that way for long.

CHAPTER 24

Mixed Parties

The Copper Mages arrived just after dawn, their caravan winding up the stone road to Red Canyon Outpost in silence. No banners, no fanfare, just a column of bronze-tinted wagons, their wheels oiled to avoid the faintest squeak, and riders dressed in layered coats of copper-threaded fabric that shimmered in the morning light.

At the gate, they dismounted not with ceremony but efficiency, each person stepping down with a worn satchel or scroll case in hand. They wore little armor, no visible weapons, and none of the rigid posturing of soldiers. Instead, they moved like librarians who had just been handed access to a forbidden vault. Their leader, a woman with slate-gray eyes and copper-plated bracers, glanced once at the fort's battlements and nodded, as if taking mental measurements of everything in sight.

Commander Blake had expected diplomats, or at least something more official. What he got looked more like a research team on the verge of an academic breakthrough.

Within minutes, they spread like ink across parchment.

One group set up tables in the central hall, brushing aside maps and reports left by the Unbound officers. Another unrolled scrolls and compared them against newly drawn sketches of the sealed dome sites that the Copper Networks had sent them ahead of time. One began taking exact measurements of atmospheric pressure near the structures, muttering excitedly about "resonants."

Blake watched from the doorway, arms crossed. Around him, his officers shifted uncomfortably.

"These people are... scholars," one whispered.

"They're definitely not here to attack," another said.

And it was true. The Copper Mages asked no questions about borders or titles. They had no interest in the chain of command. They barely acknowledged the presence of guards unless asking for clarification on a report. When one soldier tried to direct them toward the war room, the delegation waved him off and asked for access to the storage rooms that had drawings of the wild animals in the area and their mutations.

"This shouldn't happen," one Copper Mage murmured as she flipped through a thick ledger, eyes scanning faster than seemed human. "Constructs don't react like this. Not violently. Not every time. There are no precedents."

"They're... obsessed," Blake said quietly, almost in awe.

And they were. Fascinated by contradiction. Devoted entirely to solving the mystery that now pulsed beneath the domed stones outside their walls and in the Red Canyon itself. Their disregard for rank, for status, even for danger, didn't come from arrogance. It came from pure, unshakable curiosity.

To the soldiers of the Unbound Kingdom, who lived and died by the rule of order and obedience, it was both unsettling and strangely admirable.

The Copper Mages had not come for politics.

They had come for the truth.

The main record hall echoed with the sound of flipping parchment, clinking inkwells, and the low hum of whispered theories. A dozen Copper Mages surrounded the central table, its surface now buried in notes from the Unbound Kingdom's previous tests. Diagrams. Journals. Rough sketches of magical backlash patterns.

One of the Copper delegates, an older man named Veylan, whose fingers were stained nearly permanently with ink, pressed his palm flat against a torn page and muttered, "This can't be right."

A younger Mage beside him, Elsin, leaned over. "The scorch radius matches. That's the fourth entry where a non-lethal probing spell triggered a near-catastrophic reaction."

"Exactly." Veylan snapped his fingers and pointed at the map pinned to the far wall. "Every magical interaction at the structure has a unique reaction. Not uniform. Not measured. Not logical. It responds like-"

"-like it's making decisions," Elsin finished, eyes wide.

One of the Unbound soldiers standing nearby gave a skeptical grunt. "What, you mean it's alive?"

"No," said another Copper Mage, Archivist Glass, her tone clipped and precise. "Not alive. But reactive. It doesn't behave like a built construct with prebuilt traps. Not even like an ancient warded artifact. It's adaptive. Instinctive."

Commander Blake stepped closer, arms folded. "You're saying it is choosing to attack?"

"We're saying," Glass corrected, glancing up from a stack of parchment, "that it doesn't behave like a machine or a pre-cast set of detonation magic. It's reacting at the moment."

Elsin turned one of the field journals around and pointed to a hastily drawn diagram- "This reaction," she said, "was from a

Mage using a light affinity spell. Pure illumination. Not even aggressive."

"And it lashed back," Veylan added. "Not just randomly. It targeted the Mage's affinity and disrupted her senses. That kind of precise counteraction shouldn't be possible."

A silence followed, broken only by the soft scratching of quill on paper.

Blake frowned. "But it's not sentient?"

"No," she said. "But it may be built to feel like it is. Or it became that way. Either way... it doesn't follow the laws we understand."

That unsettled more than just the soldiers.

Magic was supposed to obey structure. It could be unpredictable, yes, but it followed patterns, roots, origins, affinities. This site had none of that. Every test from the Unbound Kingdom had yielded new, chaotic, and often dangerous results. Yet the Copper Mages weren't afraid.

They were exhilarated.

"This could rewrite how we understand magical theory," Glass said, voice hushed with awe. "It's not just a trap. It's a challenge."

Blake exchanged a glance with his second-in-command. "What if this thing decides that all of us are a threat?"

That quieted the Copper Mages for a moment.

Then Elsin whispered, almost to herself, "Not much we can do about that."

And for the first time since their arrival, even the scholars looked uneasy.

The records room had quieted for a moment, the sound of scribbling and rustling pages giving way to thoughtful silence, until one of the Copper Mages, a wiry man named Loric, paused mid-read.

"Wait. Here. In the scout's log entry dated Months ago."

He tapped the page urgently and looked up. "They mention footprints."

Several heads turned.

"What kind of footprints?" Glass asked sharply, already moving to his side.

Loric skimmed the passage aloud. "Upon initial approach to the rim, two sets of footprints were discovered in the mud just east of the main rise. Described as 'small, possibly a woman or an adolescent.' Slight depth. Partially eroded by wind. Direction... inward, toward the dome."

"Inward?" Elsin repeated, eyes narrowing. "As in... from outside the perimeter toward the construct?"

"That's what it says."

Glass's voice dropped to a whisper. "No animals. No signs of escort. Just two sets."

"Could it have been one of the scouting teams?" Glass asked, stepping forward.

Loric shook his head. "The log says the prints were already there when the team arrived. The site was undisturbed. No approach paths. No other tracks."

"And they led into the anomaly?" Glass said, incredulous.

Loric nodded slowly.

The room stirred with sudden tension. Quills were dropped. Pages forgotten. One of the younger Copper apprentices took a step back when he realized the significance. As if the realization had weight.

Elsin asked the next question, her voice quieter. "Are we sure it was only two?"

The soldier who had accompanied the scouts on that first trip spoke up from the back of the room. "It was hard to say. The wind had wiped most of it clean. But yeah, we are confident it was only two."

Glass's eyes darkened, her breath catching. She touched

another report and said, "And you sealed this campsite that you found under a dome of stone?"

The soldier nodded. "Yes, ma'am. One dome over the campfire we found nearby. The other over the ash field itself."

For a moment, it felt like the entire room held its breath.

Glass turned to her fellow Mages, her composure visibly slipping.

"A sealed ash field," she said. "And two small sets of prints."

Loric swallowed. "The prophecy."

That word changed everything.

Even the Unbound officers, hardened and skeptical, felt the weight of it. The prophecy the Saphrelliens whispered about. The rumors of an awakening. Of powerful stones, destined wielders, and a storm yet to come.

The Unbound soldiers had heard rumors of a prophecy, with some of their own Mind Mages even on record describing parts of the visions they remember. But even now, most believe it is just a campfire story told to entertain each other on long nights, given no more thought than the story about monsters in cities stealing babies.

She looked to Commander Blake. "If this is what we think it is… then those two prints may belong to the most important individuals in the world and possibly in many worlds."

Blake's voice was rough. "How can we find them? There has been no effort to find them since the event."

No one answered.

If they had walked away from that place… they could be anywhere.

The hall was already tense with the mention of footprints. But when the field reports shifted to the dome with the ash field under it, the atmosphere changed entirely.

Elsin unrolled the final set of parchments and laid them on the center table. "This second dome," she said, voice more measured now. "Sealed on the third day after initial contact. Described in the field notes as… 'clearing of uniform ash around a head deep.' No residual structures. No remaining flora. Just fine white ash covering a wide radius."

She looked up. "Untouched. And possibly centered at the heart of the magical disturbance."

For a breathless second, no one spoke.

Glass's eyes narrowed, her calm unraveling. "You're certain?" she asked. "Not a burned forest. Not fire damage. Ash. That uniform?"

Elsin nodded. "Yes. The ash was clean, and there was no smell of fire. It was a white field of ash."

Glass took a shaky breath, her hand going to the pendant around her neck, a sigil of the Copper Network. She met the eyes of her fellow Mages, then turned toward Commander Blake.

Glass pulled a leather-bound notebook from her satchel. She flipped through yellowed pages, stopping on one written with tight script and a faded illustration, a circle of ash beneath a night sky.

"This is a fragment of a vision recorded in the Final Index before the split. An ash field untouched by flame. Two shadows in its center. It was considered a metaphor. Until now."

Blake stepped closer. "You believe this?"

Glass looked up. "It matches. Two sets of footprints. The ash. Even the worldwide surge and visions. Did you know the Ardent Crown was not interested in the location, but interested in knowing if there were people of interest tied to the event?"

Blake's jaw tightened.

"They've expressed… interest in the event. But their main curiosity seems tied to rumors of individuals. Not locations."

The room seemed to shrink around the weight of it all.

Glass closed the notebook with a soft snap." It's long been believed that the Ardent Crown has had an ability to sense awakenings. It's very possible that they weren't interested in the location because they already knew about it. Something about it must have been different enough to spark their interest."

"If this site is what we believe it is," she said, "then the two who walked away from that ash field may be incredibly powerful."

She looked toward the doorway, where a cool wind blew in from the canyon.

"They could be anywhere now."

Glass took a step back, as if grounding herself, and then stood straighter.

"I want to see if we can find prints under the domes," she ordered quickly. "Send a team to the camp site, check for residual impressions, weight patterns, anything we missed. And another to this ash field. Test for compositions. Soil structure. Magical residue." She hesitated to say the next part out loud as if it would scare the truth away. "And probe deep in the ground. Be careful, but see if there is anything under it. Go deep."

Archivist Glass stood at the center of the storm of knowledge.

Tall and lean, with copper filigree woven into the seams of her slate-gray coat, she had the bearing of someone who never raised her voice because she never needed to. Her eyes, the color of old steel, had scanned more prophecies, pre-cataclysmic treatises, and esoteric field reports than anyone in the Copper Network's southern branch. But now, those calm, analytical eyes had gone sharp with urgency.

She turned from the records table, a parchment still clutched in her hand, and faced her team.

A group of Mages was already pulling crates from their wagons.

Glass glanced once toward Commander Blake, who still stood silently watching the whirlwind of motion. "Commander," she said. What we've uncovered here links directly to an event of immense prophetic weight."

Blake raised an eyebrow. "You're sure?"

She didn't blink. "This changes everything."

Then, turning back to her team, she raised the sealed parchment and said, "I'll be transmitting this to the Copper Network by dusk. And I'll inform our allied watchers in Saphrelle and the Ardent embassies."

Her expression had shifted fully now, no longer the thoughtful scholar, but a tactician with the burden of revelation resting on her shoulders.

"Whatever happened here," Glass said, voice low but firm, "was not an accident. And we are not the only ones searching for whoever walked away from that ash."

Commander Blake stood at the edge of the rampart, staring out across the mountains that cradled the fort. The morning mist had burned away, revealing jagged peaks and curling rivers, and somewhere out there, two sets of small footprints had vanished into the woods.

He felt the cold wind against his jaw but didn't move.

I missed it, he thought.

The prints. The ash. The impossible reactions. They had all been cataloged as anomalies, odd, but not prioritized over the construct. And now, with the Copper Mages in full command of the investigation, the truth loomed larger than anything the Unbound Kingdom had prepared for.

We thought we were guarding a ruin, he told himself. We've been sitting on a revelation.

He turned sharply and strode back into the courtyard, where Glass was dispatching another pair of Mages toward the ridge with measuring rods and sealed containers.

"Archivist," Blake called, his voice cutting through the flurry of activity.

She turned, calm as ever.

"I'm preparing a dispatch to High Command," he said. "Full urgency classification. I want to initiate a search effort across the kingdom."

Glass studied him for a moment. Then she nodded once. "Good."

"What am I even asking them to look for?" he said. "What's the profile?"

She stepped closer, her tone gentle but unflinching. "You're looking for two individuals. Young. Likely still adolescents or barely grown. Their footprints suggest as much."

"Two," Saren repeated.

Glass nodded. "They will have powers unlike anything recorded."

"Do we know what kind?"

"No, unfortunately," she admitted.

Blake felt the chill return, not from the wind, but from possibility.

"So," he said slowly, "we're looking for two newly awakened Mages. Young. Likely bonded to power no one's ever seen. But, only being awakened for a few months, they will likely be weak. And... what else?"

Glass met his gaze. "They will likely be drawn to justice. Whatever else they are, they won't tolerate cruelty."

Blake nodded grimly. "Then they'll make enemies fast."

He didn't wait. He turned on his heel and shouted for his Copper Mage, "We need to start the search now."

By nightfall, the fort was changing. The team researching the ash field confirmed it was a Wild Awakening Circle. Far beneath it, there was the grave of a long-dead, massive Dragon whose energy was spilling over into the circle itself. It was likely responsible for the wildness and beasts that this region was famous for, and it was probably powering the construct itself.

The Copper Delegation brought new life to the fort upon this revelation. They made some revelations, and the excitement was palpable.

Cartographers spread maps across long tables, tracing trade routes, forest trails, and riverways. Scribes copied descriptions of the footprints, translated the latest ash field reports, and began transmitting them to distant garrisons and outposts. They would start the search in Greyfen, which was the nearest city.

CHAPTER 25

Sacrifice

They didn't storm the gates. They bled their way in.

By the third month, Red Canyon Outpost had transformed from a rugged watchpoint into a strategic nexus. The discovery had drawn not only scholars and builders, but soldiers, reinforcements meant to secure the perimeter, and prepare for the final arrival of the Copper Network's rail. Already connected to Greyfen, the copper rail was now visible from the horizon, snaking like a scar through the mountains, drawing ever closer to the outpost walls.

In that shifting tide of movement, the Dark Circle returned.

They came not as traders or workers, but as soldiers.

Men and women with forged records, stolen insignias, and dead eyes. They wore the crests of outlying provinces. Their uniforms were correct. Their training is passable. No one questioned their arrival; there were too many new faces, too many rotations, too much movement to track. The fort was swelling, and in that swelling, they embedded themselves like rot in fresh timber.

They were assigned to guard towers, scouting rotations, and supply escorts. Some volunteered for night patrols. Others kept quiet and did what they were told. They saluted, they drilled, they followed orders.

And every night, they reported.

Not with ink and parchment, but with blood.

Each agent carried a small, obsidian Crucible no larger than a curled palm. Bound to them through ritual scarring, the stone pulsed faintly when touched. They cut themselves every night and filled the crucible to the top of its mouth, and the Crucible shimmered, receiving and transmitting wordless pulses to a twin buried in Velmirath.

Each spy had their mission.

One kept close to the domes, trying to find out what was in them.

Another patrolled near the old bunkers, listening to gossip.

A third spent her days counting who returned from field missions. Counting the growing number of troops stationed at the outpost.

They reported anomalies:

Their instructions were simple: Do not act. We only need to know what it's hiding.

And so, they watched quietly.

The Palm Crucibles pulsed with their nightly offerings.

And beneath Velmirath, something pulsed in answer.

The execution was not public.

It took place in a cold chamber beneath the Temple of Hollow Light, buried deep beneath the stone roads of the Ardent Kingdom's capital. The two prisoners, Mages barely out of their youth, were bound in silence, their hands shackled in mirrored steel, their eyes dimmed with sleepbane.

Jiran, the elder of the two, had begun to manipulate ambient sound, not just in the mind, but in reality. He could make voices blurred into static.

The girl, Selin, had burned without flame. Her fire was blue and cold.

At least they did when they were still alive.

The death cult had reached out to them first, of course.

Word came through spies placed with the Death Cult's inner circle. The cult saw promise in their uniqueness. Potential. Weapons of chaos. They offered sanctuary. Training. Purpose for the teens.

When the Dark Circle heard about them, they feared these youths could be the Twin Stones.

High above, in a vaulted chamber lit only by the pale glow of a bloodstone lantern, three Dark Circle commanders conferred over the mission's success.

"Are we certain they're dead?" asked Varek, his voice smooth, his hands gloved in silk.

"Bodies confirmed. Cremated. No remains kept," said Sova, a thin woman with no eyebrows and a mind like a steel trap. "Both were put down without a doubt."

Varek exhaled. "Good. Wild magic breeds chaos."

Across from them sat Corren, older than the other two and twice as bitter. He had once studied under the Saphrellien doctrine but turned when he saw what the prophecies might actually unleash.

"They didn't even know what they were," Corren muttered. "Children with powers no one should have. We are not in the business of waiting to see what monsters they have become."

He reached into a leather pouch and placed a coin on the table, etched with a twisted sun and a severed chain. It was smeared with blood.

"Two fewer variables," he said. "On to the next."

Across the Unbound Kingdom, the order had come down in silence, but its echoes spread like wildfire.

Across the fractured networks of the Dark Circle, the command was clear: secure the sacrifices. Reforge the Crucible.

No hesitation followed.

Agents and sleeper cells mobilized with terrible purpose. The task was monstrous, but not resisted. They clung to it with a kind of zeal, a twisted reverence for what it meant: the rebirth of one of the great weapons of their age.

Within weeks, nine towns vanished.

In the cities, their efforts were quieter but no less brutal. Sleeper Cells embedded in merchant guilds and midwife circles stole away hundreds of pregnant women under the cover of night. False clinics. Poisoned wards. Disappearing carriages. The scale of it became a myth before it was even known.

The number climbed.

Six hundred newborns.

Six hundred innocent sacrifices, and of course, sixty willing sacrifices. Those were easy to get, and many of the Dark Circle members were turned down because too many had volunteered.

Enough to satisfy the hunger of Blood Obsidian.

The women, those who were kept alive long enough to bear, were tasked with nursing sacrifices and keeping them alive long enough until the caravan got on site.

Within the Circle's secret halls, they were celebrated. Although everyone hated the constant whining that came from the nurseries.

Every Cell that contributed to the total was honored. Every successful raid was praised. Members competed to outdo one another and bring in more.

Because once completed, they would recover something not created in centuries: a Blood Obsidian Crucible, a relic of shadowed might, capable of warping life and death alike. With it, they could rebind the Twisted Shadows, control them, shape them.

Velmirath would rise again.

And those who had made it possible were proud to be the ones who had lit the fire.

The chamber was carved into obsidian, polished smooth, and veined with silver to fill the cracks.

The silence was heavy as the courier finished his report and stepped back.

A single sheet of black vellum lay on the central table. The message, encoded and direct, read:

Greyfen Operation: Compromised. At least 20 operatives captured. Local authorities alerted. Plan not exposed.

The silence stretched.

Corren, the eldest of the three, broke it. "They were sloppy."

Varek, all velvet voice and venomous smile, leaned forward. "They were ambitious. Cells that operate near small cities always are."

Corren grunted. "They endangered the timeline. We are almost ready to do the sacrifice. We can't afford delays. And we cannot afford attention."

Sova, who had not yet spoken, tapped a single, pale finger against the edge of the report. "Twenty of them are alive."

The statement hung in the air like a warning.

"Attempts at extraction?" Corren asked.

The courier stepped forward again. "We attempted to bribe

two of the guard captains. Both were intercepted. Local enforcement has been increased. Interrogations likely have begun."

Corren nodded once. "Silence them. Before they speak."

Sova's tone was colder than the stone beneath their feet. "Use internal assets. No contact from outside. Make it look like suicide or collapse."

The courier bowed.

But Varek raised a hand. "Wait."

Both Corren and Sova turned.

Varek tilted his head. "If the guards have begun questioning... do we risk exposure?"

Corren's eyes narrowed. "They don't know what the children were for. They've seen the horror, but not the reason."

Sova's voice was a whisper. "Even so... we purge the records. Any trace that connects Greyfen to us is erased. Immediately."

Another nod. Another cold decision passed like a death sentence.

Corren turned back to the courier. "Kill the Twenty. Burn the safehouse. And for the love of the shadows, retrieve any relics or palm crucibles they carried."

The courier bowed again. "It will be done."

As he vanished into the dark, Sova finally spoke what none of them had said aloud.

"If one of them speaks before they die..."

Corren's hand tightened into a fist. "Then we raze Greyfen."

The site was quiet when they arrived.

It was time. Caldreth's bones lay as they had for a decade, half buried beneath rubble and moss-veined roots, his ribcage shattered where the Dark Circle's final spell had struck. Wind cut across the basin in slow, circular currents, as though reluctant to disturb the stillness. An earth Mage smoothes the ground into a funnel with the great dragon's petrified heart at the center. The funnel was 60 heights in diameter. The Shadow Mages began manipulating the shadows and tossed all the scraps of the dragon's bones out of the way. The Carriages were arriving, and it was time.

They began at sunset.

The sixty volunteers spaced evenly around the edge of the circle, slit their own wrists, and lay with their feet up on the top of the gently sloped funnel and their wrists above their head, pointed towards the center.

The sacrifices were brought in silence. Six hundred, naked, numbered, and drugged to keep them from being too loud and ruining the ceremony.

Each one was laid down on the stone floor with their head towards the center until every drop of blood dripped freely to the heart.

No words were spoken.

The ritual did not call for incantations. It did not even require babies necessarily. Only a lot of blood and a bound beast's petrified heart. It took more babies, obviously, to fill the blood requirements, but they were what was traditionally used for this ceremony. The beast's heart did not care about whether it was innocent or not. It just wanted blood.

At the center, the six people chosen to do the sacrifice, a position of great honor, moved their blades with precision. One stroke. Then another. Then another. When every drop of blood was gathered in a pool in the center. Then the six honored slit their own throats, one after another.

That's when the obsidian heart started to drink greedily. Steam hissed through the channels in the stone until all of the blood was consumed.

The final breath came not from a sacrifice, but from the stone itself.

A soundless exhale. A long, slow tremor passed through the earth and echoed in the bones of all who stood nearby.

The ritual was complete.

Caldreth's grave had become something new. Not a tomb. Not a shrine.

A forge.

And the Blood Obsidian Crucible was reborn.

The Crucible was still warm when they carried it to the appointed carriage. And they began the march to Velmirath.

It took a full day to cool, and even then, its core pulsed with internal heat. Not the heat of fire, but something like body warmth. The transport was handled with reverence.

The path was long, winding through charred valleys and blackened stone.

Velmirath awaited.

The hidden city below the earth, sculpted from shadowed basalt and ruin. Here, the Dark Circle had made its home. Here, the old banners still hung, on them, a Crucible, caught in the open jaws of a massive, fanged mouth.

They welcomed it with silence.

There was no cheering, no drunken feast, no festival flames. Celebration here was solemn, ritualized, and absolute. In the lowest chamber, the Crucible was placed upon the Dread Pedestal, once reserved for offerings.

Candles were lit in the corridor. The chamber filled with that strange, hungry light.

High Magister Corren stepped forward first, laying both hands on the Crucible's surface. He whispered to it. "Finally, we can restart the project," he said. "To raise our army of Shadows!"

Around the room, everyone cheered.

The Crucible, always thirsty, demanded its first offering. Once it was filled with blood, they began building their army.

The creature they dragged forward was a captured Twisted Shadow, once feral, now bound in iron. It shrieked and writhed, the sound neither beast nor man, but something caught in between. Heavy collars were fastened around its neck, wrists, waist, and ankles, each connected to long dark metal rods held by Wardens, specialists within the Dark Circle trained for one task alone: the capture and containment of Twisted Shadows.

It fought. It bucked and spat black bile. But they forced it forward, step by step, until it stood trembling at the Crucible's edge.

Then came the command.

The Wardens wrenched its head downward, subduing it with trained precision. Its face was plunged toward the congealed blood pooled at the Crucible's mouth. At first, it resisted. Then, it drank.

What followed was not death, but reclamation.

Its body spasmed violently. Limbs twisted inward. Skin rippled, cracking open like bark under pressure. The wail it gave was not pain alone; it was loss, as something inside it gave way. And its body phased through the collars. Now owned by the Crucible, its natural ability to phase into shadow has been multiplied one hundred times, into something truly powerful.

The crucible stripped away its chaos. Exposed what remained beneath.

And then... it bound it.

Not fully. Not cleanly. But enough.

The beast fell still, and stood, breathing hard, its black eyes now flickering with red veins, waiting for a command. The first of many.

In the weeks that followed, others were brought forward. Some were caught in ruins. Others lured from deep caverns and hollow woods. Each drank. Each twisted. Each broke. And from each, a soldier was made.

These bound shadows would not be sent into open war, not yet. Their purpose was subtler. Infection. Influence. They would move through caves, through the abandoned places outside city walls. Seek out wild shadows still hiding. Spread the taint through a scratch. Swell the ranks.

The Twisted Awakening Circle would begin creating more Twisted Shadows again.

And with every sacrifice, the Crucible grew stronger.

Its pulse deepened. Its whispers grew louder.

The age of prophecy was upon them.

But they no longer feared it.

They intended to rewrite it.

CHAPTER 26

Night Delivery

It only took two more days for the Copper Transport Rail to reach Greyfen.

The final length of the track locked into place just after dawn. People gathered along the platform, clapping as the final spike was driven, cheering for the robed Mages and armored officials who had brought something shining and new to the edge of the wilds.

But what came next silenced the crowd.

After a brief pause, no longer than a meal break, the Copper Mages didn't pack their tools or return to the capital.

They kept building.

This time, the rail bent southeast.

Confusion rippled through the city. There were no Unbound Kingdom cities in that direction. Just hills and wilderness.

And yet, the rail stretched further each hour, each gleaming length vanishing deeper into the unknown.

Speculation lit the air like a summer storm.

"Trade with Elarith," some whispered.

"A secret settlement project," others said.

"An alliance?"

"A warfront?"

But not Cass. And not Finn.

They didn't need maps or rumors.

They knew exactly what lay to the southeast.

The Red Mound. Their mausoleum.

That evening, after witnessing the events of the construction, the teens sat down in the shade.

Cass ran a damp cloth over her forehead. "We could go," she said, voice even.

Finn didn't ask where. He didn't have to.

"The wilds are still open," he said. "If we leave tonight, it will be harder for someone to find us."

They were quiet for a while.

They had done it before. And they could do it again.

Cass looked out toward the rail.

But in their silence, they doubted if that option was something they truly wanted to do.

Finn and Cass agreed to speak with the teachers the next morning.

While they slept that night, they hadn't realized that the first transport car had already come and gone.

It arrived in the dead of night, just past the third watch, its copper frame barely catching the moonlight. There was no ceremony, no cheering crowd. Just the low whirr wheels meeting track, and the faint hiss of sealed doors opening into still air.

Only a handful stood waiting at the station.

The Captain of the Guard, stiff in his formal coat. Two city officials in neutral robes. And standing furthest from the light, cloaked in deep navy and quiet authority, was the head of Greyfen's information network, a woman few dared to name aloud.

They said little as the doors opened.

From the central cabin stepped a small team of Mages, five in total, their cloaks fluttering lightly in the night breeze. But it was the last figure off the car that drew the most attention.

An older man. Stooped, but deliberate, his eyes heavy with thought. His robes were simple. Rupart, a mind Mage, one of the capital's most senior Mind Mages, and one quietly known to oversee operations no one talked about.

He paused at the foot of the platform, breathing in the mountain air like a man testing the temperature of a battlefield.

Then he looked at the gathered officials and offered a thin, unreadable smile.

"Well," he said, voice low and dry. "Let's get to work."

Without another word, the team disappeared into the shadows, and the transport, its cargo emptied, its messages delivered, slipped back onto the rails and returned to Stonehollow before the sun could rise.

By morning, Greyfen was already waking, unaware that the first transport car had already come and gone.

The morning light filtered through the warped shutters of their rental house, casting long stripes of sunlight across the wooden floor. Finn was already up, lacing his boots with slow, methodical movements. Cass sat at the small table near the window, quietly chewing on a crust of bread and watching the steam rise from her cup of tea.

Neither of them had spoken yet about the conversation they were going to have, but it lingered between them like mist.

They were going to talk about leaving with their teachers today.

Because something in the air had shifted. The presence of the rail made them feel uneasy. It was time to move.

Finn sat across from her and picked at the edge of a dried fig. "So," he said, voice low, "what do we need?"

Cass leaned back, looking up at the ceiling as she ran the list in her mind.

"Not much," she said. "Clothes. A blade for skinning. Bedrolls. Maybe a small tent, if we feel like pretending we're civilized."

Finn smirked. "We don't need bandages or grain alcohol anymore. We really don't even need a Bow or Arrows either."

Cass shook her head. "I doubt even a Twisted Shadow could break your skin. We may be able to sleep through an attack if we want to."

He laughed softly. The ease between them felt like the last breath before a long swim underwater.

It was surprising how little they needed now. Their magic had changed more than just how they fought. Now they realized that it had changed what they needed to survive. Firewood and food could be found. Shelter, improvised. It left only the essentials, basic tools, warmth, and each other.

Cass glanced out the window, watching a child chase a kitten down the street. "I'm going to miss Greyfen."

Finn nodded. "Me too."

But neither of them said they weren't coming back. Because maybe they would. After the Red Mound. After whatever was waiting.

They just wanted Thomas, Harlen, and the others to be safe. And not to worry about them.

Cass stood, brushing crumbs from her coat. "Let's go talk to them."

Finn rose beside her, his jaw set.

It was time.

They took the usual route to the warehouse, boots patting along the cobblestone road as the city slowly came alive around them. Early vendors were setting up stalls. Smoke curled from chimneys. It was all perfectly normal.

But something felt... off.

Cass didn't say anything, but she glanced over her shoulder more than once. Finn's eyes flicked to the rooftops, the alley shadows, the corners where motion could hide. There was nothing obvious. No glint of steel. No shape out of place.

And yet.

They both felt it.

Like a gaze was pressing between their shoulder blades.

"Probably in our heads," Finn muttered.

Cass didn't answer.

When they reached the warehouse, they stopped at the door.

The teachers were already there.

That was unusual. Normally, Finn and Cass arrived first, got in a warm-up, maybe traded a few sarcastic jabs before the instructors wandered in. But today, the big doors were already unlatched, and light spilled out from the open slats.

Cass glanced at Finn. He nodded.

They stepped inside.

Harlen was waiting just past the entry, arms folded tight. Cam stood by the far wall, her expression unreadable. Bruce was pacing slightly near the weapons rack. Thomas and Sparky stood behind Harlen.

Harlen stepped forward.

"Kids," he said, voice low, steady, measured. "We need to talk about something. Please... let us speak before you act."

Finn frowned. "What does that mean?"

Cass tensed beside him. *Do they already know we're leaving?*

Harlen motioned toward the right-hand corner of the warehouse in the shadow. A stone bench and table, clearly Cam's work, had been placed there sometime before they arrived.

Sitting on the bench was a man.

Older. Gray-bearded. Average height. Normal build. His clothing was plain, clean, but unremarkable. He looked like someone's grandfather. The kind of man who sold firewood or fixed fences. If Finn had passed him on the street, he wouldn't have given him a second glance.

But now, every part of Finn's body was alert.

The man didn't rise. Didn't speak. He just sat there, watching them with a faint, unreadable smile.

"Who is this?" Finn asked.

The man said nothing.

Harlen's jaw tightened. "This is Rupart. He's here to speak with you two."

Cass slowly began to turn, scanning the warehouse, corners, rafters, and shadows. Her body was calm, but her fingers hovered near her side, where her crystal blade would form if needed.

Finn rolled his shoulders once, loosening tension the way he always did before a fight. His stance widened. Subtle. Controlled.

The stranger, Rupart, watched without blinking.

"Now, kids," Harlen said gently, stepping between them and the table, "I asked you not to act. Just listen before you do anything."

Finn didn't turn from Rupart. But he glanced at Thomas, who stepped closer to the man.

Rupart sensed the boy wonder about betrayal, and then the trust of his teacher won.

Thomas gave the slightest nod.

Not a command. Not a warning.

Just confirmation.

Cass looked to Harlen, and what she saw there stalled her next breath; his eyes weren't stern or commanding. They were… sad. And pleading.

He nodded, too. Slowly. Trying to tell her it was okay.

A beat passed.

Then another.

Finn and Cass turned toward each other.

Neither spoke.

But everything passed between them in the space of a shared glance, the tension, the calculation, the thousands of things they weren't saying.

Eventually, Cass gave a tiny shrug. "I guess it couldn't hurt," she said, her voice casual.

But her stance never relaxed.

And Finn's stance remained ready, just in case.

They wouldn't strike first.

But they were ready.

Rupart didn't move as the tension rippled through the room; he simply watched.

Cass's subtle pivot. Finn's shift in weight. The slow scan. The flexing of fingers, the timing of breath. Nothing flashy. Nothing reckless. But every inch of their bodies spoke the same language: ready.

It interested him.

No fear. Just awareness. Discipline.

These two are strong. They were young, but very dangerous.

He'd spent over forty years serving the Unbound Kingdom,

most of it in the shadows, on missions that didn't exist, for reasons too delicate to be named. He had seen strength before. Power. Potential.

He had also seen what happened when it was used to hurt the weak, when it grew unchecked, untethered. He carried those scars deeper than any blade had ever touched.

And now, they'd given him this assignment.

At first, he thought it was a soft posting. A slow descent into irrelevance. Go speak with the teens. Keep them calm. Observe. Recruit and assess if possible.

But then it all clicked into place.

It happened the moment Rupart stepped onto the transport, the copper doors sealing behind him with a hiss of pressure and finality. The air inside was still, quiet, too heavy with expectation to feel like a normal assignment.

Waiting for him on the central bench was a sealed case of dark wood. Inside was the truth, or at least the closest thing to it that the Unbound Kingdom had been able to gather.

The documents were dense. A mountain of reports and classified maps. They didn't start with names. They started with a moment.

The prophecy.

Rupart had heard it too, just like every trained Mind Mage in the kingdom, those sensitive enough to feel when the old magic stirred. Months ago, something had rippled across the leylines, and with it came those strange, echoing words. Words burned into dreams. Words no one could explain. He had woken with a pressure behind his eyes, a whisper of something that he didn't understand.

Until now.

Because here, inside that case, were the missing pieces.

There were reports from Red Canyon Outpost, accounts of ancient ruins discovered beneath a rise known as the Red

Mound, a place not marked on a formal map. Sketches of a strange, isolated mausoleum, standing alone in the wilderness like a forgotten sentinel.

There were testimonies from scouts and field Mages who had tried to approach the site and been repelled by unseen forces. Decoded messages from the Copper Network, filled with frantic speculation and diagrams. Transcripts from Ardent Crown agents, redacted but still pulsing with urgency, each one referring to a convergence, a location, a pair.

A pair.

Two figures. Possibly adolescents. Or possibly young women. That had been the initial theory.

Needles in a kingdom-wide haystack.

Until the report came in from Greyfen.

It wasn't just the rescue of the women and children that drew attention; it was the precision, the power.

When they debriefed the Police Captain, he mentioned the two who had led the effort.

"Finn and Cass," he said. "New to the city. Only been here a couple of months. Young. But awakened. Real Mages. Being trained by five."

They thought it was too perfect.

Five instructors. Two teens. A sudden appearance from nowhere.

Rupart had frozen when he read that part.

There they were, right in the center of it all. The names of every piece of evidence seemed to rotate around, even when it didn't say so directly.

Finn and Cass.

And just like that, the whispers from the prophecy weren't random anymore.

They could be real.

These children are not anomalies, he realized. They are a lynchpin. A pressure point on which multiple kingdoms are now balancing. And they had only traveled a few days from the site.

What had started as a gentle assignment had become something much larger. He was not just observing a pair of teenagers.

He was standing in the presence of an inflection point.

And they were staring back at him like they already knew everything and had expected this conversation at some point.

"Hello, Finn. Cass," the man said, voice calm and deliberate. "My name is Rupart. It's good to meet you both."

He didn't rise. Didn't extend a hand.

He simply remained seated at the stone bench, his back resting against the warehouse wall, posture relaxed. There were other benches, enough for everyone, but Finn and Cass stayed standing.

They didn't want to sit.

So they didn't.

"Hello," Finn replied, polite but guarded.

Cass said nothing. Her eyes stayed locked on Rupart, unreadable. Calculating. Like she was staring at a beast that she knew would attack at some point.

A hunter, Rupart thought. She's a natural one. And right now, I'm her prey.

The silence stretched.

"I'm not here to harm you," Rupart said at last. "In fact, I'm here because of what you did. Rescuing those women and children. That action gave us our first real break. We've been tracking disappearances like that across the southern Unbound territories for a month now."

"No problem," Finn said. "It was the right thing to do."

Rupart nodded. "Yes. It was."

Another beat passed.

Then, gently: "You know we wouldn't hurt you, right?"

Cass's eyes narrowed slightly. Finn's brow furrowed.

"What do you mean?" Finn asked.

Rupart's voice didn't change, but something behind his gaze shifted, just slightly sharper now. "We think we know who you are. Who you truly are."

He let the words hang for a moment.

"I just wanted you to hear it from me: we won't hurt you. If anything, we want to help you grow. To become stronger."

Cass's lips tightened. "So we can work as puppets for your government?"

Rupart didn't flinch. But he noted it.

My government, he thought. Not 'ours.' So they're not native to the Kingdom after all.

"No," he said. "If you two are who we believe you are, then there's no way we could control you. Nor would we try."

He leaned back just slightly.

"If anything, we'd offer resources. Training. Information. Whatever you need to accomplish your goals. We wouldn't dictate them. We'd just try to help you get there."

He paused, studying their faces.

"If you are who we think you are."

Cass didn't blink. "And if we're not?"

Rupart smiled faintly. "Then you're still the ones who saved a bunch of women and children. And that's enough for me to show you respect."

In a million years, Finn and Cass would not have expected this approach.

They had braced themselves for an ambush, a blade in the dark, or some carefully worded threat wrapped in diplomacy.

That was how Elarith usually dealt with people like them: unpredictable, powerful, unclaimed.

But instead, they found this.

An old man. Calm. Calculating, yes, but not manipulative. Cunning, but strangely… honest.

Rupart made no demands, no claims of authority. He had come offering help.

The teens stood in silence, weighing the moment.

Eventually, Cass turned, her eyes shifting back to the teachers near the wall.

"What do you think?" she asked.

The tension in the room loosened.

One by one, the five teachers stepped forward, their presence steady, solid, grounding.

Thomas was the first to speak. "We talked it over last night. Whatever you decide, we're with you."

"You can stay here," he continued, "and we'll keep sparring. Training. Just like we have been, though we all know none of us can push you anymore."

There was no bitterness in his voice. Only pride.

"Or," he added, "if you decide to run… We'll go with you."

Bruce, leaning against the weapon rack, rolled his eyes. "Oh yes. Camping in the wild. So much fun."

Finn snorted unexpectedly and immediately regretted it. Cass shot him a look, but the corner of her mouth twitched.

The moment broke the tension like sunlight through fog.

Harlen stepped forward. "And if you decide to work with Rupart here, we'll still be at your side. He spoke to us last night, told us we could remain as your guards. Not that you need us."

Cass let out a slow breath and finally moved.

She walked to the stone bench and sat down, with her back to Rupart.

Finn didn't miss the meaning. Neither did Rupart.

She was making a very clear statement.

I'm not afraid of you.

Rupart's eyes narrowed slightly, not with suspicion, but with intrigue.

Neither of them fears me, he thought. Not even a little. That either makes them incredibly foolish, which all reports say they are not, or… they're confident they could end me before I drew breath.

The thought didn't trouble him.

It fascinated him.

Finn nodded once, eyes steady.

"Okay," he said. "Let's talk."

He turned to Rupart, his voice calm but direct. "What do you want from us?"

Rupart folded his hands in his lap, thoughtful. "First," he said, "I'd like to hear your story. Just to be sure I'm speaking to the real Twin Stones."

That landed like a stone in still water.

Cass's posture didn't change, but her chin dipped, just slightly. Finn's jaw set. Neither said a word, but their silence was enough.

Confirmation.

Rupart had named them, not just as people, but as something more. Something only the deepest records, oldest myths, and most tightly held intelligence reports had hinted at.

He watched the shift in their eyes. The way Cass didn't look surprised, only resolved. The way Finn's breathing didn't spike, but settled.

There it is, Rupart thought. No flinch. No denial. No confusion. I've found them.

His shoulders eased, just a little.

There was no doubt for him now.
The prophecy was real.
And it was sitting in front of him.

CHAPTER 27

Origins

Rupart didn't speak.

He simply sat, still as stone, his hands folded loosely in his lap, his posture open but unassuming. No questions. Or prompting. Just quiet, patient attention.

Cass and Finn exchanged a glance.

Then, after a breath, Finn sat down beside her on the bench.

The teachers followed suit, circling the stone table Cam had shaped earlier that morning. It felt strange, almost ceremonial, how they all found their places without a word. As the teens sat down, Rupart began to use his abilities to encourage the teens to share. Nothing too invasive, just a light nudge. They had kept this to themselves for far too long, and the world needed answers.

Finn felt the need to share. But didn't know where to start. So he started at the beginning. "We're from Elarith."

The words landed like a hammer.

The teachers straightened, glancing at each other. That small detail shifted everything they thought they knew about the teens in front of them. But no one interrupted.

Rupart didn't react.

Not in surprise, anyway. His only response was a faint narrowing of his eyes, as if confirming something he had already suspected.

Cass picked up the thread. They didn't give precise details, just that they had traveled to a small, broken place called Varnhollow, a town they had been told was destroyed in a raid by the Unbound Kingdom. At this point, Finn glared at Rupart as if accusing him of the attack.

Rupart could feel the anger and confusion from the teenagers at this point.

There, they found two stones and a handful of documents.

Rupart's expression didn't change, but the energy around him shifted. He leaned in just slightly, as though the word documents had plucked a chord inside his skull.

He said nothing.

Not yet.

One of the documents, Cass explained, spoke of a Wild Awakening Circle, hidden far to the north. They didn't want to go to one of the formal circles in the cities. They didn't trust the King. His failure to act, or worse, his willingness to allow destruction, had cost them both their parents.

Rupert had noted the dislike for the King of Elarith, which made him like them a little more.

They had chosen to awaken alone.

They skipped the details of the journey. Just said it was long and hard. They mentioned the danger in passing, like travelers commenting on the weather.

They did not speak of the awakening itself.

Rupart nearly twitched.

He didn't interrupt, but his fingers pressed just a little more tightly together. His eyes locked on Finn. Then Cass. He heard the absence of that part of the story like a scream behind a closed door.

"And then we found…" Finn hesitated, searching for the word.

Cass finished it. "The mausoleum."

Rupart blinked slowly. The mausoleum?

That word rolled through his head like thunder. Not a ruin. Not a vault. A mausoleum. It confirmed something. Solved a riddle he hadn't even told them he was holding.

Cass continued. "We stayed the night. Left the next day. And came here."

No details.

Not about what was inside. Not about what they felt. Not about what changed in them after that night.

It was deliberate.

And it drove Rupart mad.

He kept his mouth shut, barely.

So many pieces were clicking into place. So many whispers, half-truths, and fragments of the prophecy suddenly made sense.

And still… They said so little.

Finn leaned back slightly. "That's it," he said. "That's the story."

Rupart exhaled slowly through his nose.

And smiled.

"Thank you," he said, voice dry. "That was… very helpful."

And very, very incomplete.

But enough to confirm everything.

He had found the Twin Stones. And they were sitting across the table, perfectly aware of how much they were choosing not to tell him.

Rupart was still.

Outwardly, he offered only a calm nod, the slight tilt of his head betraying nothing.

But inwardly, he was spiraling.

He had a thousand questions. A thousand. His mind raced through everything they hadn't said: what stones they found, what affinity they awakened, what was inside the mausoleum, what happened in the circle, what happened to them.

He wanted to press. He wanted to dig. He wanted to ask-

But he didn't.

He was not new to this.

So he stayed still. Focused. Measured.

His skills told him they were being honest. There were no spikes of guilt in their tone. No tells in their bodies. The story was true. But it was deliberately incomplete.

He nodded again, slowly.

Then asked, carefully, "Why did you stay in Greyfen?"

Finn didn't hesitate.

"We need to train," he said plainly. "We need to get stronger."

Cass added nothing. She didn't need to. The conviction in Finn's voice spoke for them both.

Finn continued, "We also need to return to the mausoleum. Nine months from now. That's how long we were told to wait. If we travel further from it now, it'll just take longer to get back when the time comes."

Rupart's eyes sharpened slightly.

They're counting down.

Someone told them to return in a year.

They're waiting for something else to happen.

Something that only happens when the year is complete.

He folded his hands once more, concealing his growing

urgency beneath a layer of polite approval.

"I see," he said, voice even. "That makes sense."

But inside, Rupart, Mind Mage of the Unbound Kingdom, secret-keeper and agent, was already revising every timeline, every report, every theory.

Nine months.

Nine months until something happens at the mausoleum.

And now he knew the most important truth of all:

They were preparing for it.

This shocked him.

Of all the things Rupart had prepared for, this wasn't on the list.

His training had covered a thousand contingencies, lies, half-truths, emotional manipulation, and even magical deception. He'd studied the behavioral reports, the prophecy translations that still didn't quite agree with each other.

But nowhere had it said anything about the Twin Stones returning to the site.

Why? he thought, his mind racing. Why return to the mausoleum? What happens there? What's waiting?

He kept his expression still.

His answers would come in time. He reminded himself of that. They were speaking to him now. Trusting him, even in pieces. He couldn't push too hard. Not yet.

So instead, he took a breath, reset the moment, and asked simply:

"So you're here to train."

He nodded toward the center of the warehouse, where dust still showed signs of yesterday's sparring match.

"Do you want to get started?"

The teens paused. Cass blinked.

"Really?" she said, voice tinged with cautious disbelief. "You're going to let us practice?"

Rupart gave a half-smile. "I'm not going to let you do anything."

His tone remained neutral, even relaxed.

"You do what you want. I'm just grateful you took a break to speak with me."

That brought both of them up short.

It wasn't what they expected, not from someone sent by a kingdom, not from someone who called them The Twin Stones.

There was no command in his voice. No hook behind the words.

Just… respect.

Finn nodded slowly. "Okay."

He stepped toward the center of the floor.

"Let's get to it."

What followed was the most awe-inspiring one-sided sparring match Rupart had ever witnessed.

He had watched battles between masters, seen duels that split earth and created a tsunami of fire, but nothing prepared him for this.

It began with five grown Mages stepping onto the warehouse floor: Thomas, Sparky, Cam, Harlen, and Bruce, each a veteran, each trained, experienced, and dangerous in their own right.

Finn stood alone.

Cass leaned back on the bench, arms folded, watching. Calm. Unworried.

It started fast.

Fire and ice flew in from opposite ends, Bruce and Harlen working in tandem. Cam launched stone disks like blades. At the same time, Thomas darted in low, aiming for joints, back of the knees, the ribs, solar plexus; each strike meant to stagger, to fold Finn inward. Sparky came in from behind, a full-bodied rush aimed at locking Finn in a wrestling hold, the kind meant to end a fight fast.

But Finn didn't move like a boy.

He moved like a force.

The moment the first attack hit, nothing appeared to happen. The fire and ice dissolved in the air around him in a way that Rupart couldn't understand. The ground attacks collapsed before getting close to Finn.

Thomas's quick jabs? Absorbed. Deflected. Dodged without effort.

Sparky managed to grab his arm, just for a second. Then Finn pulled it free, effortlessly. The kind of effortlessness that shouldn't be possible against the grip of an Iron Mage.

He didn't strike back.

That's what unsettled Rupart the most.

He didn't hit them. Didn't retaliate. Didn't counter.

He simply took the hits; most of the teachers' blows landed, but it didn't faze him. None of their holds stuck, none of their attacks even broke his rhythm.

It was like watching children wrestle their father. Desperate, chaotic, trying their best, while the father tried not to hurt them.

No vulnerabilities, Rupart thought. None that I can see.

And worse, he could tell Finn was holding back.

Not just physically. Energetically. His aura was dimmed, muted. He wasn't reaching. He was simply responding.

Even the ground obeyed him.

Rupart sat motionless, hands folded, his thoughts racing.

And this is only one of them.

Finn was solid, stoic, and held in restraint, then Cass was something else entirely, something colder, sharper, and refined.

Rupart had barely recovered from watching Finn when the instructors turned to face her.

She didn't flinch. She didn't take a stance.

She just stood there, arms crossed, calm, eyes unreadable.

Then the first attack came.

A flameburst from Bruce meant to test reflexes. An ice dart from Harlen, designed to pierce shields. Cam followed with a wall of jagged stone that surged up from the ground, meant to box her in.

And then, they appeared.

Her shields.

Rupart's jaw went slack. All his restraint was forgotten in the moment.

He'd been told about them the night before, half-distracted, sipping tea, listening to the instructors describe them as "efficient" and "cutting." He hadn't expected this.

They weren't just defenses.

They were beautiful to look at.

Each shield shimmered like a cut diamond, spinning slightly at the edges, refracting light as if they'd been carved by an expert jeweler. They formed instantly, without a word, without visible effort, and they did not break.

The fire and ice died against the shields.

Cam's wall was split clean down the center with one slow, silent sweep of a blade-edged barrier.

Sparky, eager and grinning, tried to rush her, wrap her in one of the classic crushing holds.

Cass didn't move.

Two of her shields manifested mid-air, pressing outward from her back like wings, slamming Sparky's arms apart in opposite directions. He stumbled, frozen in the absurd position, arms wide like a scarecrow, eyes wide with disbelief.

Thomas tried to flank her, smart, tactical.

But one of her shields moved.

Rupart nearly stood.

It wasn't static; it was tracking Thomas step for step, sliding just fast enough to cut off every angle of approach. Every time he shifted, it pressed closer. Not attacking, just… nudging. Until Thomas, a seasoned combatant, was backing up, pushed by the thing he couldn't hurt.

At the far edge of the warehouse, Cam tried to create another stone wall, taller and reinforced.

Cass's shield spun forward, faster this time, and carved through it like air.

And through it all, Cass never moved.

She stood there with her arms still folded, expression neutral, just watching her teachers struggle.

She wasn't just holding her own.

She was demonstrating control.

Mastery.

And not once, not even once, had she used her full strength, or did she attack her teacher. She just boxed them in.

Rupart exhaled, slow and shallow.

They're not just powerful, he thought.

They're beyond anything we've seen before.

These kids are monsters already, and they have only just awakened.

That was the word that kept repeating in Rupart's mind, no matter how he tried to dress it up with better language. Not beasts. Not threats. Monsters, in the most terrifying, awe-inspiring sense of the word.

He had watched Finn collapse the earth and take hits from five trained Mages without effort, without aggression, just strength. He had seen Cass divide the world into geometry and blade, tracking them like prey, her shields moving with the precision of thought.

These weren't new recruits.

They were growing beyond the scale of sparring mats and warm-up drills.

And the teachers knew it.

Rupart glanced at Harlen, Bruce, Cam, the sweat on their brows, the disbelief buried behind practiced stoicism. They were proud, yes. But they knew fighting their students was going to be too hard sooner or later.

They were no longer enough.

Rupart's hands tightened in his lap.

They need more.

They needed to be tested against generals, against war-born Mages who had stood on battlefields and bled power, not just shaped it. They needed formations thrown at them. Barrages. Real combat, not friendly duels.

They needed to be tested by an army.

If the prophecy was true, then they needed to be a lot better prepared than this.

They won't grow any more here, Rupart thought. Not without limits. Not without risk. Not without fire that could actually burn them.

CHAPTER 28

Leak

After the sparring ended, the warehouse slowly settled into silence. The teachers, Harlen, Cam, Bruce, Thomas, and Sparky, stood in a loose half-circle, panting and sweat-soaked, bent slightly forward with hands on knees or hips, catching their breath. Their pride remained intact, but it was clear: they had given everything.

Cass and Finn?

They looked exactly as they had when they walked in.

Not smug. Not boastful. Just… a little bored.

Rupart stepped forward from the edge of the room, folding his hands behind his back. His voice was quiet, but it carried easily in the still air.

"It's obvious that you're very powerful," he said. "And that your teachers have done an excellent job guiding you."

He paused, letting the weight of the moment settle.

"But I think you're both ready for something more. A greater challenge."

The teens looked at each other and nodded without a word.

The teachers did the same, though it came with a small, tired groan from Sparky, who muttered something about needing three days of sleep.

Rupart smiled faintly.

"I can help with that," he continued. "The only question is how."

He turned toward them fully now.

Rupert decided internally that taking them to the Red Canyon fort would cause more problems with it becoming an international hub.

"Would you prefer that we bring in new instructors here, Mages with specialties, backgrounds in warfare, and command? Or..." He let the pause land gently. "Would you rather come to Stonehollow and train with them at the academy directly?"

He raised a hand before they could answer.

"Let me be clear, no matter which path you choose, we'll arrange for the best to teach you. The very best. The Mage training school in Stonehollow is state-of-the-art. Its instructors include some of the most powerful and experienced battle Mages in the Kingdom."

He looked between Cass and Finn, then back to the teachers.

"This is an invitation. You choose."

Then softer, more personal:

"Whichever path you take, you won't be walking it alone."

Cass looked at Finn, then gave a small shrug, the kind that said, *I'm fine either way. You choose.*

Finn nodded once, then turned his gaze to Rupart.

There was no hostility in his expression, but there was no

softness either. Just calm clarity. Weight behind the words he was about to say.

"Listen," Finn began, his voice even. "I know you said you don't mean us harm. And I believe you."

He took a breath, eyes not leaving Rupart's.

"But I feel like I need to stress something, for your sake."

The room quieted again. The teachers, still catching their breath, looked up.

"This isn't a threat," Finn said. "I'm not warning you. I'm just trying to explain what I've figured out… so you don't misunderstand who you're working with."

He glanced around the warehouse.

"I can do a lot of damage in a city," he said. "Without trying to."

No one interrupted.

"I haven't really tried to destroy anything," Finn continued. "But I know that it's easier for me to flatten a large area than it is to control a small one. I don't know why. That's just how it feels when I use my magic. The bigger the space… the easier it is."

He shifted his stance slightly, not defensive, just honest.

"I know that probably sounds strange. But the only way to prove it would be to do something I don't want to do. And that would end badly. For everyone."

A pause.

"So just… trust me when I say this: my challenge hasn't been force. It's been restraint."

There was no boast in his tone.

Just the quiet burden of someone who understood what he could break, and chose not to.

Rupart nodded slowly, his expression unreadable, but behind his eyes, a thousand thoughts stirred.

He could feel it, deep in his mind, where his talents worked in quiet, precise ways. Finn hadn't been bluffing. That strange, heavy sensation he had picked up earlier, the ambient weight around the boy's presence confirmed it. Finn's control over a small area was very strong, so if he believed that wide-area magic was easier, then he must be much stronger than he thought.

Finn believed everything he said was true.

That was a significant datapoint, one Rupart filed away with care. It would be in his report. Must be. That wasn't just power; it was scale. And that changed everything.

Finn looked at Cass, who gave another small shrug, but this time it was different. Resigned. Accepting.

"Alright," Finn said, turning back to Rupart. "We'll go to Stonehollow."

Cass nodded beside him. "We might as well see what it has to offer."

A ripple passed through the room.

Thomas leaned back, exhaling. "Well… It's been a long time since I've seen the capital."

Cam nodded. "Could be good to stretch the legs."

Bruce muttered, "At least we might get better food."

Even Sparky grinned. "I want to see if those academy Mages are as tough as they think."

They were all in.

Rupart allowed himself a small smile. "Then I'll make the arrangements. We'll leave tomorrow. I'll summon the transportation right after this."

The teachers exchanged glances, each quietly processing what they were walking into.

They would go with the teens. Of course they would. But deep down, all of them were thinking the same thing.

We hope we don't regret this.

When the teenagers returned to their rented house, two guards were stationed just outside the door.

Both wore normal street clothes, but they were alert and trying not to look like they were watching the most powerful Mages the Hollow Realm had ever seen.

Rupart had told them it was for their protection.

They didn't argue. They didn't care.

If anything, the guards weren't there to protect them from danger.

They were there to keep track of the teens.

Cass gave the guards a polite nod as they entered. Finn didn't say a word.

Inside, the house was quiet. The same worn table, the folded blankets, the gear they hadn't used in weeks. They began packing with silent efficiency. Their needs were few: some clothes, a blade, and the maps they hadn't needed but had kept anyway.

The transport car would arrive in the morning.

When their bags were light and ready, they left the house and made their way to the estate of Lord Brenrick.

The noble opened the door himself, surprised and smiling, with his butler looking nonplused behind him. "I wasn't expecting you tonight."

"We just wanted to thank you," Cass said. "For the room. For everything."

Finn stepped forward and pulled a small object from his coat, another pre-split gold coin; its surface looked almost new, its weight unmistakable.

Brenrick's eyes widened.

"I'd like to buy it from you," he offered instinctively.

But Finn shook his head. "No. It's a gift."

Cass added, "It's yours. You've been kind to us, and we won't forget it."

The lord accepted it slowly, almost reverently. "Then I thank you. Deeply."

"We're leaving tomorrow," Finn said simply.

Brenrick gave a small nod. "The city will miss you. Know you will always have a home here."

They smiled at that.

From there, they made their way to the tavern, the one where they had first met Harlen, back when this all felt new, and uncertain, and the world didn't yet feel like it was watching their every move.

The food was warm. The people are familiar. Laughter floated around them from other tables, but they didn't join in. Not fully. They sat at the table they always sat at, sharing the same meal they'd ordered on that first day.

Cass took a slow sip of her drink and glanced around the room.

"I'm going to miss this place."

Finn nodded. "Yeah. Me too."

Tomorrow, they will leave Greyfen behind.

But tonight, they let themselves feel something simple:

Gratitude.

After the "practice," Rupart sat alone in the private study granted to him by Greyfen's city officials.

The oil lamp flickered low, casting long shadows across the scrolls and notes scattered on the desk. He leaned back in the chair, fingers steepled, mind still echoing with the image of crystalline blades from Cass and ground-warping pressure waves from Finn.

Across from him stood Georgi, a junior Copper Mage and Rupart's assigned communications officer, waiting with quill and parchment.

"Send this using the highest encryption protocol we have,"

Rupart said, his voice low and firm. "We cannot let this leak."

Georgi nodded and began transcribing.

But Rupart knew better than to hope for secrecy.

Important messages always draw attention.

And this one... was very important.

He labeled the transmission simply:

Subject: Twin Stones – Confirmed Identification | En Route to Stonehollow

The contents were precise, clinical, and heavy with implications:

Subjects Identified: Finn and Cass.

Status: Confirmed awakened. Extreme power differential.

Training: Under five advanced Mages, now significantly outclassing all instructors.

Site Connection: Referred to the "mausoleum" structure in Red Canyon.

They were directed to return to the site in 9 months (1 year post-awakening). Reason unknown.

Observed Abilities: Large-scale gravitational and crystalline manipulation. Destruction and shielding potential-territory-class.

Recommendation: Extreme caution. Direct control is not advised. Facilitation preferred.

The report was encrypted and sent on the Kingdom's copper-thread communication network designed for instant delivery to High Command.

But by the time Georgi had returned to his bunk, the message had already been noticed by other powers.

Spies embedded deep within the Unbound High Command read and copied it. The contents of this message were important enough to risk getting caught and executed.

By morning, the Copper Network, the Ardent Crown, the Dark

Circle, and the Saphrellian Sanctum all knew the same truth:

The Twin Stones had been found.

And they were moving them to Stonehollow.

By morning, four powers, each with different motives, fears, and hopes, knew the same truth.

The game had changed.

CHAPTER 29

Triggers

That morning, just after dawn, Finn and Cass slung their light packs over their shoulders and began the quiet walk through Greyfen's quarter.

Their path took them along still-sleeping streets, past shuttered windows and fading lanterns. The sky above was pale with morning, the air crisp. They moved guards, but without fanfare, just two figures heading toward a new chapter, unaware that the world had already begun to shift beneath their feet.

Because while they walked, messages were already flying across the continent.

By the time their boots touched the cobbled approach to the transport station, three of the world's greatest powers, Saphrelle, the Ardent Crown, and the Copper Network's High Seat, had already sent official communiqués to the Unbound Kingdom's inner council.

Each had the same request:

Access to the Twin Stones.

To speak with, teach, observe, and possibly influence them.

In Stonehollow, the diplomatic wings of the capital were already swamped, runners pacing the halls, scrolls flying between towers, ministers arguing over protocol and privilege. The sudden flood of attention had caught even seasoned advisors off guard.

But it was the Security Office that was in true crisis.

Someone had leaked the report. And not just a hint or a whisper, the full contents.

"How?" the Director of Internal Affairs demanded, her hands trembling above a pile of scorched paper. "How did three separate powers receive knowledge of an encrypted Level Seven communication within six hours?"

There were no answers. Just rising panic.

Meanwhile, at the Mage Academy, preparations had already begun.

The entire student body was sent home, at least temporarily. Minor instructors were dismissed. Training courts were cleared. And the cleaning and rebuilding efforts were ordered to reinforce the training grounds. They wanted to make sure that the space the students would practice in was as strong as possible. By all reports, it would need to be.

They didn't know what was coming.

They just knew two awakened individuals were arriving who would use the training yards in privacy, and they took priority over the entire student population.

◆ ◆ ◆

The Dark Circle was already in motion.

The moment the message reached Velmirath, whispers of the Twin Stones confirmed, and en route to Stonehollow, the order went out.

"Activate every embedded agent. Whether they were or were not the twin stones, they could not survive."

In less than an hour, a dozen sleeper cells inside the capital came awake, one by one. Shopkeepers, porters, stablehands, and quiet observers, all seemingly ordinary citizens, slipped into new roles. Blades were retrieved. Hidden caches opened. Identities burned.

Half were given one task: assassinate.

The other half: burn, destroy, and cause chaos.

The edict was clear.

The Twin Stones cannot be allowed to survive.

Sacrifice every agent if necessary.

A plan was already in motion.

Outside Stonehollow, just west of the outer walls, a section of the copper transport rail had been rigged with explosives.

Cause chaos.

Create confusion.

And in that chaos, they would strike.

If the rail was bombed just before the transport arrived, the resulting panic would fracture response lines, pull guards from their posts, scatter any magical response, and give just enough of an opening for the Circle's infiltrators to close in.

Meanwhile, street vendors across the lower wards were no longer selling bread and baubles. Their carts were weighted with hidden compartments. Others housed short-blade assassins trained to strike the moment the targets passed within reach.

Even members of the capital's own security force had been quietly activated, agents who had waited years for the call. Their weapons were already coated with fast-acting poison. Their orders were clear:

If you can get close, don't hesitate. Even a single wound might be enough.

The Dark Circle was not interested in secrecy anymore.

They wanted finality.

And if it costs them every agent in the capital, so be it.

Better to burn a city than let the prophecy live.

The transport car arrived just over an hour after sunrise, its copper frame humming softly as it rolled into Greyfen's eastern platform. Sunlight gleamed off its smooth curves and broad glass windows, casting long reflections across the cobbled streets.

It wasn't opulent in the way palaces were; it wasn't gilded or gaudy, but there was a subtle, quiet precision to its craftsmanship. The benches were wood, finely sanded and oiled, not designed for comfort but sturdy and new. The cabin walls were paneled with reinforced copper alloy, and the glass gave an uninterrupted view of the world beyond.

To the people of Greyfen, it was a sign of the world changing.

The whole city seemed to be there, lining the streets and crowding the platform, murmuring in wonder. Why were these two teenagers allowed to take the first car to Stonehollow? Speculation turned to celebration when the door sealed shut and the car began to move.

Cheers erupted, makeshift flags waved, and the sound of the city's joy trailed after them as the transport glided forward, smooth as sliding on ice. So smooth, in fact, that it unsettled the passengers for a moment. The motion was seamless, almost frictionless. It took a few minutes before any of them relaxed into it.

The front cabin held a Water Mage, focused on cooling the rail ahead, creating a slick, gliding surface of magically controlled condensation. In the rear cabin, a Fire Mage applied heat to the rail behind, creating a temperature differential that propelled the car forward in short pulses of force.

Slowly, gracefully, the speed increased.

The trees fell away below them. Birds scattered. The air grew thinner and clearer. Before long, they were gliding just above the treetops, moving faster than any horse could run.

Inside, Finn and Cass sat together, quiet and alert. They didn't speak much. They didn't need to. Around them, the teachers spoke in low tones, Thomas reviewing the day's plans, Cam gazing out the window with a distant look. The guards remained stoic, stationed near the windows, eyes sharp.

At midday, Rupart gave a nod, and one of his Copper aides pulled out a simple but well-packed meal: water, fresh bread, dried meat, cheese, and preserved berries, all neatly arranged for the group to share. They passed it around in quiet gratitude, the soft sounds of chewing the only break in the hush.

Then, in the mid-afternoon, someone whispered-

"There it is."

And there it was.

Stonehollow.

It rose in the distance, ringed by immense walls. At the heart of the city, high on a central hill, stood a massive castle, sharp-edged and dignified, with towers piercing the sky.

Surrounding it were hundreds of spires, chimneys, and towers, competing for airspace and grandeur. Flags fluttered from rooftops. Smoke curled lazily from forges and hearths. The city teemed with life, structure, and intent.

It was larger than anything Finn or Cass had ever seen.

From their vantage, they could see the sprawl, tens of thousands of buildings, maybe more. Stonehollow wasn't just a city. It was a world. A hub of power, knowledge, and danger.

And they were heading straight for its heart.

Just as the Water Mage and Fire Mage shifted positions, preparing to slow the car for its final descent into Stonehollow's transportation platform, the world exploded.

There was no warning.

Just a deafening boom and a wall of flames that swallowed the sky.

For one brief, blinding instant, the entire transport car was consumed, glass and wood igniting in a roar of heat as copper rails below liquefied, unable to withstand the blast. The world vanished beneath them.

Cass didn't think.

She acted.

In the same breath, the car began to collapse; she snapped into existence a massive pentagonal prism, its sides as long as the car itself, a shimmering, razor-edged structure of translucent crystal, snapping into place like a diamond coffin. The prism sliced through steel, benches, and wall panels without resistance, sealing the entire group within its indestructible embrace.

Wood splintered.

Metal warped.

Outside, everything fell.

Inside, there was silence.

At the same time, Finn's instinct took hold as soon as the car began to fall. He didn't cast. He didn't even think about it. He simply caught them in mid-air.

A gravity field burst outward, wrapping the capsule of crystal like an invisible cushion, suspending them in midair as the car and rails were vaporized beneath them.

Below, the destruction was near total.

A section of the rail, part of the city wall, and the platform edge were gone, reduced to molten slag and crumbling stone. The copper, once gleaming, had flowed like wax into the ravine beneath the tracks.

For a few seconds, smoke obscured everything.

Then, as the dust began to clear, onlookers gasped.

Floating above the devastation, impossibly untouched, was a shimmering, glass-like prism, suspended in the air, radiant in the sun.

Inside it, still seated, were Finn, Cass, their teachers, the guards, and Rupart, shielded by Cass's construct and held aloft by Finn's gravity.

From the outside, it looked as though the transport car had never exploded inside the prism, the passengers still sitting upright on benches, surrounded by carved crystal instead of copper.

Witnesses would later say it looked like nothing they had ever seen. Like they were flying in a crystal tube.

But inside the shield, Finn and Cass sat completely still, hearts pounding, breath measured.

They had survived.

Inside the car, Rupart had been reviewing the arrival plan.

His mind was on the High Council building, the escort that would be waiting, the name of the captain he'd been told to remember, what was it again? Vareen? Vardon?

Then the world exploded.

A detonation louder than thunder. Light and heat that tore through the sky. The unmistakable sensation of the car being lifted and ripped apart. And in that split second of chaos, Rupart's heart stopped.

He had been caught completely by surprise.

His worst nightmare, the one he never allowed himself to imagine, had come true.

Of course they would bomb the rail, he thought, dazed, horrified. It was obvious. Why didn't I see it? How could I have been so stupid.

He believed he'd gotten them killed.

And then, everything went silent.

Like a door slamming between worlds.

Outside: flames, molten copper, falling stone.

Inside: everyone was safe. And the chaos outside was muted.

The crushing fall halted as if caught by unseen hands. The smoke, the roar, the collapse, gone. For a moment, the only sound inside the crystal prism was the collective gasp, the quick yell, the sudden inhale of the occupants.

Rupart gripped the bench with white knuckles, eyes wide. His chest heaved. He felt like he'd been punched in the ribs.

But no one was hurt.

He looked around, and everyone was alive.

They hovered for a heartbeat, suspended in the air like a floating miracle.

Then Finn stood.

He turned toward the gaping hole ahead, the shattered section of Stonehollow's wall, the now ruined entry where the rail should've continued through to the platform beyond.

"Hold on," he said. His voice was calm but strained. "I've never done this before. And it's taking everything I have just to keep us still."

The crystal tube lurched forward, a sudden, jarring movement that made several people stumble. Then it slowed. Then it jerked again.

Forward. Stop. Forward. Stop.

Each push and pause cost Finn more. Sweat lined his brow. His arms trembled.

Cass sat frozen, not looking at the wall, not looking at the platform. Her eyes were locked on the floor, unfocused, seeing something no one else could.

She was holding the shield together. She didn't blink. Didn't breathe. If her concentration cracked for even a second, the shield would shatter, and the people inside would all drop like stone.

At last, the prism touched down.

It wasn't graceful. It was uneven, shaky, and the last few feet were dragging.

But they made it.

The platform rail beyond the wall held.

The side of the crystalline tube disappeared, and Cass, still staring straight ahead, murmured:

"Get off. Now."

Everyone obeyed at once.

The teachers scrambled out, guards following. Rupart stumbled, caught by Thomas at the last second. One by one, they cleared the capsule, stepping onto solid stone with shaking legs.

Finn, exhausted, reached down and pulled Cass gently to her feet, and picked up her pack. Her knees buckled for just a moment, but she held firm as they walked off the platform together.

The moment their feet touched the ground-

-The shield vanished.

In a sudden crash of noise, all the benches, luggage, and broken halves of the transport car that had been caught mid-destruction clattered to the platform like debris shaken loose from a forgotten world.

The crowd that had gathered, guards, officials, and civilians from the outer ward, stood in stunned silence.

And in the center of it all, Finn and Cass walked forward, alive, quiet, and entirely unchanged.

CHAPTER 30

One Sided

In the aftermath of the blast, chaos reigned.

Security teams from Stonehollow raced up the broken transport line, shouting, weapons drawn, eyes wide with confusion and urgency. But Rupart's personal guard, though shaken, held the line.

Their instincts, honed over years of protecting diplomats and Mages, kicked in hard; they formed a tight wall around Finn, Cass, and the rest of the survivors, keeping the swelling crowd and arriving soldiers at bay.

A quick headcount confirmed the unthinkable: everyone in their car had survived.

Everyone except the two Mages.

The Water Mage and Fire Mage, who had just entered their cabins moments before the blast, were gone. Vaporized in the initial firestorm.

A team of healers was waved through.

One of the guards, the young one stationed near the windows, sat pale on the edge of the platform. Blood pooled slowly beneath his boot.

Cass approached him, kneeling down. Her voice was low and sincere. "I'm sorry. I didn't realize the shield cut through-"

He waved her off with a weak smile.

"Nonsense, miss," he said. "You saved my life. This?" He nodded toward the bandage wrapping around the heel of his foot, where the razor edge of her shield had sliced clean through his shoe. "This is nothing. I'm lucky to be breathing."

Cass gave a faint, grateful smile, though her eyes were still heavy with guilt.

A moment later, one of the healers approached Finn.

"I'm fine," he said, raising his arms slightly. "No injuries here."

The healer nodded politely, stepped closer, and inspected him with clinical calm.

Then, like a whip-crack, the man lunged.

The blade glinted in the sun, a dagger, small and curved, aimed straight for Finn's ribs. It tore through his shirt and bit into his skin, but it didn't pierce.

The assassin's expression shifted from focus to shock.

So did Finn's.

The guards reacted instantly, weapons drawn.

But they weren't needed.

Finn didn't flinch.

He simply raised his hand, fingers pointed like a judge passing a sentence.

There was a sudden whump of displaced air, then the assassin was launched skyward so fast he left a blur behind him.

He screamed, arms and legs flailing as he rocketed higher and higher, until he was a speck against the blue sky.

Then, he was gone.

He never came back down.

The entire platform fell silent.

No one moved. No one spoke. The heat of the explosion still lingered in the air, and the witnesses were still in shock from seeing someone being launched into the air like that.

Harlen finally broke the silence, his voice low with awe.

"Cass… you created seven shields."

She looked at him, still kneeling by the injured guard.

Her voice was soft. "I didn't count."

"You're getting stronger," Harlen said.

Cass only nodded, eyes drifting out toward the scorched tracks.

"But we lost two Mages," she said. "That doesn't feel like a win."

A few minutes later, a team of guards escorted the survivors down the platform. A black carriage pulled by sleek, armored horses waited at the street.

As they stepped inside, Finn tugged at the torn fabric hanging from his ribs.

He looked down, sighed, and muttered, "I'm going to need another shirt."

And behind him, Bruce let out a quick chuckle.

The carriage ride through Stonehollow was not smooth.

The streets were paved in polished stone, the wheels greased, the horses well trained, but none of that mattered when people were trying to kill you.

They'd only been moving for ten minutes when the first bolt shattered a window.

It whistled through the air with deadly precision, a steel-tipped shaft glinting in the morning light, an Iron Mage Killer, designed to pierce magic-hardened flesh.

It slammed into Finn's shoulder, slicing through his coat and shattering against his skin. Finn yelled, "That hurt you, jerks!"

That was all Cass needed to hear.

She exhaled once, slow and deliberate, then raised her hand, and with a shimmer of refracted light, she conjured a simple crystalline box, clean-edged and seamless. It encompassed the entire carriage, horses, and driver included.

The next bolt, fired from a different rooftop, pinged off the shield with a dull, metallic clink and clattered harmlessly to the cobblestones.

Finn watched it fall and glanced through the crystalline walls, eyes scanning the direction it came from.

Each time a shot was fired, he noticed the same thing: guards sprinting toward the rooftops, coordinated and urgent. Someone in the city's watch was tracking these attacks in real-time.

But even so, they hadn't prevented them.

Inside the crystal box, the carriage rolled on, silent except for the rhythmic clatter of hooves and the occasional hiss of breath from Cass as she maintained the barrier.

"Let me know if you get tired," Finn said quietly.

Cass shook her head. "This one's just a shell. Easier than dancing around attacks."

He nodded once. "Still. Let me know."

Outside the walls of light, the city watched.

Some people gawked at the glowing box rolling down the avenue. Others hid from it.

Everyone knew now: the capital wasn't safe, and whoever was in the carriage was not normal.

Just as the carriage rounded the corner toward the High Command district, the street ended abruptly.

A wall of jagged stone erupted from the ground in front of them, earth magic, raw and unrefined, spiking outward like a barricade of fangs.

A second later, behind them, another wall slammed up, cutting them off from the following guards and their retreat.

They were trapped.

Inside the carriage, Cass didn't even flinch. Her shield pulsed faintly, holding firm. Finn sat forward, lips tightening.

"Cam," he said.

Already moving, Cam placed her hand to the floor of the carriage, her magic syncing with the stone. At the same moment, Finn stood, raised both hands, and exhaled.

The walls shuddered.

Then collapsed inward, like paper structures crushed by unseen pressure, falling in on themselves, their spikes dulling to dust in seconds.

The path was clear again, but the message was loud.

Finn glanced at Rupart, who had paled slightly.

"This isn't the welcome I was hoping for," Finn said, voice cool. "It was, however, the welcome I was afraid we were going to get."

Rupart's jaw clenched. "I can promise you, these are not our people."

"That may be so," Finn replied, his eyes never leaving the ruined road, "but it tells us something important."

He turned to look at Rupart fully now.

"You're not in full control of this city."

Rupart didn't answer at first.

Then reluctantly he nodded, "It appears you are correct."

After the second ambush, Finn sat back, thinking, not about fighting, but about movement.

He looked at Cass's crystalline shell, still shimmering faintly around the carriage like cut glass. It had held perfectly.

But something about being trapped, being forced to wait while others moved against them, scraped at him. It was the same feeling he'd had during the fall from the rail, the helplessness of being pinned.

So he tried something different.

Not a shield in the way, Cass made them. Hers were hard, radiant, beautiful, like walls sculpted by a jeweler.

His was… something else.

He closed his eyes and reached down, not to the earth, but beneath it, to that deep part of him that always knew where the pressure was, how heavy things should be, and how to shift them when they weren't right.

And then, quietly, he claimed the space around them.

A field formed, unseen but deeply felt. Not a wall, not a dome necessarily, a presence. Like the weight of a deep well pressing out from a central point. It radiated around the carriage, spreading in an oval shape that followed its every jolt and turn.

The horse felt it first. They jumped and lurched until the driver calmed them down.

Cass looked up and gave Finn a small, surprised glance. "That's you?"

He nodded. "I don't want us getting stuck in these streets again."

His "shield" wasn't impenetrable like hers. It didn't deflect or cut. But it was felt. Tangibly. As if the space itself resisted intrusion, a heaviness, a shifting of density, that made movement wrong for anything that didn't belong inside it.

The carriage rolled on, now wrapped in Cass's crystal and Finn's gravity well.

Together, they weren't just protected.

They were anchored, and they claimed the area around them as their territory.

And whatever lay ahead at the gates of High Command, they were going to meet it on their terms.

The carriage continued its slow, deliberate approach toward Stonehollow's inner tier, the magical shields still wrapped tight, Cass's crystalline shell glinting in the sun, and Finn's gravity field casting an unseen weight around them.

Inside, it was calm and silent.

The teachers were glancing at each other in amazement at what their young students were doing.

But outside, the city was moving.

Three more attacks happened, and almost no one inside the carriage noticed.

The most direct came just past a narrow alleyway, where ten men in plain clothes surged forward from both sides, blades in their hands.

They never made it to the carriage.

The moment they crossed into Finn's Well, they collapsed to the ground.

They couldn't breathe.

It was like stepping into deep water. Their legs buckled. The force pressing against their chests cracked ribs. Several fell instantly, coughing blood. Others clawed at the ground, trying to crawl out. None succeeded.

By the time the carriage rolled past, slow and steady, their own guards, trailing in formation, reached the alley and found ten men unconscious, barely alive, and gasping on the stones.

No one inside the carriage had reacted.

Except Rupart.

He had felt them coming, the surge of intent, and of approaching danger. He was just about to call out, to raise the alarm, when they collapsed.

Every one of them.

Crushed without a sound.

Rupart said nothing, but felt they were in immense pain.

He simply turned his head, watching the faint shimmer in the air around Finn, and felt a cold realization settle in his chest.

There was no visible effort. No motion. Just presence.

He didn't say a word aloud.

Just watched.

And wondered if Stonehollow was truly ready.

The city passed by in a blur of rooftops and rising towers, but the attacks kept coming, each more coordinated than the last.

The size and organization of the ambushes left no doubt.

There was an extensive Dark Circle network embedded in Stonehollow, more than anyone had feared. This wasn't the work of a few rogue fanatics. This was an infrastructure, years in the making, now unleashed all at once.

The next strike got through, not to the passengers, but past Finn's Well.

It started with silence. Stillness. A flicker of shadow that shouldn't have been there.

Then, without warning, the shadows on every side of the street twisted, elongating, sharpening, lifting like the spears of an ancient phalanx. Dozens of them, rising from the cracks in the cobblestone, the walls of alleyways, the underside of awnings.

They lunged.

Spears of darkness shot toward the carriage from all directions, but impacted against Cass's shield without harm.

The crystal shell flared, absorbing each impact with a resonant hum. Shards of conjured darkness shattered harmlessly against it. The structure shuddered under pressure but otherwise didn't react.

Inside, the horses screamed, hooves scraping against the stone as they leapt forward, spooked and panicked. The driver nearly lost control, struggling to hold the reins until, with gritted teeth and clenched fists, he finally got them under control again.

From behind the carriage, the guards had seen it all.

And this time, they were ready.

They charged the shadows, blades drawn, spells igniting along their gauntlets. Screams erupted as three Dark Circle agents emerged from the alleys, robes already burning under counterspells and bladework.

The attackers didn't stand a chance.

Inside the carriage, Cass closed her eyes for a moment, holding the structure firm, then glanced at Finn.

Rupart, pale and quiet, whispered, "They are throwing everything at you."

Cass let out a slow breath. "If this is everything, then they aren't strong enough to break through."

Rupart didn't reply.

He just added another line to the mental ledger he was building. Then another. And another.

Because this wasn't just a threat.

This rapidly became a war scene.

"Hmm," Finn muttered, his eyes narrowing.

Cass turned toward him. "What?"

"I think I felt something," he said, brow furrowing.

"What do you mean, you're hurt?" Her voice rose slightly, alarm creeping in.

He shook his head. "No. Not pain. But... their shadows. When they struck, I felt the edges of them. Sharp and slippery. But I might be able to grab them next time."

Cass blinked and relaxed back into her seat.

The carriage bumped over a cracked stone and slowed as they approached the High Command building.

In the quiet that followed, Thomas let out a long sigh from across the cabin.

"Of course, you can also stop shadows," he mumbled, rubbing his temples.

The other teachers didn't even look surprised anymore; they

were just resigned to the fact that their students were not normal.

As the carriage creaked to a stop, the group stepped out of the carriage.

They looked back down the street, the one they'd just traveled, and took in the damage.

Fires smoldered from the train bombing and shattered buildings. Smoke coiled up into the sky in thin, drifting columns. People were sprawled in the streets, many with injuries, others crying, others simply staring in shock. The aftermath of too many attacks, too quickly, and too much power unleashed in a city unprepared for what it had welcomed.

In the distance, they could see flashes, other unfolding across the capital. Bursts of light. Plumes of smoke. Flares of magic. The Dark Circle hadn't sent just one wave.

It looked like they had been planning this for a long time.

"Well… that just happened," Bruce muttered, folding his arms.

Then they turned, and Cass, without a word, extended a wide shield behind them as they approached the heavy bronze doors of the High Command. Just in case.

Together, with fire behind them and stone ahead, they walked into the halls of power, leaving the city behind to reckon with the fact that the Twin Stones had arrived.

CHAPTER 31

Trial Run

Inside, the marble-floored corridors pulsed with noise and motion. Guards in crested armor rushed down hallways, weapons drawn. Aides clutched scrolls, shouting over one another as they darted from chamber to chamber. Politicians in fine robes argued openly in the halls, their voices raised with panic and accusation.

Someone shouted, "There's another strike in the Southeast sector."

Another yelled, "We've lost contact with the South Spire, send a relay now!"

The stone itself seemed to carry tension, humming with footsteps and urgency.

Outside, beyond the thickened walls and narrow windows, soldiers had formed a perimeter, shoulder to shoulder, encircling the structure. Archers lined the upper balconies. No one else was being allowed in or out.

What was meant to be a place of sanctuary had become a fortress under siege.

Finn glanced at Cass, who was already studying the layout, instinctively identifying choke points, exits, and potential threats. Neither of them spoke.

Behind them, Thomas and Harlen scanned the chaos grimly, while Cam muttered under her breath, "They are all panicking; they were not prepared for an attack."

The scene surprisingly made the teenagers calm down a bit. After the trip here, they didn't know what to expect inside the building. But it appeared that the majority of the city truly wasn't expecting the chaos.

Rupart's face was unreadable, but his pace slowed.

They had walked into the center of a city on the brink, and they were in the center of it.

A flushed, middle-aged city official, dressed in deep blue, intercepted them just past the entry hall. He bowed quickly, too quickly, and gestured down a side corridor.

"Rupart, this way. We've prepared a secure room for your party. Our forces are still containing pockets of resistance across the city. Once things settle, the council will call for you."

No one argued.

The group followed in silence, boots echoing off polished stone as they passed sealed doors and grim-faced sentries. The corridor curved once, then opened into a tall set of double doors flanked by two guards.

Inside was a conference room, clean, orderly, untouched by the chaos outside.

A long table dominated the center, its surface polished to a gleam. Tall windows overlooked a side courtyard, sunlight slanting in through the colored glass.

Along the far wall, a countertop had been stocked with food: fresh fruit, loaves of bread, aged cheese, dried meats, and bowls of salted nuts. A pitcher of chilled water and several cups waited nearby.

Finn and Cass stepped inside, setting their light packs gently near a chair. Rupart's aides followed with quiet efficiency, carrying briefcases, which they set beside the far wall in a neat stack.

For a moment, no one spoke. The only sound was the distant murmur of movement outside the walls.

Then Finn exhaled, looked around, and asked:

"So now what?"

Rupart, standing near the window, didn't turn.

He simply replied, "Now we wait."

And so, with nothing left to do, they did.

One by one, the group took seats, picked up food, and waited for the city to stop burning.

The wait dragged for nearly an hour.

The food had dulled their hunger but not their nerves. The teachers whispered occasionally among themselves, while Cass sat near the window, arms crossed, eyes distant. Finn kept a quiet watch on the door, listening more than speaking.

Cass appeared to be daydreaming, staring out the window, but in reality, she was pinpointing every building and feature, adding them to the map in her head. It was not necessarily fun, but she marveled at the new markers on her map.

Then, finally, the double doors opened.

Three men in official robes and two in uniformed military attire stepped inside.

The first to speak was a tall, clean-shaven man in his mid-thirties, with a sharp chin and an even sharper smile. His tone was smooth, a little too smooth.

"Good afternoon," he said. "I'm Bob Birdhart, assistant minister of internal security."

Behind him stood a gaunt, silent figure who offered no handshake and barely met their eyes. "Dave Longtongue," Bob said with a dismissive wave. "He's more of an observer."

A third man stepped forward with a warm grin and outstretched hand. "Mike, just Mike," he said, his white eyes gleaming with a touch of harmless charm. "I work on the diplomacy end. Welcome to Stonehollow."

Then came the generals.

General Waters, a broad-shouldered man with a graying mustache and the bearing of someone used to giving orders without question, nodded once.

General Batt, lean and sharp-featured with neatly combed blond hair, followed with a quiet, respectful nod of his own.

Rupart stood to greet them, introducing Finn, Cass, and the teachers in turn. Names passed around like a ritual.

Cass asked the first question. "How's the city? It felt like a war zone when we got here."

General Batt answered. "Mostly under control. There are groups around the city that are determined to destroy what they can. We have a lot of people on the streets right now watching and willing to help. We're identifying infiltrators and dismantling what's left of their network."

There was a pause. Everyone seemed to exhale.

And then Bob Birdhart ruined it.

"I have a question," he said with a smile that didn't reach his eyes. "Who did you tell about your trip?"

Finn and Cass looked at each other, confused.

"No one," Finn replied honestly. "We didn't tell anyone."

Bob scoffed. "Then how do you explain this?" He gestured vaguely behind him, toward the ruined city. "You arrive, and suddenly everyone knows. Chaos erupts. Assassins crawl out of every hole in the wall. So either you're very unlucky..."

He paused, letting the silence hang.

"...Or you're the people who set this up."

Cass's eyes narrowed, but she stayed silent.

Bob continued, his voice turning sharper. "Maybe it's all part of your performance to convince us that you are the "Twin Stones". Maybe the attacks were just for show, theatrical, even. Meant to make us think you're victims. When really, you're making yourselves into legends. So people will follow you."

He leaned in just slightly. "Are these agents part of your following? Is this an attempt to take over the city, or is that still to come?"

Even the generals looked uncomfortable.

The room fell still.

And then Finn's expression changed.

Just slightly.

But it was enough.

Finn didn't rise. He didn't raise his voice.

But when he spoke, the room quieted even further.

"If the attacks looked minor to you," he said evenly, "it's only because Cass and I are strong. Not because the attacks were fake."

Bob opened his mouth, but Finn kept speaking.

"They blew up a transport car, destroyed part of the city wall, melted the rail, and killed two Mages. That wasn't theater. That was murder."

His eyes were locked on Bob now, calm but direct.

"And if I walked away from it with nothing more than a ripped shirt, that doesn't mean it wasn't dangerous. It means I'm alive because I'm strong enough to take it."

Bob scoffed, but Finn continued without pause.

"If you're looking for who leaked our arrival, I'd suggest starting with your own people. We didn't tell anyone. We were supposed to be protected. Instead, we were hunted the entire way here."

He turned his gaze slowly around the room, to the aides, to the generals, to Rupart.

"This isn't our city. We're guests. But even from the outside, it's obvious someone within your ranks is compromised. Maybe several someones."

He let the silence settle for a moment.

Then, flatly:

"Your intelligence network missed an entire web of what we assume are Dark Circle operatives operating in your capital. And when they finally moved, they didn't just try to kill us; they attacked the whole city. This wasn't just put together. They must have been here for a while, preparing for this."

He leaned back slightly in his chair.

"So let me ask the question now."

His voice was quiet, almost tired.

"Is this city under your control or someone else's?"

The weight of it landed like a hammer on the polished wood table.

Even Bob, red-faced and sputtering, didn't speak.

Before Bob could open his mouth, anger already rising in his cheeks, Mike raised a hand.

"Alright," he said quickly, stepping slightly between Bob and the rest of the room. "Let's all take a breath."

His tone was lighter, but his posture held the weight of someone used to stepping in when conversations turned into disasters.

"I want to apologize," he said, addressing Finn and Cass directly. "This has been a difficult day for all of us."

Bob bristled but said nothing.

"Our purpose here today," Mike continued, "wasn't to interrogate or accuse. It was to welcome you, give you a sense of place, and explain the next steps. That's all."

He gave a small smile. "Clearly, we've strayed a bit off course."

Cass nodded once, still silent, her eyes never leaving Bob.

Mike pressed on. "Tomorrow, at sunrise, we'd like you both to meet us in the main courtyard. From there, we'll move to one of the outer training fields. We want to conduct a few initial assessments, nothing aggressive. Just a way to observe and understand your abilities firsthand, with more control and less… chaos."

He glanced around the room, then back to the teens.

"After that, we'll review some training regimens drafted by professors at the Academy."

Finn and Cass exchanged a glance, then both nodded.

"We'll be there," Finn said.

Without further words, the delegation turned to leave. Bob hesitated at the door, as if weighing whether to say more, but under Mike's steady gaze, he thought better of it.

One by one, the officials exited, leaving the room in silence once again.

As the heavy doors closed behind the departing officials, a long silence lingered in the conference room.

Then Cass exhaled and sat back in a chair.

"Well," she said dryly, "that was pleasant."

Finn snorted. "Yeah. A real warm welcome."

With the adrenaline fading, the teachers gathered near the side wall, quietly discussing how best to protect the teens overnight. Within moments, they had assigned shifts: two were awake at all times, and one patrolled the apartment perimeter if needed.

"We shouldn't take any chances tonight," Cam said.

Not long after, one of Rupart's assistants appeared at the door, motioning for them to follow.

They were led through a quiet wing of the High Command, up two sets of stairs, and through a hall lined with reinforced glass windows. Their destination: a secured residential suite originally designed for visiting dignitaries.

The assistant opened the door and stepped aside.

The space inside was spacious but simple: a modest living room, five private bedrooms, two clean washrooms, and a small, well-equipped kitchen with stocked shelves. It wasn't luxurious, but it was quiet. Safe.

Finn stepped in, glanced around, and dropped his pack by the nearest chair.

"Yeah. This'll do."

The teachers moved quietly through the apartment, closing the drapes, checking the windows, and exchanging a few quiet words between themselves. Eventually, they all settled into the evening, voices low, the weight of the day pressing them into silence.

Finn and Cass slipped away into a small side room, a cozy sitting space with worn chairs and warm lamplight. They sank into the cushions without speaking at first, the silence between them familiar, even comforting.

Cass stared at nothing for a while, the firelight catching faintly in her hair. Finn could tell she was working something out, so he said nothing. He just waited.

After a few minutes, her voice finally broke the quiet.

"How are you handling all this?"

Finn shrugged, his gaze fixed on the low-burning flame. "I do not know," he admitted. "But we're okay. And that's better than... not okay."

Cass nodded slowly, lips pressed into a tight line. "Maybe we shouldn't have come here. Maybe we should've stayed in Greyfen."

Finn looked at her, calm but firm. "They were already here. All those agents, all that chaos, it didn't start because of us. It was already waiting. We just exposed it."

She didn't argue.

But she didn't look comforted either.

Another long pause.

Then: "I know you're right. I just… we didn't want to awaken in Elarith because of the politics, and now we are here dealing with exactly that."

Finn gave a dry snort, leaning his head back. "Yeah."

Cass smirked faintly, but it faded quickly.

"Let's give them one day," she said. "One practice. If it's just show and posturing, we walk."

Finn nodded. "I'm with you. We owe it to Harlen, Thomas, Bruce, Cam, and Sparky. They followed us into this fire. They deserve to know if we're leaving."

"Agreed." Cass looked at the window, now covered. "Tomorrow, then."

That night, they settled in. Cass chose a room near the window. Finn took the one closest to the hallway. The teachers remained on rotation, whispering quietly and standing near the doors, just in case.

Just after midnight, a distant boom echoed through the air, faint but unmistakable. They all woke briefly, hands moving toward weapons and magic.

But it was far off, on the other side of the city.

No alarms followed.

No tremors shook the ground.

Within minutes, silence returned.

And despite everything, the night passed without further disturbance.

For Finn and Cass, who had spent nights beneath freezing cliffs and hunted by things worse than men, it was almost peaceful.

And peace, even brief, was enough.

EPILOGUE

Rupart stepped into his room and immediately went to the small kitchen in his suite, pouring himself a large glass of whatever hard alcohol they kept in stock. He was beside himself over the day's events. He had thought it was going so well. He was bringing home his prize—the two teenagers who might have been what everyone was looking for.

At first, he'd been underwhelmed by them. Yes, they handled themselves well, but they were too short—too ordinary—to be the prophesied Twin Stones. Then everything fell apart. The damn Dark Circle and their unsophisticated, ignorant plots. It was so simple he hadn't even considered it a possibility.

He sat down hard on the sofa in his small living room.

He had thought he was dead. But then the two teenagers somehow saved them—well, all except the two poor mages driving the cart. He had seen mages do amazing things, even fly, but he had never witnessed anything like what Finn and Cass did. Every attempt to harm them failed so spectacularly that the entire battle had been one-sided.

There was no doubt now. They were the Twin Stones.

And Rupart was going to find out everything he could about them—and their purpose. He had been planning to retire soon, but now he had a new one.

To discover the information he needed, he would have to go where all information seekers went—the one place every spy, politician, and organization of any size feared. He was going to the Copper Network.

To the dragon's den.

To Virelios.

SNEAK PEAK

Book Two of The World Walkers Chronicles

The morning air still held the chill of night as Finn, Cass, and their teachers stepped out into the High Command's courtyard. Pale sunlight spilled across the flagstones, catching on dew-streaked banners and the polished bronze edges of the courtyard gates.

General Waters was already waiting, flanked by two guards in dark sashes and burnished armor. Unlike the stoic presence they'd worn the night before, both guards looked more at ease now, alert but not bristling. As the group approached, Waters stepped forward and extended a hand.

"To all of you, good morning," he said, his voice rough but not unkind. "And thank you for meeting so early. We've all had far too little sleep, but I thought it best to begin the day with clarity."

He shook each teacher's hand firmly, then turned to Cass and Finn, eyes softer than the man's rigid posture suggested. "Cass. Finn. It's good to meet you in a better light."

Finn returned the handshake, tight-lipped but polite. Cass followed, her grip steady, eyes sharp beneath her calm expression.

"I want to begin by apologizing," Waters continued. "Yesterday's reception was... not what it should have been. Tensions were high. Some members of the High Council were up through the night dealing with Dark Circle attacks. Some still are."

His gaze drifted toward the gates behind them, as if he could see the damage through stone walls. "We suffered some losses, civilians mostly, but far fewer than we could have. The targets were government buildings. We've captured several of their operatives. Enough, we believe, to start pulling apart their inner command. We hope to figure out where their command structure is housed."

"Probably Velmirath," Finn said after a moment.

General Waters turned to him, brows raised. "Why would you think they're in Velmirath?"

Finn glanced at Cass.

She gave a subtle shrug, leaving the explanation to him.

"Well..." Finn began, shifting slightly. "We've come across some information that suggests the King of Elarith was working with the Dark Circle. If these attacks are connected to them, and it sure looks like they are, then it makes sense."

He hesitated for a moment, then added, "Velmirath is one of their strongholds. Maybe the stronghold. That's where he was sending our awakening stones... before they were rescued."

The last part made him pause. He looked down for a second, a faint flush of embarrassment coloring his cheeks, a memory flickering of when he borrowed food in Darrowmere from the food vendors. He needed to pay them back now that he had real coin.

General Waters was quiet for a beat, then said, "I'd be very interested in seeing this information."

Finn only shrugged. "We'll see," he replied, not evasive, just cautious.

"Lead the way, General. We'll follow."

Waters nodded back, either missing or choosing to ignore the subtle tension in Finn's voice.

"Very well," he said. "Let's get you to the academy."

He turned, gesturing toward the row of carriages waiting by the gates. As the group began walking, one of the guards opened a door and stood aside.

Bruce groaned audibly behind them. "Another carriage ride," he muttered, "my favorite."

Cass stifled a grin.

Still, they climbed in without protest, the city stirring to life around them.

The carriages creaked to a stop as the stone road beneath them gave way to gravel. Outside the window, the view opened wide and sudden, like a curtain being drawn on a stage.

Ahead loomed the academy.

It was not a fortress in the military sense, but it looked like one. Towering white stone walls, tinged with age and time, surrounded a sprawling structure that echoed the design of old strongholds: high towers, long halls, and thick-walled keeps. It's hard to tell which was built first, the academy or the city. Moss clung to the base of the outer walls where rain gathered, and ivy traced lazy lines up toward parapets too high for comfort. Yet the grounds within were anything but grim.

The main gate, an arch of silver, inlaid stone flanked by copper-veined pylons, swung open with a low, measured groan. Guards stood on either side, dressed in pale gray uniforms marked by twin sigils: one of flame, one of a prism. They didn't salute, but nodded with quiet recognition, having clearly been informed of the guests' arrival, as the carriages passed by.

Inside, the courtyard came into view.

It was vast and green, immaculately maintained. Tiered garden beds overflowed with vibrant flowers and thick-leafed shrubs. Marble statues of historic people stood watch from pedestals scattered along the paths, some triumphant, others contemplative.

The main building stretched across the far side of the courtyard. Made from the same pale stone as the outer walls, its surface had weathered to a warm, tan hue.

As the carriages rolled to a halt at the main building, the teenagers, the teacher, the generals, and their aids all stepped out.

Five figures stood waiting just outside: three men and two women, all in robes of varying color and cut. One of the men, thin and pale, wrung his hands repeatedly, shifting from foot to foot. The two women flanking him wore expressions of faint impatience, their gazes flicking toward his hands with the sharpness of schoolmasters who'd long lost their patience. One of them whispered something to the other, who nodded, almost imperceptibly.

Of the remaining men, one was short and broad, dressed in deep black robes, his arms folded. The other wore robes of pure white and bore a long silver beard, the sun catching in the strands like threads of glass.

General Waters stepped up and made a motion toward the group. "No issues," he said under his breath, as if to himself more than to them.

Then he turned to the professors to make introductions.

The five professors stood in a loose line at the top of the stone steps leading into the academy's main hall. The early sun caught in their robes, casting long shadows across the pale courtyard stones.

The first was a man of perhaps fifty, thin as a broom handle and very twitchy. His robe, a deep forest green, hung slightly off center, as if he'd dressed in a hurry. His fingers worked in constant motion, wringing and fidgeting, folding and unfolding a strip of parchment. His name, as Finn would soon learn, was Professor Merrin, a Copper Mage and a scholar of magical theory and historical studies. At the moment, he looked more like a man preparing to give bad news.

Beside him, the two women stood like granite carved into judgment.

The taller of the two, Professor Vael, had salt-and-pepper hair tied back in a strict braid and wore robes of slate blue, fastened with silver clasps that gleamed in the morning light. Her arms were crossed over her chest, and her expression held the cool neutrality of a woman who had graded too many half-finished essays in her lifetime. She gave Merrin a side glance as he muttered to himself, and her left eyebrow twitched, just once.

The second woman, Professor Lureya, was shorter, broader in the shoulders, and wore deep burgundy robes embroidered in copper thread. Her hands were clasped behind her back with the rigidity of a drill instructor, and she gave off the sense that she'd already found everyone here lacking and was simply waiting for them to prove her right. When Merrin made a soft, throat-clearing sound, she tilted her head just slightly and exhaled through her nose, an unspoken sigh of irritation.

Further to the right stood two men who could not have been more different from one another.

Professor Haldrin was squat and square jawed, his black robes dusted at the hem with something chalky. His beard was short, scruffy. He nodded once as General Waters approached.

And lastly, Professor Alrin, clad in flowing white robes that shimmered faintly in the sun, stood with the stillness of a statue. His beard was long and white, braided neatly with silver cuffs at the tips. His pale blue eyes studied Finn and Cass with quiet curiosity, a scholar's gaze, not appraising, but noticing. Of all the professors, he looked the least surprised.

General Waters cleared his throat and gestured toward Finn and Cass as they stepped forward.

"Hello Professors, I'd like for you to meet Finn and Cass, their training is your top priority."

Merrin blinked hard, opened his mouth, then closed it again. His fingers tightened on the parchment until it tore slightly. "Just two students? All the other students were removed from their studies for these two, why?" he said.

"We'll get to that," Waters said quickly, his tone firm but polite.

Cass's face was calm, but not passive. There was a weight behind her eyes, measured, controlled, far older than her years.

"We'll answer your questions," she said. "All of them, in time. But maybe it would be easier... if we just jump into training."

Finn and Cass were as eager to test their new professors as the professors were to test them.

"Demonstration, then," Lureya said. "Very well."

She turned sharply and began walking through the main building to the inner courtyard gates.

"This way."

Cass lowered her hand. Finn glanced sideways at her, one corner of his mouth twitching upward.

Cass didn't look at him, but her voice was quiet as she walked beside him.

And the academy's main building gates opened ahead of them. It was eerily quiet, as though the building itself was still asleep.

Cass said nothing. Finn didn't look back. Their teachers walked in silence behind them, all of them alert despite the calm.

Finally, they stepped through a pair of heavy ironwood doors and emerged into the training courtyard.

The space was massive, a square roughly sixty heights across, walled in on all sides by towering stone. The walls were thick and meant to absorb hits. Along the perimeter stood pillars, thick and evenly spaced, each with a metal ring near the top, some for banners, others clearly used in combat training.

The ground was a smooth, hardened sand blend, designed to

cushion falls but firm enough for battle footing. Faint scorch marks, gouges, and impact rings marred the surface, signs of years of use. Spaced evenly around the courtyard were four stairwells leading up to an observation level. Today, the observation level was mostly empty, but not completely.

In the shade, looking down at the teens, General Batt stood with his aides and the three politicians from the night before, and Rupart, their postures stiff with expectation.

General Waters approached the group, his expression unreadable as he climbed the stairs to stand next to General Batt. His own trio of aides followed him and stood next to him as the two Generals talked.

As the group entered and took in the sight of the training field, Professor Vael, one of the professors, stepped forward.

"If you would be so kind," she said politely, "we'd like to see how you train, just for a little while. Something natural. Something you're used to."

"Just like Greyfen?" Sparky muttered with a grin, stretching his arms. "The only difference is now we've got a little audience."

Finn stepped toward the center of the yard.

Cass, meanwhile, stayed back, taking a seat near the edge beside the new professors, her arms crossed. She said nothing, her eyes tracking everything, especially how the instructors were watching her.

Finn reached the middle of the square and turned.

The five teachers took their positions, forming a loose ring about twenty heights from him, their expressions unreadable but their stances firm.

It was familiar.

But today, under watchful eyes, it felt like the beginning of something much, much larger.

KNOW YOUR CHANCES

Before you try to awaken, know what your chance is to succeed and become a Mage.

Note: Most people DO NOT survive an awakening attempt.

Clear Quartz (Light)
Common: Light sensing abilities (16%)
Rare: Light focusing (3%)
Life longevity: Normal
Chance that a Quartz awakening will result in a Mage is 22%.

Amethyst (Mind)
Common: Feeling sensing (12%)
Rare: Mind manipulation (5%)
Life longevity: Normal
Chance that a Amethyst awakening will result in a Mage is 21%.

Malachite (Earth)

Common: Material sensing (10%)
Rare: Earth manipulation (9%)
Life longevity: Normal
Chance that a Malachite awakening will result in a Mage is 22%.

Copper (Metal)
Common: Message sending and receiving (12%)
Rare: Metal manipulation (6%)
Life longevity: Normal
Chance that a Copper awakening will result in a Mage is 24%.

Iron (Body)
Common: Skin like iron (13%)
Rare: Extreme strength (9%)
Life longevity: Extended
Chance that a Iron awakening will result in a Mage is 27%.

Obsidian (Shadows)
Common: Obscure (11%)
Rare: Control shadows (7%)
Life longevity: Stunted
Chance that a Obsidian awakening will result in a Mage is 21%.

Jade (Agility)
Common: Enhanced balance (14%)
Rare: Speed (9%)
Life longevity: Extended
Chance that a Jade awakening will result in a Mage is 26%.

Sapphire (Water)
Common: Liquid water manipulation (16%)
Rare: Steam manipulation (1%)
Life longevity: Stunted
Chance that a Sapphire awakening will result in a Mage is 20%.

Ruby (Fire)
Common: Flame manipulation (14%)
Rare: Combustion abilities (1%)
Life longevity: Stunted
Chance that a Ruby awakening will result in a Mage is 19%.

Dragon Bone (Wild Magic)
Common: No control (13%)
Rare: Some control (4%)
Life longevity: Extended
Chance that a Dragon awakening will result in a Mage is 20%.

Diamond (Wind)
Common: Wind manipulation (14%)
Rare: Flight (1%)
Life longevity: Stunted
Chance that a Diamond awakening will result in a Mage is 18%.

*Warning: Some Awakening Circles have fluctuating success rates for unknown reasons. The figures above should be used solely for discussion purposes only.

RIV'EL

The Old Tongue of the Hollow Realm

Pronouns and People:

    Vi ---------- I / me

    Jo / Jon ---------- You

    Vul ---------- He

    Luv ---------- She

    We ---------- They

    Ven ---------- They (chosen / appointed)

    Tuar ---------- Twin / pair / dual

    Mar ---------- Of / belonging to

    Ul / Uv ---------- Masculine / feminine endings

Core Verbs and Actions:

Vulmara ---------- To master / dominate / rule

Ashar ---------- To rise / ascend

Tharnel ---------- To shatter / break

Krafen ---------- To craft / create / forge

Val ---------- To know / perceive truth

Tred ---------- To tread / walk / journey

Risar ---------- To rise again / be reborn

Dies'nar ---------- To die / fade / wither

Bindral ---------- To bind / entwine / interlace

Serin ---------- To bear / carry / endure

Nosen ---------- To know none / to be unknown

Modifiers, Prepositions, and Particles:

No ---------- Not / never

En / En' ---------- And / in / within

To / Tor' ---------- From / beyond / across

A' ---------- As / for / by

Vi' ---------- My / mine

Ven' ---------- Of the chosen / sacred form of "of"

Mor' ---------- Of / from / pertaining to

Thru' ---------- Through / across

'El ---------- Of time / eternal

'Nar ---------- Downward / ending / to end

'Ral ---------- In / amid / among

Objects and Material Terms:

Sten / Stenul ---------- Stone / sacred stone

Ashar / Ashen / Asharal ---------- Ash / ashes

Handra ---------- Hand / grasp / force

Bindral ---------- Thread / pattern / weave

Ruenlef / Lef'norn ---------- Remnant / what remains

Hallar ---------- Hall / temple / sanctum

Dred ---------- Dead / death

Falen ---------- Fallen / broken / cast down

Adjectives and Descriptors:

Thru'nal ---------- Ancient / of ages past

Ven'ul ---------- Chosen / divine / appointed

Falen ---------- Fallen / lost / broken

Anew ---------- New / reborn / renewed

Torn ---------- Joined / woven / bound together

Dred / Dredal ---------- Dead / lifeless / void

Sacred and Temporal Words:

Tor'el ---------- Eternal / timeless / beyond

Nura ---------- Forever / evermore / beyond life

Til'rut ---------- Until the root / until the beginning ends

Ven'ral ---------- In ashes / among ruin

Honar'Serin ---------- The High Binding

Tuar'Lethen ---------- The Song of the Two

Verbs of Motion and Journey:

Tred ---------- To tread / walk / journey

Drav ---------- To move / travel / roam

Relin ---------- To return / come back

Ascra ---------- To climb / ascend

Falneth ---------- To fall / descend

Voyen ---------- To cross / pass / traverse

Heven ---------- To lift / carry upward

Sundra ---------- To turn / shift / change course

Miren ---------- To wander / explore

Koral ---------- To flee / escape / withdraw

Verbs of Time and Change:

Tharen ---------- To begin / to awaken

Elen ---------- To end / conclude / complete

Tor'el ---------- To endure eternally

Rineth ---------- To wait / remain / linger

Saren ---------- To forget / to lose memory

Voren ---------- To remember / recall / preserve

Kalen ---------- To age / decay / fade

Morath ---------- To change / transform / shift form

Varen ---------- To renew / make again

Nuren ---------- To pass beyond / transcend

Elements and Natural Forces:

Pyra ---------- Fire / flame

Sylin ---------- Wind / breath / air

Aquin ---------- Water / river / current

Terel ---------- Earth / ground / soil

Sten / Stenul ---------- Stone / sacred stone

Solin ---------- Sun / light / brilliance

Lunor ---------- Moon / night light

Tharnok ---------- Shadow / gloom / veil

Velra ---------- Storm / tempest / upheaval

Cryen ---------- Ice / frost / cold

Myral ---------- Mind / thought / consciousness

Veyra ---------- Spirit / will / unseen force

Faryn ---------- Body / flesh / mortal form

Irun ---------- Iron / forged metal

Sorel ---------- Blood / life-force / essence

Dred ---------- Death / silence / end of breath

Curen ---------- Copper / red metal

Metan ---------- Metal / forged matter

Draen ---------- Dragon / great serpent / celestial beast

Drastel ---------- Dragon bone / draconic relic

Adjectives and Elemental Descriptors:

Pyrael ---------- Burning / fiery

Sylen ---------- Swift / light / unseen

Aquel ---------- Flowing / pure / cleansing

Teran ---------- Grounded / steadfast / firm

Stenal ---------- Hard / enduring / sacred

Solan ---------- Bright / radiant / divine

Luneth ---------- Pale / calm / reflective

Velrin ---------- Violent / chaotic / stormbound

Cryel ---------- Cold / distant / unyielding

Tharul ---------- Shadowed / half-lit

Nouns of Time and Fate:

Tharun ---------- Dawn / beginning / awakening

Elenar ---------- Dusk / ending / closure

Tor'el ---------- Eternity / endlessness

Varenel ---------- Renewal / rebirth

Morathen ---------- Change / transformation

Fatel ---------- Fate / design / pattern of life

Chronar ---------- Time / flow / measured span

Sareneth ---------- Forgetting / oblivion

Voranel ---------- Memory / remembrance

Nura ---------- Forever / beyond / evermore

Celestial and Mystical Terms:
Ethel ---------- Star / beacon / light above

Ethelen ---------- Starlight / divine radiance

Auren ---------- Sky / heavens

Valen ---------- Vision / sight / revelation

Myren ---------- Dream / vision / echo of the mind

Shalor ---------- Spirit / soul / essence

Dranor ---------- Realm of the dead / underworld

Orel ---------- Voice / word / speech

Koraleth ---------- Veil / barrier / unseen boundary

Veyra ---------- Magic / will / unseen force

Verbs of Creation and Destruction:
Foren ---------- To build / to form

Rafen ---------- To break / to destroy

Veyren ---------- To conjure / to channel

Sharen ---------- To shape / to mold

Narith ---------- To burn / to consume

Cryenor ---------- To freeze / to still

Velthar ---------- To unleash / to storm

Dranorin ---------- To bury / to seal

Morathen ---------- To transform / to evolve

Aurenar ---------- To call / to summon

Titles and Sacred Roles:

Arul ---------- Lord / master / male leader

Ar'uv ---------- Lady / mistress / female leader

Serul ---------- Guardian / keeper / watcher

Jastrel ---------- Judge / bringer of justice

Shalorn ---------- Seer / prophet / dream-singer

Tor'elun ---------- Eternal one / timeless being

Veyrun ---------- Mage / wielder of power

Tuar'ven ---------- Twin chosen / sacred pair

Honar'Serin ---------- The Bound / oath-keeper

Numbers and Quantities:

Una ---------- One

Dua ---------- Two

Tren ---------- Three

Quen ---------- Four

Penth ---------- Five

Setan ---------- Six

Venar ---------- Seven

Octen ---------- Eight

Noven ---------- Nine

Decen ---------- Ten

Vi'mar honar jo'val riv!

SUMMARY

In the Hollow Realm, where ancient stones awaken hidden powers, thirteen-year-old Finn and fifteen-year-old Cass stumble into a destiny they never sought. Haunted by loss and driven by survival, they flee a crumbling kingdom, uncovering forgotten prophecies, awakening rare abilities, and facing dark forces rising from the shadows.

As kingdoms stir in reaction to their awakening, Finn and Cass must decide not only how to wield their powers, but whom they can trust with the truth.

The Twin Stones is the first book in The World Walkers Chronicles, an epic tale of friendship, courage, and the eternal struggle between good and evil.

Made in the USA
Coppell, TX
10 January 2026

68834857R00243